BANDIT

BANDIT

A Portrait of Ken Leishman

a novel by
Wayne Tefs

TURNSTONE PRESS

Bandit
A Portrait of Ken Leishman
copyright © Wayne Tefs 2011

Turnstone Press
Artspace Building
206-100 Arthur Street
Winnipeg, MB
R3B 1H3 Canada
www.TurnstonePress.com

Turnstone Press gratefully acknowledges the assistance of the Canada Council for the Arts, the Manitoba Arts Council, the Government of Canada through the Canada Book Fund, and the Province of Manitoba through the Book Publishing Tax Credit and the Book Publisher Marketing Assistance Program.

Although inspired by actual events, this novel is a work of fiction, and a product of the author's imagination.

Most headlines appearing throughout the novel are real newspaper headlines as they appeared at time of publication. Headlines on pages 97 and 161 are from the *Winnipeg Free Press* Archives and are used with permission. Headlines on pages 43, 69, 107, 137, 215, 237, 261 and 283 are from the *Winnipeg Tribune* Archives (housed at the University of Manitoba) and are used with permission.

Back cover and photo page 3 University of Manitoba Archives & Special Collections, *Winnipeg Tribune* fonds, PC 18 (A.81-12), Box 9, Folder 299, Item 11.
Photo page 297 University of Manitoba Archives & Special Collections, *Winnipeg Tribune* fonds, PC 18 (A.81-12), Box 31, Folder 1913, Item 82.

Design: Jamis Paulson
Printed and bound in Canada by Friesens for Turnstone Press.

Library and Archives Canada Cataloguing in Publication

Tefs, Wayne, 1947–
    Bandit : a portrait of Ken Leishman / Wayne Tefs.

ISBN 978-0-88801-377-4

    1. Leishman, Ken, b. 1931--Fiction. I. Title.

PS8589.E37B35 2011   C813'.54   C2011-902370-9

for Kristen

"I couda been a contender, I coulda been a somebody . . ."
—Terry Malloy in *On the Waterfront*

Note: in 1966 gold was valued at $35 per ounce, and in 2011 at $1300, so the heist of 1966 would be valued in today's terms at approximately $16 million.

BANDIT

K en is pacing nervously back and forth, fingering his mustache, pencil-thin, like Clark Gable's, and always trim, his pride, along with his snap-brim hat, which is pulled down low on his forehead. He's walked to the far end of the warehouse without remembering doing it. Ken looks at his watch. 8:45. He's rubbing both thumbs and forefingers together, an automatic habit. 8:50. He's a family man who has a great wife, Elva, he wants to be home making popcorn and playing with his kids, unlike Harry Backlin and John Berry, who are happy hanging around in the Olgat warehouse on a frosty Winnipeg winter evening, yakking and kibitzing until all hours and then moving on to the Black Night Lounge of the airport hotel and continuing to play pool and drink into the early hours. Anyway, Ken is wary of booze, it muddles his thinking—though he takes a drink when it's the sociable thing to do or if he's under stress. He likes having a clear head, that's the only way he can keep his mind focused on the things he needs to think out, the goals he's set himself. Calculate. Plan. And he's never smoked.

A plane rumbles overhead, taking off from the airport, and he looks up on reflex, though there's no window to look out of at the back of the warehouse and what his eyes rest on is a grid of steel girders, which remind him of bars, iron bars cross-hatched by iron bars. Ken feels cooped up inside the Olgat building, a not unfamiliar feeling. He likes windows. He likes wide open spaces; blank concrete walls set his toes tapping, his thoughts jumping. The airport is not far away. The vibrations of the plane shake through the building.

It's a frigid February night in 1966 and the sounds the plane makes overhead are amplified in the still winter air of the prairies. The Olgat warehouse, once filled with cleaning supplies, echoes the vibrations from above. The company has been out of business for some months, so the heat in the building is at minimum, but things are still cooking inside its walls.

Ken puts his hand out and rests it on a table that has been turned on its side, running his thick, hairy fingers over a protruding metal leg. In a moment his fingers are tapping the metal in a staccato rhythm but he is unaware of it. Tap tap tap. Muscles mimicking thoughts. He looks back in the direction of the table where Harry and John Berry are sitting, overcoats still on, collars turned up, talking quietly, a mickey of whiskey on the table between them. The warehouse is drafty but it's a good place for them to meet and go over things, a private place. The walls have ears. Ken glances at his watch again. Nine o'clock. Time flies, the old saying goes, and Ken's minutes are flying out the window, there's so much to do, so much to get on with, another familiar sensation. He's thirty-five and he's spent almost five of those years in jail, so he wants to be on the move, he wants something to be happening, and he has to rein in the urge to dash out the door and drive to the airport, he knows that the success of what they're planning depends on timing and on not rushing into things and putting the law on to their scheme. Easier said than done. Ken runs his tongue around inside his mouth. He's been biting his lower lip again, a string of flesh is hanging loose inside, but he cannot bite it off.

He tips his hat up on his forehead a little and resists looking at his watch again. There's no point in worrying anymore about the hour, anyway. By the time he's finished at the airport and has driven home, Elva will have put the kids to bed, he'll be able to look in on them, hear their light breathing, smell the baby oil that Elva swabs on them after the bath, but there will be no chance to kneel down on the floor and play. Ken sighs. It wasn't much of a holiday season for his family. He's been out of work; cash has been scarce. Ken sighs again. He's back at the table where Harry and John are huddled without realizing he's crossed the floor of the warehouse. Though blood pounds in his temples and he blinks his eyes to relieve the headache building there.

"Sit down, would you, for Christ's sakes," John Berry says, looking up at him over his glass of whiskey. "You're antsy as a racehorse, buddy, you're making me antsy already."

Harry chuckles. "Ken's a pacer," he says. "He would have been a trotter at the racetrack." Like Ken, he wears a fedora and he fiddles with its brim for a moment.

John and Harry laugh and Ken joins in, too. He is a pacer. In school, the teachers were always chastising him for bouncing his knees under the desk. He clears his throat. "You two jokers hatching more schemes?"

John taps his temple. "Deep thinking." He smiles crookedly at Ken. His voice echoes when he says, "Trying to decide which one of us is going to get up and fetch that other mickey from the office." He laughs briefly, a sound that echoes in the empty warehouse.

Harry taps his glass on the tabletop. "Deep thinking for deep debt. As per usual." He says this wryly but the truth is all three are in over their heads and the scam they're working on is a way out from under the demands of creditors and finance companies, worries, and frets. Cars bought on time, business schemes gone bad. Ken has not checked recently but he's in hock for at least ten grand. That's more than his house is worth. His desperate finances gnaw his daytime thoughts. He and Elva had a crappy Christmas. Too few gifts for the kids. Ken wakes in the middle of the night in a sweat. He's convinced he's getting an ulcer. He has so much to make up to Elva and the kids, and instead his finances are going down the toilet.

Harry tips the rest of his drink back, smacks his lips.

"I'll get more." John has risen, pushing the empty bottle to the side of the table. "This soldier's dead," he adds, grinning.

When he's disappeared into the office at the front of the building, Harry raises his round eyes to Ken and whispers, "You can't be serious about this bullion business." Like Ken, Harry has a fleshy face and his eyes peer out, narrowed and skeptical, though his cheeks are flushed from whiskey and his voice is gritty as gravel.

"I am serious, damn serious." Ken sips from his glass. "As straight as this here rye."

"Jesus." Harry's tone is no more than a sigh. He taps his fingers on the tabletop. "Ken."

"You want out of your—your troubles? Right?"

"Of course. But, Jesus, Ken. Let's start with something a little smaller, an operation we can handle."

"We can handle this. Piece of cake."

"I was thinking what about one of the big retail outlets. They'd never expect it. Wham-bam, we're in, we're out."

"Too complicated, the in-and-out part, dashing past counters of shoppers and whatnot. Clerks and women screaming. And you never know what they got on hand for money. Actual cash. They take cheques. And people use credit cards now. You might get only a couple grand. What's that, a couple grand? A mug's game."

"It's not jail time. Probably."

"It's nothing. Peanuts. We're in another league, you and me, Harry."

"Jesus," Harry says in a half-whisper. "Why not go the whole hog, why not just break into Fort Knox?"

"You're making fun of me." Ken tilts his glass toward Harry, a narrow look in his eye. "You're turning this into a downer, you're saying it's a stupid idea."

"A bank?"

"No more banks. I've had enough of banks. Banks are how I got into all my troubles." Ken laughs, but ruefully, and strokes his mustache, on reflex.

"But Jesus, Ken. Gold bullion. How you gonna move gold bullion?"

"Easy. You pick it up. You carry it." Ken holds out his hands, imitating a man lugging a box, and laughs again. He has a deep voice and it echoes in the room.

Harry snorts. "I didn't mean that, physically carting the stuff around. I meant how you gonna sell it on?" He glances furtively toward the door John disappeared through.

"Harry. Nothing ventured, nothing gained. Am I right?"

"This is venturing a lot, but."

Ken is leaning over now, staring Harry in the eye. "Harry. Are you a man?"

"As much as any. But the risks, see. I mean, Ken, I—"

"Then be a man." Ken whispers the last words fiercely. Bent over, big hands locked onto the edge of the table, it looks as if he might tip it over onto Harry's lap. "Look. It's just sitting there. The gold. The plane flies in, drops it off, and it's just sitting there. So we waltz in and snatch it. Nothing to it. As for after, as for moving it along, we find a fence."

"Just like that?"

"Just like that. You're the guy with connections, with contacts in the East, in the Orient. You're always talking them up. Now's the time to use them, now's the time to put your money where your mouth is, my big-shot legal buddy."

"Jesus. Don't get excited. You start to sweat when you get worked up." Harry looks past Ken, refusing to meet his eye. "And another thing. There'll be cops everywhere."

"That's where you're wrong, my friend. I've checked it out, see. And I'm going to do it again tonight. Double check. The cops are inside the terminal. Outside, no one. Just the airline lackeys who shift the bars from one plane to the other. Desk jockeys with soft airline jobs who don't give a shit what happens to their shipments. It's not their gold. So."

"So?"

"So. Piece of cake. That's where the weak link in the chain is. You see?"

"There's gotta be more to it."

"There isn't, I tell you, that's the whole story, the entire narrative." Ken's voice cracks and he swallows hard. Reflexively he touches two fingers to his forehead, wipes sweat from his brow, pushes up the brim of his hat.

Harry shakes his head. "Well, Ken, there's one thing I can tell *you*. I don't wanna be there." He stares into his empty glass and then glances toward the office, refusing to meet Ken's eye. "Nowhere near there. I'm an officer of the courts, see. I wanna be miles away, Ken. Miles. You understand? Buddy?"

"You don't hafta be. You got no stomach for the action, you skip town when it's going down. Take the wife to Vegas. Out of the line of fire."

"That's right. I don't want nothing to do with no armed robbery."

"There's gonna be no guns."

"Huh. That's what they all say. Then what happens, somebody gets jumpy and ka-bing ka-bang and somebody's got themselves shot."

"Not this time. You put up the money. That's your end. I'll do the rest."

"You'll do time, that's what you'll do."

"That's the game we're into here, the gambit, that's a risk a man takes."

"No thanks, says this chickadee."

"Suit yourself. But it's a lock, I tell you. Safe as churches."

"Huh." Harry shakes his head. He pokes at the brim of his black fedora, pulled down tight on his brow. "You're always so sure of yourself, Ken. Where does that come from?"

Ken sighs, twirls his near-empty glass in his fingers. "From being poor, Harry, from having nothing, from being on the make. Being pecunious. You know that tune." Ken is so agitated his whiskey glass slips from his grip but he catches it before it falls.

Harry studies him as he repositions his big hand around the glass and takes a small sip. "I do know that tune," Harry says, gravel voice little more than a croak. He catches Ken's eye and shakes his head, but he grins, a grin of resignation, which makes him seem tired. "We both need the cash, Ken, I know that. We both got debts. We got the Man knocking at the door."

"I got kids who need sneakers. I got kids who had a crappy Christmas. A wife who—"

"You don't need to tell me about wives. Hoo boy." Harry shakes his head. "But—"

"But nothing." Ken studies him for a moment. Then he says, picking up their earlier exchange, "In here, Harry." He bangs one balled fist on his chest, indicating his heart. "It comes from in here, that drive to be a somebody comes from where it comes from in all great men."

"If you say so, Ken."

"I say so, Harry. And what's more, we're made in the shade on this one. I say so." Ken runs the back of one hand across his mouth. "Ah," he says, seeing John coming back into the room with a mickey bottle in his hand. "Let's drink to that, to our—our little enterprise."

"You bet." Harry extends his glass. "I could use a shot of that."

Ken runs his tongue around his lips. He's been talking a lot. He says, "I could use two, two shots of that. One big and the other one bigger." He laughs, a throttled snort.

In the silence they leave, John pours into each glass in turn. "Gentlemen," he says when he's done, raising his glass.

Harry snorts. "To use a term loosely."

"Let the man speak," Ken says, nodding encouragement to John. He raises his glass and looks John in the eye. "To comrades."

John laughs. "Comrades in skulduggery." He sits down and takes a quick sip. "Anyways, what you two been cookin' up while I been having a piss?"

Ken takes a sip of whiskey and blinks as he swallows. "I just been telling Harry here that we're onto a sure thing. See, the point, John, is—and I been trying to make this clear to Harry—the point is that men like us, men with imagination, with plans, with the wherewithal to execute them plans, men with moxie can have it all. I've told you before, you look at the situation, you see what's required, you take the bull by the horns and you do it, that's what life is all about. You can do whatever you want. It just requires—what do they call it in the North End, now?—*chutzpah*. Guts. Self-confidence. So, of course, we can do this. Even though Harry here may not have the stomach for it." Ken hasn't realized it but he's smacking the tabletop with the open palm of one hand.

"All right, all right." Harry sucks his teeth a moment. "Calm down, Ken. For the love of."

Ken gives him a long look, continuing to tap his hand on the tabletop. His eyes narrow, his lower lip trembles. "Don't tell me to calm down, Harry. I don't much like it."

"I'm just saying. You're jumpy as a cat. You're making me nervy."

"I don't like being told that. Calm down. Take it easy. Been told that all my life. Was beat for it. By my granddad. Bastard. At the Home for Boys too. People laughing at my ideas and calling me a fool. All my life. I've had enough of that."

"All right, no need to get sore, I said all right then."

"All right."

Harry lets out a long sigh and turns his attention to his glass of whiskey, leaving a silence. "All right," he repeats. "John and me are with you on this, Ken, we are."

Ken takes a deep breath and says in a calmer tone, "Look, boys. That's the problem with the world today. No one has enough *chutzpah*, it's like they're all beaten down and shrivelled up inside like bad ears of corn. They came back from that war happy just to be alive, they cower in their grey flannel suits, afraid for their jobs, afraid for their mortgages, for their bank accounts, their wives, their kids, they're all waiting on the politicians and the government to do everything for them, sucking on the public tit. The army suited them, see? They want socialized this, they need welfare state that. Bull Durham, excuse my French."

Harry snorts. "I'll grant you that."

"It's a matter of self-confidence, my grinning legal friend. Believing in yourself, doing for yourself. It's 1966, for heaven's sake, *Goldfinger*-mania, the world is rocking and shaking, boys, and a man who wants to be somebody can't be standing on the sidelines, picking his nose." Ken takes a deep breath. He's begun snapping his fingers and he presses them to his sides. This is a two-cup high. Three.

"You've got enough of that," Harry says. "You got a whole boxcar of that, Kenny, that there self-confidence."

"You bet." Ken glances from one man to the other. "We can do this, boys. We *will* do it." Ken grins. "And who knows, maybe after this caper, we'll pull off another. I got some thoughts about that courier carrying the army pay that runs out to Shilo every month."

"Right." Harry nods and scrunches up his lips as he does so. "You would," he mutters, half under his breath. He stares into his glass.

John Berry coughs. "We're with you on that, Ken, we're the guys, the men to—"

There's a sheaf of papers lying on the desk and Ken grabs them up, squeezing them into a shape like a flower bouquet above his fist. "Listen to me, boys. A man can get as rich as his heart desires, go wherever he wants, it's wide open, is my point. Most people actually think this in the recesses of their minds but they don't got the heart to step up and realize their dreams. You got to have the heart, you have to seize the moment." Ken throws the papers onto the desktop and looks from Harry to John Berry. "My question is, you got the heart, boys, you got the jam?"

John bangs the desk with his open palm. "You bet."

Harry bangs his open palm down, too. "By the Jesus. Me too."

"All right. Good. That's more like it." Ken checks his watch. 9:20. It's okay to go now. If he walks slowly to the car and drives slowly to the terminal and saunters into the freight office, he can time it so there's just the right number of minutes for him to chat up the guy behind the counter before the shipment comes in. Ken takes a deep breath.

"Okay," he says, "enough pertinacious palaver. Time to move. Certain sure."

Harry glances at his watch. Gold. Some flash item he got off a guy who got it off a guy. "Go get 'em, Kenny." He smirks, knowing Ken dislikes the name.

Ken's hand moves to the bridge of his nose, he scratches but does not say anything. His eyes are afire from their verbal jousting, and for a moment it looks as if he would grab Harry or hit him with his huge hands. He's been known to chop a two-by-four in half with those hands.

"Oh, come on, Ken," Harry says, seeing this, laughing a brief laugh. "Lighten up, already."

Ken says nothing for a few seconds; then he cocks a thumb and forefinger gun and points it at Harry.

"Geez." Harry shakes his head. "If you're not sweating every little thing, you're twitching about like you're about to go off like a time bomb."

Ken grins, but like a shark: all teeth.

The two men eye each other in silence. Neither blinks.

John has been watching the exchange with interest and now he says, "You sure you don't want us to tag along? A little company on the ride?" He's ten years or so younger than Ken, a single man Ken had hired some time back to handle the sales of Queen Anne cookware farther west, where Ken no longer wanted to travel, where Ken was arrested for flying without a licence back in 1952 when he was flogging cookware from a plane he learned to fly himself. Pots and pans door to door, a game that has died on him, leaving him unemployed and without cash, a small-time number, in any case. John Berry is an intense and tightly-wound guy, like Ken himself, though a good salesman and a man who knows how to keep his mouth shut, at least Ken thinks so. And like Ken, he's always broke. Flashy but broke. There's something a little dodgy about John but that's the nature of the game, that's the kind of man Ken has to hang around with. He's maybe a little that way himself, truth be told. Harry too.

"Better this way, better I go alone." Ken looks straight into John's eyes and then pulls his hat back down his brow. "More people draw more attention to themselves. Anyhows, it's better that you two jokers not be seen."

"Right," Harry says, pointing at John. "You don't want someone remembering that ugly mug."

"Screw you," John says, and laughs. "You're no prize yourself." He makes a fist and holds it up toward Harry's face in a way that reminds Ken of Bogart in a movie.

"Screw you," Harry says. An edge has come into his tone, though he's grinning. There's an odd tension in the room, the tension between men who have a lot to win and more to lose, of men who only half-trust each other.

"All right, you jokers," Ken says. "See you later." By which he means tomorrow.

"You know where to find us," Harry says. By which he does not mean the offices of the Olgat Company, cleaning products, and a warehouse Harry has access to but a business that's about to go under and take Ken's dream of being office manager with it. Ken's usual bad luck. No, Harry means the Black Knight Lounge. He gives Ken a wink. He's older than Ken, a lawyer who Ken met in the pen when Harry came out to do a little community relations when he was in law school and Ken was doing time for a Toronto bank robbery. Like Ken, a big man with big plans and big needs. Since Ken came out of the pen Harry has been a kind of big brother to him, taking him under his wing, arranging for him to land a job as a salesman, manoeuvreing for Ken to be first in line for the now defunct manager's position at Olgat. Like Ken, Harry is always broke. Big talker, no money. A man from a Slavic background who changed his name from Backewich to Backlin in order to fit in better in Winnipeg's mostly Anglo-Saxon legal community.

"Tomorrow," Ken says. "I'll find you then."

"I'll bring them guys around then," John says. "Them guys I been telling you about."

Ken smiles and nods. "The brothers Grimm?"

"The brothers Grenkow," John says, laughing. "I'll bring them round tomorrow."

"You bet." Ken grins, this time in pleasure at his own joke. "I'm looking forward to it."

You're bouncing your legs the teacher said. Everyone said this. Stop bouncing your knees! It's a bad habit it's driving me crazy. The teacher was standing over me with her one hand resting on the corner of my desk and the other raised as if to strike me in the head she had a blackboard brush clenched in the fingers says she, You can't concentrate if you're bouncing the mind wanders.

But she was wrong I could.

Forty-three, says I. And looked up at her and smirked. I did not have the mustache then so the effect was not so strong.

She had asked, What is the sum of fifteen and twenty-eight and then my head being down my mind on Tom Mix or Bela Lugosi she had strode silently between the rows of desks to catch me out. It were a kind of game between us. She wore those shoes with rubber soles designed especially for sneaking up on people. The problem was she could not catch me out. I was a whiz with numbers I was always counting things adding subtracting multiplying dividing calculating I was a walking calculator. I counted the steps from the school to the shabby little movie house, seven hundred and thirty-two. I calculated how much I would make fetching the eggs if I was paid by the egg, eighteen eggs every day one hundred and twenty-six in a week five hundred and four in a month, maybe as many as fifty more depending on which month, so five-fifty, say, per month at a penny each, say, five dollars and fifty cents but that was not how granddad worked it. He was the law around the house, as the teacher was the law at school. Here's a nickel says the old bastard at the end of a month where I'd worn the skin of my hands raw on the handle of a rake or a shovel don't spend it all in one place, ha ha, a nasty grin on his mug. Just enough for the movies and not a cent more for popcorn he did not like me granddad I was the son of ne'er-do-well Norman Leishman man with big plans no results a failure of a man and husband who brung embarrassment on the family and I also was an embarrassment to granddad and grandma.

If the teacher had asked, What is one hundred and thirty-three less fifty-eight she might of had me, she might have stumped me for a moment. But she would not think of that until the next year and by then she could have trapped me only with long division. I always been a step ahead of the law.

It's not far from the Olgat building to the airport but Ken drives slowly, drawing out the time. He fiddles with the radio in his Chrysler station wagon, tuning in CJOB, the station he prefers to listen to, they always have the news first and he likes the afternoon guy and his *Homeward Hustle* program, his quiet voice, the music he chooses to play. Ken does not like rock and roll, he prefers songs with mellow background sounds, an orchestra, not all this crashing and banging of guitars, he prefers people who can carry a tune, tranquil tones and words he can understand. Doris Day, Dean Martin, Frank Sinatra. Sweet big-band melodies, music you can dance to. And tunes you can sing along to, old country tunes, like "Your Cheatin' Heart" and "The Wayward Wind," his favourite.

It's early February and the streets in Winnipeg are icy, snow has been pushed off the asphalt onto sidewalks into thigh-high piles. When the car approaches a streetlight, Ken slows; when he brakes sharply the rear end of the station wagon fishtails. There are not many people out and about on winter nights on the prairies, and the few who are have their collars turned up against the wind. Ghosts of breath puff out of their mouths. Poor bastards, Ken cannot help thinking.

Ken approaches the airport, passing the airport hotel, where the lights in the parking lot flicker pale yellow in the late evening, the mist from the frigid air making halos around them, lending them a ghostly aspect. Harry and John will be dug in there when he drives back this way but Ken will make a point of driving past, mostly because his head can't handle drink, but partly because Elva disapproves of the company he keeps. She doesn't understand the kind of men he has to consort with.

At the long curve that leads into the airport he glances into the sky. No blinking lights up there. The flight from Red Lake is due in at ten. Ken pulls the car past the main terminal building where the tower is located, where the air traffic guys work, where passengers step off flights and wait for baggage. It was almost ten years ago that Ken stepped off a flight from Toronto with $10,000 in a briefcase that he'd stolen from a Toronto Dominion bank in Toronto. That's how he acquired the name "Flying Bandit." A reporter had dubbed him that. Another had called him the "Gentleman Bandit" because he had been so low-key and respectful when asking for the $10,000; the bank manager told the reporters he'd been impressed by the thief's good manners and quiet demeanour. That had been a sweet robbery, in and out, clean as a whistle—only he'd been stupid to take just ten thousand when he might have had forty or fifty, what a prairie chump he had been. And the ten was gone in no time, which prompted him to return to Toronto a few months later and try a second holdup, only that time the cops were waiting for him when he came out of the

Commerce branch and he was nabbed only a few blocks from the bank. The cops had handled him roughly, gentleman bandit or not. "Gunman Foiled," the headlines read. He'd been sentenced to twelve years in the pen, of which he'd had to serve only forty-four months. Concrete walls, concrete floors, no windows, the stench of other cons. A long time absent from his family. Best not thought about.

Ken drives the station wagon past the main terminal building and pulls up around the north side. Parks and pockets his keys carefully. He strolls into the area where people are waiting for TransAir flight 108 from Red Lake to arrive, but he does not linger long, he's the tallest person in sight, a target of sorts, so he tips his hat over his eyes and shuffles toward the freight office. He pauses to glance out the window toward the tarmac where the plane will land. There are lights in the immediate area but it's dark beyond the rings of light thrown by the airport's floodlights. In the gloom of winter nothing much is moving outside, and it seems very dark indeed. 9:30.

The freight office is a dingy little cubicle tucked into the farthest north corner of the building. Ken has been here before, some nights earlier when he was checking on the arrival of Flight 108, which had come in on time, bringing with it a shipment of gold bars from Red Lake. Ken had been amazed at how nonchalant the TransAir and Air Canada employees had been about the gold, at how little security there was, at how simply the bars in their rectangular wooden boxes had come out of the nose of the plane on a modest conveyor belt, at how mundanely the routine of transferring the bars into a freight truck had occurred. He could hardly believe his eyes. Each bar of gold, he calculated, had to weigh at least fifty pounds, maybe seventy, the way the employees handled them, so that made them worth twenty or thirty thousand, and there were—what—five or six of them? And yet he had seen no RCMP, no armed security, no city cops. Too good to be true. Later when he'd checked at Air Canada freight he had seen a cop with a gun guarding the bars, which were secure inside a metal cage. But at the transfer point, nothing.

He sidles up to the counter at the freight office. Behind a cluttered desk sits a young man in a fresh uniform, a guy maybe in his mid-twenties who looks like this may be his first real job. He reminds Ken of the fresh-faced clerk at the Toronto Dominion branch where he'd pulled his first bank heist.

"Hey there," Ken says. He props one elbow on the counter and leans forward, ducking his head. It reduces his height, makes him seem less imposing, less threatening.

The young man looks up from his desk. Neat, orderly. Ken can't help liking him. "What can I do you for?" The young man remains seated, returning Ken's smile.

Ken tips his hat back, knowing this puts people at ease. "Well," he says, "I got me a little problem I thought you could help with."

"Shoot." The young man clearly has warmed to Ken. He runs one hand back through his hair.

Ken tells him he's a businessman thinking of setting himself up to carry freight into northern towns. "Not the ones you go to," he says, reassuring, "I'm not trying to cut your grass, my target is the smaller, more remote places TransAir doesn't go to. But I am interested in the planes you guys use," he goes on, "the DC-3. That particular machine has caught my eye."

"Ah," the young man says. He glances quickly at his watch, pushes papers aside, and then stands up and comes to the counter. "Freight," he says, "is the business of the DC-3. Its strength as an aircraft. You're not thinking of flying it yourself, are you, mister?"

"Well, I was, yes. I got a licence."

"That's no Cessna, you know. It's a big aircraft. Needs special handling, special training."

"Training, yeah, I see what you mean. But you think it might be good for carrying building materials, things in crates?" Ken tips his hat back, surprised at how he has actually become interested in the question, though he began merely by feigning interest.

"It has a big cargo area up front, the DC-3, perfect for transporting just that kind of stuff. Now if you're looking to move heavy equipment, bulldozers and trucks—"

"You sound like an expert."

"Expert, well." The young man blushes. "I might know a little something or other."

"But look," Ken says, leaning forward, "this conversation has to be confidential." He glances back over his shoulder. "You know how it is, a guy comes up with a good business idea and before he can turn around, someone else has pinched it. You understand that, don't you, ah—"

"Chuck. Chuck Waters."

"Well, Chuck, a guy can't be too careful. You were saying the DC-3 has a big cargo hold and that's just what I'm looking for. See, there's lots of building going on up north, hydro and mining and guys developing fishing lodges, and road construction, and there's going to be a call for planes that can carry materials and equipment up there. Air cargo, air freight, if you follow me. My plan is to get in on the ground floor, to lease, maybe buy a couple of DC-3s. Not a big operation at the start, but likely to grow fast."

"The DC-3 chomps up a lot of fuel," Chuck says, "it's a heavy old bird, but it's a well-made aircraft, durable, a good plane for landing on those rough airstrips up north, some of them aren't much longer than driveways on Wellington Crescent, if you know what I mean. And the frost bubbles north of fifty are something else. The DC-3 can take all that punishment. And it has lots of cargo space, a man can stand up in the nose hold. Well, a short man."

Ken smiles. "Irregardless. Sounds like the baby I'm after."

"It's—hey." Chuck looks at his watch. "Ten on the mark. That sounds like the Red Lake flight coming in now." He reaches back to the desk for a sheaf of papers. He grabs a jacket off the hook. "C'mon, mister, I'll show you, that's a DC-3 landing out there now."

This was what Ken was hoping for—a chance to see the plane and the gold up close, check out just exactly how the transfer of the bullion occurs.

Chuck leads Ken up a short flight of stairs and out into the dark night. The plane from Red Lake is already drawn up to the terminal building, red and yellow running lights blinking, a few passengers coming down the metal ramp, the baggage hold open. When they come up to the plane, Chuck waves at an attendant and goes over to her and exchanges papers. He calls something towards the guys who are wheeling a conveyor belt toward a door that's been opened in the nose of the DC-3. In a minute he's back at Ken's side.

"Conveyor belt," Ken says, whistling under his breath. "Smooth."

"An old clunker. Cacks out half the time. TransAir, eh?" The machine has started whirring and in a few seconds a man appears in the hold with one of the wooden boxes Ken saw a few nights earlier, about a foot long, he sees now, and maybe six inches deep and wide. The guy who's placing them on the conveyor is an older man and he's wheezing with the effort. Ken thinks, At least fifty pounds, likely seventy. His mouth is dry as he watches the first little box trundle down the conveyor belt. It's bound with straps of metal and has a red seal stamped on it and some letters and numbers. Ken tries not to look too close.

Chuck Waters kibitzes with the man putting the boxes on the conveyor and the guy at the bottom end, who's taking them off and putting them on a dolly. Ken's mind is whirling. Four boxes have come out of the hold and a fifth is on its way. At seventy pounds each and at thirty-five dollars an ounce, fifty on the black market, each little box would go at almost $20,000, a shipment of ten bars would bring at least $175,000, maybe $200,000. Ken needs a drink. His house in River Heights, a modest bungalow, cost just over ten grand, a new Cadillac goes for thirty-five hundred. People speak in awe of someone who has a million. This is a lot of money coming in every week or so. A man who stole it would be set up for life.

When the boxes are all secure on the dolly, a driver starts it up and putters towards the south end of the terminal, turning a corner and disappearing into the dark. Ken watches closely out of the corner of his eye, but tries not to make his interest too obvious. He runs his tongue around inside his mouth. Goes over the numbers one more time, adding, multiplying, figures dancing in his head. Yes, almost two hundred grand, a small fortune, enough that a man might never have to work again.

"C'mon, mister," Chuck says, startling him, "let's have a look inside the ol' DC-3."

They climb into the cargo space in the plane's nose. The older man who threw the boxes onto the conveyor has an unlit cigarette clamped in his lips. He's breathing hard. Chuck says something to him about goldbricking and they both laugh. But Ken feels a flutter in his stomach and thinks, Do they know something, are they on to me? Then Chuck shows Ken how deep the cargo bay in the plane is, citing dimensions and figures having to do with weight and capacity, but Ken isn't really listening. He pokes around in the far recesses of the hold and nods his head knowingly, a man calculating; but Ken is not calculating the cargo capacity of the DC-3.

It's frosty inside the cargo space, and drafty. Ken's nose is cold, he notices that Chuck hugs his arms to his chest from time to time. He's wearing only a thin windbreaker. The guys outside had on navy parkas with company logos, bulky coveralls underneath, and their exertions caused steam to come off their faces.

When they climb down from the plane, Ken puts his hand out to Chuck. "Thanks," he says. "It was kind of you to show me around."

"Nothing to it, mister," Chuck says.

"I got some pondering to do," Ken says. "But I'm confident things will work out, this aircraft looks to be just the ticket."

"Cargo, eh, nothing fancy, the DC-3."

Ken strokes his mustache. "Kind of you."

"Well, I hope you get your freight business off the ground." Chuck smiles wryly.

Ken laughs. "I think I might, I think I just might. Off the ground and airborne even. And when I do, I'll be looking for bright young guys to run the office and whatnot. Guys like you."

"You know where to find me."

"I do." Ken tips his hat. "That I do." He gives Chuck a wink.

He walks back to his station wagon, aware of his feet moving quickly across tarmac and through the terminal but his thoughts are so abuzz that he does not remember once he's at the car if he saw anyone along the way, or if anyone took notice of him. He starts the engine. Inside the car his breath makes ghosts and condensation starts to form on the windows. He turns on the fan. His mind is whirling. No cops in the entire airport, no real cops, just the rental guy at the wire cage. Hard to believe. No RCMP. The airport is dead at 10:00 p.m., empty, no passengers, few employees. No other planes coming in at the same time as the Red Lake flight, no flights at all coming in afterwards, it appears. These are all good things, encouraging signs. And the guys unloading the wooden boxes and driving the dolly are not much interested in what they're doing—lax, in fact; it's grunt work and they know it, they have no commitment to it or to protecting the shipment. As far as Ken can determine, no one in the tower can see the TransAir plane at the far end of the tarmac. And it's so dark. At this time of the year it's cold too, so no one wants to hang around checking papers when they could be inside. Ken whistles softly under his breath and goes through the list again. All the cards are falling into place.

Just when the heater is beginning to blow warm air, Ken shuts the motor off and walks back into the terminal, this time heading for the Air Canada freight desk. It is being manned by an older guy. Behind him, near the wire cage, stands the cop. Ken registers the pistol on his hip, his burly size, his watchful gaze. The five wooden boxes, he sees, are in the cage now, secure. The only place to get at them, as he's surmised all along, is at the point of transfer, when they come down the conveyor belt at the DC-3 and are passed from TransAir to Air Canada.

Ken is sweating under the brim of his hat. He intended to turn and walk away but the guy behind the desk has looked up and the cop, a rent-a-cop, Ken sees now, has noticed him too. The antennae of suspicion are up.

"I'm—ah—I'm expecting a package," Ken says. "From Edmonton."

"Edmonton." The guy behind the desk has risen. He's almost as tall as Ken and broad through the shoulders, with a thick neck. "Name?"

"Robert, Robert Bruce."

There's shuffling of papers on the desk. "No, nothing here." The guy shakes his head.

"Damn," Ken says. "Excuse my French." He grins. Earlier his mouth was dry but he's feeling comfortable now, he talks easily with people, and they warm to him. He leans on the counter and pushes at the brim of his hat. "It's important, see, business stuff."

"Sorry, Mister. Mister, ah, Bruce."

"Not a big package." Ken gawks around, as if trying to spot it.

"Business," the guy says. "I know how important that can be."

"You got it, mister." Ken grins again, like they're in a conspiracy together.

The guy seemed wary at first, but he's warmed and is smiling back. "Maybe tomorrow."

"You bet." Ken turns to walk away.

"I'll keep an eye out. There's a flight in from the west early in the morning. I'll keep an eye out, Mister Bruce."

"Yeah," Ken says, aware he's made an impression, but also aware that the cop standing farther away has been watching and assessing the exchange. "That would be good of you."

"You bet. Edmonton, right?"

"Edmonton it is."

"I'll remember. Edmonton, Calgary, flights coming in early."

"Good. I'll be back."

Walk slow, Ken thinks, it gives you dignity. He turns slowly and squares his shoulders as he walks away, taking his time. Walking away in a hurry is suspicious. He needs to appear calm. Though inside his heart bangs in his rib cage. It's a three-cup high, he feels it buzzing in his temples, he feels it zinging in his chest, the old Ken charm at work, the derring-do, seeing how far the bluff will go. Making the gambit.

When he reaches the door that leads outside, he takes a quick look at his watch. Eleven.

When Ken closes the door at Olgat Company behind him he sees that John is sitting at the big desk behind the front counter with two young guys, the Grenkow brothers. It's another cold night in Winnipeg and Ken blows through his lips and slaps his gloves together, *whewewhew*.

"Here's the man himself," John says brightly, pushing back his chair. Three sets of eyes settle on Ken as he ducks around the counter and comes up to the desk. He takes off his gloves. It's mid-February and the winds are still blowing from the north, the wind chill was reported on the radio as thirty below.

John is standing. "Ken," he says, "I want you to meet Rick and Paul Grenkow." The other two stand, the one closest to Ken offering his hand while butting out a cigarette with the other. He has a big smile but what Ken notices about him is he's wearing cowboy boots. That makes Ken smile, and Rick Grenkow smiles bigger. He wears a fresh white shirt, too, with a smart tie, and his sport jacket is hanging off the back of the chair he's been sitting in. These days everyone younger than thirty seems to be wearing blue jeans and sweatshirts. Ponytails, love beads. Paul and Rick Grenkow are dressed like Ken, only in a more youthful way, smart, like they take themselves seriously. Rick's hair is cut short and combed back in a ducktail, which makes an impression on Ken; Rick looks more like he should be in law school than conspiring in a robbery. Ken smiles, shaking Paul's hand, and he takes a glass of whiskey when John offers it to him.

"Nice to meet you boys," Ken says.

"Pleasure is ours," Rick says, quietly but firmly. He's pulled a chair out for Ken and he and Paul both wait for Ken to loosen his coat before they resume sitting.

Ken says, "I like that. Good manners." He nods around the table.

This is a favourite theme of his, John Berry has heard him go on about it before: manners impress people, they make people comfortable, they soften defences, they win people to your side, so salesmen should hone their manners, be polite, deferential—and not just salesmen but anyone who wants to get ahead, people in business in particular; after all, aren't we all selling something, if only just ourselves?

"Oh, he's smooth," John says, nodding toward Rick. "You should ask the girls about that," he adds, laughing. "Even better, ask those girls' mothers."

Ken sees that the three others are laughing. Has he come in on a private joke? "How's that?"

"Ricky here," John says, "has a way with the girls. Anything in a skirt that moves, truth be told, anything from eight to eighty."

Rick laughs. He has straight white teeth, a winning smile, the kind of man Ken warms to.

"Anything that can spread its legs," Paul says, laughing. He takes a quick swig of whiskey, eyeing Ken, aware he may have stepped over a line. If Ken is a prude, he may not like this kind of talk, or the person who talks it. But Ken does not object.

Rick laughs lightly. "I have my share of luck with the girls, true." He leans back in his chair and chortles and takes a sip of whiskey. "Isn't that what they're for?"

"More than your share." Paul punches his brother in the shoulder. "It's got so bad," he adds, looking at Ken, "that when they see Ricky-boy here coming, mothers weep in the street. Their little girl is doomed. Her pants are about to be charmed off her squidgy little bum."

"Squidgy?" Ken laughs. "That's a new one on me. Squidgy. I like it."

When the laughter has died, Ken takes a sip of his drink. Burns all the way down, but in a good way on a frigid prairie night. He tips his glass towards the others. In the silence the four men sip their drinks. Ken clears his throat. "Well," he says.

"Down to business," John says, picking up his hint. "Ken has a proposition."

Ken looks from Rick to John. "Weren't you going to go over the set-up? Haven't you?" His eyes narrow and he cocks his head to the side.

"Yeah, yeah," John says, "of course. We've gone over the basics." He takes a gulp of whiskey and swills it in his mouth before swallowing. "But you said—"

"Yeah." Ken eyes John for a moment. "I said don't take the chicken to the chopping block until you're sure you got an axe."

"Kinda thing." John scrunches his lips. "Kenny here is fond of barnyards and such," he says to the Grenkow brothers. He grins, inviting them into a joke at the older man's expense.

Ken sniffs and straightens his broad shoulders and looks from Rick to Paul. "So what do you know?" His tone has become hard, business-like.

"Some kind of scam," Rick says. He takes a quick drag on his cigarette.

"A heist." Paul is about the same size as his brother, but his chin juts out when he speaks, like he's expecting a fight.

"Um," Ken mutters. "At the airport."

"Yeah." Rick rolls his eyes. "So what's at the airport?"

"More than you'd guess, my young friend." Ken points one thick finger at him. He turns to John and raises his eyebrows, inviting him to continue.

"Gold," John says in little more than a whisper. He leans forward, elbows on the table. "Gold bullion. Comes in bars, see, comes on a plane that flies in from the north."

"Shit." Rick looks from John to Paul. "You're putting us on."

"Shit," Paul says. "Gold? A gold heist?" He's fumbled a cigarette out of a pack and is busy trying to light it, hands shaking.

John looks to Ken.

Ken glances over one shoulder, as if he suspects someone might be listening. "In bars, yes. Eight, maybe ten per shipment. About a foot long, in wooden boxes." He taps the rim of his glass with one fingernail. "Heavy bars but not bulky. Shiny, silky, priceless gold. A small fortune." Ken's voice rises, as if he is singing the words to a song. "You boys interested?"

Rick swallows. "Yes, of course, but—"

"But?"

Paul says quietly: "How you gonna get that sturgeon into the boat?"

Ken studies him a moment. "How's that?"

"Well," Paul says, "it's just, you go after the big fish, you gotta haul that sucker outta the water. That maybe ain't so easy." He smiles after saying this and runs his big hand back through his thick head of black hair.

"You're making fun of me," Ken says, "you boys are laughing at my idea."

"No," Rick says, "it's not that at all."

Ken takes a deep breath. "What, then?"

"Sounds dangerous."

"Huh." Ken takes a sip of whiskey. "It is. A bit. A bit dangerous. John here knows that, I know that, now you know it. That scare you?"

"Hell no. But—"

"It does scare you." Ken looks at John and winks. "You said these boys were all-stars, you said these boys were hellions—"

"You bet your ass," Paul says.

Rick's tone has risen. "That's not it. It's just… it just sounds big-time, real big-time. Bugsy Malone kinda thing, guns and screeching cars. Shoot-'em-up stuff. Gold bullion, shit." He glances quickly at Paul. We never done nothing like that. We were more thinking—"

"No guns." Ken shakes his head. "No screeching tires." He leans forward, his big face looking first one brother then the other in the eyes. "That's the beauty of it. The stuff is just sitting there, out at the airport, a shipment of shiny gold, you see, just waiting for guys with the right smarts to snatch it." Almost by reflex one hand reaches up and touches his temple. Sweat has begun to bead there. He wipes at it, hand trembling.

Rick laughs, a sudden sound like a gunshot in the little room. "Snatch," he says. "I like that."

Ken's eyes narrow. "Just waiting for men with moxie to grab it up."

"No armed guards?" Rick clears his throat. "C'mon. You're shittin' us. There's gotta be guards."

"Inside, yes, a rent-a-cop guards the bullion when it's secure in a cage they got specially built to house stuff like that. Valuable shipments. But outside, where we snatch the stuff, only the airline guys, flunkies, paper-pushers, not men likely to put their lives on the line for someone else's gold, if you follow what I'm getting at."

Paul taps his glass on the table. "There's gotta be a catch." The older of the two brothers, he speaks more slowly than Rick and his voice is more measured.

"No, I tell you, it's safe as churches, boys, safe as churches. Just walk in and..." Ken's voice has become high and harsh, a rasp. He lifts his glass to his lips.

"Shit," Rick says, shaking his head. "Gold bullion."

Paul says, "You can't have this right. I mean—"

Ken sniffs. "You're scared, eh? Don't got the balls?"

"No. You got us wrong about that, we're just... Jesus."

"Boys," Ken says. "Fortune favours the daring. Am I right?"

Paul takes a quick drag on his cigarette and puffs out smoke, but neither brother speaks. John Berry clears his throat.

"Am I right?" Ken repeats.

"You're right," John Berry says.

"You bet," Ken says with finality.

The silence they leave is broken only by the sound of a plane taking off from the airport.

Finally Ken says, "Boys, this job is a lock, I tell you. That's the long and short of it." He takes another sip of whiskey and then he studies first Rick, then Paul. "I've been over the ground, see, got the lay of the land. The shipment comes in and it's transferred from one airline to the other. So that's where we're waiting. At the transfer point. See? Just walk in and the stuff is ours. It's as easy as driving up and signing a bill of lading. That's the weak link in the chain, see, right there at the transfer point. There's always a weak link." He holds his hand up, indicating what he means with a gap between the forefinger and thumb. "Well? What do you say?" His throat feels thick and his expression has tightened. He has to calm down.

"We're with you," Rick says. "Don't get me wrong."

"All right." Ken runs the back of his wrist across his mouth. "I gotta hit the can. Too much java today." He nods in the direction of the door to one side. "John here can fill you in, in the meantime. On a few more details." He turns away abruptly and crosses to the washroom quickly, his long stride eating up the space in only seconds. Inside, he sits on the toilet fully dressed and rests his big hands on his knees. They're sweaty. So is his brow. Shit, Ken thinks to himself. Shit. His heart is thumping in his chest and he practises what Elva has taught him, take in huge mouthfuls of air, count to ten on the intake before letting breath out, imagine his heart slowing. In a moment he has closed his eyes, and when the after-image of stars wavering in a ring has dissipated, he begins to hum softly to himself a few bars of "The Wayward Wind." This, too, is Elva's idea, his favourite song. She's used some fancy word to describe what he's doing, *mantra*, maybe, it doesn't matter, it's supposed to slow him down, bring him back to a place of peace. Elva's word. He thinks of it as regaining control. He gets worked up and his mind feels like it's full of barbed wire, sometimes his gut tightens and he knows that in a minute he'll have to vomit. Not good, not healthy, not productive. He hums the song through and when he's done he opens his eyes. His heart has stopped thumping in his rib cage. What he'd like to do is lay his forehead against the porcelain sink and feel the cold seep into the bone. Instead, he stands. "All right," he says aloud. "All right, then, Ken."

He's still humming under his breath when he closes the washroom door behind him and crosses to where the younger men are sitting around the table, their eyes following his progress across the room. He has a vague impression of their excited voices heard through the washroom door while he had his eyes closed, and a burst of laughter that ended with the clinking of glasses. He clears his throat. "So," he begins, "so you know the general set-up, then; TransAir's last flight of the day down from the north, the airport layout, the bullion coming in from Red Lake, the Air Canada cargo van that the TransAir guys move it to? John has filled you in about that now?"

Paul nods.

Rick says, "We're up to speed there." He takes a long drag on his cigarette.

"And who's doing what? You got that part too? The manpower aspect?"

"Right. Two guys go to the airport to grab the bullion, and you're back here waiting for the cargo. Take it off our hands. Shift it quick from one vehicle to the other."

"Exactly." Ken pauses. "We intercept the shipment as it goes from one airline to the other. Quick turnovers, fast exchanges. That's the key to this operation. The weak link."

"The weak link. We got it."

"Someone up north to tip us to the shipment."

"Got that too."

"And you're up to this?" Ken looks from Rick to Paul. "To a big-time heist?"

Paul says, "Yeah."

Their exchanges rat-a-tat, like small machine guns in the echoing room.

"It's gonna take jam, it's gonna take balls to pull this off. No weaseling out."

"You bet." Rick rotates his glass on the tabletop and holds Ken's eyes until Ken looks over at John, who's smiling.

"It's straightforward, that's the beauty of it." Ken drums the tabletop with one finger. "We'll go over the details and you'll see. Drive up, make the collection, drive away."

Paul laughs. "All right. Chief."

"The important thing is nerve." Ken leans forward, picks up his glass of whiskey and takes a quick sip. "Having your nerve and holding it. In this kind of operation you're coming on all legit but it's basically a snow-job. It's a bluff, see, you're convincing someone you're someone you're not. You have to be convincing."

"A fast talker." Rick laughs.

"A smooth talker." Ken looks from one brother to the other. "Smooth."

Paul snorts. "We been doing that all our lives. Smooth-talking. Ricky is aces."

"You gotta be so good, so convincing that you half believe it yourself." Ken pauses. "Correction. So good that you *do* believe it yourself." Ken pauses again and adds in a half-whisper, "meretricious persiflage."

Paul raises one eyebrow. "Wha?"

"Nothing," Ken says, "nothing, nothing at all."

"Just Ken talking to himself," John says. "Spouting big words."

"In any case," Rick says. He's been tapping his empty glass on the tabletop. "What if they don't buy?"

"Oh, they'll buy. You bet."

"But if they don't?"

"Yeah." Paul's voice cracks. He's older than Ken thought at first, maybe twenty-five, though he looks nineteen. "What's the backup?"

"Mostly your wits." Ken clears his throat and lets a silence build while he fingers the brim of his hat. It's chilly in the warehouse but he's hot, there's sweat on his brow. "The important thing in an operation like this," he finally says, "is to keep your nerve. You'll have a gat but it's the last thing you want to use. That's only trouble. And you use it only if you absolutely have to. You look people in the eye, you sound like you know what you're talking about, you don't take no guff. You make sure you're the one in charge. You keep talking, you don't allow time for reflection and questions. If it looks at all like things are going bad, you back off, you don't try to force the issue, see. It's a matter of nerve, of poise, and of… and, well, of nerve."

In the silence the rumble of a plane overhead draws everyone's attention.

Ken licks his lips. "It's a fast operation, see. In and out in minutes. Hardly more than an hour from the time you start out. The key is timing, which we'll go over. I've got maps and whatnot."

"That's our Kenny." John laughs. "Always prepared. A regular boy scout."

Ken eyes John and twirls his glass but does not speak.

"All right," Rick says. "Sounds good."

Ken continues twirling his glass. "We'll go over all that. The details. The key tonight is whether you're up to it. In or out."

"Yeah," Rick says. "In. You bet. It's an amazing scam."

"Yeah," Paul adds, "a real doozy. *Goldfinger* style. We're in."

"Shit or get off the pot. That's the point." Ken smirks. "Kind of thing." He nods slowly. He's got their approval, that and their praise.

There's another silence and then Paul says, "We're in, you bet, but we got a few questions." His tone rises and he glances quickly at Rick, seeking confirmation.

"Just a couple," Rick says. "Small stuff. Minor matters."

"Shoot." Ken cocks a thumb and forefinger gun at Rick and laughs.

Rick laughs. "It's a one-night thing, right, we do the job at the airport but then there's no more… no more involvement for us, no further complications. We do the job, then we're out of it, right? Paul and me, I mean."

"You bet," Ken says evenly, nodding, "that's about it."

"That's how we want it. In and out."

Paul snorts and mutters, "Rick's specialty. Ask all them girls."

Ken smiles. "Maybe one of you has to travel up to Red Lake and tip us off to the shipment. But that's beforehand, you know, call when you see that the shipment's taken on board. So we're sure the gold is on the plane before we set the operation in motion."

"That could be me," Paul says. "I don't got much stomach for hold-ups, guns and so on."

Ken nods. Touches the brim of his hat. "That'll be you then, Paul."

"But then we're out, right?" Rick fixes Ken with a stare. "We do the job, clean as a whistle, nice and simple, and then we can take off, right? Vamoose. Split the city."

"That's about it. No more involvement. For you. If that's what you're worried about."

"I've got this little piece waiting for me in Vancouver, see. Hot little number."

Ken smiles. "You'll be tussling in the sheets as fast as you can drive there."

"Good," Rick and Paul say almost at the same instant.

Ken studies Rick's fingers. They're tapping the edge of the table. "That's good, straight," he says, "it's always good to talk straight from the outset, Rick. It's dangerous, what we're getting into here. Not big-time dangerous, but risky. You should know that going in. You'll be carrying a gat, like I say, but it should be the last option. Guns. Never a good idea. You carry a gun, you end up getting shot yourself." Ken looks at Rick, making sure this sinks in.

Rick's eyes don't flinch. He scrapes one of his cowboy boots along the floor. "The other question is this: you pay us in advance, right? Two grand each, right?"

Ken shifts in his chair. "A grand up front, we're not millionaires, Harry and me." Ken takes a quick sip of whiskey. "Then a grand later, when we start to sell off the bars and bring in the cash. It's the same deal we have with John here. Right, John?"

Paul and Rick eye each other across the table.

"Of course," John says, looking from one brother to the other, "if you're not up to it."

"We're up to it." Rick nods to Paul, who nods back.

An air of ease, of bringing matters to a close, has settled into the room. Rick scrapes the toe of one boot on the floor, Paul has pushed his chair away from the table, as if he intends to stand up, Ken fiddles with the brim of his hat. John looks at Ken and nods. Ken winks back. Done deal, their expressions say.

Paul clears his throat, standing. "Just getting things clear. Just setting things straight."

"That's right," Ken says, "that's good. Keep things clear. That's good business practice." He raises his glass and leans into the table. "Here's to gold bullion, then, here's to us."

I tip my wristwatch toward the light outside to be certain I'm reading it accurately. 8:30. Tick tick. The Grenkow boys are supposed to be here they're not on time, which is not a good sign. I double-check my watch, I always been a stickler about time. I arrive at appointments between five minutes early and five minutes late, it's a joke with people who know me they call me punch-clock Ken. I take a deep breath. I'm sitting at the desk at Olgat with my briefcase on the floor at my feet, I put one hand on my knee and press down which is Elva's idea, a strategy to keep from bouncing my legs. According to her, it's a question of mind over matter, everything's a question of mind over matter to Elva. Focus, concentrate be the master of your body and you will be the master of your life says she. I glance at my watch again. 8:35.

All the songs say time is too short and there's that famous poem that legal-beagle Charlie Feagle showed to me in the pen, "had we but world enough and time." But the songs have got it wrong the poets also to my way of thinking at least. Time oozes by, anyone who's spent a stretch behind bars knows this like he knows the pattern of veins on the back of his hands. Tick-tock. On the outside, time can weigh on a person but mostly you're trying to cram things into the hours of the day shopping this appointment that pick up the kids make the call.

But on the inside you develop strategies to deal with the slow passage of time you learn how to occupy your hands mostly, lift weights, write letters to women in Australia, flip from one passage in the Bible to another and see if there's any correspondence between them, a mental game also play solitaire. One guy in the pen made finger rings out of silver the bosses gave him tools they trusted him. Some learn to shut off their mind from cares, from worries, from anything that has anything to do with the outside world, that don't matter anymore they don't exist no more thoughts no longer matter. Thought don't matter no more. Or you turn weird and become a religious nut, a born-again, blessed be the Lord Jesus, which is what I learned to do in my own way sink deep into my mind, my imagination. The lockup is a series of rooms each of which contains another room inside another like them Russian dolls, the wall that encloses the prison is the first, then come the yard, the jail, the cell, and inside the cell, the room that is the man. And inside the man his mind, the final and smallest room where he goes to get through the day, to make it through the night, to finally find out what he is and what he may become.

A hostage to time.

"You're a philosopher," says Charlie Feagle to me one day. We were sitting with our books, me flipping through a dictionary or a book about famous people from history, Charlie poring over the law of torts or some such.

"When you have a lot of time to think," says I, "you become philosophical."

"*Hostage* is the word you're looking for, Ken."

I'd said slave. We're slaves to time.

"You might try looking it up in your dictionary of quotations, Ken. Francis Bacon is the man you want. Hostages to fate."

I looked over at Charlie, a mousy little man, who nevertheless had the respect of the other cons, a source of legal information, a quiet but precise fella, a thinker. Not many of that there type in the pen, which was mostly braggarts and bullshitters and bums. I flipped about in the book on my lap. "Bacon," I said, "that's a weird name. Is there a Francis Pork Chop?"

Charlie Feagle gave me a look. "Let me amend what I just said," says he. "Cracker-barrel philosopher. Idiot savant."

That put me in my place. But he had it wrong, Charlie. What Bacon said was: "Children are hostages to Fortune."

Which I was quick to point out a couple days later.

"No," says he, "I knew what Francis Pork Chop said. I was trying to steer you to a better concept than slave, Ken. Hostage."

"Like us. In the slammer here. Stony Mountain, doing time."

"The joint, right."

"Exactly. The clink, the lockup."

"Close enough. Yeah."

Paul and Rick Grenkow are bent over one side of the table in the Olgat office, Ken and John the other. A week has passed. Almost March. They're looking at a map of the city. Smoke curls up from an ashtray in the centre of the table. "Here," Ken says, pointing at an intersection, "and here." They're studying the route between the air terminal and Olgat, the city's north end, a grid of rectangles cut through by several main thoroughfares. Ken is holding a cup of coffee, sipping, shifting it from one hand to another, his eyes darting as quickly over the map as his thoughts flit between calculations.

"Right," Rick Grenkow says. "Those two lights stop you every time." His finger points at an intersection and then moves to another. "Them others are okay. But this here one. No dice."

Ken nods. "They're in sync, them ones here and here and here?" His finger moves over the map.

John Berry says, "They've got them timed so if you make the first one, you make the next two. So that's good, that's easy. But the hitch is."

Ken makes a clucking sound. "But then you're stopped by this one?" He lifts his finger and taps it on the map.

"And the next," Paul says. "You make the first but then the yellow comes on before you get to the second. Even if you go a little faster than the limit. But even that's not enough."

Ken nods. "Limit."

Rick looks directly at him. "'Course, you could actually speed, you could jump one of the lights."

"No speeding, no jumping lights." Ken narrows his eyes and looks from one brother to the other. "By the book." He tips his hat back. "What time of day we talking?"

Rick looks at Paul. "After six. Why?"

"Sometimes they change the sequence." Ken has gone back to studying the grid of streets.

"They do?" Paul's face is scarved in smoke for a moment.

"They might. You know, according to the time of day, traffic flow." Ken drums the map with his fingers. "Check into that. When you boys been going over the route? Time of day?"

"Dunno." Rick looks at Paul again. "Afternoons—mostly?"

"Go over the route from ten to midnight, say. That's when you'll be out there, come the big night. The sequence may be different then." Ken pauses, aware that he sounds school-teacherish, and that Rick and Paul have taken a step back from the table. He doesn't want to chastise these boys. He wants their approval. "But it's what, you say, the total time?"

"Seven minutes," Paul says sharply, sticking out his chin.

"Not quite," John Berry says. "Six and something. By my watch. More or less."

"More or less?"

"Well—"

"Not good enough," Ken says. "Neither your watch—no offence, John—or the overall driving time. What you need to do is chart the times of day, you know, when the lights regularly are red or green. Down to the minute. Make a chart, judge when it's best to start out. If this light turns green, say—" he points at the intersection nearest the airport—"at 10:30, then you have to ask yourself when's the last minute you can leave the terminal to catch it while it's still green, to avoid being stopped. That sort of thing. Same with the others. If you follow me."

Paul nods. "Got it, Chief."

"Do it every which way until you've broken the travelling time down into segments, and then calculate what's the fewest minutes it can be done in." Ken fiddles with the brim of his hat. He's getting worked up, his heart is rattling in his chest. "You follow? Know what you're getting into before you get into it."

"I follow, that's good thinking." Rick taps the toe of one cowboy boot on the concrete floor. "We haven't been paying this enough attention, not really. If we knew the schedule of the lights, that could make a real difference. You betcha."

"Time to bear down, then," Ken says, his tone rising to a hard edge. "Time to get a stopwatch and find out exactly how fast you're doing it. Calculate when it's best to leave the terminal for the quickest getaway. Within a range, like. Master each and every detail. Know the layout, like—"

"Like the back of your hand." Rick holds his up for Ken to study.

"Exactly." They both grin.

"I can get one," Paul says. "Stopwatch."

"Good." Ken takes a quick breath. "It's not important how long it takes you to get there, not really, what's important is how fast you can get away. Make it back here. The transfer point. What's critical is the transfer points. Once you've got the bars in the car."

"Five minutes," John says, "I bet we can work it down to five." John licks his lips. There's a gleam in his eye, Ken sees, he feels it too, the old thrill. Selling pots and pans door-to-door has a certain excitement to it, there's that tingle in closing a sale, but it's nothing compared to what they're getting into. This is the big time, the stuff of stories and legends. Why else be alive? He tips his coffee cup to his lips.

"All right, then." Ken runs his index finger over the grid of streets. "And that's the only route that makes sense?"

Rick nods and points at the map. "It's the only way makes sense. Straight in to the airport once this turn is made. Otherwise you're diddling about on side streets and the like."

"Huh." Ken's eyes remain fixed to the map. "Back alleys?"

"Tried them. No point. Takes even longer."

"Even longer. Well, that's it then, that's the way it's gotta be done. So drive it and drive it again and drive it until it's down to five minutes and you do it each and every time in them five minutes." Ken looks at John and smiles. He turns to Rick.

"You betcha," Rick says. "That convertible of John's will do the job. It moves right along."

"It's a flash car." Ken makes a point of catching John's eye. "You don't want to draw too much attention. Low profile. Right, boys?"

"Right," Rick says. "We'll alternate between cars, one time the Ford, one time Paul's car."

"Good thinking." Ken winks at him and then studies the map. "Remember," he says, softening his tone, "what's important is the exit time. Work on that. Without drawing attention."

Rick nods. "You betcha, Chief. Without being obvious."

"Good." Ken takes a deep breath. "All right now, let's talk about where you park the car at the terminal and where they store the Air Canada van and whether the keys are in the ignition, and so on. I've got a checklist here. A description of Chuck Waters and the other guy in the office and stuff like that there." He reaches inside his coat and brings out a notebook, wets one fingertip and flips to a page near the middle.

John laughs. "Kenny's always got a checklist."

"Checklist." Rick snorts and Paul chuckles, subdued sounds in the empty building.

"Yeah. Checklist. You bet. You jokers should too." Ken glances from John to Rick. His voice has dropped to a whisper, a raspy wheeze.

Rick frowns. "How you mean?" He puffs smoke into the air.

"Organization. That's the key."

"Organization," Rick says. "Check. Checklist." He laughs at his own joke.

John taps his temple. "Got it all here."

Ken snorts. "Be prepared, be organized. The smallest slip-ups bring jobs down. You wouldn't believe the stories I heard in the pen." Ken clears his throat. "A door left open, a briefcase misplaced, an empty gas tank. Details, you see, they're the key. So don't laugh."

Hijacked
2 men escape from airport

F laubert's your man." Legal beagle Feagle had been asking me how you plan a robbery.

"Never heard of him," says I "Now in *The Asphalt Jungle* there's a guy who plots out the entire job, maps, charts, schedules, the whole works. The whole job timed down to the second. Now that's an operation. Meticulous organization."

"No, I'm not talking about some cheap crook from the movies. Gustave Flaubert, French novelist of the nineteenth century, Ken. *Madame Bovary*."

"News to me."

"Flaubert said, 'God is in the details.' "

"He had that right."

"Look it up in the book of famous quotations."

"You bet I will."

"Only Flaubert was talking about writing books. Not robbing banks, Ken. Of course."

"Certain sure, moniker like that."

"Same principle though."

"Kinda. Not much at stake there, though. In writing."

"You never know, Ken. You've heard of Shakespeare, right?"

"*Romeo and Juliet* in school. Not much to be excited about. *Julius Caesar*, now that had my interest on account of the knife fights and getting even. 'Friends, Romans, countrymen.' "

"In any event. You can name Shakespeare. A writer. Can you name one highwayman of the same period, one crook of the Ken Leishman ilk?"

I should of said I can only name Shakespeare because they make you study him in school, if teachers had made us study highwaymen same as poets my bet is you'd have more kids who could remember the names of highwaymen into adulthood than lines from Shakespeare and them others. But there you go. I did not think of it at the time, so Charlie Feagle had me. Checkmate.

"I hear you," Ken says. He's speaking into the phone at the Olgat building. Long distance. He's instructed Paul Grenkow to call from a phone box in Red Lake so the call would not have to be put through the operator. No loose ends. It's the night of 1 March and Paul has been in Red Lake for a week, posing as a salesman, but really watching the shipments of gold bars leaving the foundry and checking the times they arrive at and then leave TransAir baggage bound for Winnipeg. He's been surprised at the lack of security. He was expecting an armoured truck to carry the bars to the TransAir plane. But no. Things in Red Lake are as lax as at the airport in Winnipeg.

"Are we on time?" Ken's mouth is dry.

Paul says, "You won't believe this." There's excitement in his tone.

"Are we on schedule?" Ken's question is insistent.

"Listen to this."

Ken sighs. He can't resist looking at his watch.

"Listen to this. They deliver the things by taxi. Taxi, but. They put them in the trunk of a taxi at the, you know, the place and off it tootles to the airport."

"Paul, listen."

"Taxi, see. Sheesh. I woulda thought—"

"Paul."

"No guards, is what I'm saying. You'd think—"

"Hey." Ken's almost shouting. "Focus. Paul." They've been over this many times, the less said on the phone, the better. "Loose lips sink ships," Ken shouts down the line. "There's a plan, a routine to follow. One slip-up and the whole operation unravels. You hear me? Paul?"

"I hear you. Unravels."

"Lord. Man your post."

"Okay. It just seemed funny to me. Interesting."

"We got no time for interesting. And funny is for Wayne and Shuster."

"Geez, Ken, lighten up."

"This is not hopscotch. Paul. This is not playtime. There's only one thing that interests me, and there's only one thing that interests any of you other jokers."

"Right. Sorry."

"Good. Let's hear your report."

"She had the litter. Twelve puppies."

"Twelve?" Ken looks up and catches the eye of John Berry, who's standing at the window looking out onto the street, drumming fingers on glass.

John shrugs his shoulders. The most that have come on any previous shipment is ten.

"Twelve," Paul repeats, loud and clear. "Saw 'em with my own eyes. Eight brown and four silver. Total, twelve."

"You sure?" Ken imagines the scene in his head, Paul counting the boxes coming out of the trunk of the taxi at the airport. How far away would he be positioned? How easy would it be for an excited young cowboy like Paul to lose count?

"Twelve," Paul repeats. "No doubt about it. Baker's dozen."

"A baker's dozen…" Ken begins, but then leaves a silence. Two more bars, an additional hundred and more pounds of bullion, another fifty or sixty grand, their lucky night. Sometimes the luck is with you. And other times it isn't. Ken takes a couple of deep breaths before he asks, "And right on time?"

"To the minute."

"Great." Ken checks his watch. Just over an hour before the flight lands. "Smooth."

Only an hour until the plane lands, there's things to do. Ken's underarms are damp but his throat is dry. "All right," he says, speaking slowly, "here's what we have to do now."

"I'm all ears, Chief. A regular hound dog."

Ken hears sounds in the background. He strains his ears trying to pick something out. He told Paul to call from a phone box that was located out of doors, not in a pub or a hotel lobby, but the Grenkow brothers are young and unpredictable, likely to do something off the cuff, not in the plan. And John Berry, too, could do something erratic, he has that look in his eye, the look of the main chance. Too late to worry about that now. In for a penny, kind of thing. Ken makes sure he speaks slowly and clearly. "Get into your car now and head out to the West Coast. But don't draw attention to yourself."

"Roger. Will do."

"And Paul. No squealing wheels."

"Tires, right. No squealing."

Ken hears Paul moving the phone, crackling noises, a car horn. A look of relief crosses his face. He glances at John, who's looking out the office windows at snow piled on each side of the walkway. Ken swallows. Two extra bars of gold. "You follow what I'm saying?" he says into the phone. "Leave right away. Don't even stop to crap."

"Crap, right. I heard you first time."

"Just making sure. No slip-ups. Right?"

"You bet."

"Get in the car and go. You hear?" Ken glances around. His coffee cup is on the table, he watches steam rising from its mouth. This is a two-cup high, going higher. It's electric in his veins, each thump of his heart registers in his temples. "And remember, Paul, he who hesitates is lost."

"I read you loud and clear. All tickety-boo, Chief."

John and Rick are in John's Ford Galaxie approaching the airport. In the trunk they have two dark navy parkas that Ken brought to the Olgat warehouse several nights earlier along with a handmade stencil of the Air Canada logo, a cut-out from a cardboard box. He'd placed the stencil on each parka and sprayed it with red paint. When the paint dried they had pulled on the parkas, surprised and pleased at how authentic they looked, Ken beaming. "Remember," he'd said, "keep the hoods up. Cover your mugs. Be sure to pull on these coveralls."

March first, a cold night in Winnipeg, the wind whipping snow over the road that leads to the airport. On the radio the weather guy had said a snowstorm was coming. That seemed like a bad thing but Ken had said a storm could work in their favour, lots of fender-benders, chaos and confusion on the roads. John Berry checks his watch. Coming up to 9:40. They've got the drive to the airport down cold, the getaway to just under five minutes. The practice they've done on the route has been useful and exhilarating too: they feel in control, though their hearts are racing.

John clears his throat. "You set?"

"Ready as I'll ever be." Rick gives him a quick smirk.

John takes a deep breath. It's actually happening, actually going down. A heist.

"You good?" Rick asks.

"I'm good. But I'm glad we've got our little brown jug. It's effing cold tonight." John pulls the mickey from the inside pocket of his jacket. The blank bill of lading is in the other. Ken had managed to pinch one on one of his recent visits to Air Canada freight, pretending to be looking for a package. Lifted one off a pad when the clerk wasn't looking. Cool customer, Ken.

Rick takes the mickey and has a quick swig. "Convertible." He shivers. "Crappy car for the winter in Winnipeg."

John laughs. "But the girls like it. The girls like the air blowing through their hair on a summer drive on the way to a little schnookie out in the country. They like the Ford Galaxie." John is tapping his fingers on the wheel. "And then they like little John, you know what I mean."

"Yeah. A little poontang."

"You bet. We get this cash in pocket, there's going to be a bit of that around. Right?"

Rick passes the flask back. "Take it easy, not too fast, we don't want the cops on our tails."

"Don't worry." John looks across at him and grins. "I disconnected the tail lights."

Rick shakes his head.

"What?"

"You never thought that might attract the attention of the cops? More of a risk?"

"Forget it. Be cool. We're okay."

"If you say so."

"I say so. Trust me."

Rick grunts. "Heard that before."

"Not from me you ain't."

"All right."

"All right."

The mickey changes hands again. Small sips.

John wheels the car around the airport, a route familiar to both of them now. Rick can't resist glancing at his watch. John pulls up near the TransAir building, some distance from the main terminal, where he cuts the car's headlights and drifts slowly in the darkness towards Air Canada freight. All seems quiet. Though there's a howling north wind. It might take longer than five minutes to make the getaway if a blizzard moves in. There's that intangible Ken was talking about. John Berry strokes his chin.

"Look at that." Rick's voice has risen. On the ground floor of the TransAir building there's a light coming from one of the windows. Someone is working overtime. Maybe. Maybe worse. "Maybe a guard has a special assignment. What with that gold coming in."

"Shit." John brakes and studies the window. "What do you think?"

"Maybe it's security, maybe they're doing a monthly check or something, it's the first of the month. But maybe it's just..." Rick leans forward, peering toward the light.

"Shit." John drums the steering wheel. The car has come to a halt.

"Remember what Ken said."

"I remember, I remember. Anything out of the ordinary, anything we haven't seen before, we turn back. There will be another shipment in two weeks." John blows out his cheeks.

"Don't screw up. The gospel according to Ken."

"Yeah, Ken, he's got a lot to say about what we should be doing."

"He's the boss-man. Right?"

"So he says."

"You got a problem with that? Is that what you're getting at?"

"Our Kenny has got a lot of talk, is what I'm getting at. For somebody not taking any risks here. For a big talker not out here with a gun."

"Not many risks. He's not taking many right at this point. But later—"

"None's the way I see it. Ken talks a big talk, but who's putting their butts on the line and who's back at the warehouse, safe and out of the line of fire? You follow?"

"Well." Rick sighs. "We're here now. Right?"

John has lit a cigarette and is puffing at it nervously. "Want one?" He offers the pack.

"No." Rick has his eyes fixed on the window. "Nothing's happening in there."

They sit in silence, the car motor ticking over, watching the wind blow streams of snow over the tarmac. By morning there will be drifts, the streets will be plugged. John checks his watch. 9:50. It's now or never. He eases the car forward. When they pass the window, they both look in, someone is sitting at a desk, back to them, hunched over papers, an accountant, maybe, clearly not a cop or a guard. They glide past. No reaction from inside. John cracks the window of the car and chucks out the cigarette. "We're on."

They bring the car to a stop and hop out. In a moment they're popping open the trunk, pulling on the parkas and the coveralls. The temperature is falling fast. The gloves Ken has bought for them are thin and the wind freezes the fingers. Rick is wearing cowboy boots, John oxfords with leather soles. They scuttle toward the Air Canada hangar, slipping and sliding on the icy tarmac, breath fogging out of their mouths. When they arrive there they find a side door that's open and John runs inside while Rick begins to slide the hangar door open. At the rear of the building is a boxy white cargo van with AIR CANADA stencilled on it, and John hops in and begins to back it out while Rick looks from side to side into the darkness, glancing at the sky from time to time. So far, so good.

The van eases out through the large door. John checks to both sides. Rick slides the door closed again.

Inside the van John is breathing heavily. When Rick hops in he asks, "The keys were in?"

"Yup. Same as when we did the trial run the other night."

"Right on cue, then."

"See anything?"

Rick is puffing too. "There was an old guy crossing toward us at one point but then he turned back and went into another building."

"Huh. You think that's a problem?"

"No. But keep an eye peeled."

"Check." John is driving slowly, trying to recall which gate the Red Lake flight comes in at. He's sweating inside the parka, wondering how many eyes are watching from the observation deck, wondering if the flight is on time, thinking for the first time of how many things can go wrong. Who was that person working late? What about the old guy Rick saw crossing between buildings? But there's no need to worry because TransAir 108 is taxiing toward them, its lights lost in the floodlights playing on the tarmac, which the van has just entered. John pulls the van over and glances across at Rick. Rick is chewing his lower lip. Both of John's hands squeeze the steering wheel. The two men breathe in silence while the plane comes to a stop and sits while the ground crew hustle about with their wheel blocks and flashlights. John clears his throat. "Hard to just sit here, what?"

Rick is sweating inside his parka too. They're pretty obvious out in the floodlights and anyone who knows the routine may be puzzled that they're there. It's usually the dolly that picks up the shipments and takes them from TransAir to Air Canada cargo. "Should we move?"

"No. Give 'er a few more minutes. If we rush in we give them more time to identify us, more time to wonder why the change in routine, more time for questions. Ken said wait until the moment the cargo hold opens and then move in fast, make the exchange occur as quickly as possible, keep everyone off-balance."

"Right. Transition point. Keep everyone off-balance."

"Transfer point." John has another cigarette lit and is puffing at it. The little multi-step ramp has been unfolded from the door of the plane and passengers come down the narrow metal steps and scuttle toward the terminal building. The cargo hold at the side of the plane has been opened.

"Look." Rick points. The conveyor is being wheeled up to the plane and in a moment two guys are positioning it under the cargo bay.

"Now." John wheels the van around and then backs toward the plane. Easy. His heart is racing, hands clamped on the wheel. Don't back into the conveyor. But don't stop too far away from it either. Don't look like you don't know what you're doing. Don't look like rookies. His eyes skip from rearview mirror to side mirror. "Okay?"

"That's got it." Rick's words are still echoing in the van when he leaps out of the van and hits the tarmac. "Okay. You're good right there."

John sees the guy Ken called Chuck come out of the freight area and make his way to the plane. He has papers in his hand, as Ken said he would. John wipes his brow with the back of his hand. Makes sure the hood of his parka is up. He hears Rick's feet scuffling at the back of the van, and in a moment the rear doors swing open, bringing in a blast of cold air. Time to roll.

When he comes around the back of the van he sees that a couple of the wooden boxes are already on their way down the conveyor belt. Thunkathunka. They're smaller than he thought they would be, the way Ken talked up the weight, but when the guy at the side of the dolly stoops and lifts one he sees that they're heavy, the guy grunts putting it on the dolly.

"Wait," John calls out. The wind is blowing and the conveyor grinding, the plane's engines still whirring, words swirl away in the snow. He has the bill of lading out and waves it in the air. "Hold on a minute there."

The guy at the dolly looks up. He's stocky and burly, his eyes quizzical.

"Rush job," John calls out. "The guys down east want the shipment going there straight away."

The dolly guy puts the second box on the dolly but looks relieved that he might not have to shift the others coming down the conveyor belt. A frigid wind is blowing but there's sweat on his brow. "All right by me," he says, "but you have to check with the boss." He nods toward Chuck but begins to put the boxes coming down the belt into the back of the van. Rick steps forward and hoists one himself. Heavy. It slips in his grip and he almost drops it. The dolly guy snorts. He indicates with a curt and dismissive head gesture that he'll take over.

Chuck has scrambled down from the cargo hold. "What's going on?"

"The guys in Ottawa want the shipment there tonight," John says. "Rush job." He holds out the bill of lading. His hand trembles. For once that night he's thankful for the strong wind.

Chuck looks surprised. He takes the paper from John and studies it. The signature at the bottom seems to satisfy him. Everything seems okay. His eyes wander over the parkas that Rick and John are wearing, shift to the white van with the AIR CANADA logo.

John raises his voice. "It's freezing but. We should get moving."

Chuck pats the pocket of his shirt. "Shit," he says, "forgot my pen. We'll have to go inside."

Rick stares at John and John stares back. Why is he wearing those cowboy boots? John should have said something. They're a dead give-away. "Here," Rick says. "I got one." He puts his hand into his coat and brings out a pen. His hand shakes as he passes it across.

Chuck looks at the pen and then the papers.

"It's effin' freezing," John says. He hops from one foot to the other.

Chuck holds the papers down on his knee to keep them out of the whipping wind. "Shit," he says, shaking the pen, "ink's froze."

"Crap." John looks at Rick. This is what Ken meant. The smallest thing can screw up a job. Details. He should have brought a pen, a second pen as backup, he should have thought. His heart is in his throat.

Chuck is stamping his feet. "C'mon, let's go inside." He turns but just then the conveyor belt makes a high-pitched whine and comes to a grinding halt. One of the last wooden boxes shivers on the belt, halfway down.

"Damn." Chuck slaps the papers on his thigh. "Useless old piece of crap." He shrugs at John. "Cacks out all the time. TransAir, you know? Not like your outfit. All the newest gear."

"We've heard." John's voice quavers.

"It'll just be a minute." Chuck is glancing toward the terminal building. Is he suspicious, or just cold?

"We're in a hurry." Rick's words are almost a wail.

"Yeah," John says. "The guys down east, eh?" He is aware of the pistol in his coat pocket. Plan B, he had called it. *Plan Be-likely to get you shot,* Ken had quipped. *Keep the gun out of it.* But Ken himself had used a gun in the Toronto robberies. You gotta do what you gotta do. And Rick had said he'd see if he could get hold of a pal's .22 pistol.

"Jaysus," the guy at the dolly calls out. "Don't stop working, you crappy machine. Not tonight." He bangs on the motor of the machine with his open palm. Whack whack whack. "C'mon, you piece of old junk. TransAir crap."

Chuck shrugs. "Freezin' out here. Let's go inside." He's wearing only a thin windbreaker.

John looks at Rick. Rick stares back blankly. Did the kid bring the gun he said he could lay his hands on? "Let's load up first," John offers. "Get that over with. Paperwork after."

Chuck studies him. Did he say something that's tipped him off? Naturally suspicious?

John doesn't even know if the gun works. Ken said it would never come to that. Waving the gun in their faces would be enough. Still.

Rick's face is red and not from cold air. John feels sweat on his upper lip.

Thunkathunka. The conveyor suddenly comes back to life, making a grinding noise. The dolly guy has a big grin on his face. He slaps the motor again, then rests his big hand on it. The belt grinds into action, the last two wooden boxes clunking down.

"Look at that," Rick says. "She's moving again."

John raises his voice. "Let's get this show on the road, let's get this done."

Chuck bends over the papers again, scribbles fast back and forth. Ink starts. He positions the papers on his knee and signs quickly, passing them to John. "Here. Christ almighty, it's cold as a nun's tit tonight." John scribbles a name on the papers, passes them back. Chuck nods at the dolly guy and waves once quickly at John and Rick as he hustles back to the terminal building, arms hugged around his thin windbreaker.

John exhales a deep breath. Catches Rick's eye and nods at the doors of the van. "Thanks," he calls out to other guy, who is moving quickly to the seat on the dolly.

"Nothing to it."

"Saved our asses," John yells into the howling wind.

"C'mon." Rick is already scrambling to the passenger seat of the van. He bangs the door shut. Inside John sits for a moment feeling the warm air from the heater on his face. He turns to Rick. "Shit," he says.

"Yeah. Close call. Thought we'd have to use the gat."

John laughs. "The gat, is it?"

"Yeah." Rick laughs. "Ken's gat."

The van's lights pick out the far corner of the Air Canada freight building but John does not pull in there, he drives past and continues on to where he has parked the Ford. He wheels the van about and backs toward the rear of the car. It's dark and the exhaust of the van swirls into the air behind it, John is aware he could hit the Ford. "Let's move," he says when he brakes. Rick is already banging the door behind him. In a moment they're both between the two vehicles, popping the car's trunk, flinging open the doors of the van. Rick grabs one of the boxes but it slips his grip as he crosses between the vehicles, the box slides down his leg onto his shin.

"Fuck!" Rick has grabbed his foot.

"Jesus." John picks up the wooden box. It's heavier than he thought and he almost lets it slip too. And he's shaking with nerves. The few steps across to the car trunk are almost more than he can make. The box thumps into the trunk. He mutters. "Crap."

Rick is rubbing his leg, hopping about, cursing loudly. "I've broke the fucker!"

"Quiet." John elbows past him. "You'll wake the whole goddamn city." He wobbles between the van and the truck with two more of the boxes. Rick is rubbing his shin. "Can you for Christ's sake give a hand here?" He looks at Rick. It's clear he's hurt. He's leaning against the side of the van, now, sweating. Cursing.

"Stand back!" John sprints toward the front of the car, hops in and fires the ignition. He looks in the rearview mirror. Trunk's up, he cannot see anything behind the car. He throws open the driver's door and begins backing up, eyes on the rear of the van, the elbow rest gripped in one hand. In a moment there's a sickening crunch. The open door has caught a wooden post, buried in a snowdrift. Crap and double crap. John eases the car forward, then backs slowly to the van. When he's happy with how far he's gone, he jumps out. There's only a few feet between the two vehicles. Rick has hoisted himself half into the trunk, and when John climbs into the van, they can pass the wooden boxes across. They're both sweating. Condensation rises off their faces. John pushes back his hood to feel the cool air. The wind whips against his cheeks. The storm is on the way.

In five minutes the boxes are in the trunk. "Christ," Rick says, easing himself out of the trunk and onto the tarmac. "This effing foot." He's pulling off his parka and coveralls, hobbling around, teeth gritted. Every now and then he lets out a suppressed moan. John follows his lead with the clothing, stuffing the suits on top of the boxes. His heart is hammering in his chest, as if he's run three city blocks at top speed, there's a sharp burning there. Is this what a heart attack feels like?

"Get in the car!" John runs back to the van, pulls it over against the nearest building, shuts off the engine and sprints back to the car. The rear of the Ford slumps low on its springs. Ken said it would be a heavy load, eight hundred pounds, maybe more. When he's back inside the Ford, John Berry sees Rick is bent over, grimacing. "Don't take the boot off."

"What?"

"It's going to swell. If you leave the boot on it will keep the swelling down. Then ice."

"Ice?"

"It brings down swelling."

"Ice is for drinks." Rick laughs, a kind of snarl.

"It works, I tell you."

"Shit. Just move out."

"Right." John starts the car away slowly, checking the mirrors. On the way back to the car he's seen that there's a dent in the driver's door, a piece of metal near the handle has broken off in the collision with the fence post. Should he tell Ken about this? It's evidence, evidence they should not leave behind. And Ken's fussy about that. He won't be happy about Rick's foot, either. Stupid bugger probably should go to hospital. Ken won't be happy at all. Screw-ups in the plan.

"Hey," Rick says. He's grinning. "We did it."

"We did it." John brings the whiskey flask out of his coat, passes it across. He looks at his watch. Just 11:00. If he goes slightly over the speed limit they'll catch that green light and be back at Olgat in five minutes. John glances down the road. Snow is beginning to swirl about and gather at the side of the road. If it comes down like this for a while it will be a real blizzard.

"Hey," he says in a minute. "We did it. Shit. A heist. Like in the movies. You and me."

"Yeah." Rick tips the remains of the whiskey down his throat. "A couple dumb cowboys like us. Us. We got the booty."

"We did, my young friend. *We* did."

"That's what I said."

"Yeah, and what do we get for it? What's our cut?"

"A cool two grand, by my measure. Up front." Rick bangs his fist on the dashboard.

"Yeah. Quite a slice."

"I'm heading out west. Got a little gal there. A gal keen on her Ricky-boy."

"Yeah. Our share is two grand and Ken's and Harry's is two hundred grand."

Rick whistles. "That much?"

"You figure it. You get two grand and Kenny a thousand times that much."

"Jesus."

"Maybe more. And you were the guy held the gun."

"I'm beginning to get the picture."

"Yeah. The point is we're being stooges here. We did the work—the robbery, man. We held the guns."

"So to speak."

"We pulled the heist and Ken and Harry walk away with a couple hundred grand. Sound fair?"

Rick raises his voice. "Watch it, now. Make the right up ahead, eh?"

"I got it covered."

"That's our turn."

"The point is, it's not our turn, you follow me. But it should be. It damn well should be."

"You're getting yourself worked up. I'm okay with the two grand. Paul is too."

"Unless we make it our turn. That's my point, that's what I'm saying, my fine young friend."

You're bouncing your feet on the floor.

It's the new teacher saying this, he's substituting for the regular woman away in Winnipeg for some mysterious operation the mothers talk about in whispers behind hands held over their mouths sitting in the parlour with its doilies and antimacassars and cushions covered in plastic. Mr Cavello? Something like that. He has a head of thick black hair and a brush mustache, also he's younger than the regular teacher, much younger than my grandparents certain sure, from the city, he is, a man who studied chemistry at the university and worked for a big chemical company but had not stayed with that job but had become a teacher.

He's called me to the front of the room where he is sitting behind the desk, eyes darting over the classroom. You're nervous. He says this the way he says most things, in a cool flat voice. I do not like being at the front of the room, Peter Scarsby is always at the front of the room, *Pansy Scarsby,* it's not good to spend time with the teacher, you get beat up, teacher's pet.

Not a bad habit, a nervous habit, Mr Cavello corrected himself. Bouncing your feet that way. He wears glasses and he pushes them up his nose.

Like that, thinks I, a nervous habit like fidgeting your specs on your nose but I keep my gob shut, adults don't like to be taken up on things. Backtalk. They call you a smart aleck.

Don't be self-conscious about it. But be overly conscious of it. Try to temper it.

My granddad is always at me about it. After church on Sundays. What I don't say, he had raised his voice, threatened to hit me, only my speed at ducking and running had spared me.

It bothers people, it unsettles them. Mr Cavello pushes his chair back the better to see past my shoulder and keep an eye on the other students. Unlike the regular teacher, he does not need to box ears to maintain order. He does this with his voice alone, the threat of violence rings in his tone, though otherwise he is a quiet man. After the lesson at the board, he says, Do the maths problems and everyone bends their heads to their notepads, even them who have no clue how to answer questions one and two, much less imagine what is being asked in nine and ten.

Is it a distraction? His eyes fix on mine a second. For you? The knee-bouncing?

No one has ever asked this before. They either want me to stop because I am bothering them or because they already decided it is a sign of moral weakness, which is a favourite theme of Granddad's. Mr Cavello has brown eyes, almost black, he must be Italian, irregardless no one says so. I do not know what to say so I stand mute.

No, says he, I thought not. He keeps his eyes on mine and smiles. He holds the smile for a moment. I have a brother, he goes on, same thing only different, taps his fingers on the tabletop, the arms of chairs, his knees, whatever comes to hand. He imitates with his fingertips tap tap tap. Mr Cavello smiles again. He's a businessman, my brother, a stockbroker, younger than me a tall fellow. Always he was unhappy where he was, wherever that happened to be. He was not so much nervous as restless. Always he wanted to be somewhere else. So now he's in New York, big New York stockbroker. Makes a lot of money. The gifts he sends my mother, you wouldn't believe, and not just on her birthday and at Christmas.

New York, says I, with a sigh. That's where the Bowery Boys live.

Mr Cavello laughs. He has big white teeth, a whole mouthful of wonderful strong teeth. You are like my brother, he says, after he's stopped chuckling. Ambitious, restless, your mind racing off in all directions at once. Nothing is going to stop you, Kenneth.

Ken. Everyone calls me Ken.

Of course. Ken.

Nothing was going to stop my brother either. He purses his lips and shakes his head. But is he happy, Ken, is it a good thing, in the end, this restless energy? He has picked a pencil off the desk and he points it at me, smiling the whole time. That is the question you must ask yourself, Kenneth. Ken. This is the question that will define your life. Is it a good thing?

The Galaxie drifts up to the Olgat building. Ken can tell by the way the rear end sags that the job has come off. He puts the cup of coffee he's been drinking down on the counter fast, sloshing liquid onto the countertop. He's closing the door behind him in a second, waving for John to back the Ford toward the rear end of his station wagon. The wind is whipping, snow pelting down, not a lashing, stinging snow of January but a wetter, heavier snow, a March storm. Ken glances at the sky. For his money, the snow could stop anytime. If it continues through the night, the city will be brought to a standstill. He wants to keep the gold bars on the move, he needs to shift them fast and to that end plans on storing them first at Harry's house and then hiding them in an old out-building on his grandfather's land near Treherne. Snow-blocked streets will be a problem. Too late to worry about that now. Reproachments.

When the two vehicles are back to back, John hops out and throws open the trunk of the Galaxie. "Put those there," Ken says, pointing to the suits and then at the ground. "We'll use them to cover up after." He looks at John. "What's with Rick?"

"Dropped one of them boxes on his foot. He's fucked."

"Bugger." Ken throws open the hatchback of his car, grabs a box.

"They weigh a ton." John laughs and then snorts as he moves a box across. He and Ken work feverishly, silently, intensely. When half the boxes are in his car's trunk, Ken pauses for a moment, puts his hand over his heart. "Buggers are heavy," he says. John laughs. Ken reaches for another. They're both blowing hard when they're done. Rick has climbed out of the car and he gathers up the coveralls and the parkas and pushes them on top of the boxes. Ken slams the hatch door down. He stares at the rear end of the car, sagging on its springs. "That's a load."

"That's some stash," John says. "About to become some cash." He laughs.

Ken is moving toward the driver's door. "I'll call in the morning," he shouts at John. "Early. You should have your money in the afternoon."

"Check." John laughs. "I'll tell you, though, I'll be happy never moving another one of those things."

"Lord. You won't have to."

"A man could break his back."

"I'll take care of it now. You're out of it."

"I'm out of it." John has produced another flask of whiskey and he's pulling at it, grinning and offering it to Rick.

Ken's mouth is set as he slides in behind the wheel. His heart is racing. It's a four-cup high. John may be out of it but he's just jumped in. Both feet. He and Harry both. That's where he's headed. The plan is to transfer the boxes to the freezer in Harry's basement across town in Riverview, far away from TransAir and Olgat and Ken's house. Moose meat, he's to tell Harry's mother-in-law, who is looking after the kids while Harry and his wife are down south. Ken smiles as he wheels the station wagon along the snowy streets. They've done it. He's the master thief. He touches the brim of his hat. In just a few minutes, he thinks, he'll be at Harry's. He's been over the route a dozen times. The traffic on Ellice at night is not heavy, he can make all the lights down to Maryland, but that's where things might get complicated. There's construction along Maryland and the last time he drove the route, there was a water main break. Traffic often gets hung up at Broadway and Osborne. One time he was stuck making the turn there for two minutes. But he mustn't speed, mustn't risk attracting attention. Go at a nice pace, though his thoughts are flying ahead to Harry's house. Twelve bars at seventy pounds each could make the take some four hundred grand. On the black market it could fetch as much as twice that much. It's enough to make the mind swim. Ken's thoughts are jumping every which way. He cannot resist the urge to glance at his watch. 10:50. All going according to plan. The least the drive has taken him is fifteen minutes and the most nineteen. What's four minutes? Ken has both hands on the wheel. He whistles under his breath as he drives along. "Go slow," he says aloud, "don't attract attention." He does not look in the rearview mirror or he would see a Ford Galaxie following at a distance, speeding up when he does, braking when he does, but showing no red glow of taillights.

You like to use big words, you've been in love with words since you were a kid in school and looked them up in a dictionary, or parroted grown-ups you heard using them. It was the feel on the tongue and the look that came into the eyes of people you were talking to. Words made you a somebody. So you repeated them, big words, fancy words: *irrelevance, gambit, narrative.* They impressed people, they took notice of you, it was a way of flying past the looks of contempt and dismissal and the hushed tones when you entered the room, Leishman, son of Norman, no-good, old lady on welfare, pack of snivelling kids. Words. They give a man an air of education, of polish. Using words out of the ordinary sets a man above the average run. They were free, all you had to do was look them up in a book and bandy them around and they gave you a kind of power, they put you in control, they put you on top. If clothes make the man, then words make the man impressive. There were times when you stretched their meaning and other times when you invented new ones, that was a kind of game, gaining power over the words themselves, making them do your bidding. Charlie Feagle said it was showing off, but isn't that how new words come into existence, anyways, someone has the moxie to stretch the meaning, or coin a new one?

"The what?" Corporal Scotty Gardiner of the RCMP shouts down the line. It's early in the morning of March 2, but he's at his desk, shuffling through papers, answering the phone. His grip tightens on his coffee cup as he listens to the voice on the other end of the line.

"The airport." It's a city cop on the other end, a detective, he says. His tone has risen and become urgent. "A shipment of gold has been stolen, from the Winnipeg airport."

Scotty groans. He can see the headlines already. "You're sure?"

"Right under the noses of Air Canada."

"Not surprised. Bloody government flunkies." Scotty laughs but it's a painful sound. He pushes the coffee cup aside and slides his chair back.

"Yeah. Clean away. Those bozos at Air Canada and TransAir just let them drive away with it. Right under their noses."

"Yeah, airport guys. Not smart enough to work for the post office." Scotty laughs again and scratches his temple. A dozen questions flash through his mind. There will be a hundred more before the hour passes, he knows it. He feels sweat start under his armpit.

"You guys have to come in." The detective on the line is agitated, voice insistent. "Chief Maltby says both the city detectives and your lot have to come in. And smartly."

"Uh-huh. I follow. Could be international implications."

"Exactly. All hands on deck. It's a big deal. Hundreds of thousands of dollars. Maybe half a million."

"Uh-huh. Half a million. And maybe a flight over the border. I get it. Interpol." Scotty covers the mouthpiece with his hand and presses the receiver tight against his ear. He signals to the sergeant at the front desk. "Get on your bike, my friend," he says. "Big doings out at the airport." The sergeant's eyebrows go up.

Scotty turns back to the phone. "I'll meet you there. Half an hour, sure. Maybe twenty minutes, could be ten if we turn on the siren." He puts the instrument back in its cradle. "Well, well," he says, "somebody's pulled a robbery at the airport."

"Robbery?" the sergeant says. "They stole a—a what?—an airplane?"

"I wish. Gold."

"Say what? I don't follow."

"Gold bullion from Red Lake. You never heard of Red Lake? What they teaching you guys at the academy these days, anyways? Gold bullion. Whisked off a plane coming down from the north." He stands and pats his pockets. Starts to head for the coat rack near the door.

"Krikey." The sergeant's eyes are round. "Gold bullion. That's big time."

"Gold bars. Ten or twelve bars of pure shiny gold. Gone."

"Bars?"

"Yeah. Each weighing—well, I don't rightly know—a lot anyways." The sergeant whistles. "But it adds up to half a million bucks?"

"This city cop on the blower says so. He may be exaggerating. But a real haul."

"And a real stink-a-rooney for us."

Scotty snorts. "You got that right." He sighs. He knows what's coming. Headlines, reports to fill out, radio interviews, recriminations, accusations. Criticism of police competence. Hopefully not one of those investigations, or a commission with *experts* poking their noses into police business. "Get your coat," he says. "Check your weapon."

The sergeant raises his eyebrows again.

"You never know." Gardiner pulls on his coat and says with a sigh, "And I bet I can tell you whose work this is."

The sergeant gives him a quizzical look.

"Ken Leishman." Scotty shakes his head and snorts through his nose again. "No one else would be so brazen. Just walk in and snatch the gold like that. And at the airport yet. Probably flying somewhere by now himself. Yeah, it has to be Ken Leishman." He shakes his head again and laughs bitterly. "Flown south, most likely. He'll have crossed the border already and be long gone into the States, Mexico maybe, or Cuba, if I know the Flying Bandit."

The sergeant asks, "Say what?"

"The Flying Bandit. You never heard of Ken Leishman?"

"Who is Ken Leishman?"

That's a lot of bullion
$383,000 in gold hijacked
2 men escape

It never rained. We prayed for rain ordinary folk at night before going to bed down on knees at sides of beds, please God, and not just the womenfolk men too hardened in the fields we looked up from the stooks and uttered silent prayers for the crops for a day off so we could go into town even. But it did not rain. A cloud would go by high overhead and a few drops would fall not enough to wet your face even, pissing in the wind someone says like pissing in the wind.

Better, someone says, than dying over there in the mud of France or Italy, shot in the gut blown to pieces.

No, says someone else. That ain't it at all. The boys over there are saving Europe from Hitler, the Nazis gotta be beat down. Them boys is heroes.

For a minute work in the field stopped, everybody had an opinion everyone were prepared to raise their voice, hats was doffed, brows wiped. Nazis this, Winston Churchill that. Were the Yanks coming in? If the Yanks come in, the Krauts were up shit creek for certain sure.

I was stooking along with boys my age, also the cutter had gone before cutting the grain and leaving it lying flat on the field our job was to use the rakes and make stooks, which stood like tiny pyramids in the field waiting for the grain to cure also for the man with the horses and the threshing machine to thresh the grain from the chaff few farmers could afford a tractor. Also the straw was not thrown away it was kept for the cattle for winter bedding in the barns and rough fodder for pigs. When you didn't have a pot to piss in, as the fella says.

Martin De Vlieger done the shovelling into the buckboard box he and three or four older boys beards beginning, Sandy who also played the mouth organ at night before we bedded down and the man with the guitar and the heart-wrenching voice no Wilf Carter but he sung good.

It was long days. We were up before the sun six maybe earlier dew beaded on grass, and the farmer's wife had laid out bacon and eggs and toast on tables near the back door of the house and we sat on benches makeshift chairs overturned wooden crates and drunk milk and coffee in gulps, we was always in a hurry out to the fields it was so dark you tripped in the rutted earth getting down from the buckboard wagon that delivered the gang to the pendulous field.

Hats, those who could afford them bare hands the calluses soon developed also long pants long shirtsleeves some of the men took them off towards noon tank-top undershirts sweated to skin beneath, white stained brown under the armpits and around the collar, the standard issue of the day our khaki some wag quips, our army issue, stand easy boys!

Many in shoes a few in boots those lucky enough to have them most in bare feet. Shovels, rakes. Under the blazing sun the handles grew so hot the men spit on them. Water in Mason jars, cool in the morning but tepid by afternoon cold tea in jars too it did not matter quench the thirst sluice the water around in the parched mouth, no booze, work be work and schnapps be schnapps.

It never rained. That is the memory. All through the 1930s and into the '40s. In church on Sunday the preacher prayed for rain, a special prayer offered right at the beginning of the service and then also again at the end just before the peace that passes all understanding guard and keep you in Christ Jesus. It did not work, there were those who begun to say there were no God but these unrighteous was shouted down by Bible-thumpers who elucidated the plagues that befell the children of Israel.

You looked up into the sky. Is that a cloud? A few drops and you took off your hat and turned your face up to the sky in the early days sometimes a cheer went up, but then came the days of silence, silent staring at the heedless sky it cannot go on but irregardless it went on and there was nothing else for it, it was that kind of kick in the teeth.

Sandwiches for lunch, chicken, egg salad, pork, stringy and full of fat. Mustard on bread. Celery sticks, carrots. More water in Mason jars brung by the wife and the girls of the house if there was any and aunts and neighbours also on a buckboard at noon. Cold tea for the men. I was always hungry.

It was August maybe September so we were not yet back in school, I was twelve maybe thirteen but a big boy who needed the money, pennies a day but something better than nothing as the fella says. The sun dropped to the horizon and a breeze come up some days and you fanned your cheeks with your hat, straw flew up in your face and went down the collar of the shirt and itched and you scratched and made red welts on your chest red oozing sores the size of nickels you did not complain. You thought, better than in them trenches over there.

Then the sun dropped on the horizon and the horses pulling the buckboard wagon come and you climbed on board and jolted across the rutted fields and fanned your hat on your cheeks and wiped the sweat from your brow with a handkerchief from the back pocket of your pants, red or also blue with white polka-dots and set in silence on the ride back, exhaustion. A hawk riding on air currents high above clouds streaked with purple and yellow. You don't see that in your city, says an older fella with broken teeth and a crooked smile he smelled of dung also bad bread and I thought to myself even then, not this chickadee, it's something else for me.

Behind the barn there was a wood frame built to hold thirty-gallon water barrels and there was hoses running out of these and you stood below with a bar of rough soap and felt the cool water hit your skull as you soaped up and the rougher men swore, by the Jesus. Some of the older men did not bother to wash up. Men with tanned faces and fore-arms almost black some had been working gangs since June bringing in hay but their chests were white like the bellies of fish though the muscles of their arms were hard as rope and they had no bellies, also their ribs showed through, they was skinny as a race horse, them was hard times, you was lucky to eat.

For supper there was hard-boiled eggs and cabbage rolls and bread and roasted beef. Mrs. Peterson was known for her dill pickles and Mrs. Grienke her cabbage rolls and Mrs. Olsen for her fried chicken, stay on the gang until the Olsens', that was the word, stay for the fried chicken and potato salad also coffee, apple pie, at Mrs. Spelchak's blueberry muffins, another treat you were loath to miss, there was this at least for a hungry belly plentiful provender.

Storytelling begun round the tables and went on as the sun set and the sky darkened and the men begun to move to the granaries, four-teen-by-twelve wooden buildings that would hold ten or twelve army cots some men fell asleep immediately still in their boots but most set around laughing at something Charlie Chaplin had did or the Bowery Boys, waiting for the guitar or the mandolin also the banjo to come out, homemade entertainment after homemade food, a fella had a mouth organ and he played all the sad old tunes you felt lonely and full in the chest all at once. Lights out at ten though the men drinking whiskey outside stumbled in sometime after and fell onto cots in their work clothes snoring within seconds talk of the Bowery Boys stilled.

I don't know where it begun my love of the movies. I remember being at a silent picture but I do not know where it was some shabby small room in Treherne or Rathwell, certainly not in Winnipeg, which was a big deal for kids growing up in the stony earth between the two big lakes, one-horse towns, people used to say. Who was I there with? Not my father long gone leaving Mother to raise me and the other kids alone, maybe the kind preacher from the Lutheran church, he'd took a liking to my ragamuffin self. I do not remember. What I remember is Tom Mix the pianola rattling in the background, images of a cattle drive, cowboys, boots, holstered pistols, also some kind of argument, angry faces, a fist fight, hats flying off and rolling in the dust, a dust-up. All in black and white, images jumping crazily, a scene half-missing also white spots like plates dancing across the screen. It did not matter. There were a paper bag of peanuts offered to me, it must of been offered to me for some time because I only became aware of the bag when my elbow was nudged—hard—and I jerked as if awakened from a deep dream, a trance—what? Who are you? It should of been obvious right then for certain sure. I was living among quiet, hard-working farmers straight in their business dealings, church on Sundays, good men strong women, simple folk who worked hard and listened to the crystal set on weekdays and the preacher on the Sabbath and voted dutifully for whatever gang of imposters were currently in vogue, and every now and then went into town and enjoyed the pictures by gum. Irregardless someone should of known, maybe the kind preacher-man he done lots of good around, to me also, known that he'd given me the poisoned apple that day, when we walked out of the shabby place that passed as a movie house and I was like a stunned cow, eyes wide, hardly able to walk down the street much less articulate the sounds that set us off from the simple beasts of the fields. But how could he of known? Because I was drownded already, what had taken me was a thing much bigger than he'd ever known or ever would lively as lust stronger than moonshine. The sedulous intoxication of images on a silver screen had commenced.

They carved their initials into the desks, the kids. If you was caught the teacher strapped you. Miss Sanders? So initials had to be scratched inside the little slot where books and tablets were stored at night. *GB*, Gary Bigelow, he was two grades ahead he was goofing off one day pulling Janice Smith's pigtails and Miss Sanders chucked a blackboard eraser at his head and he blocked it with one hand and picked it up in an instant and threw it back at Miss Sanders and she come down to where he set and boxed him in the ears. That's the story we told, that's what were passed down, boxed him in the ears. It was a school with two classrooms Rathwell maybe one of them towns, my mother farmed me out to relatives also friends she could not manage to take care of all of her kids on the welfare money, *relief* it was called, she never stopped singing that song. Up to grade four in one of those two rooms, five to eight in the other, the occasional bookish girl went to high school, the university was like God you approached from a distance you spoke of it in the tone of Noah being instructed to commence the ark. I was in grade five and Gary Bigelow in seven when he done that with the blackboard brush.

Says Larry Thompson, The balls but to throw it back at Miss S.

For certain sure but the old man did you hear that part?

I heard. Five on each leg.

Ten!

Five says Monk McNult.

I ain't arguing with Monk.

Smart move that boyo.

Old man Bigelow he has them arms come from driving fence posts, so says the old man.

The balls but says Larry Thompson. Gary done the same at church. He's got the yap.

Them that do always pays. Soon later.

Says Larry Thompson You're right about that boyo.

LT & *DW*. Dawne Whitelaw.

Dark-eyed and dark-haired Dawne, at home I scribbled *KL* & *DW* on the inside cover of the science book I'd snuck home but in pencil before going into school the next day I erased it gone, disappeared no one to ever know. She married Willy Sutton knocked-up they said and on the day of the wedding Larry Thompson bridegroom pissed as a newt on beer drove the old man's Buick off the highway into town and were killed along with Jerry Sharper when it rolled. By then I'd went from there shuffled back to my grandparents' farm in Treherne, where I worked like a donkey for nothing except the occasional lecture on wickedness and sin both attributed to me in large measure by the Lord Harry, as the fella says. Irregardless I heard things on the grapevine. Gary Bigelow went hard of hearing by age thirty.

Alvin Gorman is standing directly in front of Jon Levy and Doug McNult and me. Brown nose, says he. One corner of Alvin's mouth sags down so it looks as if he's sassing you out of the side of his face even when he ain't, a birth defect says Grandma tapping her temple.

Jon and Doug and me are friends, kind of friends, I like Jon because he has the comic book collection also when I go over to his house his sister Debbie who has red hair come into his room to make faces at me also laughs and then leaves and comes back with cookies she's stole from the cookie jar. Jon's father is the town doctor, he was in the Great War according to Granddad also a lot older than Mrs. Levy according to Grandma. Jon wears glasses and has a quavery voice he gets picked on on the schoolyard by boys like Alvin Gorman and Jack Kramer. No one picks on Doug McNult 'cause Doug's older brother is Monk McNult no one knows how he got the name it's actually Andrew but Monk is tall and has a thick neck and a bright pink face to go with his red hair and everyone seen how he put both his big hams on Bobby Cox's chest, two years older and shoved him down on the dirt, hams for hands as the fella says. So no one picks on Doug McNult, me neither, since Doug and me are together all the time we shoot marbles and whittle whistles from poplar branches, come recess recreation there was one baseball and one bat and you weren't getting into a scrap with Monk McNult over the use of them there.

Brown nose, says Alvin again, he shoves Jon on the shoulder an unexpected blow and Jon staggers backwards. Jon doesn't say nothing he adjusts his glasses, which have slid down his nose. Jon-a-than, says Alvin in a sing-song voice kisses Miss Sanders' ass. Jack Kramer stands behind him blocking the way to the school steps and safety, a smirk on his face, which is dirty. He sniffs, Jack Kramer seems always to have a runny nose. Alvin shoves Jon again, harder this time, Doug and me standing silent to the side. Ass-kiss, says he.

Hey. The sound is out of my mouth without me knowing it lay on my tongue.

Alvin turns to me. Well now says he look who's got summat to say.

I'm looking past his shoulder at the school door it's almost time for Miss Sanders come out and rung the bell.

Leishman, Alvin says, what kind of a name is that anyways?

I been wondering if that's a Jew name. Jack has a squeaky voice and poor eyesight, if it were him alone he'd be spitting out teeth. I'm a big one, they say, but Alvin's two years older.

That's right. A Jew name.

It's English, says I. We're mistaken for Germans sometimes but never Jews we're English from England where the King sits up high on his throne. I want to say this but I know better, engaging Alvin, confronting a bully is just what he wants get your goat. I know already that the best course is to dodge around the Alvin Gormans, they'll get theirs soon later certain sure.

Cat got your tongue? Jew boy? He must of swung at me 'cause I never would of first but I soon felt the wind go out of my chest and my knees wobbly but through good luck or skill I don't know which I got him by the neck and we thrashed to the ground near the scrub willows how he bellered to be brung down, I smelled cat piss on his shirt up that close also the sting of my elbow jammed onto rocky ground

Alvin's hand gouging into my neck my own nails digging into his ear and eyeball until he hollered out more but I was not letting go, then there's a whack and an *ahhhh* from voices gathered around and Miss Sanders has Alvin by the collar dragging him off me and striking him on the shoulder with her yardstick, whack whack whack. You little turd says she.

And at home Granddad says to me, That was all there was to it, he called you a name?

He torn his shirt, Grandma says. She's been hovering near the table, flitting like a bird. An expensive shirt. Make him pay for that.

Woman, hush. Granddad puts up one hand. And you come out of it okay? You're not hurt?

Yes. There's a scratch across my nose, which they know about also my elbow stings and still has pins and needles but I will not say nothing about that.

That ain't all. Grandma snorts. There's more, there has to be more to it. I bet he begun.

What name did he call you? Ken? What did he?

This boy is a troublemaker. Just like his father, that Tiddles, Tiddles Leishman, that's what they call him, an old alley cat. Brung this family nothing but grief. A no-good Irish.

Hush woman. Granddad's eyes are fixed on mine.

He's lazy. Irresponsible and lazy.

The boy's not all bad. He wants to please.

He wants everything but he's not willing to work for nothing.

He's good-hearted, he's not all bad.

Lazy as a pet pig. Mark my words, he'll come to no good, that one. Leishman, it's a curse. May as well lock him up in jail right now.

Hush woman. Grandad's eyes narrow at me, I'd better not find out you begun.

Grandma snorts again. That's it? You're going to take the word of this… this lying boy, this son of that. My tongue can't even be brung to utter the name.

And you come out of it okay, Granddad says in a flat tone, a state-
ment a pronouncement. I nod. He's told me before stay clear of it with
boys in the schoolyard but once you're into it you got to show yourself
a man.

Oh. Grandma makes this sound, which is more an *umph* than a
word and she busies herself at the sink clattering plates and silverware.

Granddad drinks the remainder of his tea and sets the cup carefully on the table, a tiny chink of sound when the enamel strikes the
Arborite, there is silence as he regards me, his hazel eyes not blinking
lips tight closed. There's more to it than I'm saying, he knows it and
he wants me to know he knows. What he's chiefly concerned about is
that I'm not hurt that I'll be able to do my chores that he won't have to
muck out barn shit and shovel straw from the loft and gather eggs and
slop out the pigs and feed the horses also throw hay bales and and...

After a moment he clears his throat. Alvin Gorman, says he with a
snort, son of that no-good Larry Gorman, a drunk who cannot control that she-devil of a wife he done married.

It's just a movie says he, people acting before a camera. He laughs but
it's a nervous laugh as if he's frightened of something, a small thing
but important nevertheless, a thing that gets under his skin.

I nod and look him in the eye a glance before I avert my eyes, it's
the kindly preacher with the crooked nose, broken says he playing
lacrosse, a sport he thinks I might of been good at. Sports are good for
you, says he, and adds something in a language I do not understand,
sounds like corporal sandy. Or maybe rugby another game I never
heard of.

Play-acting, he says, and laughs again in the same nervous way,
nothing to be afraid of, he pushes the plate where his sandwich
had been away from him and takes a sip of coffee. It's quiet in the
diner stuffy and steamy with cooking. I'd rather not be there I feel

uncomfortable around grown-ups but he brung me with him to the movies.

Says he, the man was not locked into the coffin, he was not going to suffocate.

I know.

He smokes a pipe and he busies himself with a pouch of tobacco and the bowl in which he tamps the tobacco carefully also then the match he strikes on the side of a small box of wooden matches, Eddy Match Company is writ in red letters on the box. The tobacco lights and he draws in once quickly and the tobacco glows red and then he sucks in the smoke and lets it leak out of both nostrils thin streams. He smiles at me. Nothing to be frightened of his smile says but I seen he's nervous, not understanding me. Who was this boy who had dived behind the seat in the movie house when the fella was sealed in the coffin? He blows a stream of bluish smoke over my head I like its smell.

Movie characters smoked cigarettes but always nervously, I was to make a study of it later, Bette Davis with her white palm turned to one cheek at the side of her head, long cigarette holder pinched between thumb and forefinger, smoke billowing from the painted mouth, salacious.

No need to be frightened. Ken.

When the coffin lid had been brought down over the man inside him still breathing I could no longer stand the pressure around my heart, I had closed my eyes but then they had betrayed me and opened on their own and the coffin were shut then the man sealed inside and I'd dropped off my seat and hidden behind the one in front of me heart knocking knees on the floor brow pressed against the metal back of the seat, it was too much for my young heart to take what would become of the man, he'd suffocate certain sure. Who was sealed inside? Lon Chaney? Bela Lugosi? I seen the names on the screen at the start but in my distress could not remember.

No need to be frightened.

I know. I know.

He draws on his pipe and then pushes the glass of Coke closer to me. My sandwich lies uneaten on the plate at my elbow. Eat, says he.

I take a bite. Dust in my mouth cardboard I reach for the glass of Coke and swallow back a long gulp. Coke it's a treat I should be enjoying it, instead I'm choking back tears, I wanted to impress, to gain approval and all I've done is show myself a weakling.

You have too much imagination. He says this the way he says, It's a bad time for folks on the prairies now but it will be better, the Lord will see to it, a voice full of calm and confidence. Too much imagination is a bad thing. I been told this before but that day I feel the truth of it, the tightness in my gut, the trembling in my legs, weakness, I'm a weak boy in a world that requires me to be tough. He also means, You should not allow this to continue you must change it you must change yourself.

Here boy, says the fella jabbing the cigarette toward at my face. Go on.

In the dim light thrown by the hurricane lamp closest the cigarette looks like a pinched straw only short. The smoke is a roll-your-own and it's the fella who done the rolling who is offering it a short man with a hooked nose the little finger of one hand has been chopped off.

It is some time after nine and those of us who sleep together in the granary are gathered together sitting on the edges of cots like army cots, knees up to our chests, some smoking some talking quietly. We are enjoying a pause in the music, which is being made by a tall man on a guitar and a thin red-haired boy on a mouth organ everyone calls him Sandy. The man with the guitar has long thin legs, he has treated us to "Red River Valley," and is coming to the end of "Streets of Laredo," a high quavering voice that squeezed emotion out of every phrase he sung, a voice that wrung my heart. There's sweat on his lower lip and as subdued talk begins he drinks water from a chipped enamel cup the farmer's wife has provided and winks at me.

The men who are sharing a flask of whiskey are outside, sitting on the stoop of the granary the resonance of their voices rises and falls like wind in the tops of trees occasionally interspersed with guffaws of laughter, raw, but irregardless comforting not threatening.

Go on, says the fella again leaning toward me. On me, boy. He has thin hair and his teeth are a crooked jumble in his mouth. Even in the dim light thrown inside the granary the yellow stains are obvious, it's the stains make me hesitate. George Harbison, town druggist, has stained teeth and every time he smiles at me I go all sick inside. There are so many reasons to escape.

The man with the guitar puts down the enamel cup and begins to strum the strings, slowly, quietly. I am trying to bite back the tears I feel welling in my eyes. "For I'm a young cowboy and I know I've done wrong." The words have stung my heart and I'm biting my tongue to hold back the tears, I'm hoping they'll not be seen in the gloom of the small poorly lit space thankful for that now. I do not want to bite through my tongue but am prepared to rather than lose face in front of the other boys and men. I'm too sensitive Grandma says, he has too much imagination Granddad adds.

We're working on a threshing gang. I'm going to use the money I make to catch a bus to the city and sit in a real movie theatre if there's enough a bag of peanuts too. I'll have to make sure Granddad doesn't steal my little stash he thinks he has a right to it since I'm not doing my chores when I'm out here on the gang by the Lord.

He's too young. Grandma says this sharp and hard, little strikings of hammer on anvil but she's not concerned about me for her it's not having her slave there to fetch eggs and sweep the walks and hoe the garden.

He should get out among men. Time the boy brung money into the house. He's what, fourteen?

Right, Father. How many years we been feeding him? Eats like a horse.

He should of been out among men by now.

This is a familiar argument, Ken is a dreamer, he'll turn into a ne'er-do-well like his father, an embarrassment to the family if he's not pushed to become a man. Another nobody Leishman.

Truth be told, I liked the threshing gang, I wanted to get away from there, from them as fast as my feet would fly also there was the money, little enough but something better than nothing. In the city I can see movies every day, Uncle Henry and Aunt Agnes will put me up, they've told me so, they have no children and have promised to take me to Assiniboine Park and Lower Fort Garry, let down our hair, says Aunt Agnes ice cream also.

I'm reaching for the cigarette when a voice behind me says, No, and I feel a big warm hand close over my shoulder. The fella who is speaking rises behind me and comes to sit beside me, not letting loose of my shoulder, his fingers clamped to my thin boy's bones. Put that away, says the fella to the man with the stained teeth, who looks across at him for a moment then rises with a snort and goes outside to join the men drinking whiskey and telling stretchers.

The fella beside me says, I know your granddad. The cot sags, taking his weight. Kenny, right?

Ken.

Ken. Right.

I nod.

I'm Arno de Vlieger's son. Run the John Deere dealership in town. Martin.

I'd thought from the sound of his voice and his grip on my shoulder that he was a growed man but I seen now that he's only a few years older than me, twenty maybe, thin blond hair and a round face. I seen him around town at the dealership maybe wearing a green and blue checked shirt, always smiling and laughing. They're a Dutch family and in winter Martin skates on these queer long skates on the town rink speed skates I heard them called.

You don't want to start that, says he, meaning the cigarette. A bad habit. Weakens the lungs. Give you that smoker cough soon later. He draws a deep breath and exhales at length.

There's nothing to say to this so I say nothing but I draw a deep breath too. In the silence someone outside says, Maybe in Hell the priest replies to the rabbi, and then there is a burst of laughter. When it dies away Martin says, You liked that song. About the dying cowboy. I did too by gum. I wish I could sing that good.

I've recovered and say, On Sundays the choir does "Little Church in the Vale."

I like that one too.

There is another pause. The guitar is being strummed quietly, the man with the long legs reclining back on a cot and playing with his eyes closed, a tune I never heard before.

Miss Sanders says you're a good scholar.

It was a surprise to me how adults knew each other, I was always surprised at who knew what about who around town, it was a shock that they would have found my ragamuffin self fit subject for their private conversation. But I felt a flush of pride too just to be noticed, to be mentioned.

She doesn't like me. She thinks I'm a smart aleck.

Martin laughs, a light tinkling sound unlike the laughter outside, which is raw and loud and comes like gun bursts. She doesn't like much. He laughs again. But she's got a good eye for human nature. You know what I mean by that?

I do. I've recovered my voice and say it with authority. She knows Gary Bigelow is a liar and Tammy Johnson a flirt.

Martin laughs again. Yes, she's a good judge of character. He pauses, then adds, And you know what she says about you, she says that young Ken he's going somewheres. Martin looks away when he says this, he's looking at the doorway. Light has gone out of the sky except for a stripe of purple above the treetops but fireflies flit by the doorway, tiny sparks of gold flitting past the rectangle of the door, warm air from the earth like the land is breathing long and low at the close of day. Me too, I hope says he. Soon later. After a pause he adds, Going somewheres.

But your family runs the John Deere.

That's a good living. True. My brother Eddy wants to take that up, settle down in town. He pauses and looks down. The toes of one foot are tapping the floor. Me, I'm heading for the city. I'd like to do something else. Don't get me wrong. Selling tractors is a good living.

But.

But I have the feeling there's bigger things on my horizon. Not so small town.

Dead as a doornail around here?

Martin studies me a moment. Yeah. You've seen that one, then? The angels movie?

Angels with Dirty Faces. I never miss the Bowery Boys.

No, me neither. Though Jimmy Cagney stole the show in that one.

He did. Don't be a sucker. Whadya hear, whadya say? Dead as a doornail. I like the way he says stuff like that. Bigger things on my horizon. Be a somebody.

Martin laughs again and this time me too, we chuckle and the fella strumming the guitar stops the strumming of his fingers and opens one eye lazily and looks at us and grins.

Rocky Sullivan is finally cornered by the cops, he don't have a chance for certain sure. Cagney is good at showing this working his mouth from side to side pacing with the pistol up like he intends to fire it, flashing his eyes here and there in desperation. He's robbed and he's shook down politicians for money and he's killed people shot them dead, he's a criminal and his old pal from school days the priest who started off stealing from the corner store with him and was sent to reform school with him but who become a priest where Rocky become a gangster has tried to get him to go straight. But Rocky is too far in, he's cast his lot with the criminal element besides he thinks going straight is for suckers. Says Rocky throughout the movie, Don't be a sucker.

The kids in the neighbourhood think he's a hero. He is. When he comes back to visit, he drives a fancy car and splashes money around and talks big. He's used part of the money he's got through robbery to pay for the community club the priest has been building, the old store that the two of them used to steal stuff from when they was kids. The club will be a place where the kids can hang out and play games and so on away from the criminal element. The kids in the neighbourhood are the Bowery Boys, toughs, in the movie the priest calls them angels with dirty faces. They're bad but not really bad, they can be reformed, he believes they're good inside, the priest believes in the goodness of human nature just the opposite to how Rocky sees things.

It all goes wrong in the end. The girl Rocky had a crush on in school refuses to accept his gifts, the priest tells him he cannot take dirty money for the club, the cops close in on Rocky and trap him in his old neighbourhood hideout. It's curtains for Rocky. He starts to sweat and shake. Cagney is brilliant, his facial expressions alone worth the price of admission but then there's the way he fidgets around the set, energy, intensity, fierce determination and a kind of controlled rage. Though the priest comes to intervene there's nothing can be done, Rocky is captured even his shyster lawyer cannot save him from the law, he's sentenced to death, crapped-out.

The priest comes to see him one last time. Rocky sticks out his jaw. He brung this on himself and he'll go down spitting in the eye of the law the hell with cops the hell with judges the hell with everyone, he'll go down as he lived, cursing and defiant. Don't, says the priest. Remember when we was kids and we did each other favours? Do this one last favour for me, for the kids, the neighbourhood. Beg for your life, when they take you to the electric chair, show them that crime don't pay. Rocky hesitates. He's a tough guy always has been he's gotten a reputation, he wants to go down spitting in the eye of the law. And he truly does think there's only one way to make it for kids from the neighbourhood, the way he's went from his childhood onward. For the kids, the priest argues. Do this one good thing. You done bad things but Laura and I both know you're good inside. What can Rocky say?

And then there's a final scene where one of the Bowery kids is reading the paper: Rocky Sullivan, tough guy gangster writhes in dread in his final minutes and begs for his life, is writ in the paper, Rocky pleads for mercy. How about that?

I lug the last side of beef that were passed me by Mike through the back door into the meat locker and hoist it to an empty hook, also take a deep breath and watch steam condense in the air in front of my face, wipe both hands on the apron, shut the meat locker door behind me. Sixteen, Granddad says, but big as a horse. And eats like one too says Grandma.

That it? Tommy is up near the front counter checking the stock, 5:40, almost closing time, come a few minutes Tommy will have me cover the cuts not sold with damp cloths.

That's the lot. I reach down under the cutting counter and grab up the cloths used to cover the meat over night as I pass from the back of the shop to the front.

Good take, Tommy says, we had us a good day. He goes over to the cash register and opens the drawer and studies the bills inside. You wanna head out, Ken, leave me to close?

I'll put the cloths down. I say this as I slide the glass door to one side, preparing to cover the two unsold chickens first also livers and miscellaneous bits. Hang around until close-up.

Tommy nods. He's a short stocky man, big hands, strong wrists, it's all in the wrists, he's explained to me about wielding the cleaver and using the saw, mastering the butcher trade. Good work with those sides of beef, says he. You kinda showed up that delivery fella.

I did? I didn't mean nothing.

I know. You're a big kid, Ken, you use your size well.

I don't think he took no offence.

No, he's a good fella, Mike, a good Ukrainian boy who don't take himself too serious.

I have a washcloth out and am wiping the top of the meat counter, don't want to cover up too much of the meat too soon someone may walk in at the last minute every sale counts.

Tommy is leaning against the cutting counter. You're a good kid, Ken, a hard worker and you learn fast. Most of the kids I've had in here... Well, the less said the better.

I like the business. It has a steady pace. And you're doing something for people.

That's right. People like you, Ken. You're a natural with the women. You're a born salesman. Know what I mean?

You mean I spend too much time chewing the fat. It ain't by intention, just gets the better of me. I enjoy joshing with folks. I'll try to keep the yapping down.

No. Not at all. That's part of running a butcher shop, any shop. Making all the old biddies feel they're important, taking the time to answer questions and whatnot. You're a natural. The women like you. I ain't good at that but you got the gift of the gab, you do.

I could learn more. You know, the finer work with saw and knife. And the money side.

That's right. I been thinking that too. I been thinking you could work out real good here, Ken. I could send you on a course to the city even meat cutting and such you're a quick learner. Tommy has stuck a cigarette between his lips unlit because smoking is against health regulations so his speech comes out slurred. I could maybe take you on in the business, you know, after a few years.

You would? No one has ever said nothing like this to me, my grand-parents spend all their time telling me I'm a slacker and sinful the devil's own work, the few times my mother come to visit she spends all her time telling me how the other kids are, how tough things are for her. The last time she was with a fella, I think she was going to marry him, he stayed out in the car while she talked with me and then with Granddad and Grandma. She has no money. The cleaning work she done for years has dried up, she has to go back on relief, a lousy fourteen bucks a month to buy food and pay rent and heat her cramped apartment. How is she going to make it? Trembling and tears, I feel a lump in my throat but irregardless storm out the door without saying goodbye, even, she brung me too much pain in the past sending me to work for this one and that one.

Tommy looks at his watch. Well, let's pack up for today.

I'll lock the door.

And don't forget what we was talking about. I can use you here at Tommy's Meats. Your grandparents, they would like to have you around. Close to home. Know what I mean?

One of these eggs is cracked. Look here, boy. Can't you be more care-ful? I told you a hundred times.

You said to hurry, you said—

Why don't you pay attention to what you're doing? To waste is a sin.

I—but I was just—

Na, na, na. No backtalk. Honour thy father and thy mother. You know what that means?

You're my grandmother, not my mother.

See. It means you do what I say with no backtalk. You're a wicked boy. You always been, with excuses and dodges, Kenny. And a smart aleck to boot. I have half a mind to send you to bed without supper.

We'll have no more of that talk, Mother. Let the boy eat.

Let the boy eat. You got no idea how much he eats, Father. It's sinful, it's greed. He don't need to make a pig of himself.

For certain gluttony is a deadly sin.

You see. And the slapdash job he does in the barn is a wickedness too. Did you see the mess in there? I had to go in after and pick up all the hay on the floor. Slapdash. I set him one simple job but ain't he the prince? He done such a awful job.

The devil finds work for idle hands, Ken. You don't need to rush through. You know that.

He knows it but he pays it no heed. He's his father's son, a wicked seed. An Irish. The sins of the father. You know what that means, child?

My father, I—

A lesson you could learn by heart.

Our cross to bear, Mother. Yes. But Christian charity, the Lord advocated too.

Humph. It's not enough we took him in when no one else wants him. Well, tonight we will fall down on our knees and we will pray for the Lord to purge you of your wickedness, child. To help you walk the straight and narrow, the path of righteousness for His name's sake. Amen.

He will learn, Mother, he will be taught. One way or the other.

Now go wash your hands and face. Scrub. Cleanliness is next to godliness. And you need a good purging, boy. Ain't soap enough in heaven.

Go now, boy.

And that cracked egg, that will be your breakfast tomorrow, and if he's sick on it that will be the Lord's sign for marking a sinful child to be punished. No sneaking off to the movies come Saturday.

When I leave Tommy's Meats I go out the back door and down the alley and turn into the main street, it's closer to take the back streets but I like walking down Main nodding at people on the sidewalk looking in the front windows of the other shops sometimes I stroll down to the John Deere on the edge of town and go inside and yak with Martin. We stop in at the drugstore for a Pepsi on ice and go to the movies together on Saturday afternoons. He tells me about books he's read, descriptions of places he seen in them books, and other things too, how to influence people and get ahead in business.

Tommy's proposition sings in my mind, I'm flattered, no one has ever said that I do a good job before, no one has said I wasn't a bum, and my steps feel light as I amble along. Also I like talking with the people who come in the shop, I like serving customers also wrapping parcels of meat in brown paper but cutting the guts out of things that's another story, I never had an easy time with blood I feel light-headed when it spurts out of the throats of chickens and splashes on the wrists sometimes the face I could faint then. And sausage. The meat sticks to the fingers between the fingers, hunks of white fat fly up from the grinder and hit your cheeks, sickening, so when Tommy's doing that I make an excuse to go outside where I can take a few deep breaths. All in all, the butcher shop may not be for me, I'm maybe better suited for a white-collar job, bank teller or selling life insurance or whatever. Bigger things on my horizon. Irregardless no one else has ever offered me a job in all my sixteen years and more no one has ever made my big clumsy feet feel light as air on the walk home.

I pass the gas station and cross the street and take the side street to the house at the end of the block where my grandparents live. I pay them room and board, the food is no better than it was when I didn't pay, and there's never enough, but Grandma curls down her lip if I utter a word. Greed, says she. Gluttony, says Granddad, one of the deadly sins. When I come close on to the house I see there's a strange car parked in front of the house, a new Ford Meteor it turns out green with shiny bumpers the kind of car Humphrey Bogart would drive in the movies whitewall tires, a car that calls attention to itself gleaming and new. Granddad has a rundown Chevy in the winter it won't start and in the summer it's always getting flat tires.

When I come up to the car a man gets out he's wearing a topcoat and a wide-brimmed hat which shades his eyes so at first I don't recognize him. Hey, he calls out.

I stop. I drop my eyes. A moment ago my heart was light, Tommy's words of praise sung in my ears but the sound of this voice. Now my gut feels like there's a lead ball in it.

Hey, say he. You got nothing to say to your old man?

He stretches his arms wide like he means to give me a hug. I step backward. He drops his arms but then puts out one hand, a big mitt like my own. You won't shake your old man's hand? Have I treated you that bad?

There's nothing to say to this so I say nothing. The lights are on in the house, Grandma will be fussing in the kitchen, Granddad insists on eating at 6:30 sharp, he hit me with the back of his hand when I come in late one time when I was a kid he wouldn't dare try that now.

My father takes a step toward me, hesitates, then another step. He's smiling a big grin that takes up his face, slickly shaved, he's been wearing leather gloves to drive and he's folded both of them into one hand, tapping his thigh. Look, says he, I'm doing good now, I've got my own business, elevator repairs and maintenance. I'm doing good, real good. He looks sideways toward the car. The evening sun catches the shiny bumper, which glints and winks light. I study his topcoat, new, and the brown leather gloves. In the city, says he. He glances up and down the dusty street, a clutter of houses, rusty cars driven up on side yards, crumbling sheds, tarps thrown over abandoned machinery, chickens pecking in the gravel, mutts pissing on trees, all shabby and rundown when I see it through his eyes, the eyes of Norman Leishman. He takes another step forward. C'mon, says he, let the old man buy you a nip and a Coke at the restaurant, let me make you a business proposition. I need a bright young man to help me, start at the bottom but work himself up as the business grows, be the office manager in a couple of years, a desk to sit at, a pretty little secretary with a cute behind. C'mon. You wanna be stuck in this one-horse town all your life? He glances around. You're my son. I'm proud of you. You're a comer. Your mother says so. You like the pictures, I know that. Kenny. Your mother tells me. In the city you can go to the pictures every day if you want. All the new shows, Cagney, Bogart. You like Bogart? There's a new one on now. And a Clark Gable coming. C'mon, I'll treat you to a nip and lay out my proposition, it's good money to start and a lot more to be made soon for a bright guy like my only son.

I'm so taken with *The Maltese Falcon* that I sit in the darkened theatre while the rest of the audience files out and then I watch it a second time through. Sam Spade wears a fedora and a dark suit and carries a gun, talks in a slurry slang that cuts through nicey-nicey speech and has a hard-boiled attitude to everyone he meets trusts no one, dames, he calls women he isn't taken in by their wiles and silky movements, which he lets them know. The fast talk of other men don't impress him either. He smokes cigarettes one after the other. It's in watching Sam Spade that I seen that smoking cigarettes is never just a matter of getting tobacco smoke into your lungs, it's a style, an art, a way of dealing with the world. There's cheek in the way he inhales while listening to someone tell their story and in the way he blows smoke out when they're finished whatever they have to say, before he says anything. Lighting, inhaling, exhaling, butting out are their own language, they say as much as the words Spade says. There's a swagger in the way he butts out a cigarette that is only half smoked. Smoking is a language it's brilliant. The taste of success, of power is in my mouth, I consider buying a pack when I leave the theatre but then I remember old people with stained teeth. Not for me. I'm vain. I'm good-looking and I will not jeopardize that irregardless.

When I leave the movie house I'm half in love with Sam Spade. I stop for a cup of coffee and sit in a diner and go over the scenes in my head, so many to remember. I need a hat. I want to learn how to sip coffee and look mysterious and earn respect because I talk tough, hardboiled.

There are things that bother me. Throughout the movie Sam Spade says *egad* when things go bad and *blast* when he discovers he's been betrayed or double-crossed and there's lots of that in *The Maltese Falcon,* part of the reason I stay to watch it through a second time is that there are so many twists in the plot. Sam Spade is a rough customer he behaves like the kind of guy who knocks back half a bottle of whiskey without thinking about it he calls women *dames* and carries a gun, which we're to understand he's used in the past, maybe even killed someone. He makes a fist in a woman's face he throws punches and takes them and wipes his mouth with the back of his hand like it's something that has happened before and you can see by the look in his eyes that he'll bide his time but he'll get even. He's not the kind of man who says *egad* when he could say *crap*, or *blast* when there's *shit* and even *fuck*, talk more likely to come out of the mouth of a tough guy. I wonder who's been cleaning up the talk in the movie, and I wonder why and I wonder if the plot has been cleaned up too that would be just like prissy Hollywood types.

But mostly while I sit sipping coffee I think about which day I'll go back and see the movie again. The scene where the bad guy offers Sam Spade a spiked drink goes through my brain over and over, like a reverberation. The bad guy wants to knock Spade out so he commences by saying that real men hammer back shots, whereas pansies or whatever he calls weak men sip at drinks. He pours Spade a whiskey. We don't see him spike it but we guess that's what he's did, something tells us, it's movie magic. Spade holds the glass a while but does not take a drink, he's suspicious and rightly so. The bad guy sips yapping the whole time trying to put Spade at ease, get him to go for the whiskey. Sam sets the glass down. The bad guy sidles over and pours in a little more whiskey, like they both been drinking. Spade picks up the glass and eyes it coolly but still does not drink. His eyes follow the bad guy the whole time, scrutinizing, assessing, The bad guy sidles over again, splashes a little more into the glass. That's when Spade takes a sip, not a big one but it does the trick in a few seconds we're seeing the room through Spade's eyes growing blurry and tilting sideways. Villainous perfidy.

He shoulda used his brains better. He was clever, Sam Spade, but not cagey enough.

Bogart, I think, what an odd thing to call a kid. Did he make that up for the movies? Also *Humphrey*. Not the kind of name that goes over on the schoolyard. A few bloody noses in that moniker. But maybe Humphrey went to a classy school in a big city the kind of place where no one made fun of Jonathan or Anthony or whatever a school with ties and blazers, ticket to an Ivy League college and silver spoon in the mouth. Jimmy Cagney, that could be an actual name. But Clark Gable? Ken Leishman. William Kenneth, actually, quite a mouthful. William Kenneth Leishman. Esquire.

Hoaxers Grab $400,000 In Gold

Ken is pacing along the corridor of a Canadian Pacific rail car, bound for Vancouver. He's carrying a copy of the *Winnipeg Free Press* folded in one hand. He was trying to read it while sitting in his roomette but he could not concentrate on the words. He'd struggle through two paragraphs and then realize he'd lost the thread of what he was reading. That's why he's given up and is making his way to the club car. Maybe a drink will settle him. He tried having breakfast earlier but could not say now what kind of food was put in front of him. His head is abuzz. It's a three-cup high. He's hardly slept since leaving Winnipeg on Monday night, eight days after the robbery, though the roomette is comfortable and he knows he should sleep. He needs to be alert for the days ahead, the trans-Pacific travel, the negotiations, the courier he hopes to hook up with overseas. He pats the money belt around his waist. It's become a reflex. As has a nervous twitch in one hand.

Ken's mind is whirring with numbers. The bullion, the newspapers say, was valued around $400,000. According to Harry, they should be able to get eighty cents on the dollar for it in the Orient, even allowing for fences' fees and courier charges. He and Harry would each come out with as much as $200,000. But being conservative, minimum $150,000. You can buy a River Heights house for $15,000, a grand one on the river for $25,000 and a little business for the same, say a restaurant or car dealership, he'd be good at selling cars. That would leave more than $100,000. Ken could have a Cadillac, he's always liked a cream-coloured Cadillac, he could buy Elva diamonds, get a cottage, buy a new Cessna, a powerboat, send the kids to private school. But not right away. That's the mistake thieves always make, splashing the cash around. The trick is to lie low for a while, a year or two, before spending any of the money. It takes patience, it takes discipline, it takes a man with self-control. But that leaves—what?—$100,000, maybe $120,000. More than anyone needs. Enough to impress the likes of lawyers and bankers and that lot. Ken could buy bonds and stocks, be a guy who muckity-muck bankers would have over for supper—well, take out to lunch. What would the interest on $100,000 amount to in a year? Is the going rate 5% these days, 8%? Ken calculates. Whistles under his breath. He'd never have to work again. A car dealership would just be fun, gravy.

It's morning, Wednesday, 9 March, and the train is due into Vancouver in a few hours. Ken glances out the window. They've passed through the Rockies, which were spectacular, but their beauty was lost on Ken. He cannot remember anything but a blur of tall pines and rock. They're into the flatter lands around Chilliwack, something like the prairies, Ken thinks, though always in the distance there are the peaks of mountains, covered in snow. Beautiful, Ken thinks, this is a beautiful part of the country, as soon as this caper is over, he will talk to Elva about moving out here, he's heard Chilliwack is a city on the move, yet quiet and folksy. A good place to raise kids, a place where a man could wake every morning to bracing air, the smell of snow-capped peaks, to boundless blue overhead, white clouds scudding like sails, the sun bedazzling up above, where the world seemed fresh and new as Adam and Eve, space for a man to walk in, for the mind to wander about and be at peace, nothing holding him in or back, no boundaries, the ease of emptiness. Chilliwack. Or maybe the interior of B.C. Buy that little business, hardware store, car dealership maybe, it would not matter, raise the kids in style, become a respectable member of the community, he's always wanted to belong to the Chamber of Commerce. He's imagined himself as the mayor of a town. It's a cinch he'll never make a life in Winnipeg after this.

The club car is the next one up. Ken pushes open the door and crosses between the two cars, the soles of his shoes sliding on the two interlocked tongues of metal that connect the cars. There's a bit of engineering. He wonders who invented those tongues, made himself a million, probably. Ken's something of an inventor himself, he designed an easy-to-inflate air bag that could be thrown on the ground below the windows of burning buildings for people trapped above to jump onto. He cannot understand why the air bags did not go over. The test run with the fire department seemed to work out okay, though there was some shaking of heads when the stunt guys jumped from a greater height than the second storey. Ken suspects the fire department had something against him, maybe in cahoots with someone else, it's possible they even stole his idea. Whatever the case, like most of his inventions, this one just didn't quite work out. But Ken will not stop trying, he's an optimist. When he's in the clear after this caper, there are a number of ventures he would like to try.

In the club car there's a couple of empty tables but they expect you to eat a full-size meal if you sit down where they have menus and white cloth napkins, so Ken takes a seat beside a man at the counter. "BLT," he hears someone in the kitchen, hidden from view, call out. Ken nods at the waiter moving toward him on the opposite side of the counter. "That's for me," he says. "BLT. And a beer." It's early in the day for him but what the hell. He glances at the guy beside him, who's nursing the last of a glass of lager, then back at the waiter. "And another one here." He gives the guy a wink.

The guy raises his eyebrows but does not say anything. He's smoking, and he takes a drag on a roll-your-own cigarette, inhaling deeply.

"Hey there," Ken says. He touches the brim of his fedora. The newspaper rests between them, folded in half to conceal headlines.

"Cheers," the guy says. He raises his glass and tips it towards Ken. He looks like Peter Lorre, kind of a pasty face and a pudgy nose. A dangerous man in *The Maltese Falcon*. He scrapes his cigarette on the edge of an ashtray before speaking. "Thanks," he says, "for the beer."

"Nothing to it." Ken gives him a quick wink. "One fellow passenger to another."

"Yeah," the guy snorts, "one inmate to the next."

Ken laughs uneasily. "You got it. Kills the time, does a glass of beer."

"You're right about that." The guy takes a sip, then asks, "Where you from?"

"Winnipeg."

"Hoo. Quite a storm out that way. Surprised CP was able to make it through."

"Just. They clear the tracks with these big tractor things got snowplows out front." Ken's beer has arrived and he tips his glass at the guy. For a second or two the other guy's face goes in and out of focus, and it's not just because of the cloud of smoke scarving his face. Ken realizes his head is buzzing, he has slept poorly, he's at his nerves' end. He blinks as he listens to the other man going on.

"Radio said feet of snow came down on you guys. Feet! The Great Blizzard of Winnipeg. Drifts more than ten feet high. Cars buried. Cops riding around on snowmobiles. Chaos and confusion."

"Lord." Ken laughs. "The wife took some pictures. My son standing on a snowdrift, high as the roof of the car, which he's standing beside".

"You don't say. I'm from Castlegar myself. Got on just back a bit."

"Drifts right up to the eavestroughs. Eight, ten feet high." Ken taps the newspaper, but the other man is going on.

"Lots of shovelling."

"No end of that, no. They're saying it's the biggest snowstorm ever."

"On TV they showed people on snowshoes going for groceries. Schools closed?"

"Schools, city offices. The whole shebang. But then when did those government guys ever do an honest day's work? They got the union, they got the pension. Who needs work?"

"Right about that. Messed up the city, I bet. Not much happening in the way of business."

Ken nods. There's a part of him that's happy that the first thing the guy is talking about is the blizzard and not the robbery. But part of him is disappointed too. He's the Flying Bandit, the man the headlines are all about, the man John Harvard on the radio can't stop talking about, though not by name. Him, he's the thief of gold, Winnipeg's desperado, an all-star, a big-time operator. One of the papers said the operation at the airport was smooth. Another called him clever. People are talking him up like he's a big-time gangster, Al Capone or Bugsy Malone. He pats the belt on his waist again. If he rests his hand in the right place he can feel the tiny bar of gold bullion stashed there, probably as much as five pounds, at least three thousand dollars worth, a good sample for a prospective buyer.

"But you got out?" The guy is stroking the bridge of his pudgy nose. He's a short man with beady eyes and he seems suspicious, not Ken's type at all. He lets cigarette smoke curl out of his nostrils, then says again, "But you were able to get out of snowbound Winnipeg?"

"Just." In fact, Ken was trapped in his house for two agonizing days while the snowdrifts plugged up the streets and brought traffic to a standstill. In that time he could think of nothing but the gold bars in the deep freeze in Harry's basement. What if someone stumbled across them, stole them, reported to the cops? He contemplated walking to Harry's place, a distance halfway across the city, it would have taken only an hour or two, but what would that have accomplished, other than drawing attention to Harry and himself? Instead he spent much of those two days frenetically shovelling snow—walkway, driveway, part of the back lane—in expectation of the first moment when he'd be able to take out the car. Kept his hands busy, burnt off anxiety raging inside. It worked, but there were still nightmares, sleepless hours, a knot in the gut as big as a bowling ball. At times he felt panic rushing to his chest and clamping his heart. If only he'd got the gold out of town, as planned. Damn snowstorm. The luck was just against him. It was with him when there were twelve gold bars instead of ten. But that's how things worked. Sometimes the luck was with you, sometimes against.

The guy sips his beer. "You got business in Vancouver?"

"Not quite in Vancouver. Meeting a man in the Far East." Ken glances at his watch. There's sweat on his arm, glinting through the thick hair of his wrist. "I got a plane to catch at four."

"Huh. The Far East, you say?"

"I'm flying on to... to Australia." Ken puts one hand on his knee to still the bouncing. He almost said Hong Kong, which would have been foolish. You can say too much, one of Ken's weaknesses, something Harry has warned him about, blabbing on. Rule Two in the lawyer's handbook: keep your mouth shut. Rule One: get the fat retainer up front.

"Huh." The guy busies himself butting out his cigarette.

"Yeah," Ken adds, "little jaunt to the Orient, check out a prospective buyer, make a few contacts, kinda thing, and set the wheels in motion for a bit of business later."

"Uh-huh, business." He gives Ken the quick once-over and sips his beer thoughtfully.

"We're trying to get in on the ground floor, see, of a little... a little enterprise, let's call it."

"Uh-huh."

"My partner and me..."

Ken can tell the guy doesn't believe him, thinks he's a bullshitter. If he's a mover and shaker, a businessman on his way to Australia, why is he travelling between Winnipeg and Vancouver on the train and not flying? Harry's idea, Ken could tell him, keep a low profile, fly under the radar. But he bites his tongue. He mustn't shoot off his mouth. It's the thing he finds most difficult about being a thief. Not the planning of jobs, not the hard work of trial runs and the like, not carrying the gun, driving the car, not the difficult followup, lying low and going about the day-to-day. Preparation and grunt work come easy. They're not work at all, not compared to hefting sides of beef or cleaning greasy elevator parts. What Ken finds most difficult is keeping his mouth shut after a job has been done. He wants to lay out the whole narrative, to tell people, That's me, I'm the guy who pulled the whole thing off, a regular highwayman, scarpered with the bag of loot, made fools of the cops—look, here's how we did it, first we...

Downtown intersection, desolate and snowswept.

Schools, services closed down

Blizzard brings city to halt

When the train pulls into Vancouver, Ken is standing at the door with his suitcase in hand. He looks around at the platform, first one direction, then the other. Quiet. Passengers bustling off the train. Harry was right. The cops would have been watching the Winnipeg airport, they would have stopped him. On the train they don't check papers, they don't ask for ID, all they're interested in is whether or not you have a ticket. There's enough to worry about with the flight to Hong Kong. Harry has arranged a ticket for the flight across the ocean but Ken does not know what he's going to do once he's there. The Orient is crazy for gold, that he knows. But they need to make contact with a courier. Harry has given him the name of a lawyer he thinks may be able to help them dispose of the gold bullion, but if that guy doesn't come through, then what? That's the unknown. Every plan has an unknown, a head-scratcher, and the head-scratcher of this plan is what do they do if he cannot locate someone in Hong Kong to take the gold off their hands? Fly on to Japan, Harry has suggested. Maybe Indonesia? They all love gold, apparently. Everyone wears gold. Rings, bracelets, necklaces. You can't have a proper wedding unless lots of gold is exchanged. But it's a big chance he's taking getting on to that plane, flying here and there with a sample of bullion, breaking his parole, trusting Orientals he's just met. But that's the game they're now playing, that's the gambit. It's no wonder, though, that Ken's hands on the suitcase grip are sweaty, that his heart knocks as if he's downed a pitcher of black coffee. He's abuzz.

Ken comes out of the station and flags a cab. "Airport," he tells the cabby. He checks his watch. Almost four hours before the flight to Hong Kong leaves. He's jumping parole being out of Winnipeg but he knows his parole officer well enough to take the chance. Veccione will cut him a little slack, and Elva will cover for him, if they come after her. He tells her as little as possible about what he's doing, it's their mutual protection pact. What she doesn't know won't hurt either of them. But hopefully they won't come after her. He's been a model parolee since he's been out of the clink. Has a job, reports in on time, a family man. And he gets along with everyone, he can tell Veccione feels comfortable with him and proud in his dutiful social-worker way of Ken's progress. He's not like other ex-cons, he's thoughtful, he speaks like an educated man, he's not surly and angry and withdrawn, he has ambitions and plans. Ken Leishman is a gentleman. Besides, he's served his time. And the Toronto bank robbery is ages past, five years.

"Where ya from?" The cabby has adjusted the rearview mirror and glances at him.

"Winnipeg."

"Stranglehold."

"You what?"

"On the TV. They said stranglehold on the city. That snowstorm out that ways."

"Oh, yeah, we get Colorado lows. They dump these piles of snow on the prairie."

"Shut everything down, the TV said."

"You bet." Ken tips his hat down to shade his face.

"Snow halfway up the doors of people's houses. Stranglehold on the whole city. TV showed office workers trapped downtown and sleeping in the furniture departments of the Bay and Eaton's. Army called in to shuttle pregnant women to the hospital on toboggans."

"Snowmobiles. It was something, all right. "

"So much snow. I never saw nothing like that."

"Lord." Ken grunts. "Colorado lows, they call them, they just move in and dump snow."

"They had it on TV though."

The cabby's words have brought an image to Ken's mind, a picture of him and his son standing at the front window watching the snow pile up in the street in front of his house, wind blowing it around the wheel wells of parked cars, neighbours standing thigh-deep in drifts and shaking their heads. He's also thinking about the gold bullion. The plan was to move it from Harry Backlin's freezer. There's an abandoned barn on the edge of a field of what once was his grandfather's farm near Treherne. A good place to hide the gold bullion. Ken had planned to drive out there the day after the heist and hide the bars. Keep one but leave the rest for a couple months, more if necessary, until the heat died down. But the great blizzard messed up that plan. Cars could not get around on city streets. His station wagon was trapped. The RCMP closed down the highways. The gold had to stay in Harry's freezer. As he stood watching the snow pile up, Ken grew more and more antsy by the hour, at times he felt as if his skull was going to explode, it was a four-cup buzz, only the buzz of antsiness and anxiety, not of excitement and pleasure. And now a whole week has passed. The bullion could not be moved.

"You okay, buddy?"

The voice of the cabby startles Ken. He realizes he hasn't heard what he's been saying. He blinks and runs his hand over his forehead. "Geez," he says, "didn't sleep so great last night."

"I was saying we don't get that much out here."

"You what?"

"Snow. Except in Whistler. You know, ski resorts and the like. No Colorado what-you-call-'ems."

"Lows. Huge dumps of snow. Big winds too. Guess they only hit the prairies."

"Only in the mountains round here." The cabby laughs. "High up in the Rockies."

"Yeah." Ken puffs out his cheeks. "Sorry. I—"

"I talk too much, eh? At least my wife always says so. Got the gift of the gab."

"Me too. Usually. It's just that today—"

The cabby laughs again and taps the steering wheel with both hands. "That can get a guy in trouble, though, all that gabbing. Motor-mouth."

Ken pushes down on his knee to still his tapping foot. Looks out the window. Spring is already in full swing on the West Coast. Cherry blossoms, snowdrops, others whose names he does not know. This would be a nice place to live, to raise kids. Ken's eyes grow misty for a moment. If he pulls this off, he's going to buy the kids enough toys to fill up the house, a cottage at the beach where they can spend summers swimming and playing in the sand. He has not been a good father. The kids would not say that, nor Elva, but he knows better. Maybe he'll risk a phone call later, just to hear their voices. A surge goes through Ken's chest.

"And that gold robbery." The cabby's tone shoots up. "Geez, I just about forgot about the gold robbery. That was an eye-popping caper, wasn't it?"

Ken leans forward. "You heard about that out here?"

"How could you help? Headline-grabber, that one. Just like what's-his-name, you know, the one they're always talking about, big-time thief."

"Al Capone?"

"No, he was a mobster, the other one, bank robber, man of the people."

"John Dillinger."

"Yeah, that one. All over the news, radio, papers. Quite the opera-tion, quite the eye-popping caper. Hoo boy, made the cops look bad, I can tell you that, did that one. Whoever pulled off that job, he was one sharp cookie, that one."

"They saying that on TV?"

"Slick. A real operation."

"Operation. I like that word. Classy."

"Planning and daring. Those guys got some balls."

"You think?" Ken has heard this on CJOB's phone-in show, regular folks full of admiration for the audacity, for the way the job went off. In Winnipeg, a blue-collar city, sticking it to the Man goes over big, even when what's been done is illegal. So long as nobody gets hurt. That seemed to be the message on the radio: so long as nobody's hurt. Also Ken's cardinal rule.

"Probably off in Mexico or somewhere by now," the cabby is say-ing. "Argentina or wherever all the Nazis went after the war. They're not too picky about who they take there, in Brazil and so on. Long as you got the moolah. Money talks, right? If he figured out how to steal the gold, that one there, he also figured out how to whisk it away. Oh, yeah, he's a schemer, he's far away from here and sipping cool drinks, that one, bronzed Brazilian babe on each arm. A mastermind."

"Mastermind?"

"You bet."

"Hadn't heard that," Ken says, leaning forward. "High praise for a thief."

"More than a thief," the cabby says, drumming his hands on the steering wheel. "You bet. This was a little guy sticking it to the big guys. Everyone knows that lawyers and bankers and businessmen are ripping us off all the time, nothing anyone can do about it, just how the system works. And the politicians. They've got their hands in the public pocket, they're in on every dodgy deal that goes down. Take this St. Lawrence Seaway business, you can bet your bottom dollar the politicians are all taking their slice of the pie. And this Olympic thing coming up in Montreal." The cabby looks back at Ken, makes a gesture with his hand, rubbing his thumb on his forefinger. "Lots of brothers and brother-in-laws and friends of friends getting rich on that one, you can bet, politicians, bankers, lawyers. The fat cats, right? But this gold heist, this is different, now, this is the little guy, not a fancy-pants politician with a college degree."

"Huh," Ken says.

"I'll tell you something, I'd like to meet that guy. Folks may not agree with me about that there, him being a criminal and all, but I'd like to meet that guy. Find out more about him, how he pulled off the robbery, what makes him tick as a man."

"Just a regular guy, a guy who..." Ken stops himself. "At least, so I'd guess."

The cabby eyes him in the rearview mirror. "Sounds like you may know more than you're letting on, friend."

"Well, you hear things, eh?"

"And you, my friend, you hear...?"

Ken's clutching the back of the cabby's seat as he leans forward. "Well, just between you and me—"

"Yeah?"

"I hear that guy did a lot of planning, I hear he got together the right little team, cased the set-up out, knew where the cops would be and how to snatch the gold, I hear the whole business came off smooth as a well-oiled machine." Ken taps his temple with one thick finger. "Brains, eh?"

"Huh. Like the Great Train Robbery. Schedules, timing."

"Exactly. Smarts, not muscle."

"That's the ticket. Beating the shysters at their own game. What else you hear?"

"I hear that gold will be on the move, and soon."

"Yeah, that's smart, that's clever, keep it moving. You know where that gold is headed?"

"Well—" Ken drops his voice. Beside them a car honks loudly and the guy driving it shakes his fist at the cabby, whose car is straddling two lanes. Ken swallows hard. For a moment or two the cabby is distracted by his driving. Ken leans back and closes his eyes, runs one hand back and forth over his mustache. His heart is beating a tattoo in his chest. Jesus, he thinks, slow down. Shut your trap.

Past the next intersection, the cabby says, "You were saying?"

"Aw, nothing," Ken says, shaking his head. "Rumours, you know, loose talk at the bar."

The cabby drums his hands on the steering well. He changes lanes, glances at Ken in the rearview mirror. "Well," he says after a few minutes pass, "I can tell you this. For once the little guy has done the system over. Outsmarted the whole works and got away with the gold. I'll tell you another thing, too. Regular folks are all behind him but you better believe the powers that be are mighty sore about it."

"Sore?" Ken blinks his eyes. For a moment he lost the cabby's thread. "Regular folks?"

"No, no, the cops. The whole judicial system. Prosecutors, judges, police chiefs. They'll stick it to him if they ever catch up to him. Hang 'im high."

"Huh." Ken's fingers are tapping on his knee. "Never thought of that."

"But I'm thinking they won't."

"Me too."

"Which, I better say, I'm hoping they won't. I'm *hoping* he gets away, clean away."

Ken runs his tongue around inside his dry mouth. "I'm with you there."

"'Cause he's a luminary in my eyes."

"Luminary," Ken says, smiling. "I like that. Star. VIP."

"Uh-huh .Lots of regular folks think the same. Robin Hood, kind of thing. The dashing rogue. The little guy making good. We're pulling for him, you betcha."

You need heroes, nothing raises your flagging spirit like a story of courage and derring-do. The Greeks and Romans knew it, they told the stories of Jason and Hercules and Achilles, and before the Greeks—what?—the Bible. In biblical times there's David and Samson and even Jesus is a hero, a special kind, the man not celebrated for brave and daring exploits but the man punished for the message he brings, though a hero nonetheless a moral hero, a hero of the human spirit. Not everyone would agree. But his story touches a truth about hero stories, people like the tale of the underdog, the one who rises above his station and becomes the champion of the common folk. King Arthur of Camelot, the little guy who became king by pulling a sword out of a stone. Also Spartacus, a slave who defied his cruel masters, the good man challenging the bad man or system, and Jesse James, guys that become the idols of regular folk who see themselves as downtrodden and cherish the story of the fella who dares to challenge the bosses and ask the question they most hate to hear asked, which is: Why you and not me?

These are your heroes, the not-so-good men who rise from deprived circumstances, like your own clay-eating self and whose conduct is not exactly exemplary, the ruffians on the edge of the law, or outright outlaws, like your scalawag self, they carry the banner of everyone who feels they do not have a chance in a rigged system, that the only way for them to come out on top is to bend the rules, also set their own rules, Rob Roy, Louis Riel, the impecunious, the irrefragable. The dictionary ain't going to agree, it says something a little different about luminaries and heroes, less inclusive, so it's a reach to include some of them there names but that's what you do, isn't it, you stretch, you give things your own meanings and connotations, you have your say.

Ken is in the Richmond airport. Two hours before the flight to Hong Kong. He's checked to see that it's on time. He's bought a newspaper and has sat in a waiting area, trying to read it. The words are a blur. What does he care about Vancouver municipal politics? Sports teams he's never heard of. He's tapping his toes and looking at his watch. Tick. Tock. Time is not on your side. He rises and goes into the washroom. Instead of standing at one of the urinals, he goes into a cubicle and locks the door behind him. He sits on the toilet, shifts about in his coat and moves the money belt around so the little pouch rests on his belly. He pats it and then unzips the pouch, unwraps the soft cloth folded inside.

"Come here, baby," he whispers. He feels like a kid stealing a look at a dirty magazine, the thrill of the illicit.

In the dull light of the cramped public toilet the small chunk of gold gleams bright. Ken feels blood surge from his chest into his face, a rush of childish delight. He cannot believe he's pulled the job off, but here is the evidence, his treasure, the way out of his money troubles, the key to making his kids happy, Elva, the meaning of his life in one tiny chunk of gold he sawed off one of the bars. It had taken him longer than he had expected. Labouring with a hacksaw in his basement office, he had worked up a sweat by the time the little piece had come away from the bar. Someone had said that gold was soft, and maybe it was compared to steel, but it had been work, hard work. His arm is still stiff from the effort; for a day after the sawing his biceps trembled. Felt like rubber. Ken rotates the stumpy bar in his hand, tests its heft. Three pounds, four? Maybe as much as five. A good sample for someone to study and test. After he'd sawed off this little taster, he had put the remainder of the bar from which he'd sawn it into a briefcase and given it to Harry Backlin when Harry had come back from his vacation down south.

Harry's arm had sagged under the weight. "What am I supposed to do with it?" Harry had looked puzzled at first and then pissed off. Didn't want to get his hands dirty. But happy to split the profits.

"Use it as a doorstop," Ken had said with a smirk.

Ken wraps the bar carefully in the cloth and zippers it back into the money belt, closes his eyes and smiles. He's done it. He's pulled off the biggest heist in the country's history, he's John Dillinger—no, better than that, Doc in *The Asphalt Jungle*, the mastermind who beat the system with brains, not brawn. He's the Gentleman Bandit, a folk hero. Smarter than the cops, than any other thief in history, more daring than the lawyer, Harry Backlin. He'd be the envy of those highwaymen he's read about. He's bested them—and on their own terms. And he's going to be rich for the rest of his life. He's made it, the ragamuffin kid from Treherne whose parents did not want him, whose grandparents treated him like a servant, who beat him and laughed at his dreams. Ken Leishman has superseded any hero that Bogey has played, or Clark Gable, he is the ultimate outlaw. He checks his watch. Only a few minutes have passed. He's had a cup of coffee already but going for another one could kill a half hour if he dawdles. That's the upside. The downside is the caffeine will set his heart racing and he doesn't need that. He's already a nervous Nelly, what with his hand twitching crazy out of control.

Why, he wonders, do the minutes slow when you're in a hurry to get on with something? Feels like time in the slammer. Tick, tock. Is this his fate, to be always waiting?

Including the stint for the furniture theft, which occurred so long ago now that it seems when it crosses his mind to have happened to someone else, Ken has spent almost 1500 days in jail, over 37,000 hours, according to his calculations, more than two million minutes. It's lost time, Ken figures, hours he might have spent walking streets in sunshine, smelling the green air along the city's two rivers, advancing himself in the business world, doing things with Elva. It's time that he owes her, time he owes himself, time that he feels he must make up somehow, so for the remainder of his days he has to cram in as much living as possible, live intensely, seize every moment. It is no wonder, then, that he finds himself restless to get on with things, anxious, he suffers from headache during days, and wakes from nightmares, maybe not even aware why he's impatient, of what is at the root of his restiveness. He's a man who cannot stop checking his watch, who cannot still the tapping of his feet. He has heard that only four hours of sleep are required each night for both body and mind to regenerate, and he's intending to begin a program that reduces the hours he spends in bed in order to make the most of the time he has left. There can never be enough now. He's been cheated. Elva and the kids, too. Their faces come to him. His family. A sudden weight descends on his chest, deflates his buoyant mood.

Instead of having another coffee he puts in a call to Elva. It's late afternoon in Winnipeg, he'll hear the voices of the kids. Tell them the joke about the grasshopper and the windshield. His toes tap as he listens to the rings, waiting on the click of the receiver, Elva's sweet tones.

When she hears his voice, Elva shouts into the phone: "Where are you? The cops have come around. The phone's ringing off the hook. Ken, Ken. City cops. RCMP. Ken. They're crawling all over the street."

"Hold on, hold on, baby, give me a second here."

"Your parole officer wants to see you. John Veccione. He's called twice."

"Jesus. Jesus Lord now."

"I'm going out of my mind here. The RCMP. Photographers. The neighbours."

Ken is sweating. "Here's what to... Put Veccione off. Tell him—"

"You're supposed to call him back within the hour. No, he's calling you. No. God, I can't remember, my head is in a buzz, I just know something bad has happened. Ken."

"Tell him… tell Veccione I've gone to Treherne to visit my grand-father who's sick, on the point of dying. Tell him I'll be home tonight."

"Ken, Ken, you promised."

"I know. You don't need to remind me."

"Where are you?"

Ken's throat has constricted. "I'll be back tonight. Tell Veccione."

"Ah, so it is true. What the cops say."

"Hold on a second."

"No. You won't tell me where you are or what you've done. So I know it's true. You're in trouble again. You've done something crooked."

"I will tell you. It will be okay. Baby. I always do tell you."

"Yeah, always unless you don't."

"But."

"No buts. Just get home."

"I'll make it okay with you. The kids. Make it up to you. Elva."

"We need you. I'm going bananas here. The kids, Ken, the kids."

"I know, Elva. Geez."

"You promised."

Ken puts down the phone. His soaring spirits have gone through the floor. Everything seems to be unravelling. Has Harry talked? Have the cops got to John Berry or the Grenkow brothers? Ken needs time to collect himself, to think, to come up with another plan. There has to be a way out of this mess. He's the famous Flying Bandit. He just has to have time to think it all through. The one thing he can count on in any tight corner is his mind, which works like lightning, a blaze of inner circuitry, an imagination that sniffs out possibilities. That and the audacity to attempt the improbable. That's what has made him the famous Bandit. He finds a waiting area and sits down. Tries to still his racing thoughts.

Bogart holds the steely-eyed stare for a long moment. He's playing a man named Steve, who is being talked into one last job, a run on a boat out of the Florida Keys, helping the Free French, he's been told, an adventure but he's suspicious he thinks it's maybe guns or drugs. He has been an outlaw all his life Steve but he has his standards, there are rules he plays by. The scene is taking place in a hotel room and Steve is listening to what the spokesman of the French has to say, standing with his back to the wall. An unlit cigarette dangles from Steve's lips. He's not convinced by what he's being told, it's clear in his eyes something is fishy but this is a big chance for Steve, a last chance for a man down on his luck so he's listening.

The movie is based on a book by Hemingway, *To Have and Have Not*, and I know the story, I read it as soon as I heard the movie was being made. In the books of Hemingway there is not a lot of speaking, which is to say not a lot of speechifying, his is a world of men of a certain kind, the strong silent type, laconic, this part could have been played by Gary Cooper, he would of been good, but Bogart is perfect for the part the dark eyes his black hair slicked back and shiny with oil the set of his jaw his look of anxious desperation. Cooper's face is softer, he's the good man forced to do a bad thing, like in *High Noon* but basically he's a good man, the kind you want your sister to marry.

Bogart is dark and mysterious. Playing Steve, he's straight, he does the things he does by a set of rules but he works on the edge of the law, a dark hero, not preacher-good, irregardless he's a good man at heart, down deep, there are rules he will not break things that are important to him—loyalty, grace under fire, things a man is prepared to die for. It's not easy to explain. And you always seem to be pulling for him because he's at the end of his rope. It's a last chance.

In this movie Steve has to do something illegal also risky, it's almost a certainty his run is going to come to grief, we know it, he knows it. But his hand is being forced. And he thinks he can slip away this one last time, maybe get the loot and the girl and help the French at the same time. Though there are doubts. There are other forces at work and not just the law, men on the other side, women prepared to use feminine wiles to get what they want, pirates, ruffians who do not live by Steve's rules or any rules. Betrayal waits around every corner.

Bogart screws up his lips as he ponders what the other man is saying. Risky, it's all risky. He'll have to carry a gun and he hates guns. Steve's motto is you carry a gun, you end up shooting a cop. Or you end up getting shot. You can see in Steve's eye the foreknowledge—he may be killed on this venture, this may be his last run in a totally different sense than he first thought, this may be the final run for Steve. Inside him something doesn't care.

The men continue to eye each other and sip whiskey—always with Bogart there is whiskey, Hemingway too, whiskey and cigarettes and dangerous undertakings. Women are not often part of the scene though in this movie sexy women keep showing up but they are not a major interest, which is risks and difficult decisions, betrayals, painful choices, deaths, the failure of will and the triumph of evil.

This is why the movies hold the attention, grip the heart, cause sweat to break out on the brow, even when you know the outcome, even if you've read the book.

Bogart is nodding in agreement but his eyes betray him. He's agreeing on the outside but not the in but it's not fear that we see there. Bogart does not show fear. His jaw is set, his eyes steady. He's calculating the odds. He knows, Steve, that being a winner this time out is unlikely, this job involves risking all. He calculates the risk, anticipating the worst, putting it all on the line. One last time, Steve is thinking, one last throw of the dice. And if it doesn't work out, well what the hell.

Ken jumps up from the bench and goes to the CP counter. There's a flight to Winnipeg in an hour. A young woman stands behind the counter, a brunette wearing the navy blazer of the airline. "Hey there," Ken says. He gives her a warm smile.

"Hi," she says.

She's about to add something but Ken says, "I swear the gals at CP are getting prettier by the day. Are they hiring you right off the floor of the Miss America show now?"

The woman laughs. She tucks a fallen lock of hair behind her ear. "How can I help you?"

"The name's Leishman," Ken tells her. He'll take a one-way ticket to Winnipeg.

The woman says, "Mister Leishman is it? We have a Leishman going to Hong Kong. Is that you?" She smiles in a crooked way that brings to mind June Allyson in *Days of Wine and Roses*, was it?

"You bet it is. In the flesh." Ken gives her the smile. Touches his mustache. He knows what effect this has on women, this gesture has gained him more than one sale in the past. So many lonely housewives looking for someone to show a bit of interest. Ken knows about loneliness and neglect. It rushes back to him in a flush of remembrance whenever a memory of his grandparents comes to him, a childhood of neglect and solitary hours, criticism and censure, a life of isolation and defeat.

The clerk is saying, "Just a moment. I have a… a something else here for you." The lock of her hair has come loose and she tucks it behind one ear.

Ken is tapping his fingers on the counter. "The ticket was arranged for me by my business partner. He was to wire money too."

"Yes. Mister Leishman. I see. Yes, there is an envelope here for you." She fusses with her hair again, a thin woman, pretty in her own way, pale skin, alabaster, Ken thinks.

"Good." Ken puts out his hand. The clerk seems nervous, she keeps looking down at her hands and does not make eye contact with him. Ken clears his throat.

The clerk clears her throat, too. "I also have a message for you: you're to report to the RCMP desk when you arrive, Mister Leishman. Just over there, you see those glass doors?" Her hand trembles as she indicates an area behind him.

Ken has been leaning on the counter and he turns his shoulders slowly, following the direction she's pointing. There are two glass doors in the distance, with stencilled words on them.

"RCMP," Ken mutters. "What's that all about?"

"No idea. They just said—"

"Hmm." Ken pokes at the brim of his hat. "Probably some business thing."

"No idea. They just said to report."

"Oh, yeah. I'll do that." Ken is having a difficult time swallowing. He runs his tongue around inside his mouth. He puts the ticket in his pocket and heads toward the glass doors, moving slowly, seeming preoccupied with the wire, which he's studying as he walks. He can feel the eyes of the clerk on his back but then senses they've shifted away, so he lets the wire flutter from his hands and in stooping to retrieve it, glances back. The clerk is busy with some papers. Go slow, Ken thinks, preserve your poise.

When he nears the glass doors Ken can see the office of the RCMP. He can just make out the figure of a burly officer sitting at a desk behind a counter. Sweat is building up in Ken's armpits. He turns abruptly before reaching the glass doors and goes down a corridor that takes him into an open area where he spots a shop selling paper goods and books. He buys brown wrapping paper and a small shipping package. In another bathroom he goes to a toilet where he brings the bar of gold out again and wraps it and addresses it to Harry Backlin, using string he bought at the shop to tie the package. He throws the money belt into a trash can and then leaves the toilets and locates the air cargo counter of CP Air. It's a cramped counter in the basement where air conditioning or something is whirring in the walls. The air is dense and smells of a kind of must, like a library. The clerk, a smoker with long brown-stained teeth, tells him the package weighs six pounds and Ken pays for the shipping and heads back to the glass doors and the RCMP desk. He's still sweating. The digression has taken only fifteen minutes. He pauses and sits on a bench looking out on the tarmac, waiting for his heart to slow. Should he call Harry? Risk making a run for it? At least the gold is safely out of his hands.

One finger rests on his wrist. He counts the pulse. High. He looks around. There are cops wandering in the airport. Big burly guys. A run would be a foolish play. But what to do, what to do? Ken feels pressure building in his chest. He tries to remember what Elva said about relaxing the mind. Willpower, yes, but also thinking about something he enjoys. Drift, she told him, that is what the magazine article she read had advised, be a cloud, learn how to drift. Ken closes his eyes, he imagines lying on his back in a field with a straw of hay in his teeth, like he did when he was a boy, the big prairie sun high in the sky overhead, he imagines flying low over trees, then toward an unending horizon, he imagines a life free of worries and betrayals and guilt. In a moment his eyes pop open again. His heart hammers. His mind jitters with jangled thoughts. Ken does not think he would make a very good cloud.

In the end Steve does not seem to care. He's only taken the boat out on the escapade because he's desperate for money, he's been cheated and he's at the breaking point but he's stuck to both the word he gave the French partisans and the schedule he has set for himself. The boat cuts through the water. Steve is at the wheel, steering and peering into the darkness because this is an illegal operation, it is being done under cover of darkness. That suits Steve, it suits Bogart too, who looks dark and handsome in shadows, his jaw set, his eyes fixed on the ocean, the horizon. Occasionally he bites his lower lip in thought. He's troubled. If it were daylight we'd see how beautiful the seascape is around the

Florida Keys, we've been treated to glimpses of the dancing waves in earlier scenes, the bright sun, the lush vegetation. Hemingway lived in the Keys and his descriptions bring them to life on the page, he loved the sky and the trees and the surf. He loved daiquiris too, lime daiquiris, which he drank every day. Steve we see drinking whiskey only, straight whiskey, probably bourbon it's a hard drink as befits the rugged character of Steve, a dangerous but sympathetic outlaw, a man we pull for even though we know he's doomed, maybe because we know he's doomed.

Near the end there is a shooting. Steve tries to keep the boat going, he's made a deal, he's committed to seeing it through but the bad guys close in and Steve is shot. This is the part of the movie I do not like, Steve wounded also Steve struggling to keep the boat on course, a hopeless endeavour and a lost cause. At points Steve seems to flounder, to struggle to go on, it's writ on his face, he has been betrayed and he's on the verge of losing his will to live. I turn my eyes away at points. Seeing Steve go down is painful, seeing Bogart bleeding and gritting his teeth. It's a movie, it's play-acting but I'm gritting my own teeth and taking shallow breaths, this shouldn't happen, but Hemingway is true to his vision, things don't work out for the little guy and Steve is a little guy who goes down, and Bogart is true to his art, he shows how a man can be an outlaw and defeated but still be a hero irregardless. That's because he lives and dies by his word and the rules he sets for himself, there's honour in him and grace under pressure and these are good things even though Steve is doing a bad thing. It's complicated, it's not easy to explain how Bogart makes you feel sad for Steve and yet at the same time proud of him, the little guy with the big heart who does the courageous thing even though he knows the odds are stacked against him. Like Johnny Cash, a hero but an outlaw at the same time.

Ken takes a deep breath, stands and goes through the glass doors. The guy at the RCMP desk is young, fresh-faced. There's an energy emanating from him that Ken instantly warms to.

"Hey there," Ken says. He tips his hat back. "I understand you're looking for me. Ken Leishman." Ken puts out his hand.

The corporal stands, wiping his palms on his thighs.

"Oh right. Mister Leishman."

"In the flesh."

"Ah, Winnipeg has asked us to detain you. Can you wait here a few minutes? Mister Leishman?" The corporal riffles through some papers on the desk. His hand trembles.

"Sure." Ken touches his hat again, tries to look nonchalant. "What's up?"

"Don't know. Winnipeg hasn't given us more info. Just that we should detain you."

"Detain."

"Ah, a few questions."

"Odd." Talk slow, Ken thinks, it gives you authority. "Odd," he repeats. He leans on the counter. His throat is dry but he speaks slowly and confidently. "I'm on my way to Hong Kong, you see, business about a new fleet of aircraft that me and my partner are thinking of buying. We've been using DC3s, see, flying cargo up north, but we're looking for new aircraft, the DC3s are a bit clunky, use a lot of fuel, and this Japanese firm is trying to establish themselves in the business, offering a good deal because they're coming in on the ground floor and we're just getting going, too, so it's a natural fit, a couple of what you might call your germinating business ventures. We've been exchanging letters and documents. I wonder if it has something to do with that? Some papers maybe gone missing somewhere along the line?"

"Just don't know."

"That kind of thing. Maybe."

"Ah, maybe." The corporal holds up his hands, purses his lips in a crooked way.

Ken smiles at him. He's not angry, his smile says, just a bit confused. "Huh," he says, "can't figure that. I was just." He shakes his head.

"Yeah," the corporal says, "I know. It's kinda odd. But."

"It's okay. I'll wait. You bet." Ken studies the corporal's mouth, the way his shoulders slump forward. He's embarrassed, Ken thinks, embarrassed that he doesn't know more and has been made to look a bit of a fool, and embarrassed for Ken, clearly a busy man, maybe a big shot, somebody significant on their way to do important business.

Ken looks at his watch. Sighs. He knows he has to keep talking, that's the key, bullshit baffles brains. "Missing my flight."

"Ah. I wish I could help." The corporal shrugs, looks at the papers on his desk.

"My partner won't be happy. We're just getting going, see, and every minute is important, deals can make and break in missed connections and whatnot, it's dog-eat-dog out there, as the fella says." He states this calmly but his mind is a-whirr, jumping from thoughts of Elva to the gold sample to the ticket in his pocket. Detained for questioning? What do the RCMP want? Has Harry been arrested? One of the Grenkow brothers or John Berry? They're young bucks and likely to crack under questioning. Has Ken been fingered? He wipes sweat off his upper lip. He could use a coffee.

The corporal sits back down, begins to flip through papers on his desk. Reaches out his hand to the phone. Is he thinking of calling a superior? Winnipeg? Ken wipes the back of his hand across his brow. Taps his fingers on the counter. The corporal does not look up. There's a cigarette package on one corner of the desk, an American brand, Marlboro, maybe, Ken thinks the Marlboro Man is a triumph of advertising, the guy who put that together really was a mastermind. In the corridor behind him Ken hears the squeaking of wheels as a cart is being pushed from one place to another. He glances in that direction. A cleaning lady with a mop and trash can.

Ken studies the clock at the back of the office, red second hand slowly circumnavigating the numbers on its face. Ken looks at his hands. There's hair on the backs of his knuckles, thick black hair, the hands of a butcher, not a banker. Charlie Feagle had told him, It's down to your hands, Ken, you may think that who *you* are as a man, the essential *you* is your mind, or if you're religious, your soul, but that's not how it is. Who you are is your hands. What have they done? Where have they been? These are the questions. Have your hands nurtured a child, struck a woman, pulled a girl from a fire, strangled a cat, forged legal papers, waved a gun in the face of a bank teller? That is the measure of your life, the only measure that counts. No point in talking about why your hands did what they did, what you intended, how sorry you now might be about what your hands have done. They're the issue and there's no escaping it. What have your hands done, actually done? *Mano* they're called in Italian, and that's good to remember—a man is his mano. Ken's mind jumps to thoughts of his kids, to Harry Backlin, the gold bars in their wooden boxes at Harry's house, the briefcase with the one mutilated bar in Harry's office, John Berry, Rick Grenkow. Where has Rick gone with his pocket full of cash? He's a flash kid, likely to land himself in trouble. One thought leapfrogs to another, a blur of images, a static broadcast of words in his head. Try as he might, Ken cannot still his mind. This corporal has the same eyes as Charlie Feagle, bright blue, peaches-and-cream complexion, Celtic blood there. Charlie Feagle told him he'd visited Ireland one time, a place with a name that made Ken laugh: Macgillicuddy's Reeks. "Gotta go there," Ken had said, "just to be able to say I'd been there when I came back."

"Where you gotta go," Charlie had told him, "is to kiss the famous Blarney Stone. The Blarney Stone has your name written all over it, Ken." That had made them both laugh.

"Maybe so, Charlie, but I can tell you where Robert Ford is buried."

Charlie Feagle looks up from his book, pale blue eyes, thick glasses, he's in the slammer for cooking the books at some company, for fraud, so now he's boning up on the law. Says he, "Robert who?"

"You know, Bob Ford."

"Is this some kind of game—a bad joke? I don't get it. Some reclusive scion of the Ford Motor company whose life history I should know about? What are you on about this time, Ken?"

"The man who shot Jesse James. Bob Ford. You know, famous leader of the James gang, Jesse James. Train and bank robbers of the western territories, low-life miscreants and bastards, pardon my French, jokers, like you and me. I know where he's buried."

"Jesse James I've heard of, Ken. Kind of a highwayman. Your kind of guy."

"Ours. Mendacious, a dastardly mendicant."

"I knew you'd get one of those in, Ken, a fancy dictionary word. But okay. Ours, then."

I smirk. "Everybody's heard of Jesse James, Charlie. Like Shakespeare. So throwing you Jesse's name would of made it too easy for you. But I know something about him too. I know Jesse James is buried in St. Joseph, Missouri."

"I thought out west somewhere, Ken. California or whatnot. You sure now? You play fast and loose with facts sometimes."

"Most people think that. The James and Younger gangs did not operate in California and Arizona and so on, the Mexican territories. They robbed trains and banks and the like in Kansas and the Dakotas and Missouri. The West was not the West Coast but what we call the Midwest. Almost our own backyard, as the fella says. Which is where most of the wild west outlaws come from. Right here in our own backyard. Our heritage so to speak."

"Do they now? And the Hole in the Wall Gang?"

"Well—"

"Got you there."

"In any case, Jesse James in St. Joseph, Missouri and scummy Bob Ford in Crede, Colorado. Shot Jesse James in the back, did Bob Ford. No manliness in that. And in turn was shot in the throat himself years later by a member of his gang. Which he richly deserved for certain sure."

"No surprise."

"You're saying what goes around comes around?"

"I'm saying no honour among thieves. You ever weasel out of this slammer here, Ken, and think of doing another job, you remember my words. Everyone will betray you."

"Everyone?"

"Your very own grandmother, mark my words."

"She would, miserable old witch. Choke her in her bed, if I had the chance."

"In any case, Ken, everyone will betray you."

"You, Charlie? My old cellmate?"

"Your old cellmate? Your cellmate most of all. Soon later."

"I ever get out, I'm going straight."

"Yeah. So you say, my friend. What odds you give Jesse James thought that too?"

Fifteen minutes pass. Ken doesn't mind missing the flight to Hong Kong but would like to make the one to Winnipeg, he'd like to be back in the bosom of his family. The kids always lift his spirits. He repeats their names: LeeAnne, Wade, Ron, a kind of mantra, maybe saying their names will bring him luck, maybe they carry a kind of magic. He glances at the corporal and taps the counter with his fingertips. "Mind if I get a coffee?"

The corporal looks up. "I'll walk over with you." He stands and comes out from behind the counter. He is young but he's big and sturdy, thick neck, massive hands. To Ken his uniform fits over his shoulders as if he's still got the coat hanger in under his shirt. Though he looks green, he's not someone to mess with.

At the coffee counter, Ken takes out his wallet. "Care to join me?" He studies the young man's eyes. The corporal looks away and shakes his head. He's not sure he's doing the right thing. Orders are orders but he doesn't want to look the fool. He's the picture of ambivalence. There doesn't seem to be a reason for holding this well-dressed and polite man. What if this guy raises a stink? Calls a lawyer. Why hasn't Winnipeg given him better orders? He lingers near the coffee shop entrance, watching Ken but aware that he's abandoned his post. What if the phone on his desk is ringing at this second? He's being pulled in two directions at once.

Ken takes a seat and holds the sugar dispenser over his cup. Stirs slowly and takes one small sip, then another. He can tell by the way the corporal is shifting his gaze from Ken and then back toward his office that he's divided about what to do. Stay with his detainee? Go back to his desk? He doesn't want to miss a ringing phone and be called on the carpet for that. But he doesn't want to leave the detainee alone, he could walk off. Which is worse? Ken guesses he could use one of the Marlboros on his desk about now. He stares at the counter, then watches other men and women buying coffee and things to eat wrapped in shrink-wrapped plastic. In the glass facing the drink machine beside the counter Ken scrutinizes the corporal's unease, and in doing that he catches the reflection of his own face.

He smiles at himself. He can't help it. He's vain, good-looking and always has been. He has strong cheekbones and a pencil mustache and a mouth that flashes into a winning smile. Clark Gable, housewives told him when he turned up on their farms in his plane with his Queen Anne cookware and the well-practised patter, dashing in the style of Clark Gable. That was the kind of stuff that could turn any man's head. Ken smiles at his own reflection, he cannot help it.

Most days Ken wears a soft-brim fedora, sometimes a porkpie hat, which narrows his wide brow and gives a dark cast to his eyes.

Shadowy. Mysterious. People like mysterious when it comes to looks, women especially, and if the hooded look of mystery can be transformed in an instant into a roguish smile, you're in there like Flynn. Or Clark Gable. They're not far off, the women who flatter him with that, and he's learned to carry himself like Gable, studied the way he squares his shoulders, the tilt of his head when he's listening to someone, the way his eyes widen and then narrow as if understanding has just dawned, the set of his mouth. How he pauses before answering, which gives him the pose of superiority, puts him in control; control over other folks comes down to the waiting, making them wait, too many make the mistake of thinking it's the opposite, dashing about, trying to force your will on them, but it's in the waiting that power lies. He's studied Bogart too, the way he curls his top lip down when he's troubled, how he holds one hand in the pocket of his suit jacket, fingers inside but thumb just out. Ken has worked so hard at miming him that he doesn't only look like Clark Gable, he comes off as Clark Gable, dark but handsome, dangerous but sexy, full of fun but deep, like the old-time highwaymen, the rogues, the dashing outlaws the ladies can't resist. He catches women looking at him and knows what they're thinking. They're thinking, just once, I'd like to try that just once, the danger, the passion, then back to solid and predictable Norm or whatever, Normal Norm, the guy women marry, but not the guy they dream of having sex with, hot rough animal sex in a steamy motel room.

It's their self-possession I cannot acquire. I can stand like Gary Cooper, hands loose at the sides, shoulders squared but in the way of cops or recruits on parade, at ease but alert, the posture that says, I am so in command of myself that I can look relaxed while being ready to spring into action at your slightest flinch, grab your throat, finish you, so I got you in my power. That look I can acquire, I got that one. *Spring.* it's the only word to describe how the muscles tense, ready for one lightning strike, the blow of death. But it's a momentary thing, a pose, a second of calm just prior to sudden and violent action that bespeaks raw force, the big cat about to pounce. Gotcha!

I can touch my lips like Clark Gable, draw the end of a fingertip along my mustache, a long silent movement where the eyes do not blink or the jaw muscles flinch, it's the steady stare gaze of the sphinx which says I done everything, you can't even think of also I know everything about you, your one strength, your fatal weakness, so don't mess with me, move on, I am not your man, I am not anyone's man, impervious, I got you by the throat.

That too is a stilled moment, the moment caught by the camera lens, frozen in time. It's mine, I possess it. But what I cannot acquire is self-possession, the calm at the centre where the whole body is relaxed, the entire person. *Being* is a better word than *person*, being touches on the mind as well as muscle mastery, spirit as well as body, it reaches to the very soul, the centre of a man where he is what he is and nothing greater or lesser, the still centre, relaxation, peace, calm. The entire being is relaxed. Fingers stop twitching, toes cease tapping. Mr. Cavello was right, I'm restless at the core of my soul. Impulsive and impetuous. My spirit cannot sit still.

In a few minutes the corporal sidles off. Ken waits, sips coffee, presses his hand on his thigh. His knees have been bouncing. He lets five minutes pass. His heart thumps in his chest when he stands and goes along the corridor that takes him to a flight of stairs and down to the CP cargo counter where the same clerk is riffling through papers, cigarette smoke billowing out of his nostrils.

Ken asks, "Is it too late to get that package back?"

The clerk raises his eyebrows, an unusual request, not standard practice, but reaches under the counter. "It's still here. Yeah. Change of plans?"

"I just talked to my partner. Seemed we made the wrong call."

"No problem." The clerk lays his cigarette on the edge of the counter, smoking ash end projecting over, curling a thin stream towards Ken's face.

"You know how it is with business deals. One minute this, the next that."

The clerk retrieves the package, sets it on the counter, where it makes a dull clunk. "There she be." He smiles at Ken.

"You know how it goes in business, one minute on, the next minute off." Ken feels his heart hammering in his chest. He shouldn't be blabbing on, but he can't stop himself. It's as if the coffee has control of his mind, his tongue. "First we're doing this, then my partner wants to do that. Partners. Always a dodgy business. You ever go into a business venture, my friend, be wary of partners, choose your partner as careful as you choose the gal you're having kids with."

"Right." The clerk has reached back under the counter. "We'll need to fill out forms for you to get the money back."

"Don't worry. Keep it." Ken turns the package over in his hands. "For your trouble."

"Hey, thanks, mister."

Ken winks at him, then strolls away with the package in his hand. He's trying not to move fast, trying to look calm and collected. There are cops everywhere, it seems. He's never noticed them before. Have there always been this many in airports? He cannot remember. They're big, broad through the shoulders, they look fit and powerful, their belts are thick and black and weighted down with short-wave radios and night sticks and handcuffs and guns, the whole lot must weigh fifty pounds. His watch says 4:10. He's missed the flight to Winnipeg. Everything feels like it's coming apart. He's not going to Hong Kong, he won't be seeing the kids tonight. But he has to remain calm. That's what he and Charlie Feagle agreed. Don't give it away. Stay in control. The biggest mistake to make is to jump the gun. Too many guys break and run, like rabbits in the forest. They're moving targets. Ken smiles. Don't jump the gun. He's heading toward the airport's main exit, where the cabs and buses line up outside the door, he realizes, so he turns and walks down a corridor leading away from the main exit and finds an unmarked side door that seems to lead out. He pushes at the door tentatively, fearing he may set off an alarm.

In a moment he's in the fresh air. It feels cool on his face and he looks up as if on reflex, watching a commercial airliner take off. Someone will soon be far away from here. Lucky bastards, Ken help can't thinking. But he's made his bed. The luck has turned on him, and now he has to make the best of things. Ahead the tarmac stretches out toward the runways. To one side a series of low buildings, airport vehicles coming and going, lights flashing, the usual bustle. A van bearing the AIR CANADA logo. Ken can't help smiling. It was perfect, wasn't it, the heist? *Mastermind*, the cabby said. Even if nothing comes of this trip to the Orient, even if they're caught and the whole works goes up in smoke, there will always be that: they pulled off the biggest heist in history. He's a legend. Kenneth William Leishman. The Bandit.

The low buildings are on one side and to the other side is a stretch of lawn bounded by a chain-link fence, but the lawn ends after a distance and gives way to an area of grass, knee-high, resembling a prairie field. Ken strides toward this field, tapping the package against his thigh as he walks, smiling to himself, a lightness to his step. The ground is uneven but he does not break his long stride. He glances back over his shoulder once. No one in sight, no one has come after him. The control tower looms in the distance, someone would have to be looking for him to spot him. One thought keeps tracking through his head: without the gold, the cops have no evidence, at worst he's broken parole. No big deal. Let them detain him, let them question him.

Gold found; charge laid

Find 10 bars in snowdrift

K en is staring at a concrete floor, cinder blocks, steel bars, a room within a room within a room. He's sitting on a bench with wooden slats. Across the tiny room there's another bench, in one corner a sink, a grey piece of soap, tap dripping. Pock pock pock. A place not unfamiliar. It's a tiny room, so small that when he closes his eyes he feels that if he puts out his arm he can touch the wall across from him with his fingertips. He can smell the concrete mortised between the cinder blocks, the rough texture of cement reaching out to his skin, little knobs of cement that would prick when touched. He blinks and stares. The room is more narrow than it was earlier, the gap between the toes of his shoes and the base of the wall opposite has diminished, and he has to breathe in and out slowly to ease the rising throb of blood in his temples.

It's evening in Vancouver and Ken is being held for skipping parole back home. He's been questioned about why he was travelling out of the country. And about the gold robbery.

Ken is thinking about his last session with the cops. An RCMP officer from Winnipeg had joined the Vancouver cops and local RCMP, Scotty something, a young corporal who whistles his words when he gets excited. He and the other cops have been telling him a story. They've arrested John Berry, they tell him, in a motel in Vancouver. John has told them that he stole the gold bars at the airport, that he was part of a gang, not the brains behind the operation, but he took one of the gold bars from the deep freeze of Harry Backlin and hid it along the Assiniboine River near Headingley. He's told them where. Rick Grenkow has been nabbed too, in the arms of a girl in a motel room in Vancouver, real Hollywood stuff, a role Bogart could have played, door bursting open, sheets flying. The other gold bars have been found, too, buried under snow in Harry's backyard, Ken has no idea how they came to be there. The cops knew Harry was involved because a Winnipeg cop stumbled across the mutilated bar while searching Harry's office. It's this mutilated bar that interests them. Where is the missing piece, the one that's been cut off, worth, they estimate, as much as $5000. Harry, they say, has given up the whole story, where the gold was hidden, who was in on the heist, the whole works. Interesting, Ken told them. But he knows nothing about gold. He is Harry's business partner, true, but the business they're in is aircraft, he was on his way to Hong Kong to look into purchasing aircraft, intending to fly on to Japan, he knows nothing about gold. No one can show otherwise.

Ken has stuck to his story. He's convinced the cops are bluffing him. Word in the pen is this is how they work it: try to break you down by claiming they know more than they do, trying to pressure you into giving up the story, giving up your mates. Though he's furious at Harry for breaking—if he did break—Ken has stuck to his story. Harry he will deal with later. The weasel. Lawyers. Finks, the lot. Likely to betray you to cover their own butts. Scrofulous perfidy. It's a grey downer, grey headed towards black.

There was a drunk in the holding cell with him for a while and even though they took him away, the odour of rotting vegetation hangs in the air. Just a minute ago another guy was put into the cell, a man with a cigarette in his lips.

He gives Ken the quick once-over. "Got a light?"

"Don't smoke." Ken shifts on the bench. There's just space for two to sit. But the new man takes the bench opposite Ken.

"No matter. Bosses probably make me butt out anyways." The guy leans back, resting his head on the concrete wall.

Ken nods. "They get their own way, the goons."

"They're the bosses."

"Beat it out of you if you don't talk. Unless you got a good lawyer."

"Jew lawyer. They're the best. Gift of the gab. But pricey." The guy laughs bitterly.

"Gift of the grab." Ken chuckles at his jest, thinking of where his famous gift of the gab has landed him.

The guy laughs too. He has a good haircut, a nice smile. Pressed pants, but an ordinary windbreaker. A regular guy. He leans the back of his head against the wall and closes his eyes. Sighs. "Sure could use a cuppa joe."

"You got that right. Even instant."

"Or a shot."

"Yeah," Ken sighs. "A shot."

After a minute the guy opens one eye. "Where you from, then?"

"Winnipeg."

"Hoo boy. Big storm out that way."

"Yeah, biggest ever, they say. For the time of year. Biggest ever."

"Bet you're glad you're out of there."

"Lord, yes. It's a crazy place. Lots of crappy weather. Not like here. Nice here."

"Depends on what you like. Here it's long winters without sun. Warm but gloomy."

"Never thought of it that way." Ken's hand twitches at the end of his wrist and he stills it by placing it on his knee.

"Which is better," the guy is saying, "cold and snow, or cloud and rain? I miss the sun."

"I like the sun too and the big blue sky of the prairies. It's beautiful here though. The ocean, the mountains."

"Get in the way of the view. The mountains." The guy chuckles. "I'm Del, by the way."

"Ken."

In the silence the dripping of the tap seems louder. There's a smell, too, like sewage, a whiff of swamp water that reminds Ken of the farm in Treherne. Animal dung. Somewhere in the distance the echo of boots striking concrete, hurried walking. Ken resists looking at his watch, which he realizes in the instant of denying himself a peek at it is not there, taken away, shoelaces, too, and his belt. He will have to get a lawyer, and a good one. He's heard the name Harry Walsh.

Del clears his throat. "Could use that cigarette. Seem to need them when you're in here. The old Crowbar Hotel. Cigarettes, coffee, they keep a man going."

"Crowbar Hotel." Ken chuckles. "That's good, hadn't heard that one. I miss the kids."

"Family man, then?"

"Mouths to feed. Why I'm in here, you could say. Keepin' the wolves from the door."

"Yeah." Del runs one hand back through his hair. "What'd they nab you on?"

"Robbery. Armed robbery. Conspiracy, they're saying."

"Whew. Big-time. Me, I'm just a little fish. Suspicion of burglary. They stop me with a tool box and a crowbar in my trunk and suddenly I'm in the can accused of burglary. Jesus H. Christ. You know? I'm just driving along the street. Cops. Burglary. They think they can hang that on me, they got another think coming."

"Bad enough, though, burglary."

"Yeah, but it's not armed robbery. But I ain't heard of no robbery around here."

"In Winnipeg."

"Right. I forgot." Del puffs out his cheeks, studies Ken for a moment. He's not a big man but he looks like he could take care of himself. He sniffs before speaking. "You don't look like no armed buggering robber. Pardon my French. Them guys are thugs, rough bloody customers. You look like a guy who got caught passing bad cheques. Paper hanger. That's how I got you figured." Del scratches his nose and studies Ken, mouth turned down in skepticism.

Ken narrows his eyes. "Think what you please. It's a free country."

"Huh. But there was a robbery in Winnipeg, come to think of it. All over the news. Gold or something."

"Gold bullion at the airport."

"That's it. A shipment. Scooped up by a gang of some kind."

Ken makes a pistol out of his index finger and thumb, points at Del. "That was me."

Del has been leaning back, eyeing Ken, tapping one hand on his knee. "Yeah? The papers said that was a lawyer. Did the gold robbery. A gang led by a lawyer."

"Not a gang exactly."

"That was a slick job in Winnipeg, real professionals in on that. You know, slick operators with flashy suits and topcoats. You don't look like that, not the way you're dressed."

"Maybe not. But I did that job." Ken drops his cocked thumb, imitating a shot. "Twelve gold bars, my friend."

"They said a couple of young guys. Picked them up here in Vancouver. Young guys. Not a family man wearing a plain suit and tie. Squealing like pigs, I hear though, them young guys."

"Squealing. That's what they say?" Ken can't help clearing his throat.

"Spilling their guts. Blabbing out the whole story."

"It was me. They were working for me. Rick and Paul Grenkow. I engineered the whole thing. Not a gang, just the four of us."

"Shit." Del leans forward. "You're shitting me."

Ken clears his throat. "Believe what you want." He drops his gaze to the floor.

Pock. Time is the gap between the drips of water in the oriental torture chamber, a cupboard opening to nowhere, an abyss. Pock. Time is the drips. The moment. Pock. When you. Pock. The treacherous but beckoning moment, just when you think you've begun. Pock. To forget, to let the mind ease back into itself, let an image take form and move toward. Pock. An image to come into focus and begin to resolve itself so you can see not just the frame, the background but the outline of the swelling flesh, you begin to sense, yes this is the curve of a. Pock. Soft giving flesh, a curve like a. Pock. Leg, that round smooth calf muscle but it could be the softer curve, the rounder, fleshier curve of a. Pock. And now you can't help but anticipate, you want more than an image, you crave the curve, it's a memory thing, maybe a muscle memory thing, you can feel it, taste it on your tongue, you know it's an act of imagination, you're fooling yourself, it's the reflex of the mind intent on the porn magazine, you know the beckoning babe with the swelling breasts is not real but she excites you anyway, you feel on the tip of your tongue the delicious soft curve, but the other is coming, you sense it, still you want it now, the curve, the cleft is there also, but the other is looming too, you have the. Pock. Pock. Pock.

"So you're the guy, the very man himself." Del's shaking his head and looking Ken straight in the eye. "I have to tell you, the guy who pulled that off was a mastermind. Like one of these guys in the movies, Stewart Granger or the other guy, what's-his-name, Cagney, Jimmy Cagney. Big-time operators."

"I'm Ken Leishman and I'm the guy who did that job." Ken glances into the corridor, cocks his ear, listening for sounds outside the cell. Nothing but the high-pitched hum of fluorescent lights. Ken lets some seconds pass. He pats the bench beside him. "And let me tell you, ah—"

"Del."

"Right. Forgot. Let me tell you, Del, that heist, it was beautiful, it was like something you'd see in the movies. Archetypal pulchritude."

Del crosses the cell and takes the space on the bench beside Ken. The cigarette still dangles from his lips. He moves it from one side of his mouth to the other. "Tell me more," he says.

"I'm Ken Leishman. The Gentleman Bandit. Robbed a bank in Toronto."

"You don't say."

"Two, actually."

"Can't say I ever."

"The Flying Bandit."

"Yeah. That I may have heard. That may ring a little bell."

"That's me. In the flesh."

Del sniffs. "All right. I'll buy that. Tell me, then, tell me about the business in Winnipeg."

Ken takes a deep breath, puffing out his chest. "Well, it was a gold shipment. From up north of Winnipeg. A place called Red Lake where they make the gold bars. It's a mining town but they've got a kind of refining place there, too, a foundry, a place called Madsen something or other. They fly the gold down to Winnipeg and then on to the mint in Ottawa, where they... where they melt the bars down again and make coins and whatnot. The mint, you know. Smaller bars. But the ones at the airport are big suckers. Heavy. Seventy pounds, they say. There were twelve in the shipment and we nicked them right under the noses of the cops. Zip. Just like that. A sweet job, let me tell you. Smooth."

"A holdup? Now, that does sound like Cagney. 'You dirty rat.' Bang bang bang."

"No, no. No guns. Brains." Ken taps his temple and grins. "Planning, see, using the mind to catch people off-guard and get the better of them through cleverness and fast thinking. Guns are for guys who got no brains."

"I prefer the crowbar myself." Del snorts.

"Each man to his own."

"Huh." Del sniffs. In the silence he scrapes the toe of his shoe on the concrete. "You're a con artist, then?"

"Sort of. I wasn't actually out at the airport myself. That part you heard right. It was two young guys I hired who did the actual robbery. The grunt work, you could say."

"That's how the game's played? Send in the young punks to do the dirty work?"

"You bet."

"You were the brains. The guy pulling the strings. The guy with the seed money. Now that sounds impressive."

"Yeah. Me and another guy."

"A banker."

"A lawyer, actually. The lawyer you heard about. A—a business associate."

"You don't say."

Ken leans forward and drops his tone. "A deal this big you gotta have a partner with some pull and some cash. Lawyer helps. Knows the legal ropes and whatnot. Maestro of the mouth."

Del nods. Down a corridor a door bangs and he jumps. Laughs. "Jesus. I'm jumpy."

"Me too." Ken rests his hand on his knee. Takes a deep breath. It feels good to talk, he's had a lot bottled up inside for a couple days. He would have liked to talk to Harry. But Harry has ratted him out. Maybe. Maybe not. Most likely the cops are bluffing. Who can you believe in this kind of business? Who can you trust? He thought he could trust

Harry and Harry may have ratted him out. Or the Grenkow brothers. Or John Berry. Or all of them. Ken knows the old saying: all for me, and me for me. There's nobody you can trust but your own self.

Del taps his fingers on his thigh. "So what were you gonna do with gold bars? Walk into the showroom and say, I'd like that Caddy, you got change for a gold bar?"

Del laughs and Ken does too but he doesn't say anything.

"They're heavy, eh? A man just doesn't walk around with a gold bar in his pocket."

"You got that right." Ken leans toward Del. "That's why I was out here, on the West Coast. Catching a flight to the Orient. They're crazy to buy gold in the Orient, see, pay twice the face value on the black market. I was looking to connect with a courier who'd come here and collect the bars from us. The Orient, see, that's the ticket when a man's talking gold, they can't get enough, the Orientals, they got the endless predilection for it, as the fella says."

"More than face value, you say. That doesn't make any sense."

"Communist countries, see. Restricted market. The government only lets a little of the gold it buys out at a time. Dribbles it out to friends of the party and whatnot. High-up commie muckity-mucks. All bent, of course. So if regular folks want to lay their hands on gold, for jewellery or just as a safeguard against bad times, they gotta go to the black market, and that drives the price up."

"Yeah, I see now, I get it."

"Supply and demand. You're talking business, you're always talking supply and demand, my friend."

"And they nabbed you with a gold bar?"

"No. Lord, no. Not this cowboy." Ken looks over his shoulder and drops his voice. "I was carrying this small sample, see, in a money belt, just enough to show prospective buyers we had the real goods. Couple pounds. Five, six maybe. Just a little taster. That's the way to do it, see, cut the bar into smaller pieces, sell it off bit by bit over a numbers of years. Brains."

"And they got that, the cops?"

"No, no. Listen. I was in the airport, see, and I had an idea the cops were closing in on me. So I slipped out with the gold sample and headed into this field out back of the terminal, which led to the river or whatever out there behind the runways." Ken taps his temple with one finger.

"The ocean, you mean? It's a distance from the terminal."

"Ocean. Could be. A stretch of water."

"You mean the Fraser River? There's a creek runs through there,"

"Could be. I don't know from the Fraser River. Looked like ocean to me. Anyhows, it don't matter. I tossed the thing into the water, that little gold bar. Gone, see. Oh, they have an idea what I done. I bet the cops are out there right now, combing the area on their hands and knees, search dogs sniffing around, all that. They won't find it. Long gone, that gold. Only I know where." Ken taps his temple again. Puffs out his chest and basks in a big smile.

"I'm glad to hear that. Glad to hear a little guy's gonna get away with it for once."

"That's me," Ken says. "Man of the people."

"A go-getter. But with brains."

"Anyone can have the brawn. It's the brains that really matter." Ken winks and tips his hat. "It must be coming up to midnight. I'm bushed."

"Me too." Del yawns. "You think if we curl up on these benches we can catch some shut-eye?"

"I don't put much store in the movies." Charlie Feagle blinks behind his glasses. I been telling him about a scene where Jimmy Cagney is on the run from the law, racing his car up dangerous mountain roads, a look of desperation in his eyes, sweat on his famous pugnacious brow. Things have gotten bad, the cops are closing in.

"No surprise," Charlie says. "The cops always get their man."

"In the movies, anyways."

Charlie laughs. "Not only there. Look at me. Look at you. What's the lesson, Ken?"

"The lesson is the cops and judges and powers that be broadcast their successes loud and keep quiet about the guys they don't nab. The ones that get away."

"Like the famous one who got away, the mythical fish, is that it, Ken?" Charlie spreads his arms wide to indicate a huge fish and smiles almost that big. "Here's one for you: gargantuan."

"It's like battles you read about—and wars. Who gets to tell the story? That's the question to ask yourself, Charlie. Who writes the history books? Whoever comes out on top, that's who. According to them, they're the good guys, and the losers are always the bad guys, from the Bible on down. Cops, generals, it's all the same. Got a lot to say when they win the upper hand. And they don't tell you about the times *they* broke the law."

"In any case, I don't go to the movies much. Maybe a Chaplin or a Laurel and Hardy."

"They're diverting. Diversions."

Charlie smiles. "I knew you'd find a way of working that one in. But, Ken, the movies are like novels, made-up things, somebody dreaming while they're awake. Not very practical. For me, it's history and biography, the world of facts and information. Practical value. Something I can use."

"I've read a few of them biographies. They're as much fiction as fact, a lot of puffery, some, some outright bullshit, excuse my French, a tapestry of stretchers. The biographies written by the guys themselves, especially. You telling me that's facts?"

"Autobiographies, they're called, when you write about yourself."

"I coulda sworn—"

"In any event, I enjoy biography and history because they give me information, they inform me about the world around me and make me a better citizen."

"Oh, now, Charlie, let's not get carried away. *Citizen*?"

"But, Ken, what do you see in novels and movies, why are you so... so enamoured?"

"Somebody said that nonfiction gives us answers about things but fictions ask us questions about life—our feelings and whatnot."

"Cute, Ken, a pithy saying. I wonder who it was who said that. Not a scientist or historian, I'll wager."

"I'll look it up."

"And I'm not sure I believe it, pithy as the saying is. A bit too pat, what?"

"You don't think it's a good question, *What if*? What if I worked at that job rather than this, what if I tried living that way rather than this? Aren't these the questions that lead to change, to people better-ing themselves, greater happiness? Columbus thinking, 'What if the Indies lie to the west?' Abe Lincoln saying, 'What if the black man is the same as the white?' "

"Now who's getting carried away? But Ken, as often as not that question leads only to upset and unhappiness, it's a bad thing."

"Would the black man have gotten the vote if it weren't for *Uncle Tom's Cabin* and Huck Finn and his pal, Jim? Ain't that where human progress comes from, dreaming and wishing?"

"These questions lead people to do foolish things, more often than good. Put ideas into their heads that make them unhappy and rest-less and often destructive, end up getting guys like you and me in jail. Maybe movies are actually bad for us, Ken, turn us against loved ones, cause social discontent and make us unhappy people. The imagina-tion, Ken, can be a bad thing, it can make us want more than we're supposed to have."

"I can't agree. No way I can see that."

"Ask yourself this, don't the movies promote bad behaviour, civil unrest? Wouldn't most of us be happier taking what we're given and not scrabbling after more? Accepting the good life as what we've been allotted?"

"Allotted?

"Yes."

"Allotted by who? That's the point."

"Oh, Ken, I can see where this is going. The downtrodden man of the people."

"We'll have to agree to disagree about this one, Charlie."

"We will, Ken, we will."

They could have had a good life, he and Elva. If he'd been willing to stay in Treherne, take over the butcher shop, buy a little house. Quiet, homey, serene. Raising the kids in a peaceful prairie town where they could ride their bikes on the street, swim at the swimming hole, look at stars in the night sky. But Ken had to have the Cadillac, Ken had to eat steak at the Town and Country, Ken had to buy suits at Hanford Drewitt. Elva would have been happy baking bread, going to Women's Auxiliary, winning prizes at Fall Fair, the kids would have flourished in the sun and clean air, and grown up proud of their dad. Poor but happy. But that was not to be. Ken is a bum, a ne'er-do-well, his own father all over again. He feels tears welling up in his eyes and trembling in his shoulders. He is not a man who regrets things, not one to dwell on the past and wallow in remorse. But he senses his life is unravelling. All those dreams he shared with Elva, the plans, the ambitions. He was too ambitious, too cocky, too self-confident. He wanted too much, he dreamed too big. Elva was right about that, as she has been about most things. Ken sighs. He's been betrayed by his own imagination.

"What if your lawyer guy really does talk?" Del's words come out of the quiet of the night, an echo in the silent cell that momentarily bewilders Ken. He must have been dozing. The lights in the cell and the corridor are still on. Del is going on. "They do say he's spilling the beans."

Ken stares at the wall. His back is to Del, who is back on the far side of the cell. Ken can smell the concrete, a dull metallic odour he associates with the lockup. An unpleasant odour but a familiar one. "Dunno about that. Puts me in a pickle, I guess."

"You know how it is with shysters. Can't keep their traps shut."

"You got that right. First they cover their own asses, then they look out for you."

"Yeah. They're somethin' all right."

"Bad as bankers."

"You can say that again. Bankers, lawyers, always sticking it to the little guy."

"Don't want to be struck from the rolls." Ken turns toward Del and looks at the ceiling. "Is that what they say, the rolls?"

"Sounds right. Doctors got the College of Physicians. It's the bar with lawyers."

"Bar. That's a joke. Guess I'll have to find another."

Del, Ken can see, is lying on his side, facing him. "It's a cinch you're gonna need a good one. They're not letting you walk away on this one. The powers that be."

"They say this Walsh guy is a good shyster. Got a killer off last year."

Del grunts.

Ken's thoughts are suddenly far away. He's picturing an abandoned barn on the edge of a field, seeing himself carting little boxes from his car into a dark corner, a tarpaulin, bushel sacks. Those damn gold bars. If only he'd been able to move them. That had been the plan. Keep one to cover immediate costs, pay off the Grenkows and John Berry, and to use to cut off samples to flog in the Orient. That's why he'd given Harry the bar in his briefcase, he'd made a joke about it, but it was a good plan, actually. One bar would have fetched them thirty grand, maybe more, plenty to pay off some debts with lots left for daily expenses. But that damn storm intervened and then it was time to get to Vancouver and head on to the Orient. But the RCMP were waiting for him. If only it hadn't been for that stupid snowstorm.

The luck of it. If he'd only been able to drive out to the country and stash the gold. Crap. Crappy prairie snowstorm. That's the thing has dogged him his whole life. Bad luck. Everything always seemed to go against him. Now even the weather. Crap and double crap. Ken's heart is pounding, a four-cup buzz, only it's the buzz of frustration and fury, not the good buzz of sticking it to the Man.

Del clears his throat loudly. "You all right there, buddy?"

"Gimme a second," Ken says. He's lost the thread of the conversation. He runs his hand over his brow. "Haven't been sleeping so good lately." His voice is little more than a croak.

"I hear ya," Del says quietly. "This place gets a man down."

"The tank."

"Yeah, the hoosegow, the slammer, the can, the joint."

"The clink, the big house." Ken takes a deep breath. "Anyhows. You were saying?"

Del's face is hidden in shadow. But his voice is clear. "How were you going to explain the fact you suddenly had money?"

Ken chuckles. "I was going to take the wife to Las Vegas. Claim I won it at the tables."

"Huh. Just might have worked."

"Might have. All part of the big plan. Never know now."

"Yeah. You know what they say: crime doesn't pay."

"Yeah. Crime don't pay, but you can't beat the hours."

They both laugh, chortle, bitterly.

"Look." Del leaves a pause, listening. Only the hum of the lights, the whirring of a furnace or a fan in the distance. "Look, Ken, I'll be out of here in the morning. I'll make my call, my shyster will have me out. I got contacts out here, you know what I mean. If you tell me where that gold is I can help you out. Dispose of it. Put a little cash your way. You're gonna need it. Bail. All that. Hiring up a lawyer."

Ken studies the ceiling. There's a damp patch directly overhead. "Not easy to move, gold."

"My contacts are good. I know a guy."

Ken inhales deeply and exhales through his nose. This is a nerve-wracking moment. Who to trust? Momentarily he sees the face of Harry Backlin. John Berry. Who has ratted him out? "Naw," he finally says. "Not a good idea. Not a good idea for you, Del. You walk out of here, they'll be all over you, they'll be watching your every move."

"I'll take the chance."

"It's my partner, see."

"You scratch my back, I scratch yours. Kind of thing."

"It's tempting, Del, I have to say, bu... my partner, see, it maybe would be that he—"

"Your partner? What's he done for you? Other than sell you down the river?"

"Still. I gotta keep my word. It wouldn't feel right if I didn't."

"Could be a break for both of us. The way I see it."

"No offence. But—"

Del lets a long exhalation out of his nose. "All right. Your call. Just thought I could help you out, Ken. Help myself a little too."

Ken has been thinking that. Tell a crook where the gold is and he'll nick it away and you will never hear of it again. Or him. Don't be a sucker. He clears his throat. "More likely to get yourself in trouble." Ken clears his throat again. He likes this Del, but he's in enough trouble as it stands. He says, "They'll have the area staked out. They'd nab you, like as not."

Somewhere down the corridor there's a metallic *clang* and then the sound of footsteps receding quickly. Ken glances in that direction. Cinder-block walls painted a dull yellow, a concrete floor painted green, a narrow corridor, grey ceiling. A place too familiar, the smells, the dead colours, the sounds and silences of the tank.

Del clears his throat. "It's your call, Ken."

"No offence. But thanks."

"You bet. But look, good luck, my friend, good luck to you."

Ken is standing at the door of his house and he's looking at the door, which is part open, he was sure he locked it, he promised Elva he'd lock it, and he knows when he looks inside that everything that should be behind him will be gone, golf clubs, sewing machine, stroller, armoire, stolen because the door was not locked as he'd said it would be. Elva is screaming at him, "You promised, Ken, you promised!" Her face is as red as her hair, a face of flame, screaming, "You promised knowing that you'd break the promise and that you'd come begging forgiveness and that I'd give it, so breaking the promise is twice as bad, three times over, double double bad!" And a giant 2 flashes up neon red on the wall followed by a giant neon red 4. The voice is Elva's but coming from above, deep as the voice of God but with the accents of his grandfather, furious and accusing.

And blood races through Ken's throat. His teeth clench in his jaw, he strikes out with a bat, only the person he hits is his grandfather, whose face is blotched red, he hits his shoulder, once, twice, he feels the repercussion in the shoulder, three times, the old man's face is distorted with pain, but it's like hitting the punching bag in the gym, just a dead *thunk* against a dense and inert mass, and Ken is hitting, hitting, only he's behind the barn striking a rabid raccoon that wandered onto his grandfather's farm, he's got a fence picket in his hand, the white paint chipped off, he's hitting hitting hitting, blood flies from the raccoon's mouth, mucous from its eyes, fur, it spatters on Ken's bare feet, and Ken is hitting, kill kill kill.

And he thinks, Oh it's a dream, open your eyes, wake up from the dream, Ken.

He lies staring at the ceiling, cons groaning and snorting in the dark. His heart thumps, his knees tremble. The raccoon's blood and guts splattered his bare feet, he can almost feel it, though he knows it was only a dream, the blood was wet and cool on his toes. This has become a recurring nightmare, except the person he's striking out at changes, sometimes his father, at others his mother. Grandmother. All people he'd thought he'd made his peace with. Lately he's started to sweat profusely, waking with wet forearms, with pools of water on his chest, and lying awake for hours, questions buzzing in his mind like angry flies. Where does this jumble of nonsensical fragments arise from and why does he wake from them breathless and weak kneed? How could he be so enraged in a dream? Does Elva think he betrayed her like that, making promises he knew he'd betray even as he made them, letting down the kids and her, knowing in advance that he was going to break his word and hurt them, a deceitful and conniving cad, a low-life of the lowest order?

What a rotten man he must be.

He took her completely by surprise. He came up behind her. "My God," he whispered close to her ear, "your gorgeous hair." They were at a funeral in a small town in southern Manitoba, her hometown, he was to learn later. He had not even seen her face. But he'd always been a sucker for red hair. Hers hung halfway down her back, that brilliant orangey red that usually meant a face of freckles. "I'm a sucker for red hair." That's what he told her, his very next words. He was standing behind her and she turned to see who had said this in such a voice. *Devotion*, she was to think later, *reverence*. A tall, square-shouldered man stood next to her, a man who wore a hat, soft-brim fedora, who touched its brim when she turned her gaze to him. A gentleman, then, with pressed slacks and a business suit, not a farm boy. He reminded her of a movie matinee idol.

Elva was not a beauty. She was overweight, *fat* her mother constantly told her, you'll never land a man. But her smile. It was not the coy smile of a city girl, not the simpering smile of the flirt, but a straightforward smile that spread from one side of her freckled face to the other. Here I am, it said, take me as I am. It was a smile of openness and wonder. She was a farm girl with a farm girl's virtues. A hard worker, a woman prepared to do what she was told, a good cook, a hearty laugher, a woman who wanted to get along with others. A simple girl. She did not have the affectations of city girls or their put-on manners.

She understood immediately, intuitively what Ken needed. He needed love, he needed approval. It was written in his searching eyes, the guarded set of his mouth. He was used to being hurt. He hid it well behind his cheeky grin and city boy's clothes and the swagger he had acquired watching movies. But he was a wounded kitten, he was wary. You had to approach slow and give unconditional affection. He was an open wound, this city boy pretending to be a big shot. He had been hurt and hurt often, he knew what it meant to be lonely, he was alone. At heart he was a naïve boy, a farm boy at that. He came from Treherne. A one-horse town.

She understood that right away, took it in in the first moments. She'd seen wounded dogs, she'd nurtured wounded cats. Approach slow, take a lot of time. She understood that from the start and she learned soon enough the story of the poor boy who needed to prove to the world that he was a success, a somebody, the poor boy who spent his nights dreaming about making it and his days making it happen. It was a dream she could sympathize with, a life she could share, she admired determination and did not balk at hard work. Ken Leishman was the same.

He took to visiting her home in Somerset, a farm. Arborite table, plastic covers on the parlour sofa, vegetable garden, dogs in the yards, cats in the barn, a rusting Ford, apple pie, three pigs, a heifer, a table where there were always bananas out and chocolate-chip cookies, and at night pot roast and fresh potatoes from the cellar. He consumed food, breathed it in, her mother said, and laughed. He helped wash up. Elva's father showed him the leak in the barn roof. *Rafters, shingles, slats, beams, shiplap.* These words, the words they bandied on the stoop, she had no idea what they meant, only that they sat together afterward drinking water, smudges of sawdust on their coveralls, her father and the man who would father her children. She did not know from rafters and shiplap but she saw that he ate what seemed like half a roast, a dozen potatoes, a loaf of bread, a jar of pickles, and then an extra slice of pie. All with a grin, innocent, disarming, infectious.

He could eat and he could talk. Talk the ears off the elephant, her mother said. Such plans for a boy in a threadbare suit. Combines were forever breaking down in the field. He was working on a gizmo that prevented this or that bearing, bushing from wearing out, he would make a million. The city was overcrowded, there were not enough houses, there were not enough apartments. The thing to do was put up buildings that were made up of six, eight units, giant duplexes, *condominiums* he said they were called in Chicago and New York. He drew diagrams on scrap paper, he scratched down numbers, calculations. It required big money. Or he would build a fishing lodge up north and cater to wealthy Texans, he would fly them up there and provide meals and booze, there was no end of big money to be made. So many plans, ambitions, schemes. He wanted a house in River Heights, a Cadillac, an airplane of his own. A boat, a this, a that.

Elva listened. It was like a song heard at a distance, she could not decipher the words but she knew the tune, the music wove a web around her heart. She would have been happy on the farm, but if the city is what he wanted, then the city it must be. Where they lived did not matter.

"You look like Clark Gable."

He was full-tilt into one of his schemes when she said this, telling her about leasing something to someone somewhere, it might have been bulldozers to Natives in the north. It stopped him in mid-sentence. He'd taken to combing one lock of his dark hair down on his brow to resemble the way Gable's fell over his eyes. He had the pencil mustache. When he stood in a doorway, leaning against the frame, he tilted his head the way Gable did when someone was talking to him. He paused mid-sentence and grinned at her. "That's the nicest thing anyone's ever said to me." He smiled in his innocent schoolboy way and she laughed. She knew him. She loved him and she knew she could always have him.

Ken is with Elva outside the Town and Country, he's just opened the door on her side of the car but she's screaming at him. "You say you love me but it's not me you love, what you love is Bogart on the screen." Her face is as red as her hair, a face of flame. "You love pretending you're Clark Gable, you think you're a big shot, so superior and smart-looking, a dandy, the ladies' man. Oh, you're Ken Leishman, the famous Flying Bandit." A giant red neon BOGART flashes in the sky, like on a movie marquee, followed by a giant red neon GABLE. Elva is screaming, "Only when the scene ended on the screen—the heist, the scam, the deal gone bad—Bogart walked off the set, Gable went home or out to eat clams with his pals, but suckers like you, Ken, did not walk off the set, you walked into the arms of the law. You went to the slammer with the cops pinning your arms behind your back. That's the part you never did quite get, you thought you were in the movies but you were in real life, where there were consequences to furniture stolen from a warehouse, to guns waved in bankers' faces. For Bogart the movie ended. But for Ken Leishman the wife and kids went on into poverty and humiliation."

Blood flushes through Ken's cheeks, his fingers clench into fists, he punches out, only the face he hits is his grandmother's, once twice three times, he's hitting hard, stop saying, stop saying, only it's like hitting the plastic toy that bounces away each time you strike it, grinning face bobbing back for more and Ken is in a hot fury, only it's the growling boxer behind the fence on the way home from school that always scared him with its bared teeth, Ken is hitting hitting hitting, the boxer's muzzle turns into a mash of blood and bone, its tongue lolls out of its mouth spraying mucous, one of its eyes dangles from a socket, a red fluid spatters Ken's throat and cheeks, kill kill kill.

And Ken thinks, Oh it's a dream, open your eyes, wake up from the dream.

He lies staring at the ceiling, the snores of cons around him, the tic of a leaky water tap in the distance. His heart thumps, sweat pools on his chest. The boxer's black blood flew up onto Ken's cheeks, he can almost feel it on his skin, wet and cold. Why such rage at a growling dog? Ken does not think of himself as a violent man. He's never struck his wife or children. He prefers persuading to threatening. Yet up from somewhere—a buried life he'd prefer not to think about—roil these images, burst such burning furies at people he loves. He does not understand it, he's puzzled and alarmed. Frightening questions drone through his head. Do his own children dream of him this way? Elva? Did Elva really say he was never in love with her but with the notion of himself that he'd made up from watching the movies, that he was in love with the Bogart in himself, that he was in love with himself?

What a pathetic man he must be.

Police Nab 3 In Airport Gold Haul

City Men Arrested In Vancouver

The elevator goes up from the ground floor, smooth and fast. Ken studies the elevator permit near the controls for a moment, an old habit: 1957. Ken is wearing his best suit, but not his flashy suit. He has three. The one he wears to make his sales calls in the country, he calls the "rack." It's made of a fabric somewhat worn, he wants to look like an ordinary guy, not too much like a banker or a lawyer, a city smoothie slumming in the backwoods. Country folk are suspicious of men in slick duds. The women in their aprons that he sells Queen Anne cookware to should see the difference between him and their husbands but they should not think of him as flashy, likely to take advantage. They should trust him. That suit comes off the rack at Eaton's. The flashy suit was custom made at Hanford Drewitt, Winnipeg's posh men's shop, the tailor with pins clasped in his lips while Ken stood in front of a mirror, no end of measurements. He wears the "flash" out to the Town and Country where he notices the other wives admire it. The one he wears today is in between, a good fabric in blue and grey pin stripes, Ken's suit for doing business.

"Solid citizen," Ken calls this suit. It says he's an important man, but not showy.

The office he walks into on the seventh floor has wood panelling. There's a receptionist who smiles at him and asks him to take a seat, Mister Campbell will be out in a minute. Ken sits on the leather sofa and leafs through a copy of *Maclean's*. There's a smell of lemon in the air, the smell of worn leather, the smell of money. Ken smiles over the top of the magazine at the receptionist. In a minute a ruddy-faced man in his forties appears from a corridor Ken had not noticed. He extends his hand. "Fraser. Fraser Campbell." Wedding band, signet ring on the middle finger of his right hand. Firm but not overpowering grip. His suit is like Ken's, well-made but not ostentatious, a worsted kind of fabric. There's a faint whiff of aftershave. Black oxfords that squeak on the walk to his office.

Coffee is brought in by a secretary. She wears a business suit. Her hair is done in a smart bob style that accentuates her long throat and draws attention to her pierced earrings, which catch the light coming in the large window of Fraser Campbell's office. Maybe they're diamonds. Ken cannot help thinking that they say the same things to the outsider as the oak-trimmed panels on the walls of the offices and the silver-framed family photographs on Fraser Campbell's desk, things about substance and reliability. Before speaking, Campbell sips his coffee. He's put in a little cream but no sugar. Ken does the same. "So it's a loan you're looking for, Mister—ah—Mister Leishman."

"Ken. Everyone calls me Ken. I have a proposition, I think you'll find it interesting." Ken has placed his briefcase near his feet and he opens it up and brings out a typed sheet. Numbers, a paragraph or two of sentences Ken sweated over at the typewriter, calculations, projections. He passes it across. He clears his throat.

"Go on." Campbell stirs his coffee, takes a tentative sip.

Ken gives him a big smile and waits a second, fussing with his own coffee.

Campbell smiles back, then glances at the paper Ken's handed him. He studies it. "Hmm. In the north, I see."

"Not too far. Just past fifty." The hand Ken holds the coffee cup in shakes and he steadies it with the other, then places the cup on a little side table. "Moar Lake, virgin territory."

Fraser Campbell looks puzzled a moment, then smiles. "Yes, just beyond latitude fifty."

"Lots of activity. Burgeoning up there." Ken leans forward. He explains where the fishing lodge he's building is located. He has forgotten to bring a map. Details. He should have remembered. When Ken is done speaking, Campbell nods. He knows where Powerview is, he knows the country there is rich in small lakes that are ideal for fishing lodges. He likes to fish himself. A brother-in-law has a place in the Lac du Bonnet area, a colleague a place on Lake of the Woods. He likes to get away with the boys, he understands the attraction.

"Americans," Ken explains, "they love to fly in. Men from Chicago, Minneapolis, Texas. Oil executives, lawyers, bankers like himself, businessmen. A weekend of fishing, a weekend with the old boys, cigars, Canadian Club, telling lies around a roaring fire. They call pickerel *walleye* and take photographs of their buddies holding up northern pike on a line for the guys back home to admire, they carry a roll of greenbacks in their pockets and they give the Indian guides more in tips for a weekend than the lodge owner can pay them for a month." Ken stops, aware that he may be talking too much, maybe overselling, blabbing on. His heart flails in his chest. He feels the coffee buzzing in his temples, a three-cup high. This isn't quite the same as selling cookware. He feels a little out of his water, a little out of place. He wants this man's approval and senses it's slipping away.

Fraser Campbell smiles. "I can see you love it."

Without realizing it, Ken throws his arms wide. "It's wonderful up there. The lakes, the air, the big sky. So much space. There was a guy on the radio just the other day said the North was the West of our time, says the population north of fifty is going to double in the next twenty years. It's the happening place, the place where the action will occur. Towns like Dauphin and Grande Prairie and Prince Albert are going to expand into real cities, twenty thousand plus."

Campbell nods. "Dauphin, hmm."

"The thing is there's money to be made. If you get in on the ground floor. A housing boom, mortgages, building supplies. Schools and hospitals and whatnot. And a presence to establish in the early years for—well, for a bank, for instance. Get in on the ground floor, kinda thing."

"It all sounds pretty exciting, when you put it that way."

"Space," Ken repeats, "room for a man to do things, take the initiative. No walls, no—"

"No boundaries?"

"That's it. No limits. A man can do what he wants, follow a dream, start a business on his own and make a life without restrictions and so on around every corner. It's… it's wide open, see, a man can make his mark." Ken drops his arms and his voice. "It's not just about money."

"It's a good idea." Campbell nods, looks at the figures again, pinches one earlobe between thumb and forefinger, tugs it down. "Clearing land, cutting timber and building a lodge. Heavy construction, a lot of this. How do you get all that equipment up there?"

"Winter roads for the big stuff. Fly the lighter stuff in."

"I see. And who do you get to do all this, this heavy work?"

"Indians." Ken is warming to the subject. "Some of it has to be done in winter when the lake is frozen. You bring equipment in on winter roads, cross the lake ice and clear the lodge location with a bulldozer, then chainsaws. They make these little earth movers now, *BobCats*, they're called. The men do the grunt work after it's finished, the clearing, limbing fallen trees, burning brush, stumps. Chainsaws, pickup trucks. It's a whole organization. An enterprise."

"How do you live up there? While the lodge is in progress?"

"Tents. It's bloody cold in December. The Indians are used to it. But I fell asleep one night without a toque and damn near froze my head, pardon my French." Ken taps his skull. Laughs. "Not much fur, not much protection from the elements, when you got as little between the ears as me. And not a mistake you make twice."

Campbell leans back, smiling at Ken's reference to his growing baldness. "I can see you're a man of determination. You've got a dream and you've got the will to see it through."

"Exactly. Get hold of the thing and run with it."

"Make your fortune."

"I believe in the system. I believe that if a man shows initiative he can do great things. This country is wide open, the opportunities for success are boundless. I want to be part of all that."

Campbell strokes his nose, his index finger moving up and down its bridge. In the silence there's the sound of a phone ringing in the distance, ticking in the walls. Campbell clears his throat. "It's a question of collateral. For us. The bank."

"There's the land itself. I've put almost five thousand of my own in already."

"You own two planes, I see."

"Yes. I have a man working for me. John Berry. He flies one, I fly the other."

"And they're worth?"

"Maybe three thousand. Together." Ken picks the coffee cup off the table, considers sipping but then changes his mind. His head is already buzzing with caffeine. He feels sweat forming in the tufts of hair above his ears.

"You've done well for yourself."

Ken smiles. "I'm a comer, they tell me."

"This three thousand that the planes are worth. Do you think you could write that up? Procure an official assessment? We've got some forms you'll need to fill out."

Ken nods, shifts in his chair. "There's the house, I guess."

"Yes, you have some equity there. Hmm. River Heights."

"There's a lot of money to be made." Ken leans forward. "I'd do the flying myself, you see, from the city here up there to the lodge once it's been completed. Fly the guys myself, I mean, Americans and so on, land the plane on the water, a plane with pontoons. Lay on good meals and Scotch and liqueurs. I've made contacts up north. I understand how things work and how to keep them working. What wheels need greasing, that sort of thing."

"You've done your homework. I'm impressed. But the north is a risky place. It's not the usual sort of business that we do here. Car dealerships, restaurants, that sort of thing. We know that territory. But this is a little out of our line. Fishing lodges and such, they start up great guns and then something happens and they're folding their tents. Risky stuff. We're into commercial property."

"This is commercial. We'll charge a hundred dollars a day. It's a commercial enterprise."

"Yes, yes, in a way."

"People trust me. I pay on time. I bring in food. Let me tell you, those Indians can eat. It seems to me sometimes I'm feeding the whole reserve."

Fraser Campbell smiles. "They're good workers?"

"The best. Happy, easygoing. Long as they're well fed. Long as there's no booze." Ken is sweating. Bouncing his knee. What he hasn't said is that he's already borrowed from a finance company and that he's been paying for things on credit—generators, stoves, septic tanks. If he doesn't land the bank loan, he's in trouble. He has difficulty sleeping when he thinks about it. If he's turned down by the bank, he doesn't know where he'll turn next.

Campbell looks at the paper in his hand. "Ten thousand dollars is a lot. Toronto is likely to want a say about this. It's the north, you understand, not something we usually deal with, not a place we have a handle on. Hmm. Not exactly a commercial property." Campbell looks out the window. He studies the sheet of paper again and drums his fingers on the desk top. He lifts his coffee cup to his lips. "But this idea has a lot going for it. A lot of promise. And you've done your homework, Mister Leishman. I'll just hang on to this, if you don't mind."

"Keep it. I made a carbon."

"I'll have to pass this on to Toronto. And in the meantime, we'll need you to fill in those forms, an application for a loan, references, that kind of thing." Campbell passes a handful of papers to Ken. "I'll be in touch."

They walk to the reception area together. Campbell's tie, Ken notices, is a red and blue stripe with a crest on it, letters stitched in white, which he cannot read, a college tie, or maybe one from a golfing club.

When he passes through the reception area, Ken tips his hat at the woman behind the counter. She's on the phone but she smiles back. At the elevator an older man in a suit and a red-and-blue-striped tie nods at him. Ken taps his toe on the carpeted floor. In the elevator his free hand twitches. His head is buzzing, he feels the same jolt of adrenaline running through him as when he makes a sale. It's a good proposition, he knows it and Campbell knows it. There's money to be made in the north, everybody says so. Even crazy Diefenbaker is getting in on the act. His Vision of the North. But something is wrong. Though Campbell knows the lodge has every chance of making it big, though he smiled and nodded and gave Ken the impression he was on his side, Ken feels as if a bowling ball is in his gut, he knows that he will not hear back from Campbell, that he will have to call him and that when he gets through the answer will first be we're still looking into it and finally will be a polite but chilling no.

You only ever wanted to be a businessman. There was a certain strut to the businessmen you'd seen in the movies. Not just the clothes, which spoke of wealth and having been to the right schools. The way they spoke. Quietly, you had to lean in to hear what was being said, you had to pay attention. They way they stood and carried themselves. In Cadets you'd been told that posture was the man. You didn't know if you believed that, Bogart and Gable came off pretty well even though they sometimes slouched. But spine straight, shoulders back, there was a lot to that, the look of authority, the carriage of a man who knew what was what. With good clothes and commanding speech came confidence, a kind of mastery. You posed in front of the mirror before going out and practised tipping the brim of your hat. You bought a new hat, a fedora with a grosgrain ribbon, the kind of hat a businessman wears.

You only ever wanted that. Businessmen exuded wealth and confidence. They stepped into a room and voices ceased. They spoke and everyone listened. There was the money, yes, very early on you'd learned the maxim, Money talks and bullshit walks. You liked the jewellery and the sleek cars, the fancy suppers at the best restaurants with good red wine and brandy and cigars afterward. The women. You did not want the women, not that way, you were not a man for *pieces of tail* or even a fling. You liked the way women looked at you, you loved the way they smiled, you needed their approval. They were the ones who dressed their husbands and told them which aftershave to buy and where. They understood style. You wanted them to see that you had it. Yes, there was the money. And the approval of a certain kind of woman.

There was the manipulation of money. In the movies businessmen talked of millions, they made deals—fleets of ships, airlines, office towers in Manhattan. They flew across the country in private jets, some flew their own planes, and they brokered deals in the restaurants and lounges of hotels you knew the names of. The Ritz, the Carleton, the Waldorf, the Brown Derby. Once you were rich to a certain extent, it was not the money itself that was important any longer, it was the manipulation of money, the hobnobbing with the other men who had their hands on money and moved in certain circles, flew here and there, consorting, competing, having a snifter of brandy afterwards. It was not the money, pure and simple. It was the aura around money.

It was power. You intuited it early on. With money went fame, yes, that was important, that meant people looked at you, nudged the person next and said, "Look who's just come in," yes, fame was important, as was money. But what was more important was power. Businessmen had it. With it they controlled other businessmen, they had politicians in their pockets, they could have whatever women they wanted. If you cared about that sort of thing. People at your beck and call.

That was what you had wanted. You didn't need the millions. You knew who you were and where you came from. Certain doors were closed. That was all right. You did not need to be at the top of the pyramid, you just wanted to labour somewhere near the middle. But you wanted to be there. On the pyramid. Wearing the suit, making the deals, driving the sleek car. You couldn't understand why they wouldn't let you. Wasn't America the land of dreams realized, couldn't anyone go from rags to riches? You were prepared to work and work hard. But it never seemed to happen for you. The luck was always against you. You saw a movie once. A man approached a glass door, carrying a briefcase, square shoulders, the look of authority. He put his hand out and the door swung open. Another man approached the door. He was dressed differently, no briefcase. When he put his hand out the door did not open. But he had seen the first man go through, he was expecting it to. His face smacked into the glass. He looked puzzled and hurt, he kept rubbing his nose. That was the story of your life. More bad luck than good. For other men the glass door swung open, but for you there was only the smack on the nose, the look of bewilderment. You think you saw that in a movie. Maybe it was a dream.

You had a dream. All you ever wanted was to be a businessman.

On the screen the man named Doc has just been released from prison but already he's planning another caper. It's *The Asphalt Jungle,* and the caper is a big jewellery heist. Doc wears a white shirt and tie, a dark rumpled jacket. He looks like a businessman and he meets with a businessman to discuss the heist. Doc needs seed money, quite a bundle, he plans on using a safe-cracker and a getaway driver, guys he thinks should be paid up front and not told what the actual value of the haul is to be. The guy Doc meets with has a German name, a big man with a hatchet face and shifty eyes, he keeps looking around, as if he suspects someone is eavesdropping on their conversation. There's another man in the scene, too, a man with a thin pencil mustache, a lawyer, maybe, he nods and smiles approvingly, all the while sipping from a cocktail glass and fingering his mustache. Doc remains cool. He tells Emmerich that even if they sell the jewels at a quarter of their face value to some fence Emmerich knows that the haul will still bring them hundreds of thousands, maybe as much as a million. They talk in hushed tones, businessmen planning to close a big deal, conscious of their importance.

According to Doc, the key is the *boxman*, named Louis, the safecracker.

Doc has the whole thing planned out. He has maps, he has timed the drive required to and from the jewellery store, he has determined the tools necessary, the movements of cops on the city streets, the time it will take for Louis to go down a manhole and creep through the sewers and then jackhammer through the brick wall that leads to the jewels. He has a diagram showing where the other gang members are to be. He has sketches and lists, timetables, schedules. A budget. He needs fifty grand. A heist like this requires certain things to be paid in advance. It's not a shoot-'em-up robbery where a gang of thugs with guns blasts their way into a bank with pistols blazing, it's a business operation, calculations and planning. The plan rests on brains, not brawn. Though Doc is prepared for violence. The men will carry guns and use them if they have to. He and Emmerich eye each other

as they go over the plan in Emmerich's fancy living room, stone fire-
place, crystal cocktail glasses, generous windows overlooking a wide
lawn, the other man nodding and fingering his mustache.

There's a girl of course. Marilyn Monroe as Angela. You wouldn't
kick Marilyn Monroe out of bed for shedding hair. She sashays
around Emmerich's place in a tight black dress, teasing the men with
her full breasts and ample behind, talking about how she's going to
buy a French bathing suit, a green bikini, and then lights out girls, the
fleet is in town. She's aware that she's flirting, and she has fun doing
it. Emmerich smiles and Doc stares. She's a hot piece. A lot younger
than either of them but worldly in her own way. Dangerous, maybe.
She might betray them to a younger more virile man, a man like Dix,
who's the muscle and brawn of the operation. Doc has his fears. Doc
is kind of dowdy, he's a small man, the brains of the heist but not a
mover and shaker like Emmerich, or a man of derring-do, like Dix.
Dix is a rough-and-tumble sort with a two-day beard who is going to
use his share of the loot to buy back the family ranch that was lost on
mortgages, a place he grew up on riding ponies and watching golden
sunsets and the like. He doesn't have the brains of Doc or the style
of Emmerich, but he's the type to see the heist through, a man of
action. But also one of those men who can bring an operation to
grief—passionate, wild, unpredictable.

It's the early scenes in the movie that I like best. Doc has everything
planned: he knows how the alarm system works, what kind of safe the
jewels are kept in, every last detail, and he's laid out the whole operation, it's timed to perfection. Emmerich listens to Doc as he talks. He
has thin hair and he runs his hand back through it as Doc explains
how the whole heist works. He looks like he could be a banker. His
shirt is white and he wears a bow tie. He says he knows men who
might be interested in backing Doc's scheme, respectable people. It
sounds as if the two men in suits are talking about a commercial venture. Emmerich says you can't trust cops, the minute you think you
can count on one he goes and turns legit. Everyone laughs. He tells

them that crime is just left-handed business dealings, the left hand of the free enterprise system. Emmerich is a bit of a joker.

But when he looks at Angela his eyes are the eyes of a wolf. He exudes power, Doc senses it and Dix does too. And Angela. She threatens a man who comes banging on her door, she tells him that if he doesn't buzz off he'll have to deal with Emmerich. Go away, you big banana-head, she says. Men are prepared to die for a night in the sack with a babe like Angela.

The heist is amazing, the most stunning thing I ever seen in the movies. Louis, the safe-cracker, goes down the manhole and jackhammers through the brick wall. The tension builds as the gang waits for him outside, aware that they could be spotted at any moment. Then Louis is into the building, but he has to slide along the floor on his back to keep from being detected by the alarm system. He's sweating, the audience is sweating along with him. What Dix and the rest of the gang don't know is that the jackhammering has set off the alarms in nearby buildings, the cops are on their way to the site. This is the one thing Doc didn't take into account, a bit of bad luck. It's going to be touch-and-go whether the gang can pull off the heist. Tension mounts. The robbery has been carried out coolly and calmly but Dix begins to show signs of stress as things go awry. The other gang members too. Louis's hand shakes as he prepares the vial of nitroglycerin that will blow open the safe. The members of the gang glance at each other, there's sweat on everyone's face. This is the part I do not like. I sense the operation is doomed. There's a watchman hobbling around the neighbourhood. Will he stumble across the heist? It seems inevitable. It seems inevitable that something else will go wrong. And it does. One of the gang members knocks the watchman's gun out of his hand when he blunders into the heist and it goes off and wounds Louis. There's panic among the gang members. Are the cops closing in? What to do about the bleeding Louis? The whole scam is unravelling. Maybe they should drop the scam and hightail it. Abandon Louis to his fate. My eyes wander from the screen, I study the floor. In the final few minutes as the cops close in, I get up and go for popcorn and a Coke.

But I do not leave the theatre. I stay while the audience files out, and join the new crowd when the lights go down, watching the way Emmerich moves around in his house, the way he studies Angela from a distance, how he talks. I mouth some of my favourite lines. I rest my hand on my crotch when Angela shimmies onto the sofa. I study Doc in particular, the cool he maintains, his poise even when the scam is going all bad. At the point where the watchman is about to stumble onto the robbery, I stand up and leave the theatre. Outside I go into a café and sip coffee. I've known men like Dix. Charlie Feagle is the Doc type. I myself think like Doc but I'd actually like to be Emmerich. Can one man be both?

"Either a knave or a fool."

Sometimes, he gets off these kinds of sayings, Charlie Feagle, snappy epithets. I ask, "And which is what?"

"Knaves, Ken, is those businessmen types you're so fond of, high rollers, the guys in the newspaper headlines who get the biographies writ about them. Knaves is men who put success first, success above everything else. Men willing to do whatever it takes to get to the top—cheat, lie, betray friends, turn their backs on their families, step on the other guy."

"Ruthless, you're saying."

"Slit their own grandmother's throat."

"I'd of slit my grandmother's throat before you could bat an eye."

"Just a saying, Ken. Applies to people who like their grandmother. That's how far they'd go to get to the top, is the point."

"Miserable old witch."

"In any case, if you're a knave, you put your ambitions first and foremost, your feelings, you forget about. You don't have feelings, except maybe if greed can be called a feeling."

"Power-hungry, you're saying. Politicians."

"Politicians, businessmen, that lot, the movers and shakers of the world. Anyone, really, who's after the main chance."

"And fools?"

"Fools is who the knaves take advantage of, fools is those who put other things before raw success and personal aggrandizement."

"Swanky word, that, Charlie, aggrandizement."

"The man who puts his family high on his list, doing right by friends, that kind of thing, this is who is called a fool. The softer types, who do the right thing rather than the thing that most quickly or easily leads to the money and the fame and whatnot."

"The babes, the broads."

"If you say so. Men of integrity, Ken, almost by definition find themselves being fools, see, because the knaves perceive them as weak, they take advantage, they sense that here is a man who will hesitate before seizing the main chance, so they go for the jugular of that man."

"And—what?—you can't be both?"

"Oh, the Golden Mean, well in theory, yes, you could be part knave and part fool, but it hardly ever works out that way. Most men find themselves in one camp or the other. You sort of have no choice, is what it comes down to, you end up being one or the other."

"And you're saying—what?—that I'm a knave?"

"I'm saying that most men imagine themselves as knaves, that's what they sort of picture for themselves from the time they're boys onward, without knowing it or reflecting on it. Being a success and becoming a somebody, making the big score, leaving an impression. They think of themselves as tough and ruthless but I'm not so sure very many are. See, Ken, the heart gets in the way. You got any heart at all, the heart gets in the way and makes a fool of you."

"So to get to the top, you gotta be a heartless bastard."

"Seems so. But don't take my word."

"And you, Charlie?"

"Oh, fool for sure. Here I am in the can, correct? No bigger fool than the man in the can."

Ken glances out the little porthole window of the airplane. Below lie the endless fields of the prairies, suspended in March between winter and spring, wind-blown, runoff lying in shallow lakes, marshy in places, deserted. No evidence on the land of the frantic activity soon to begin: the planting of seeds, the start of new life. The plane is beginning its long descent into Winnipeg. Flying usually brightens him, but Ken drops his chin to his chest. He is shackled to the cop beside him, an RCMP officer who came to Vancouver to join Corporal Scotty Gardiner, Ken's constant companion over the past several days. Ken knows nothing about the wiry Scot, but Gardiner knows much about him. Too much, Ken feels. He speaks of Elva and the kids as if he actually knows them. He bandies around Harry Backlin's name like he's an old pal, he tortures Ken with dates and times and places that Ken once thought private and sacred: Elva's parents' names, the birthdates of his children, his mother's hometown, acquaintances from jail, the Grenkow brothers and John Berry. Ken feels sick to the stomach when Gardiner prattles on about details like these. He knows that is what Gardiner is trying to do: wear him down, make him sick of the business, bring him to the point where he spills his guts in the hope that the cop will finally shut up and leave him be. Ken has not done that, spill his guts, but he's sick to the stomach nonetheless. It's a grey downer, a black turning to jet. Jet. Ken smiles ruefully to himself. He realizes he's been rubbing the thumb and forefinger of his free hand together: there's a crack near the nail of his thumb and a trickle of blood is oozing out.

Going back to Winnipeg. Ken sighs. Never made it to the Orient, never got to flash the little bar of gold, never got to cash in. Just his luck. It's only ten days since the heist but it feels like ten months have passed. Time does that: compresses sometimes, and then at other times seems to balloon. Maybe some professor can explain that.

The drone of the plane's engines subsides for a moment as the pilot manoeuvres, then the whine rises again, filling the cabin. A woman sitting in the seat one ahead and across the aisle gasps aloud and then sighs. She reminds him of a woman Ken sat beside on his journey to Toronto years ago to rob the bank on Bloor Street, she too was apprehensive and only became calm under the spell of Ken's running chatter. So many important moments in Ken's life have been linked to planes. When he was a kid in school the war in Europe was on, dog-fights over Britain, Lancaster bombers, night flights into Germany. He'd dreamed of becoming a pilot and flying a Spitfire, shooting down Messerschmitts over France, returning to Treherne in a smart serge uniform to be fawned over by the girls and admired by the boys. School had been a trial for Ken. Though he was big, he was ever the target of teasing. Picked on because he lived with his grandparents, laughed at for the hand-me-down clothes he wore, his awkward manners, all the memories make his neck flush and his stomach hurt. Coming back from the war a hero would have changed all that. Being a pilot would have made him special. Everyone looked smart in a service uniform, and there was glamour in being in the air force, a flyboy.

All his life Ken has felt bound down. His father abandoned his mother and her kids when Ken was still in grade school. His mother worked hard to feed her family. She took in sewing and laundry, she toiled in a café to keep the family together. But it was all doomed—too many bills, not enough money. The road she was on led to welfare and the humiliation and despair that accompanied it. As a child Ken did not have toys, did not eat ice cream. Other kids travelled to the West Coast on family trips and talked about the Rockies. Ken did nothing but work. He didn't mind. Slaved for his grandparents, delivered groceries, went to work for Tommy Reece in the butcher shop. He did not mind working but it weighed him down spiritually. Having to keep body and soul together bent his back with worry, turned his legs to lead. He did not bounce about as a child, in one respect he never was a child. His young life was trammelled up in cares and concerns, fretting about money. So when he saw a plane in the air it took his breath away. One spring day he lay on his back in a grassy meadow and watched two single-engine jobs circle and swoop, they were barnstorming and had touched down in Treherne, giving people rides for a dollar. How Ken would have loved to have gone. The freedom to be in the air. Fly towards the sun. Rise above Treherne and go on toward the horizon and never return. Above the problems and entanglements of school and work and adults, the sky flying away and the high clouds ships on a blue sea, far, far distant, an ocean for him to float into and then drift away on, unending space where there was no longer separation between his body and the endless blue but a boundary-less melding of the him and not-him. Peace. A place to breathe deep breaths and listen to thoughts criss-crossing each other in boundless ease. One day, Ken told himself, one day. Above it all. Impervious. Flying would not only be a job, a way to make money, it would be an escape from his dirt-farm background, an escape from who he was.

He wonders what his own kids will dream of. They're too young yet to have such thoughts but time rushes past for children and soon enough they will have their own wishes and desires. Thinking of them makes Ken flush and grow hot. He remembers the embarrassment of hearing his father called "Tiddles Leishman," of overhearing his grandparents say he was a bum, a layabout, a ne'er-do-well. Ken had set out in life to walk a different path but he has become precisely what he set out not to be, his father's son, a bum. He's failed his children and he's failed himself. Is it something in the blood?

The nose of the plane drops slightly. Below lies Winnipeg, the ashes and elms that will soon be in bloom, a grid of streets, the towers in the city centre, the rivers. Places Ken should feel good about. But his gut is in a knot. He has not talked to Elva. She'll be in a state. He's let her down again. And he's not even sure quite how it happened. It's as if he's been in a dream that he cannot wake out of. He will have to ask forgiveness. Supplicate. He will have to stick by his story, insist on innocence. So far the cops have not broken him down, they have very little on him. Parole violation, peanuts.

Though Scotty Gardiner and the other cop seem pretty satisfied with themselves. Well, the hell with them. He's stuck to his story and will continue to do so. He's a businessman, he just happened to be in the Richmond airport. Yes, he jumped his parole, he'll do the time for that, slap on the wrist time. He's become used to that. He's used to time off for good behaviour. He's not only the Gentleman Bandit, he's the model prisoner. He's a sharp cookie, he knows how to work the system. When he's back in Winnipeg, Harry will put him onto a shyster and things will turn out okay. He's got a good story. Though he feels a little abashed he shot his mouth off to that Del guy in the cell in Vancouver. A major character flaw he will have to work on. He needs praise. But what he should do is practise the old stiff upper lip. *Hold your cards close to your chest.* The words of Charlie Feagle. Good advice. It's the thing that Ken has found most difficult about being on the left-hand side of the law. He wants to explain to admirers how he did it, pulled off the big job, he wants to see that look in the other guy's eyes, amazement, awe, admiration: *Geez, you don't say, what a masterpiece of thievery!*

The first time I brung the Stinson down in a farmer's field the fella thought I'd dropped in from the moon or somewheres. It was the late summer of 1952, harvest time and I'd flown from Winnipeg to just south of Yorkton in one go, a sunny day on the prairies blue sky dotted with fluffy white cloud the kind of day that convinces you that God has picked this land as the final resting place for mankind, the blessing of warm prairie wind, the glory of golden sun, the miracle of sky.

It was so grand up there in the clouds I wanted to fly forever, out beyond beyond, where the sky and the earth meld together, a place only those who have soared in a single-engine know, a place where only a privileged few ever go a place you don't find on any map a place in the heart. But there were pots and pans to be sold, shoes to be bought for the kids, farm wives to be charmed. I brung the Stinson down in a grassy field not wanting to land on a crop aware of where the farmer was working the land. He'd seen me circle, he'd looked up and I'd dipped the wings and I set the Stinson down smooth as silk near the house, I had hardly hit the dirt before he was headed toward me in his truck also waving his cap. I stood for a moment beside the whirring propellers not yet bringing out the case with the cookware, don't jerk the reins of the running horse as the fella says. QUEEN ANNE was stencilled on the fuselage, the name of the cookware. Minutes later, we had hardly set down at the kitchen table, the farmer's wife the farmer and me three cups of coffee steaming in our faces when first a truck and then a car come down the road trailing plumes of dust, the folks jumping out says, "What's going on?"

The plane was a sensation. They wanted to crawl up onto the seats, to fondle the controls, study the dials. What does this do? How fast can it go, how high, what does it cost? *Dazzled*, that was the word. I'd thought it might be so. They're farmers, the boss had said, practical dull people, why fly a plane to farmers but he'd growed up in the city, he had no idea that the men and women who till the soil are dreamers and lovers, in their hearts beats the romance of wide open spaces. Irregardless they were farmers in love with machines. How many valves, how much horsepower, what kind of oil? Just the one engine? The wives liked the paint job. Why Queen Anne? Says I, a solid name, a name with history, a name that bespeaks substance and value. Did they know who Queen Anne had been? They'd heard of Elizabeth, Mary Queen of Scots. I gave them the story we'd worked on at the firm, I embroidered, gave the tale an exotic twist or two, the point about telling stories, Charlie Feagle and I agreed, was that people did not really want the dull and boring truth, the bare facts, they wanted a *story*, drama and colour so I embroidered the Queen Anne story, led up to the pitch, which was the name of this new line of cookware, which we're sure you're sure to like. Terms available.

In the office we'd practised what to say, the patter the boss called it, the stainless steel, the lifelong guarantee, the solidity, quality, value. *Cookware* it was always to be called, never pots and pans, though that was what they was. I knew the lines knew what to say, what was more important was what you did not say, using silence pregnant pauses leaving the buyer time to think to ponder but not too much. The art of not overselling, I'd learned to call it if you came on too strong you scared people off, the trick of it was to make them think you had something good here, limited supply, and they was special too, getting in on the ground floor, if they did not buy they'd be passing up the chance of a lifetime. Limited supply, there was never such a lie told, limited to how many we were capable of selling, maybe. Smiling, changing the subject. You have kids? How many? Girls? I'll bet they're as pretty as their mother. Boys? I'll bet they make the old man proud. I carried snaps of Elva and the kids, this one is learning to ride a bike, last week that one said the cutest thing, the art of misdirection. Play the wife and the farmer. Use misdirection. Did he belong to the curling club in winter, was she the one winning the prizes at fall fair? It's amazing how far a little homespun flattery will go. Laying the groundwork laying out the limited time offer the introductory offer the buy-on-time terms.

The patter was good also I was charming, I looked like Gable and I played on it. People seemed to warm to me, it was that simple, some people affect us that way, they walk into a room and everyone brightens, in a crowd they're the one everyone wants to talk to first, that was me the golden boy the old Ken Leishman charm. Early on I'd came to understand that women made these decisions, that women make most decisions around most houses, it was certainly true in my own, so it were the women I turned my attention to. They were starved for it they lapped it up, even the ones who were not going to buy and you knew it right away, the crumbling steps, the shabby furniture, what could they possibly afford but even they wanted to fondle the samples and meander through the catalogue. I did not brush them off, I treated them the same as those who were likely to buy, laid out all the options, tried variations on the patter, I told myself it was practice for closing the real sales but I knew in my soul it was a kind of courtship, I was wooing them with words, shameless how I loved to use words, it was the art of verbal seduction.

There was smiles and waving when we stood by the plane, the wife brought out the Kodak and stood beside me under the stencilled QUEEN ANNE, I put one arm around her doffed my hat. Then it was time to go. The engine coughed into life, I fumbled with the ailerons, commenced the taxi also checked the altimeter, brung everything into line, felt the surge of power and the lift, eyeballed the distance to the nearest treetops. It was a rush second only to sex. Below, the farmer waved his cap. Above, the sun glinted off the fuselage. To be in the air. Sometimes the surge of it took my breath away, I thought I sold the pots and pans just to do the flying at times I felt I'd fly forever and never come down never look down even the earth was a shabby place compared. Whenever I took off I felt such a rush of adrenaline I sometimes thought I'd open the window and jump out and float to earth, it was such a sensation, glorious. At the flying club there was a poem tacked onto the notice board: "I know that I shall meet my fate somewhere in the clouds above." Glorious words. I put that poem to heart.

My fate was in the skies. I had the jump on the guys peddling door-to-door because I had the Stinson, the glamour and excitement it alone brought to my visits, never mind Ken of the Clark Gable mustache, I was exotic a creature from another place another planet it seemed on some days. I'd set a target to earn $10,000 in a year. In the *Free Press* they said that a family of three could live comfortably on $3500 and I was way ahead of that. The company was offering a trip to Hawaii for the salesman with the highest numbers that prize was mine I was the best and I wanted it and had the gumption to make it mine and wasn't that the winning formula? I never lacked for self-confidence you could say that certain sure.

So I had spent a few months in jail. The one thing about Ken Leishman was resilience. I'd bounced back when a horse kicked me in the head as a kid, I'd survived falling off a wagon onto the ice and cracking open my skull and bounced back, irregardless my parents had abandoned me but I'd got on. What was a little jail time? It was not grinding through the Great Depression eating carrots and potatoes every night, it was not incarcerated in a prisoner of war camp in Hong Kong, emaciated. I was knocked down many a time but I always bounced back up. No welfare for this cowboy. I'd made a mistake in that furniture store but I had moxie, I'd not only landed a job selling the best cookware in the country, I'd made myself the best salesman of the best cookware. Screw all those who had said I'd never make anything out of myself, I was flying high the earth could not hold me I was the creature of the heavens I would soar to the sun, I could say as the poet says, "The years ahead seemed waste of breath in balance with this life, this death."

He is not a thug, a shoot-'em-up gangster going in guns blazing, no Bugsy Malone or Machine Gun Kelly. This is what Ken thinks, what he admires in himself. The Gentleman Bandit.

In 1957 he flies to Toronto on a commercial airline. He could have flown himself in his own little plane but decides against that course of action. He would have had to touch down somewhere and refuel, he would have been exhausted from the flight. Better to let some other pilot do the work. He needs to be fresh and alert when he gets to the bank on the next day.

He checks into a downtown hotel and has a shower. Trims his

mustache, then rests with his legs crossed on the bedspread. Drifts off despite the fact his mind is abuzz. Circumstances have forced his hand, he tells himself. It's mid-December and Christmas is coming; he has no money to buy gifts for the kids. Debts are piling up. He's a disappointment to Elva. To himself. He's been going straight for eight years but things have not worked out despite his best efforts. There seems no way out of the increasing pressures. And now his sales job with Queen Anne wares has dried up. Bad luck following on the heels of bad luck. He finds himself exhausted every day from worry and fret about making ends meet but he cannot sleep at night. His mind is in a whirl, he cannot keep his hands still. The dawn hours are filled with nightmares. In the mornings he has headaches. It was his plan to build the fishing lodge up north and run it and make an honest day's profit, but the banks would not back him. He had to take loans from finance companies, he got into debt, the fishing lodge was slipping through his fingers. Not to mention feeding the kids, buying shoes, all the costs of a household. The mortgage, the car, the plane. And that muckity-muck Campbell at the bank turned down his loan application. What was left for him to do but get the money on the left-hand side of the law? He wasn't really to blame, then, was he? It was the system, the system had let him down.

When he wakes from a doze he takes the elevator and visits the bar downstairs and has a beer and a yak with the bartender. There's talk of major-league baseball coming to town. The bank he picks is a branch in the city centre. He's cased it out, noting the set-up of the manager's office, where it is located in relation to the tellers' counter and the main entrance, the back exit where employees come in and out. He is thorough, he makes notes. He times the walk from where he parks his rental car to the door of the bank, and he times the drive back to the hotel. Writes down numbers, scribbles notes. These things do not matter much but they give him the feeling of control. Which is important. The job he has in mind requires calmness and self-posses-sion, things that grow with familiarity and routine. Ken knows these things, he has learned them as a salesman. Knowing the groundwork, the lay of the land. Comfort comes from routine and feeling in control grows with comfort.

From a phone in the hotel he puts in a call to the bank and asks for the manager. He's told, Mister Lunn is in meetings all afternoon.

"You close at three?" Ken sounds nonchalant. "Set me up for 2:30 tomorrow, then. I'm Mister Price, from Cleveland. Mr. Lunn knows me."

He spends a restless night, sweating, fighting off nightmares, and wakes early in the morning with a grainy headache and a dry mouth, which he tries to scrub away in the shower.

Before he heads out on the final run he checks himself in the mirror, touching his wetted fingertips to one lock of hair in the style of Clark Gable, adjusts the brim of his hat so it is at exactly the right angle, smoothes the mustache. He puts his hand in his jacket pocket in a certain way. Bogart. The car he's rented is a recent model, it glides down the streets and avenues of downtown Toronto, slides into the parking space two blocks from the bank. He checks himself in the mirror one last time. Checks the heft of the briefcase as he steps out of the car. The pistol is there, he feels its weight.

The walk to the bank entrance passes and Ken could not say if anyone else was on the sidewalk. He strolls in and explains he has an appointment with Mister Lunn. The bank is busy, Christmas activity. Ken leans on the counter and yaks with the man nearest him, glances around the interior of the building. Heavy desks and chairs, hardwood trim, the appearance of wealth and substance. In a minute a young man who was bent over a desk when Ken came in leads him in back to the manager's office, a young man who returns to his desk not far away once he's left Ken with the manager.

Ken puts out his hand. "Hey there," he says. "Garth Price, Cleveland."

The banker puts out his hand. He's an older man, grey at the temples, a man with small hands and a light grip. Gold watch, gold ring, a married man with pictures of his family on his desk, a man unlikely to risk his life for a bank, to play the hero.

"I'm a businessman," Ken says. "Construction." He lays on his best smile.

Lunn nods and smiles back at Ken. "Williams said something about a loan."

"Startup funds. Leasing equipment." Ken tips the brim of his hat up. He's removed his coat and thrown it over the back of a chair. It's warm in the office.

Lunn is reading his mind. "We're having trouble with the heat system. Workmen coming in tomorrow."

In the main area a clock chimes for 2:45. Ken glances through the open door of the office. He can see Williams at his desk, the backs of the tellers. No one is looking in. He chuckles and says, "They're always coming tomorrow, workmen."

"Isn't that the truth?" Lunn chuckles. "Well, what can I do you for? Mr.—ah—Price?"

Ken has placed his briefcase on the floor. He has the feeling Lunn has warmed to him, the old Ken magic is at work, everyone seems to take a liking to him. "Mind if I close the door?"

"Suit yourself." Lunn shuffles some papers on his desk while Ken crosses the room.

Ken closes the outer door, carefully. "I've got something here I think you'll find to your interest."

The manager is relaxing in his behind his desk. He's reaching for a phone. "Should I call in Leavers? He's our expert on loans."

"Let me show you this first." Ken stoops, opens the briefcase. His heart is in his throat. He fumbles under the file folder he's placed at the top of the briefcase. He brings out the gun.

The manager's mouth drops open but he does not say anything. Ken is standing only a few feet away from him, the pistol pointed at his chest.

"It's a holdup." Ken leans forward, holding the pistol close in to his own body. It's only a .22. He bought it on a recent flight into the Dakotas. He's never fired it, he does not like guns. Ken clears his throat. "How much you got on hand?"

Lunn says, "Me? I have nothing. The cash is out there."

"And?"

"And I don't usually have anything to do with it. I'm paperwork." Lunn glances at his desk, covered with folders and files.

"But—"

"But we could go out there. The tellers are in charge of cash."

Ken eyes him. Is this a trap? Is he supposed to wave the gun around out there? He's not Machine Gun Kelly. "All right," he says, "I'll tell you what we're going to do. We're going to go out there. Calm and relaxed. Buddy-buddy like. A couple of businessmen doing business. You can make out a cashier's cheque, right? Business loan kind of thing. You do it all the time."

"Every now and then."

"Often enough. It will not raise suspicion."

"All right." Lunn has been eyeing him carefully. He can tell he's serious. This is not a cowboy he can bluff into going away.

Ken nods. "So that's what we're going to do. Nice and calm."

Lunn says, "I have to reach into the drawer. For the cheque pad."

"You're a smart man. You won't make a grab at a gun, now will you? Push the alarm?"

"No."

"Good." Ken touches the brim of his hat. "We're doing well, you see. No violence, none of that. We're doing business, see. If you do as I say, you'll go home tonight to your wife. No one gets hurt. Right? The bank will get its insurance. I'll be a problem for the cops. You'll be out of it. Right?"

"I guess."

"You bet." Ken has dropped the barrel of the pistol. "Write the cheque."

Lunn's hand shakes as he produces it from a top drawer. He looks at Ken. "What amount?"

Ken's mouth is dry. What would a bank have on hand? He thinks maybe as much as fifty thousand, but what if that isn't the case, what sort of a tangle-up will they get into if he asks for more than they have on hand? And he can't ask Lunn. He'd look like a bumpkin. "Ten, ten thousand," he says. The words croak out. This is a detail he should have thought of, a detail that has led to a mistake. Once the words are out of his mouth, ten thousand doesn't sound like much.

Ken reaches for his coat. When the cheque is written, he drapes the coat over one arm, concealing the pistol beneath. "We're doing real good," he tells Lunn in a calm voice. "Smooth as silk. I'll tell you what we're going to do. You get your coat now and your hat. What's your name, by the way?"

"Albert. Al."

"Get your coat and hat, Al."

"I need to stand and breathe a moment. Look at me. I'm shaking."

"All right, then, take a couple seconds. Ken smiles, reassuring. "You got kids?"

"Grown up. Our daughter out west just had a baby."

"Christmas baby. Nice."

"It is. We're flying out to visit."

"You bet. Christmas and kids, that's what it's all about." Ken takes Lunn's elbow and ushers him out the door, like they're old pals going for a drink.

They stand in line at the teller, Ken behind, his hand resting on Lunn's shoulder, which is trembling. "Geez, Al," Ken says in a loud voice, "that's good news about the new baby."

The woman in front of them in line turns and smiles. Ken gives her a wink. He's calm on the outside but his heart is pounding so hard he can feel the blood beating in his teeth.

"I bet you're a proud granddad." Ken keeps his hand on Lunn's

shoulder but looks around the room, catching the eyes of other customers. People are nodding and smiling. Lunn is no longer trembling.

When the woman in front of them has closed her purse and walked
off, Ken says to the teller, "Hey there, young fella, we're kinda catching you at the end of the day." He nods toward the clock on the wall.
"Sorry about that."

"No problem," the teller says, returning Ken's smile.

"Well," Ken says, "that's good then, certain sure." He looks at Lunn
and clears his throat.

Lunn passes the cheque to the teller.

The teller looks at it. "That's a hefty amount, sir." He's young, fresh-
faced, a college graduate doing his first job. "Sir. I don't have that
much."

"It'll be in the vault." Lunn clears his throat and nods toward the
back. "Just go fetch it."

The teller walks away. Ken feels sweat run from his armpits. He
fears that Lunn has signalled the teller somehow, though Ken has seen
nothing. In a moment he'll hear the sound of a siren. Will he use the
gun? Will he run? He shifts his eyes to the rear exit, calculating, how
many running steps to the door? He's been a fool, Lunn has tricked
him.

But in a moment the teller is back, with a roll of fifty-dollar bills.
He begins counting them off. When he reaches two hundred, he stops.
What he's taken off has hardly made a dent in the roll. Ken has been a
fool. He should have asked for more, he should reach out and snatch
up the wad and run. It must be a hundred grand. The clock chimes
three. Lunn flinches. So does Ken. He asks for an envelope and puts
the money in his briefcase.

"C'mon, Al," he says, his tone loud and confident, "I'll buy you a
drink. You can tell me about this new grandbaby."

Outside they take the sidewalk. "You're doing great," Ken says.
"This is the easy part. I'll tell you what we're going to do. We'll walk
a couple of blocks and then I'll let you go. Easy as pie. You wait five

minutes and then do what you wish. Call the cops. You're home free. I'm their problem now. Right? You're out of it, fair and clean. The bank gets insurance. A simple business transaction. You and I, nothing to sweat about, no problems. Right? Al?"

"Right." Lunn is trembling and struggling to keep up to Ken's long stride. They both puff ghosts of breath into the chill December air.

At an alley, Ken indicates they should turn. Halfway down they stop. "This is it," Ken says. "You wait five minutes before moving." He shifts the arm with the coat and the pistol. "You don't want to do something dumb now, do you? Get yourself shot? You want to see that new grandbaby."

Lunn nods.

"I thought so." Ken tips his hat. "Goodbye, then. It was good doing business with you, Al. You're a smart man."

Lunn nods at him. "So are you. Clever. And a gentleman."

"You too, Al. Nice doing business with you."

The Flambouyant Flying Bandit

You're an animal, aren't you? A tiger in a cage, a monkey staring through bars. The holding cell they put you in on remand is fifty by fifty, you're in with thirty other guys, some of them smell, most of them don't give a shit, they're dirty, foul-mouthed, their lives are nothing and they know it. The day is spent pacing. A goon comes to get you and take you so you can shave at a dirty basin in a dingy corner. Water has pooled on the floor, bits of paper stick to your shoes, the smell is of sewage, there's grit on every surface, you want to puke. No point in even mentioning the food. You're constipated, you cannot shit.

Hours pass and nothing happens. The dripping of a tap somewhere: plick, pock, blip. You look at your watch. Two o'clock. You sit in a corner and ponder your fate. How many days has it been, how many weeks, months? At the Town and Country they cooked the steaks rare, they came on the plate with a baked potato and asparagus and a sprig of something green—parsley? Cocktails, beer, a glass of red wine. Elva smiled and laughed, the guy beside her told a joke

195

and seemed to be flirting but it didn't matter, that night in bed she'd be yours and yours only. The Cadillac sat outside, big and flashy, a convertible, the plane was in the hangar, your monthly cheque was in the mail. You were made, a success, a somebody. When you stood in the parking lot later, the women's eyes sparkled as you talked and the men reached out to say goodbye and fondled your elbow. Everyone wanted to touch you.

You looked up at the moon. You were there, high as the moon. You were the Man, you read admiration in every eye turned your way, approval, love, it was a three-cup high.

2:15. Pock, plick, blip. You're sick at heart. A kid with long dirty hair, a scruffy beard and pimples pukes in the corner. The boss comes in and fetches him, says the kid has to go to the infirmary, he laughs and says he'll send someone in to clean up. He knows and you know he'll wait to the last possible minute. You sit as far away from the fetid green pool as possible and think of girls you've seen on TV, the one who does the weather forecast, Lana Turner in those tight sweaters, other guys are thinking the same, some are rubbing their crotches, a kid turns toward the wall and moans. An older con walks over and kicks him in the ribs. Another guy stands up. He and the one who did the kicking eye each other at a distance. Everyone else shifts back toward the wall. A moon-faced guy wearing glasses calls out, Guard! His speech is shrill in the cramped space but no one comes. Nothing else happens. No one moves. You look at your watch. 2:30. Pock, plick.

Her sweaters are angora, Lana Turner's, snug in the right places, tight above the elastic at the waist, if you were to slip your fingers under that elastic, slip your hand along the white back, the alabaster curve of. Plick. Pock. Blip.

The image of Lana Turner fades, replaced by Elva's. If you concentrate, you lose it, the trick is to not think too hard. You remember the smile, you remember the curve of a breast, the way a nipple pokes out the fabric of a sweater. Sweat forms on your lower lip, you shift where you sit on the concrete floor. You stand. Another minute of this and you'll go bonkers. You've seen it happen. Stir crazy. A man bangs his forehead against the wall until he splits his skull and blood pours out and runs into his collar. A guy grabs the guy beside him and squeezes his neck until they both pass out and collapse on the floor. Two kids are sitting in a corner humming and one of them starts to scream, he doesn't stop even when the guards come in and slap his face, his cries echo down the corridor as they drag him off to the infirmary, heels kicking.

You swallow hard and try to keep your thoughts in order. They fly here and there.

No one is immune. The older cons, the ones who've been in and out all their lives say it doesn't affect them. But they smoke. They smoke and smoke and smoke. They drag on their cigarette, as if the idea were to choke the whole tube inside their lungs, tobacco, paper and all. They growl in the corner, they spit on you, they say, "Later bub," and they mean it.

What time is it now? It does not matter. Pock, pock. When is supper, a relief from this, though the food is crap. How long to lights out? The relief of sleep. If you get some. Another day ticked off the mental calendar. One hundred and three, one hundred and two, ninety-nine.

How many days before they take you before the judge for sentencing? A week, ten days, a lifetime it might as well be. If you had a magazine, a book, a place to sit and read, a place to sit and write. Letters you get, letters they'll let you write. But nothing more. The only thing you can turn your thoughts to is the outside. A salesman is visiting a prospect right this minute, a guy in a suit, a housewife coming to the door in her apron. Good afternoon, ma'am. Queen Anne Cookware, best in the world. Small-time stuff, in the end. Why didn't you go into real estate? That's where the real money is. Pots and pans. Peanuts. Somewhere right at this time an agent is closing a deal. His buddy is in the bar at Hy's Steakhouse, in a half-hour he'll be there, too, drinks on me. In a hotel room across from Hy's a guy is screwing a secretary, another is getting a blowjob, cock stiff and thick, it's Lana Turner, it's.

You've never been into that. Tried it once, did not understand the attraction. Women have let you know they're yours for the asking. You never asked. You're a thief but you don't philander.

Somewhere a father is picking his kids up from school. Not you. You're a disgrace, a bum. You'll be lucky when you come out if they remember what you look like. You'll be lucky Elva doesn't remarry. Stepdad. You've been there, turned away by the creep your mother took up with. You've done the worst thing a man can do, you've failed your kids. You're a fiasco, a debacle. But where do thoughts like this get a man?

Pock, plick, blip.

The only thing your mind can focus on is escape.

It can be done. It can't be done. It can be done.

You're watching, you're waiting. Every day you make a note on some aspect of the jail routine. Is the weekend staff the same as on the weekdays? How long does it take a boss to respond to a call? Which goons are in the best shape, who are the slackers? When do the slackers come on shift? Who opens which door? Where are the keys, what size what shape opens which door? When does the superintendent leave? Is there a fence around the parking lot? Can a car be hot-wired, driven away from the jail? Do the goons leave their keys in the ignition? These thoughts hurt the head.

You stroll across the cell trying to maintain your cool, you can feel your teeth grinding on each other. You picture Doris Day, a serious piece and try to whistle "Que Sera, Sera." You know the words but you daren't sing, a suppressed whistle brings a dozen looks, to sing aloud would be to risk a beating. You look through the bars. You breathe through your nose and grip the black and worn iron until your knuckles turn white but you do not notice. Down a corridor somewhere the sound of feet moving fast. Boots. Shoes squeak, sneakers go swish swish swish. A hinge squeaks, a door opens, the one that leads outside, it brings a whiff of outside air, fresh-turned earth, mulch. Inside the smell is a mixture of oil and greasy food, human sweat, and piss.

The smell is of puke. The day is pure shit.

You are shit. Instead of this pile of crap, you might have made something of your life. By being straight and true and honest you could have made Elva happy, the kids, but you had to have the steaks, the car, the house in River Heights. You wanted to be somebody, a big shot, a mover and shaker like Harry Backlin, with an office, respected, admired, praised. You had dreams, you had ambitions. But everything you've touched has turned to shit.

You're a failure, a thief, a bum, a deadbeat.

A bell goes off somewhere. A guy has come up beside you. He has his fingers wrapped on the bars like you. An Indian, tall, big through the shoulders. Joe Dale. He doesn't say anything. Joe says little. He can sit in a corner for hours without speaking. You've tried to do it. Crossed your hands in your lap the way he does. Took deep breaths and tried to think of nothing. Your mind leapt to this and that. Before you realized it your fingers were tapping on your knees. Ideas flitted through your head, plans, schemes. How does Joe do that? Why can't you do it? He sits in a corner quiet but you fret and pace. You try not to think, to blank out the mind, find peace, but an idea flits into the emptiness, an image, and it leads to the next and that to another and soon your head is buzzing. Your heart hammers in your chest. Your jaw hurts from grinding your teeth together. Your gut aches. You have trouble shitting. You develop headache during the day and cannot sleep at night. You're an animal in a cage, a monkey behind steel bars.

Ken is looking at a concrete floor. He's wearing pokey-issued shirt and pants. He's in a box within a box within a box. A not unfamiliar place. Ken breathes out slowly, counting to five, when he closes his eyes he sees an after-image of cinder blocks, one row atop another, straight and precise lines, a uniform and unending pattern of rectangles separated by joints of white mortar, a repeating grid that shimmers as it pulses toward him with each deep breath he takes, and then recedes, only to quaver back with the following exhalation. He feels the room is closing in on him, and when he opens his eyes the walls are closer than they were before, he has to draw longer and deeper breaths to quell the beat of blood in his temples.

The air is stale, cigarette smoke and human sweat, every now and then a whiff of sewage. The Assiniboine River is not far away, you can catch glimpses of the sun dancing on water when you're in the yard. It's fall, six months after he was arrested in Vancouver and flown back to Winnipeg for parole violation. Since then Harry Backlin, John Berry and the Grenkow brothers have been arrested and, like Ken, face various charges in connection with the gold heist. The air is cool, leaves blow around his feet when they take Ken out for court appearances in the city. When it's quiet and he strains his ears, he can hear semi-trailers on the highway leaving and coming into the city, rumble of rubber on asphalt, the throb of diesel engines. On a clear day the contrails of jets can be seen far up in the blue sky overhead, from time to time a smaller plane winging over the prairie. How he longs to be up there.

The fall air is filled with dense smells. Farmers are burning straw in their fields, to the south dark clouds loom in the sky. Ken loved these days on the farm, threshing gangs, geese flying by overhead, the frantic rush to bring in the harvest, fowl suppers in church basements. It seems like so long ago that he lived on a farm and at the same time just yesterday. The simple life, Elva's girlhood garden, fixing the barn roof with her father. A place he can never return to.

The judge has sent Ken to Headingley Jail on remand, awaiting sentencing. He will get at least six years for the robbery at the airport, his lawyer has informed him. Del, the guy he met in the cell in Vancouver, it turns out was Allen Richards, undercover RCMP agent. When he took the stand in court Ken knew the gig was up. Up to that point he had been optimistic. He'd stuck to his story. Even though Harry Backlin had confessed his part in the robbery and ratted Ken out. Even though everyone advised him to give it up, come clean, follow Harry's lead. Ken's lawyer said he had a strategy. He too had been optimistic. But Allen Richards had undone all that. In his smart RCMP uniform he had recounted Ken's tale of the robbery word for word, he had taken copious notes, and the judge took copious notes of Del's copious notes. It didn't seem right to Ken, the cops had cheated, they had set him up, and John Berry and the Grenkows, too, who had also been tricked by an undercover cop into telling their stories. They had been trapped. But that's how the system worked: the cops were allowed to cheat, the judge had no trouble with that. The system was bent.

It's September 1, 1966 and Ken is waiting for another prisoner to return from a preliminary hearing. If the charges against Joe are dismissed, Joe will be free, he will not be returning to the lockup. Ken will be disappointed. He likes Joe, he has plans that involve himself and Joe. Joe has a knife. Though a quiet man, he's charged with robbery and rape, a tough customer. Joe has the look in his eye of a man who when he says he'll cut a guard's throat to get out of Headingley will do just that. At the same time he can sit in his cell quietly for hours at a time, a silent Indian who has inner strength to match his powerful frame and fierce determination. Joe is the kind of man Ken has been looking for. Joe is desperate and powerful. And Ken is not about to spend the next ten years of his life in the lockup. He's not yet forty years old. If he spends ten or twelve years in the pen he'll be an old man by the time he's released. His kids will have grown up, Elva will have found another man. The world outside will be a different place. So much is happening so fast: rock music, protests against wars, rocket ships into space, medicare, love-ins, long hair. He won't fit in. Black, a black downer. Ken has become desperate.

Ken paces his cell, then strolls out into the common area where the cons mill about during the day. The inmates at Headingley Jail are housed on two tiers, connected by short flights of stairs. From the place where he pauses at the nearest set of bars there are two further sets of barred doors that lead to the outside. The first is a hundred feet away and around a corner to the left. Ken has paced the distance out. The barred doors there are manned by a guard and they lead into the administration area, where the super has his office, where the weapons are stored in a special room, where the kitchen is located. A single guard is at that door. The final door is not manned by guards. But a key is required to open it and it leads directly outside to the parking lot. Ken has made the walk through the three sets of doors a number of times himself on the way to court hearings, and he's made mental notes. He has studied distances and times the same way he studied them for robberies. He knows how many guards are on duty at any given moment, he knows the size and shape of the keys that open each door, he knows the prison routine changes at 5:30 when the super goes home for the day and the night shift comes on. There are no more than half a dozen guards on in the evening. Headingley is a minimum-security jail. Ken knows the area immediately outside the prison is a parking lot where the staff park their cars, he knows a gravel road leads straight out from the Jail to the main highway, about a mile distant. Word has it that Headingley is an easy place to break out of. Cons do it all the time. Only they always get caught and almost within hours of busting out. There's an RCMP detachment just east of the prison, toward the city. And the cons always run toward the city, toward their girlfriends and wives and pals, towards beer and smokes and burgers with fries. These are mistakes Ken does not plan to make, the errors of men with less brains than brawn. But brawn is required. The brute force of big Joe Dale with the knife.

Shortly after 6:00 Ken sees Joe's big frame sauntering down the corridor toward the cells. Ken jumps up but then sits back down again. Takes a deep breath in and puffs air out of his cheeks. He has learned to tell by the way a person walks whether they're bringing good news or bad; it's a salesman's trick, you look at the shoulders, you study what the eyes are doing. Women who are going to buy the cookware look you in the eye, a con whose appeal for release has been denied studies the floor. Joe Dale is looking down. His shoulders are hunched in. He's been sent back to remand. Ken's heart flutters. He senses his fingers are drumming his thigh. He jumps up and takes two steps forward, but then lets out a deep breath and steps backwards, then sits on a bench with his eyes closed to the count of ten. He does not want to appear too eager, so he waits until the bars have clanged shut behind Joe, until Joe is seated on a bench on the opposite side of the large holding cage before he stands and crosses to him.

"Not good then?"

"Ever hear of an Indian who got a break?"

Ken taps his foot on the floor. His heart is thumping wildly. He feels sweat in his armpits. "We're still on, then?"

"Yup."

"When?"

"Tonight. The sooner the effing better, eh?"

"Right," Ken says, "strike while the iron's hot."

Ken feels a surge of blood in his throat. He checks his watch. 6:30. Shift change must be occurring out there, goons exchanging keys, cars being started in the lot, the super putting away his papers and pulling on his coat. There's stuff to do. Where is the knife stashed? Do they tell everyone or make the bust-out in a small group of two or three? Who will grab the guard and snatch the keys? Thrusting knives into guards' ribs is not Ken's style but he's desperate, the system has forced him to it. Georges LeClerc, a man not afraid to kill, says the tighter the gang the better, but Ken says tell everyone, create a scene of pandemonium, start the guards and cops running this way and that, trying to sort out how many have escaped, chasing their own tails. There are crazies in the cells, letting them free will create confusion and mayhem. "All right," LeClerc says, "but we stick together, you and me and Joe. I'm the balls, Kennet, you're the t'inker." LeClerc is French-Canadian, he's learned English as a second language, it's sometimes difficult to tell what he's saying. But he's used a gun before and he will not hesitate to use one again.

Probably they won't have to. Headingley is a minimum-security jail: many of the inmates are there on remand, awaiting trial notices and preliminary court appearances, so they inhabit a kind of grey zone in the incarceration world, not outright convicts yet, and the relation between them and the guards is more lax than in a penitentiary. There's kibitzing between inmates and guards, and the inmates enjoy a degree of freedom.

Word of the breakout spreads like fire through the cells. The volume of talking, of laughter rises sharply. Ken begins to sweat. Will the guard on duty notice that there's more noise in the pen than usual? He goes to the bars and peers out. At the desk sits a young man named Mac, he's engrossed in papers. Ken takes a deep breath, as if he's calming himself before taking on something important. Behind him a commotion has begun. Barry Duke is a guy whose lawyer got him off a murder rap by pleading insanity. He spends the day doped up. Barry is a crazy, no one knows what to do with him; he's too dangerous to be put in a mental hospital, but he'd be chewed up alive in a penitentiary, where there are real toughs. So the goons keep him under control with pills. He's howling and other cons are shouting for the guard to help, Barry is going nuts, a seizure. Ken places himself near the front of the holding cell. Joe takes a place near the door, opposite him. When Mac opens the door, Joe grabs him and thrusts the knife blade to his throat. Ken grabs his keys and takes his gun out of its holster.

In a moment the cons have surged forward. Ken is making motions like a baseball umpire calling safe, calling for quiet. The guard is trussed up and pushed into a cell. Two groups of men move quickly, one to disarm the two guards at the head of the stairs on the upper tier, the other, with Ken in the lead, toward the basement, where two more guards are located. Among the cons is Barry Duke. He was not having a seizure, he was faking it, part of Ken's master plan. The cons are loose in the prison now. Ken and Joe make a dash toward the basement stairs where the two guards are reading magazines, not paying much attention. It doesn't take long for the cons to overpower them, seize their pistols, truss them up. Ken calls for a halt. They stand and listen. No sirens, no commotion in any other part of the jail. There are only a half-dozen guards on duty at night and no alert has been sent out. The cons have a few minutes of grace.

With Joe Dale and several others, Ken goes back up the stairs to the prison's main level, running toward the door that opens into the administration area, manned by a single guard. It's located down a hallway and a corner. It seems no one is breathing and yet Ken's heart thumps in his throat, he can feel each beat of his pulse in the finger crooked around the handle of a guard's pistol. Ken goes ahead toward the left-hand corner, the other cons hold back.

One more guard between the men and freedom. When he reaches the place where he's stationed, Ken catches the guard's eye.

The guard half rises. "What you doing outside the cage?"

"Mac said it was okay. I got information."

"Mac let you through? Jesus. I got to talk to him about that."

"I got information," Ken repeats, voice rising, "need to see the chief. Right away."

"It'll wait," the guard says, resuming his seat. He drops his gaze.

Ken is sweating. He hopes the guard does not notice. He raises his voice. "This could be important. Is important."

"See the chief tomorrow. Tomorrow." The guard's eyes looking up are flat, uninterested. Ken opens his mouth but before he can speak, the guard says sharply, "Buzz off." He returns to the papers on his desk. Ken's fingers are tight on the bars, knuckles turning white. Does he risk taking a shot from this distance? Minutes are ticking by, precious minutes.

There are men crowded in behind him. Ken can hear their breathing, slight shifting of sock feet on concrete. He fiddles with the pistol in his hand. Just then a workman comes out of a corridor on Ken's side of the door carrying a bag of tools. He's been repairing something in the kitchen. When he arrives at the door the guard stands and moves toward him, toward the door. He drops his head to put the key in the lock and when he looks up the muzzle of a gun is in his face. Ken and two other men push the workmen through and grab the guard, then disarm him. Someone says they'll gag and tie him up. Now they're moving. With the keys they've snatched, they throw open cell doors, releasing more cons on the upper level. The guard and workman are bundled into a cell, trussed with sheets. Georges LeClerc is beside Ken, Joe Dale too. They're running now, first to the room where the weapons are kept; they snatch up .22s and .45s, they leave the rifles but grab handfuls of ammunition. Then back to the basement where their street clothes are stored, tagged with their names; they throw off pokey pants and shirts and put on shirts and trousers and shoes. Ken pulls on the sweater that he was wearing when he arrived in the winter, grabs his hat and jams it on his head, checks his watch. Not yet 7:30. He cannot help thinking that at any minute he'll hear sirens. His palms are wet, heart racing.

Quite a gang of men have been let loose but only a dozen or so have followed Ken into the basement to put on street clothes. The rest are standing around in the administration area on the main floor, look- ing uncertain. The exhilaration of getting out of the cells has been replaced by fear of getting caught. They cheer, they shout encourage- ment, but they stay rooted to the floor. Ken nods at Joe and Georges. He knows they have to move fast. That last guard may have put in some kind of call to the RCMP. The escapees have only minutes. An RCMP squad car could be on the way already.

Ken sprints out the front door. The staff cars huddle in the park- ing lot, as he remembered. He jumps into a Chevy. Joe Dale has it going in seconds. Ken stamps on the accelerator. The rear doors swing as Georges LeClerc and Barry Duke throw themselves onto the seat. Gravel scatters from the wheels whirring down the road, dust flies up behind the Chevy. Ken pushes his fedora down onto his head. He has the window open. The air smells of burning straw and the rich bot- tom land of the Red River. Meadowlarks call from the ditch. The sun is going down in the west, a ball of orange spreading purple through the thin clouds on the horizon. Beside him Joe Dale sighs. "Huzzah," Georges LeClerc cries from the back seat. "We did it, Kennet, you're amazing, you're beauty."

Ken feels tears welling in his eyes, immense relief. But he senses too the enormity of what they've done, if they're caught years will be added to their sentences, it will be decades before Ken sees the outside world again. If that happens, he may as well forget about Elva and the kids. He'll die in the joint. The thought shoots Ken's heart into his throat and for a moment the car bounces crazily along the gravel road that leads from the Jail to the highway, almost out of control. Then Ken pulls himself together.

At the highway Ken turns west, away from the city. He's headed toward Warren, a small town to the north, a town with an airport. He and Georges LeClerc have talked things over. The plan is to fly south, out of Canada, past St. Louis, into Texas, then Mexico. Maybe put down somewhere not far from the Mexican border with the United States, maybe go farther south. LeClerc thinks they're men with something to offer, Ken has brains, he's a schemer. A guy like Castro might be interested in men of their fibre. Fly on to Cuba. Or if that doesn't work out, Jamaica is a wide-open place. Men with an airplane can be of use. Men with guns, with moxie, with nothing to lose. LeClerc makes it sound as if they're characters from a movie. LeClerc has some words of Spanish; it's like French, he tells Ken, *hombres*, he says, *dos cervezas por favor*. He and Ken laugh. Georges says they've got the brains in Ken, the brawn in Joe, and the derring-do in LeClerc himself.

The Chevy turns north off the main highway. Ken is driving fast, the Chevy shaking and shuddering. They whisk through farm country, past St. Francis Xavier. In ten minutes they come to a gravel road and Ken pulls onto it, heading east for a distance. The gas tank is almost full. The sun is still above the treetops. Farmers are out in the field, bringing in the last of the harvest. Geese fly over, giant vees high above the trees. Every now and then a truck or a car goes past in the opposite direction. Ken calls out, "Heads down, boys." Drivers going past tip their caps, lift their index finger off the wheel, rural forms of greeting. No one seems interested. The escapees do not have a map but Ken knows the lay of the land, he's flown over all this country, or driven most of it in the cookware days. Warren is to the north and the east. It may take an hour to get there. But the airport is a good size, they'll find a small plane to their liking, hot-wire the engine, head south. Freedom. The chance to start all over again.

What about Elva and the kids? When this thought crosses his mind, Ken lifts his foot off the accelerator without knowing he's done it. Once again he'll have let them down. But if it all works out, he can send for them later. That's the ticket. He was going to be away from them in the pen for years anyway. That time can be shortened. Things will work out for the better this way. Elva loves the sun and heat, Cuba or Jamaica would be to her liking. He'll send for her and the kids. Things will work out. The accelerator goes down again.

The roads criss-cross the prairie in regular grids. Ken drives as fast as he dare. He knows that by now the alert will be out, the cops will be at the Jail gathering names and questioning cons about who escaped and how long ago. His name will cause a certain sensation, excitement, but Joe is a killer and Barry a crazy man. Without his pills, he might do anything. The other cons were afraid of him. Georges LeClerc has a gun cradled in his lap as if he expects to use it, he's been a con man in his time but he's also a shoot-'em-up type, a desperado. They're armed and dangerous, no one knows what they intend, what might happen. Ken doesn't either. The cops will be anxious, on high alert, marshalling forces. Once the news hits the radio stations, there will be general ferment and fear. Panic, possibly. Calls for the army to be brought in, maybe. At any moment Ken expects to hear a helicopter or spot a single-engine looking for them. His eyes keep scanning the sky. Perspiration runs from his armpits. The sweater is a bit tight and he's hot.

Georges is tapping the pistol on his thigh and looking out the car windows nervously. "Could use a cig," he mutters. A bluebottle fly buzzes around his head and when he shoos it away, it lands on Ken's hand where its legs become entangled in the thick hairs on the back of his wrist. He shakes it off.

It takes more than an hour to spot the sign for Warren. Ken does not head straight to the airport but drives past it some distance before pulling the Chevy onto the verge of the road. Joe Dale and Barry push it off the gravel and into the bushes where it will not be spotted. Ken leads the others through the bushes and across a field toward the hangars. A few planes sit outside the buildings, easy pickings. It won't be long until they're into the air. Ken checks his watch. Nine o'clock. The shadows are deepening. Darkness will fall soon and he thinks it's better to wait until then and fly when they won't be so easily spotted. Just as they're about to emerge into the open and make for one of the planes, there's the sound of a car approaching fast. It pulls up in a cloud of dust. It's an RCMP squad car, two cops jump out and begin an animated discussion with the men who've come out of the hangar to see what's going on. The cops wave their arms, point at the planes, then the hangars.

Ken knows what it means. The cops have his name. The alert has gone out: The Flying Bandit is on the loose. Lock down the airports. That RCMP corporal, Gardiner, knows him too well, has anticipated what he will do. The squad car roars away in a cloud of dust. The guys at the airport begin to shuttle some planes into hangars and lock down the wheels of the planes left outside. Ken and the others confer. Barry Duke wants to storm the Warren airport, use the guns and steal a plane. Ken and Georges are dubious. There's too much to risk, they have to move on. They shouldn't have ditched the car, but that's spilled milk now, they'll have to hoof it to St. Andrews airbase near the city; Ken knows how to get into the hangars there. The others nod their heads, though Barry kicks the ground in disgust and mutters curses.

Ken takes the lead but soon Georges passes him and strides on ahead. Ken's mind is buzzing. Do you walk as fast as five miles an hour? Probably not. And the city is how far south? As much as thirty? Maybe forty, say forty. That's eight hours of walking, that takes them to somewhere early in the morning, say 2:00 or 3:00 a.m. If they make five miles an hour, but they probably won't, in the dark. But then St. Andrews is on the edge of the city, so that makes the distance less than thirty. So the one balances off the other. But if… Ken sighs. What's the use? He should be concentrating on the next step he's taking, on not stumbling and injuring himself, not on numbers and calculations, but it's as if his mind is on automatic pilot, he cannot help himself, thoughts keep grinding through his brain.

As darkness falls the four men cross fields and struggle through woods and bushes. Their breathing is heavy. They curse when they lose their footing and fall, stumble and stagger into each other. Bushes snag them, they lurch into depressions and holes. At times they find a gravel road and make better time. Ken figures it's about thirty miles to St. Andrews, if they keep at it they could reach the airbase by dawn. But when full darkness comes they're slowed to a crawl. They're thirsty and hungry. They snap at each other. Barry has begun to fall behind, humming and singing to himself, and then bursting into loud curses. Georges is tramping ahead and Ken calls out to him to slow. Georges and Joe bump into each other in the dark and there's cursing and muttering. They have to find a farmhouse, Ken says, overpower the occupants, steal their car. But every place they come near has dogs that start barking. They veer away.

Barry has fallen farther behind. Ken pauses in the middle of the road. "Barry," he calls out, "can you pick it up? Georges is a way ahead up there."

"Jesus, Ken." Barry looms closer in the gloom.

"C'mon now, we gotta make time."

"I don't got my pills. I'm feeling shitty."

"Lord almighty. You got your legs."

"I don't got them pills."

"You're doing fine. Just keep moving, keep focused now."

"I'm not doing fine. Listen to me. I'm doing shitty."

"Look. I was just saying."

"What the hell are we doing out here anyways? Stumbling around on gravel roads. In the middle of the goddamn night."

"We're fugitives from the law. We're doing what we have to do."

"It's crap, Ken. It's a dumb idea. Traipsing around in the dark. We shoulda used the guns at Warren. Turned 'em on the guys at the airport there."

"No, Barry. Bad idea. Guns are always a bad idea. Even Georges agrees."

"No, Ken, this here is dumb. This is a dumb idea. Stumblin' round out here in the dark."

"The dumb idea was you coming along. You shouldn't never have come along."

"Don't give me that crap, Ken, that mental incompetent crap."

"I was just saying. For your own good, like. You got no pills."

"I got a right same as you. I did my bit."

"You did, yes. You bet."

"We'd all still be back there in the clanger if it wasn't for me. I got us out. That was me."

"All right."

"Don't forget it, is what I'm saying. I was the one got us out, eh? Even though I maybe don't got your brains. I got what it takes. I woulda used them guns at Warren."

"Lord. I said all right already. Just try to keep up."

"Just lay off the crap talk, Ken."

"All right."

"All right."

Hours pass. Feet slip on the gravel. Joe trips and lands on his knee. Curses. Every muscle in Ken's back and legs aches. His shirt is matted to his back in sweat, he should ditch the sweater but it's a gift from Elva. Out in the fields there are combines bringing in the harvest, lone dots of light in an otherwise black panorama, like ships on a sea,

bobbing, seeming to make no progress. They'll be out there until two
or three in the morning, Ken thinks, maybe work through to dawn, if
rain is in the forecast. The land is a cruel mistress, it exercises a stranglehold on these people, promising much but defeating dreams and
grinding its occupants down, more often than not. His father tried to
break out of that cycle, moving to the city, working with machines.
Maybe, Ken muses, that's what his fascination with flying is all about,
breaking the hold of the land. And yet Ken loves the north country, its
trees and rocks, its lakes and silence. The two ideas don't fit together,
and Ken cannot puzzle out the contradiction with his head buzzing
thoughts, like flies rattling inside his skull, and his legs and back cry-
ing out in pain with every step he takes on the stony road.

Ken sighs. He's not given to philosophical speculations. He runs his
tongue around his mouth. They need to drink. Georges has stopped
to rub a calf muscle that has cramped. Frogs croak in the ditches,
crickets chirp. From the bushes come the sounds of night birds, occasionally sudden rustling that ends as quickly as it began. A kill going
down in the depth of night?

Down a dusty road they spot a place where there are no dogs.
They've walked maybe ten miles, Ken calculates. A light is on in the
yard of the farmhouse but otherwise the place seems deserted. They
approach cautiously, look in the windows. No one around. They try
the door, force it open. The house is inhabited but no one is home.
Ken runs a drink of water, Joe and Barry raid the refrigerator, LeClerc
keeps an eye on the road. The furniture in the house is old and worn,
the curtains dusty. Poor people. Ken turns on the radio in the kitchen,
tells Georges to turn on the TV. They're not news yet. Maybe the
cops fear that news of the breakout will instigate panic. More likely
they prefer not to admit they've been made fools of. Again. The Flying Bandit has had them again. If they can nab the escapees before
the breakout becomes widely known, they can appear heroes rather
than bums. "Keep them both on," Ken says, "with the volume low."
He checks his watch. Almost four o'clock. He sits in an armchair and

chews on a piece of bread and drinks more water. Barry has collapsed on a sofa, his arms and legs splayed every which way. He's a good-hearted kid but he suffers from mood swings, he shouldn't have come along, Ken shouldn't have let him come along. He needs medications, at any moment he could go off the deep end, injure himself, hurt others. Ken feels responsible. He got Barry into this, he'll have to get him out. Ken tips his hat over his eyes. A little shut-eye and he'll be able to figure things out. One more drink of water.

You're making it up as you go along. The thing is, you can plan a breakout and execute it to perfection, we did, it worked, we overpowered the guards, we hot-wired the car, we were gone in a matter of minutes, things could not have gone better and Bob's your uncle. But what you cannot do is plan out every single move. You don't know what the cops are thinking, you can't anticipate bad weather and crappy luck, an unexpected thing like an engine blowing out on a car or a guy going berserk, there are too many little wrinkles, too many variables brung into play. If we had gone for the plane at Warren five minutes earlier we'd of been flying high when the cops arrived. It was that close. If you'd of known the whereabouts of another airport closer to the Jail but you didn't, you'd set your mind on that one so that was it. It's a crap-shoot. All of life is. A car whizzes through a red light just in front of you and your eyes bug out, your heart leaps to your throat, one second different and you would of been killed, you weren't, but it was that close. So much depends on luck—sometimes it comes out good, mostly it turns out bad. You cannot anticipate everything. So you make it up as you go along, you saw that was how it had to be right away, even though you're a planner by nature, a calculator, you'd rather have everything laid out nice and clean, a plan to follow from beginning to end. But then Barry starts to fall apart. Who would of thought that dumb kid would of jumped into the getaway car, a crazy who might do God-knows-what, no one could of anticipated it, no one. Also you become thirsty and hungry and also cranky, you can't go on because darkness has fell and everyone is pissed off at everyone else and you feel it's your fault, you feel responsible, somehow you got to be the leader. On your own you could of made it to Selkirk and the St. Andrews airfield. But four guys thrown together at the last moment is like a four-horse team heading off in every which direction, sawing and yawing all over creation, as the fella says. You have to change your mind, let Barry rest, locate food and find water, locate a car so you don't have to stamp across the countryside, mud up to your ass, pardon the French. So you give up the idea of getting to St. Andrews before dawn, irregardless you know that not making it all the way there in one go complicates things, you may as well give that idea up altogether, the cops will be crawling all over the place come daylight. If you stop and rest, which you have to. You got to be flexible, you got to go with something else. But what? Maybe what you gotta do comes clear when you sit down and take a long cold drink, let your brain rest a few minutes in peace, consider the options, commence with something new, it's all you can do, it's all you got. Flexibleness.

Armed, dangerous

Five fugitives still at large

KENNETH LEISHMAN

Huge dragnet

en wakes with a start. Light is coming in a window. 7:30. Barry snores on the sofa, Joe and Georges are collapsed in beds in nearby rooms. Not much of a cutthroat gang. The cops could have snuck up on them and nabbed them while they slept. Ken locates frozen bread and a package of hamburger in the freezer. They eat both partly thawed. On the TV there are pictures of them now: Georges's ears sticking out of his head so comically they all laugh, Ken without his hat, a boiled egg needing salt, he quips. Joe's mug shot is out of focus, Barry's face creased with dark lines that appear to be scars. They look like hooligans, like the treacherous men the reporter claims they are. Do not approach. Armed and dangerous. They're silent as they stare at the TV screen. For a while after they have trouble looking each other in the eye.

They wait out the daylight hours. Every now and then a car approaches on the road, a swirl of dust coming toward them. They duck down, watch through a crack in the curtains. The cars move on. In mid-afternoon a tractor chugs past, they could run out and hijack it, but what is the good of a tractor? Ken studies the sky. The contrails of commercial jets high up, but no single engines are flying. No helicopters either, though. They doze on the armchairs, chew hamburger and dry bread, drink water. On the news they are still the lead item. The TV does an interview with Scotty Gardiner. Nothing to report, the airports have been locked down. The gang is still at large. The important thing is to stay clear, don't make contact, immediately call the RCMP.

"Gang," Ken says aloud. "We're a gang. Like Jesse James."

"Like the great train robbers," Barry says. He's got a huge grin on his face.

"John Dillinger." Georges holds up both hands with index fingers and thumbs like pistols, waves them in the air. "Bam bam."

"The Leishman Gang." Joe laughs.

"You like dat," Georges says. "You like dat one der?"

Joe nods. "I never was part of a team before. This is my team." He swaggers around the room, rolling his shoulders. "Leishman Gang. Big bad Joe Dale."

"Look out," Georges says, "bad guys on the loose. Le Gang Leishman *dangereux*." He struts around too, pretending to shoot his imitation guns.

"Hey," Joe says, "maybe Johnny Cash will write a song about us."

"*Mon dieu*," Georges says, "Stony Prison Blues. Hear that train a-chuggin.'"

Joe sings: "I'm stuck in Stony Prison, 'cause they won't let me freeee—"

"All right, you guys, geez," Ken says. Though he too is smiling.

When daylight ebbs out of the sky Ken says they have to move. He's found a little cash in a drawer. Georges found a hundred dollars stuffed between the pages of a Bible. Enough to buy gas if they can locate a plane. While they've been sitting around Ken has decided that's still the best plan. Get hold of a car somehow, maybe a farm truck, overpower a farmer if necessary, locate a small-town airport,

hot-wire a single-engine, get airborne and stay airborne far into the
States. It's their best play, their only play. They ransack closets and
come up with clothes for Georges. But everything in the house is
too small for the other three. Hats and sweaters, though. Before they
leave, they wash up and shave. Do they look less like the desperadoes
on the TV? Those mug shots stunned them into silence, but they're
feeling better after cleaning up. Ken would like to call Elva and tell her
he's okay, but that would be sheer madness.

They head out on the gravel roads again, walking fast and hard in
the dusk. Soon after they start Ken feels tightness in his calves, stiff-
ness in the neck, he notices that Georges up ahead is limping slightly.
One of Barry's feet drags in the gravel with each step, step scrape step
scrape step. Only Joe seems unaffected by last night's gruelling trek.
As close as Ken can figure, they're somewhere to the south of Warren,
and they're heading south toward the city, which they must avoid. His
mind is whirring. They cannot be spotted. When car lights approach
they duck into the ditch. The plane is the key. Where else might there
be an airbase, an airport of some kind? The night becomes dark. A
moon shines down, just enough to illuminate the gravel road. Briefly
Ken looks up at the stars. A warm night, a night to sit out with a drink
and enjoy soft prairie air, maybe the last of the season.

Joe is walking beside him, somewhat behind. "Nice, eh?"

"Still of the night." Ken says quietly, slowing so they can talk. He
whistles a few bars of music softly.

"Yeah. 'Stars begin their twinkling'. Always liked that one, eh."

"You bet, 'Deep Purple.' Wish I knew more about the—the—what-
do-they call them—constellations. Big Dipper, that's about it."

Joe points into the sky. "North Star."

"That one too. A whole world up there. Beautiful."

"Been a long time."

"Lord, yes." Ken nods. "Long time."

"Freedom, eh?"

"Nothing like it."

"I ain't going back." Joe has been looking at the stars. He stumbles slightly.

Ken feels the same way. "Whatever it takes." He taps the butt of the pistol shoved into the back of his pants. He's always hated guns. But a man is driven to desperation sometimes.

"They don't take me alive, eh."

"I hear you there."

They're silent for a minute, then Joe says, "You got us out."

"It was luck."

"It was brilliant."

"Hmmm." Ken strokes his chin. "This is how I got life figured, Joe. There's bad luck and there's good. We had the good luck in getting away from the lock-up, but then we got the bad luck when the cops pulled up at the airport. All of life is like that." Ken holds his hands out at his sides, like he's weighing the scales of justice. "You just gotta hope you get more good than bad."

"I 'spose," Joe says. "That's one way to look at it. But I still think the escape was brilliant."

Ken sighs. His heart feels light in his chest. He feels close to Joe but does not know what to say to him, so he says nothing, basks in the other man's praise.

Joe hums as they walk along. Ken counts paces, an old habit. He counts to ninety-nine and then starts over again. Ahead Georges is setting a fast pace. Barry is already having difficulty keeping up. He's breathing hard and scraping one foot in the gravel.

Ken looks into one farmyard and then another. Dogs bark when they hear feet stirring the gravel, voices. An hour passes. They cross mile intersections, head farther east. How far can they walk before it becomes pointless? Ken takes off his hat and fans his head. He's sweating. Once again they have no water, no food. He's a detail man and it irks him that he's forgotten these simple requirements. He listens to Barry's feet scuffing the road in the rear, he's falling farther and farther behind.

Ken looks back. Barry is little more than a form in the gloom, dragging one foot wearily. Come on, Ken thinks, put your back into it, man. Show some drive. Some guts. This is the problem, too many men with big plans but not enough moxie to follow through. A man has to put his shoulder to the wheel if he expects to get anywheres. A man can achieve anything if he sets his mind to it. The problem is... the problem is not enough men have the imagination to see what they can achieve and the wherewithal to reach out and grab it.

They come around a bend in the road. Up ahead there's a car parked on the verge. A tiny glow of pale light comes from the interior. Georges puts out one arm and they slow, whisper.

"Piece of good luck," Georges says.

"Finally," Ken sighs.

Georges asks, "Do we take them?"

"Yes," Ken says, "grab the bull by the horns."

When they come closer Ken sees the windows are fogged. A couple has chosen the spot for late-night activity. The gang approaches carefully. Georges has his gun drawn. Ken signals that he'll go to the driver's door. Georges circles to the other side. When Ken springs the door of the car open, the girl inside screams and the boy cries out.

"Hush." Ken leans into the car. His eyes fix on the boy's.

"Take what you want. Don't kill us." The boy's eyes dart from Ken's face to Georges's gun. The girl is staring at Joe, part hidden in shadow.

Ken laughs. "Sorry to catch you at a bad moment."

The girl trembles. She's a blonde, maybe eighteen, maybe younger. Tears well in her eyes.

"It's okay," Ken says. "We won't hurt you."

The boy is zipping up his pants. "Take the car," he insists.

"Nobody's getting 'urt." Georges waves the gun in their faces. "Long as yuz behave."

"Take my wallet."

Georges grabs it and looks inside. A few bills, a driver's licence. He nods at Ken.

"Take the car." The boy keeps his eyes on Ken. "Let us go. Please."

"One minute." Ken motions for the couple to step out of the car. "I'll tell you what we're going to do. You're going to have to come with us. You're going to have to be our companions. But you won't get hurt if you do as you're told. See? So first, what are your names?"

"Heather. And Ross." The words are barely whispers in the dark.

"All right, Heather and Ross. This is what we're going to do. We're going for a little ride. No one will get hurt if you do as we say. Right?"

"We will." Ross nods, looks at Heather.

She nods back. "I have some money too."

"That's good, that will come in handy. That's the idea." Ken motions with his head to Ross. "You come in front. Your girlfriend can sit in the back. No funny stuff. You look like a couple of smart kids, kids with bright futures. Now, you don't want to mess that up by doing something stupid. Trying to be heroes. Am I right?"

Georges waves the gun in Ross's face. "Die young, eh. That would be stupid. Eh?"

Ross nods.

"Prolly haven't even had a piece of tail yet." Georges laughs. "Excuse my French."

Ken wheels the car onto the gravel road. This time he drives at a good pace but not fast. He does not turn on the car's headlights. The night is black, the road lit by moonlight and stars. It's a lovely night, the soft air of the long prairie evening wafting into the car. The roads are deserted. Who's out driving back roads past two o'clock? They head south. Ken is watching for signs of airports. He has one in mind now. The farmers down south are wealthy, and they love to fly over the border into the States. He's come down in little airports when selling the cookware. Clean little airports, efficient, new and bright Cessnas and Mooneys. To get to those country airports in the south, the gang will have to cross the Trans Canada highway to the east of the city. Ken taps the wheel with his fingers. In the car there's silence. Georges clears his throat from time to time. Ken can hear the shallow breathing of Heather in the back. She's frightened. On the radio Barry was depicted as a killer and Joe a murderer and rapist.

As light comes into the sky he looks into the back. "It's okay," he tells her. "No one is going to be hurt. You'll come to no harm. We'll be with you for a couple of hours and then we'll let you go. You'll be back with your folks by noon."

"Just drop us off anywhere," Ross says. "We'll walk."

"I'd like to but it won't work." Ken feels sorry for the kid. By now his parents and hers will be alarmed. The boy will be the one to answer for this. Ken says, "You have to stay with us."

Georges taps the pistol against the window glass. "You're our safety, eh, our insurance."

Ross sighs.

"We need gas soon." Ken looks across at Georges. "How we gonna work that?"

From the back Barry says, "Kick 'em out. Get rid of 'em."

"No," Joe Dale chimes in. "They're our safety, Georges is right."

Georges spits out the open window. "Split them up when we get to the gas station?"

Ken nods.

"Keep one in the car. With you. While we others... Lemme t'ink, Kennet."

"I'm too visible, I'm the one they've all seen on TV. So. When we spot a pump that's working, we'll go through town, then a little past town the three of us and the boy will get out while you and the girl, Georges, drive back to the pump. That way no one tries anything stupid."

"I won't," Ross says.

"No." Georges pokes him with the pistol. "You're too smart for that. I'll have your girl."

In the rearview mirror Ken studies Heather in the back seat. She's chewing her lower lip. He asks Ross, "You in high school?" Ken's tone is softer than Georges's.

"Last year. Going to college."

"Hoo boy. You hear that, Kennet? We got the smart one here. Brainy boy."

"Good for you." Ken glances quickly at Ross and grins. "We're a bunch of ignorant bums, us."

"On a scholarship," Heather offers from the back. "Track."

"Impressive," Ken says. "College and a track scholarship. Smooth."

"Maybe we should pull over," Joe says. "Let the boy do a little training beside the car."

Ken laughs. "Sounds like you want to join him."

Joe laughs. "That's me all right. Jigaboo sprinter. That's the one thing Indians can do. Run fast. Specially near a white man, specially to get away from the white man." He chuckles and Georges laughs aloud. It breaks the tension in the car. Ross exhales.

You did not get to attend high school, you were never offered a scholarship. You might have played for the Blue Bombers, a big kid with huge hands and a back used to work. You could have been a hero, a somebody. But those doors were closed, they clanged shut in front of you the same way the doors in the clink clanged shut behind you. Whatever you got, whatever you achieved, you did it on your own hook, it was you grinding it out day to day at selling pots and pans or cleaning elevator parts and making the best of things, whatever you got was from your own doing. No fancy education, no set-up in the old-man's business, no old-school tie or fixed-up job. It was all down to your own plotting and planning and putting your back to the wheel, as the fella says. At another time, in another place, you might have had a scholarship. Everyone said you were bright, a hard worker, everyone liked you. But your tuition was paid to Crowbar College, the only break you've ever had was a break out of jail.

They gas up at a little town north of the Trans Canada. When Heather pulls up at the side of the road so they can hop back into the car, she is smiling. It's a caper, she's having fun. Georges gives Ken a big nod. For a moment Ken had wondered if Georges would run off with the girl, but he knows, too, the Ken magic, people like him, they don't betray him. It's a gift of a kind. He's nice and people are nice back. By the time Ken is behind the wheel again, they're all laughing, even Heather and Ross. They pulled it off!

"Smooth as silk." Georges has tucked his pistol into the top of his pants. "She was cool, this one, here." Georges chuckles. "Guy at the pumps had no idea."

"Thought so." Ken tugs at the brim of his hat. "Girls, women, they got the softening effect."

Georges snorts. "To mention just one t'ing."

Barry coughs. "I could use a smoke."

Joe grunts. "I could use a burger. A steak. Onions. Potatoes."

"Soon." Ken points the car south. To the east the sun is climbing over the treetops. As they drive along, Georges whistles a tune. Then Ken hums some bars of "Wayward Wind."

"Like that one," Joe says. "And 'Jambalaya' by Hank Williams. That one's peppy."

"How about 'Kaw-Liga,' you like that one?" Ken laughs.

Joe snorts. "Wooden head," he says bitterly. "Not so much, not so much that one. Who says Indians got wooden heads?"

"Ah c'mon," Ken says. "Catchy tune."

It's a Sunday morning. The roads are quiet. They drift through the town of Ste. Anne and then a tiny place called Blumenort. It's a quiet morning and the land stretches out around them, flat under a big blue sky. Ken sighs. "Gotta love the prairie," he says, "gotta love that big blue sky." Just outside Steinbach there's an airfield. Ken turns in and drives down the road slowly. Birds are calling from the roadside, red-winged blackbirds, frogs call in the ditches. The sun is a golden ball coming over the treetops to the east. Dew is on the grass along the roadside.

The windows are rolled down and Ken takes in deep breaths. Odours of new-mown grass, ditch water. "Jesus," he says aloud. "Lordy-O. Months in jail dropping off me like a snake's skin."

"Been a long time," Georges says. "Sun, grass, ditch-water. Let me out here."

Ken looks over at him.

"I lie right down in the ditch here and die."

Ken lifts his foot off the accelerator, glances at Georges quizzically.

"A joke, a blague, Kennet." Georges laughs. "You English, you English never know when a man makes a joke. You're all so serious." He laughs again, broken and crooked teeth in a small mouth. "But it's tempting, Kennet. It's real nice hereabouts. A man could die here and be happy. *Heureux.*"

In the back Joe says, "Let me out, Ken. Let me die here." He and Georges laugh aloud.

Ken shakes his head. "Geez, you guys." He steers down the gravel road toward the airport.

"Look." Joe Dale points into the sky. A hawk is circling overhead, swooping and rising on air currents.

Ken peers up through the windshield. "Nice."

"*Magnifique,*" Georges says. "Beauty."

"The freedom, eh?"

"Lord, yes. Flying. Above it all. Free to go where the wind she blows."

"Been a long time," Joe says.

"You got that right."

"I ain't going back. Come whatever."

"D'is *hombre* neither," Georges say. "Prison, eh? *Tabernac.* They don't take me alive."

Though the RCMP have sent out the call to lock down all small aircraft from Winnipeg to the west, there are a number of single-engine planes sitting outside. In the morning sunlight with dew glistening on their paint they look to be straight from the factory. "Huzzah," Joe calls out from the back seat. Ken drives close to a Mooney four-seater. No one seems to be around. They hop out of the car.

"Only a few minutes now," Ken tells Ross and Heather. He looks down the road they came in on. Concern wrinkles his brow. They came so close in Warren, only to be thwarted. His hand is tapping his thigh. There's no one around but Ken starts at every sound, a plastic bag flapping at their feet, a branch falling from a tree. As Georges works with a screwdriver to remove the cover over the instrument panel inside the plane's cabin and then Joe fiddles with electrical wires, Ken can't keep his eyes off the road: no plumes of dust. Every few seconds he glances at his watch. What is taking so long? Ken wipes sweat from his brow with the back of his wrist. His hand is twitching. Ross and Heather are standing by the car, conversing in hushed tones. Geese fly overhead. Frogs chirr in the ditch. Ken paces around, then looks over Joe Dale's shoulder. He paces away and then is back peering at what's happening again. "Geez," Joe says, "you're as antsy as a long-legged horse in fly season."

After about fifteen minutes Joe has hot-wired the engine. Sweat is running down Ken's back. "All right," he says to Ross. "Here's your wallet back, your keys. We'll have to pay you for the gas another day." Ross laughs, waves his hand. Ken tips his hat and smiles. "Sorry we inconvenienced you last night. Sorry if this lands you in it with your folks. We had no other choice. You know?"

"It's all right." Ross takes Heather's hand. "No harm done. You kept your word."

"We'll be okay," Heather says.

Ken purses his lips. "Just want our freedom. We're just ordinary men. We never meant no harm."

Heather nods. "They'll be happy we're safe. Our folks."

"Just like I said, no one gets hurt." Ken smiles.

"Yeah. Thanks," Heather says. "You kept your word."

Ross jangles the keys in his hand. "You're okay." He smiles, a tight grin. "Whatever you done, you're okay, Mister."

"I hope so," Ken says. "I feel bad about what we done to you two kids—a little contrition."

"It's okay," Heather says. "No harm done."

Ken touches the brim of his hat. "One more favour. Give us half an hour now before you call the cops. Give us a running start. We kept our word, right?"

"All right," Ross says. "You did. Half an hour."

When the plane is in the air, Ken looks down. Heather and Ross are standing by the car, waving. Ken dips the wings, then points the plane south. It skims the treetops. Ken's fingers are tapping handles and knobs in the cockpit. He's giddy. When he closes his eyes he sees red-rimmed after-images weaving on his eyelids. It's a four-cup high. But he's jumpy. He's barely slept in two days. Hardly a minute has passed when he hears a loud crack. Ken starts. Did one of the wings break loose? Is there something wrong with the plane? Is that why it was sitting unattended?

He leans over and shouts, "What was that?"

"*Sacre bleu.*" Georges has rolled down his window. He fires his pistol in the air again. "I never been in a plane before, Kennet. *Tabernac.* So beauty. It's hard to describe."

In the back seat Joe and Barry have grins on their faces.

"It's like we could be going to the moon." Georges puts his head out the window. The rush of air sweeps back his hair. "I can't believe it. *Mon dieu.*"

Joe and Barry are gawking around like kids. "Look at that river, Kennet. Look at that truck. Just a speck. *Mon dieu* but it's beauty."

"Geez," Ken says, "you guys. But no more firing guns. Those bullets come down somewhere, you know. They could hit someone."

Georges laughs again. "*Tabernac.*" He looks into the back seat, grinning at Barry and Joe. A kid at the fair.

"I mean it." Ken's voice has risen and become hard.

"All right, all right." Georges holds up one hand. "You English, *mon dieu,* so serious all the time. Where's your *joie de vivre*?"

Ken laughs now too. "All right," he says. He takes a deep breath and taps his fingers on one knee. "You still want to die in that ditch back there?"

Georges shakes his head. "It's beauty up here. Eh, boys? *Magnifique. Mon dieu* but."

From the back seats Joe and Barry grunt approval. They're still gawking down at the fields below, nudging each other, pointing.

Ken clears his throat. "'I know that I shall meet my fate somewhere in the skies above.'"

"What's that?" Georges has a smile on his face.

"Oh, nothing." Ken shakes his head. "Just some verses a guy wrote."

"Poetry," Georges says. It comes out sounding like *poultry* and Ken laughs.

"Say more." Joe Dale has leaned forward.

"Let's see." Ken pushes his hat up his forehead slightly. "The guy is talking about flying, eh? Let's see if I can remember how it goes. 'I measured all, brought all to mind, the years to come seemed waste of breath, in balance with this life, this death.'"

"Hah," Joe says. "That's good. That's a good one, isn't it, Georges?"

"That's our Kennet. Busts out the can one minute with guns blazing, and then quotes poetry the next."

"You bet." Ken laughs. "Works wonders with the ladies, poetry. You oughtta try it, boys."

Ken keeps the plane low, flying just over the treetops. It's scrub land, a lot of rock piles on the edges of fields, sloughs, extensive stands of bushes. Though it's a bright and warm morning, only a very few farmers are out on the fields. It's Sunday morning and this is Manitoba's Bible belt, Mennonites, and even more orthodox types, the women wear little skull caps. Ken cannot recall the name of the sect. Every little town has a church, some two or three, spires glistening in the sun. The Mooney moves along fast, twice as fast as a speeding car, three.

In less than an hour, they cross the border into the United States.

Nothing below looks different. Scattered farmsteads, gravel roads, sloughs, here and there a small town or a village. The occasional car stirring up dust on a gravel road. He locates what he thinks must be the main highway going south, then bears to the east of it. He glances around the cockpit. "Check that compartment." He points near LeClerc's elbow. "There should be a navigation map."

Howard Hughes that's his name, big shot so enamoured of flying he begun his own airline and flew around the world it was on the news every night, Howard Hughes in Paris headlines in the Saturday paper Howard Hughes in Moscow. First though he flew across the entire States, Los Angeles to New York City also across the Atlantic, like that other guy, Lindbergh also Amelia Earhart. Odd when you think of the way that name is pronounced, *airheart*, 'cause I knew a guy in the slammer who ran a fishing lodge name of Whaley and two brothers who were safecrackers the Locke brothers. I wonder how often that happens, your name has something to do with what you work at in life? Leishman, man on a leash, man with a leash on his life. In any case Howard Hughes a man I understand because once you been up in a single-engine there's nothing else you want to do it's a drug. With me it started much before that as a kid, that's probably where it starts for most, romance of the wild blue yonder as the fella says. All those war aces, the Red Baron and his like just enjoyed being high in the sky most probably, which I understand because in a single-engine no one's holding you back, calling you to account, there's no horizon the prospect is endless there's no limit to where you can go and what you can do. No leash on you. There is a horizon true but as you move toward it the horizon moves too so it's as if there's no end and that's the feeling that gets you, the infinite. Below, everything looks puny like ants people say and like ants on their hill all that frantic human activity down there seems tiny and pointless from above, pathetic.

Whereas the sun high overhead, the endless blue, the rush of air, these are things to live for a passion greater than filthy lucre or lust of the flesh. All that other the rushing to work office infighting career responsibility climbing the so-called ladder, keeping up with the Joneses bullshit, ants on an anthill is how you come to see it. Man commenced as a wanderer, I read that somewheres, restless on the move peripatetic, a fancy word for wanderer. There's the freedom of the seas and the freedom of the open road, I've experienced that one, I understand men who throw over friends and jobs for those but none matches the freedom of the air, you're above it all, that's the point, so far above the trials and tribulations that you just want to fly into the sun. They say some war aces done that near the end of the fighting. For years they'd had the greatest adrenaline rush known to man, flying the single-engine and added to it the thrill of the kill and of cheating death then one day their planes just crashed—into the sea the Dover cliffs a field in France—when the war was near ending, it never made sense. Why was that, the most experienced pilots, the best that had ever been seen? They must of thought, An office job after this, the nine-to-five, a boss, kids to feed and send to college. No thank you ma'am. Better go down in a blaze of glory than die with smoker's cough and chained to a desk with nothing to look forward to but the pension and the wife getting fatter by the year. I understand that, I have to fight the urge to fly on forever and just let the plane come down somewheres, even if somewhere is a cliff face or the sea, the same way you have to fight the urge to jump when you're looking down from the tenth-floor balcony or into the canyon, something in you wants to leap, it beckons, it calls like a seductive song, you have to fight off the malevolent impulse of that great unknown.

LeClerc has the map on his lap again. They've just taken off from Tyler, Minnesota where they had to stop to refuel. Just after ten on a Sunday morning, the guy at the little airbase in Tyler had not heard the news. Desperadoes from Winnipeg in a plane. Maybe what happened in Canada never made the news down south. Americans, Ken's discovered in his travels to Texas and Arizona, know nothing about Mexico, a hundred miles to the south, and little about Canada. "Cold up there." That's it. "You guys like hockey and you say *eh*?" Ken had a good look at the map when they were on the ground, refuelling. But he glances over toward LeClerc every now and again. They're still heading south but on an eastern slant.

Below they see what must be the Mississippi River, a broad strip of water snaking north to south, wide as a lake in places, glistening in mid-morning sun. Big boats, steamships they look to be, as the plane skims above them; logs lashed together, floating armadas of hydro-pole length trees, tugboats, two sets of train tracks winding along beside the river, sailboats. Away from the river, extensive areas of dense bush and equally extensive segments of field under cultivation, tractors and combines on the land, cars and trucks stirring up the dust on gravel roads. Tarmac highways winding like snakes. Towns dotting the landscape, nice-looking places beside the river, hamlets and villages on ridges. Big barns and dairy cattle in meadows. Minnesota and Wisconsin, maybe Iowa. Ken calculates. At the speed they're going they are somewhere east of the Minnesota border but also a couple hundred miles west of Chicago, maybe more than that. Three hundred, say. Somewhere to the east of Minneapolis and maybe as far south as Iowa, yes.

From the back Barry Duke says, "Pretty here. Drop me here, Ken, I'll die here. It's cheese country, right? Find me a little farm girl."

LeClerc laughs. "Find me a fat farm girl, Kennet, *la fille forte*. I like 'em that way. Fat girls appreciate a man, appreciate attentions."

"Any girl," Barry says. "Hoo boy, it's been a while. How 'bout you, Joe?"

"I'm hungry. When was the last time we ate?"

LeClerc looks into the back seat. "Lockup grub starting to look good? Granny's old leg?"

Joe chuckles. "Bring on the dung pie."

Two flies are buzzing around in the cabin, making ellipses around Ken's head, and then Georges's.

Ken looks at the map. It's going in and out of focus, leaving after-images on his eyelids. He points at the map. "I'll set 'er down soon. We get past Wisconsin, over in this area, maybe some farmer won't have heard about the Canuck hoodlums on the loose. Chicago. Toledo."

"Yeah," LeClerc says. "Look here. Gary, Indiana. I heard tell of a guy dere."

Ken glances across. "What kind of guy?"

"A guy who can maybe help us out, Kennet. Let me t'ink now. Paulo? Pablo?"

Barry leans forward. "We need help?"

Ken says over his shoulder, "We don't got much cash."

"Shit." Joe raises his voice. "Why'd we have to come across dirt-poor farmers back there? And then a couple of kids with nothing more than pocket change? My stomach's been growlin' for an hour."

"Pablo." LeClerc has the lobe of his ear pinched between thumb and forefinger. "Yeah."

Ken is sweating in the sun. He really should get rid of the sweater. Nice argyle pattern, though, a Christmas gift from Elva and the kids. He glances at the map again. In Tyler he'd been thinking they would put down again in Springfield, but he's been wavering now about whether to continue south, so they're heading on a diagonal, as much east as south. "Gary," he says, "maybe hook up with a guy named Pablo, Gary's just past Chicago and looks to be a few hours away. I calculate three hours, maybe four at most. We're making good time." He glances at the air speed indicator. Just over a hundred an hour into a slight headwind. If Gary is 300 miles away, that's three hours, maybe three and a bit. If the wind stays the same. But maybe he can push it a little, get a little more speed out of the Mooney's engine. So maybe less than three. Maybe. "Three hours," he calls toward the back seats. "Can you hold out that long, Joe?"

Joe laughs. "It's what Indians know best. Tighten the belt. Hold out."

"Three hours." Ken pushes his hat back. "Maybe less."

Joe laughs. "Probably more."

LeClerc laughs. "If it was any other man than Kennet, it would be more, that's for sure, but you know Kennet. Always calculating, always figuring the angles. Five minutes early or five minutes late. Am I right?"

"Maybe." Ken laughs. "Maybe on this auspicious occasion, *mon ami*, not."

The thing of it is, flying to Cuba or Mexico sounds like a good idea when you're sitting in the cells plotting with Georges LeClerc but after a few hours in the air certain unpleasant realities begin to emerge. It's thousands of miles to St Louis, much less Havana, and your shoulders and legs ache already, those two nights stumbling around on gravel roads in the dark are beginning to talk back to you. So pain, yes. And who wants to be a communist anyways? You've always been a staunch capitalist, a believer in the market system, are you ready to work for the common good? Socialism means everyone gets to share whatever you've earned. And on the topic of cash, how are you going to pay for fuel-ups along the way? You hold a hundred dollars and a bit. In Canadian money. How far will that take you? When will the Canadian cash tip someone off? There are four mouths to feed and Joe can put back as much as any three ordinary men. And there's Barry. Barry could go off at any time, the kid hasn't had a pill in almost two days. You've got a headache. How long is it since you've had a good night's sleep? Any night's sleep? Eyes feel grainy, thoughts going everywhere,

a skipping record when you need to concentrate. You've been squint-
ing into the sun hour after hour, no sunglasses. Your neck aches.
There's a lot of stress in keeping the plane just above the treetops but
below radar. The excitement and exhilaration of slipping out of the
dragnet, of skimming the treetops, of getting the best of the cops
again wore off hours ago. Now you're hanging on and hanging in
there, trying to keep your thoughts straight while your brain buzzes
and your ears ring. By now everyone knows you're on the lam, by now
who isn't on the watch for the plane? That cop Gardiner will have
figured it out, he'll have sent out a general alarm, Interpol will be on
alert. The Flying Bandit. The last time you put the plane down, a place
called Tyler or something, the guy who refuelled told you the name
but you cannot remember, you watched his every move. Was he going
to turn you in? You're an unlikely crew, so even if a man hadn't heard
the news, he'd naturally be suspicious—a big Indian, a kid with rolling
eyeballs, a guy with a French accent. Odd clothes, scruffy, an unkempt
lot. You gave him the line about being an Alberta oil exec flying to
Texas to check out rigs. You kept up the patter while the guy worked
the nozzle and wiped with the red rag, luckily you've spent a lot of
time around rural folk, selling the pots and pans, you can yak about
the weather and machinery, you can spin a story about where you've
come from and where you're headed to. You've studied at the University of Bullshit and your credentials are impeccable. Still, a plane with
four odd types, who wouldn't be suspicious? Canadian money. You
finger the bills in your pocket. That's the head-scratcher. You can't
possibly make it to Mexico on a hundred bucks, can you? What then?
When the cash runs out. Joe Dale won't qualify for credit. Barry Duke
can't ask for a loan. Do you start holding up banks and grocery stores,
LeClerc waving the pistol, Joe snatching fistful of bills from registers,
getting gunned down in a shootout, John Dillinger style? It's a lovely
day, there is that. Big prairie sun, blue sky. The land below is a patchwork of yellow and green fields with rivers running through. This is a
land you love. Still, you're done in, you need to eat, need to rest.

Collect your thoughts. Cuba sounded like a good idea when you were in the car stirring up dust on gravel in the back roads of Manitoba, but now that you're in the air with an aching back and ringing ears the grim realities begin to hold sway.

Hostages, car seized
in dash to Steinbach

Leishman flies away

Stolen plane

T his looks good." Ken has made a long looping circle over a farmer's field not too far from Gary, Indiana. The afternoon sun is beating into the cabin of the plane. Ken feels clammy all over his body, his left knee throbs from a twist he gave it on the gravel road south of Warren. Sweat glistens on Georges LeClerc's cheeks and brow. "What do you say, boys?"

Joe leans forward. "Looks good. A lot like home. I like farms."

Ken nods. "Me too. They always got food. Sometimes a pretty redheaded daughter."

Joe grunts. "Eggs, bacon. Been a while."

LeClerc looks into the back. "What'd I tell you? Kennet has made it over to here in just about three hours. It's just early afternoon."

Ken chuckles. He has done it. And not just got them to their destination in time, either. He's pulled off the biggest gold robbery in history and he's escaped from prison. He's not only the Flying Bandit, he's the Houdini of Headingley. It's a four-cup rush. "And this Pablo?" he says. "He interests me. He could help us."

"Paulo." LeClerc looks out his window as Ken begins the descent. He's biting his lower lip. "I'm sure Paulo."

"Or Pablo," Joe Dale says.

"No, no. Paulo. I got the phone number in here." LeClerc taps his skull.

Barry Duke leans forward. "You sound confused to me, Froggy. You got anything else in there, Froggy? Like a way outta this shit-ass mess?"

"*Tabernac.* It's not so bad. We're free and away the can."

"It's bad. We're nowheres, far as I can tell. It's a shithouse mess."

"*Mais non.* I was just saying."

"Crap. Crap is what it is. And I got no pills."

"*Non, mon frère,* but I got a gun you don't shut your face, mister foggy brain."

"You're not the only one packin'. Just remember that, Froggy."

"All right," Ken says. "Geez. Settle down, boys. You're getting all nervy."

"We're cool," LeClerc, says, tapping the pistol in his lap. "We're cool, Kennet. Froggy and Foggy." He laughs in a bitter way.

Ken sets the plane down in a grassy area not too far from a farm-house, smooth as glass. They've seen the farmer out discing a nearby field. Ken dipped the wings at him as the plane circled, the old sales-man's calling card. Only he isn't selling pots and pans this time. LeClerc has his pistol stuffed down the back of his pants. Joe is still carrying his knife. They get out of the plane but wait until the farmer comes up on his tractor before starting toward the farmhouse.

"Little engine trouble," Ken tells the farmer. "Gotta make a call."

"Russ," the man says, sticking out a big, weather-worn hand. He reminds Ken of the guy in *The Grapes of Wrath*, something Brennan, Ken's mind is jumping about, he's having trouble focusing his thoughts and remembering things. Russ pauses a moment. "You boys come far?"

"Alberta." Ken tips his hat up. "I'm a rancher, Garth Price, and these are my hands. We were heading to Texas to check out some beef. Longhorns."

"Must be nice up there." Russ glances at the sky.

"The best." Ken has taken off his hat and is fanning his face. "Bit hot, though, today."

"Nothing like it." LeClerc is walking behind Ken and Russ, Joe and Barry behind him.

Russ points toward the back door of the house. "Bet you boys got a hunger on."

Joe grunts. "You got that right, friend."

"Bet you could chow down on one of the wife's old-fashioned fry-ups."

"Wouldn't say no to that either, eh?"

At the house Russ's wife scurries about. As Ken tells Russ about his herd of Angus, the spread near Lethbridge, a patter he knows well from having dreamed of owning a ranch since he was a kid, coffee, eggs, and toast are prepared. The food smells so good Ken almost passes out. He sees Barry lick his lips. Ken knows he has to keep talking so Russ can't ask questions about the plane, the way they're dressed. Barry could say anything. This would be much easier if he were on his own. Accomplices make complications. It's an old saying but a true one. Once the others have begun to eat, he asks to use the phone.

In the hallway he has to put his hand on the wall to steady himself. The inside of his head could be broken glass. His eyes burn, legs feel like rubber. How many hours since he's slept? Eaten a solid meal? The one thing you forget when you're on the lam is how the needs of the body keep asserting themselves. You think the will to go on conquers all but the body gives out and the will succumbs. It's not mind over matter, the matter always has its say. The flesh is weak. One of Elva's favourite sayings. Only she's the one who always says mind over matter.

LeClerc has given him a phone number. He dials. Out of service.

Ken hurries back to the table. At any moment Barry could be asked a question and give a bewildering answer. He could have one of his fits. Why did Georges bring the kid along? There's a silence when they're done eating. Ken can tell Joe could eat as much again but they dare not ask and arouse suspicion. To Ken's eye their motley clothes and general dishevelment are dead giveaways that they're on the run, but the farming couple seem to be taking them at face value.

Ken rises and helps gather up plates. "Do you mind if we wash up?" he asks Russ's wife.

"No, no. Upstairs. Help yourself."

"We left in a bit of a hurry." Ken turns on the old Gable smile, the charm.

"Use my shaving kit," Russ offers. "Feel free."

The boys clump up to the bathroom. Ken sits on the stairs while the others shave and wash; he listens to the muted conversation of Russ and his wife coming from the kitchen. The radio is not on. They have no suspicions. Ken rests his head against a wall and closes his eyes; blood surges in his temples, red after-images, spots and dots dance on his eyelids. He's had a headache since he woke up, stiff from sleeping fitfully in a chair. His shoulders ache, he twisted one ankle getting down into a ditch the night before and it throbs. Both ears ring. So this is freedom.

When they come down to the kitchen, Russ is standing with his boots on and ball cap in hand. He'd like to give the boys a ride to Gary, he says, but it's the first sunny day in a week and he has to finish the discing. His wife will drive them to the nearest bus stop. She's wrapped cinnamon buns in a bag for them. Joe has taken possession of it, one big fist gripping the paper bag.

When they stand outside saying goodbyes to Russ a vee of Canada geese goes by overhead. Russ chortles. "Those buggers are always going one way or the other. Restless suckers. Me, I've never gone nowheres. The stay-at-home type. You," he says to Ken, "you're a lot like them, I can tell by the way you jiggle your leg under the table. You're a man on the move, a man who can't keep still. No offence."

Ken laughs. "None taken."

The sun is still above the treetops. It's past four o'clock. Russ can work for three or four more hours. "I'll keep a good watch on the plane," he tells Ken.

Ken laughs. "If we don't come back, you can learn how to fly it."

"Fly that?"

"You betcha. Man with your practical knowledge. Easier than the tractor."

"Me, up in the air. That's a good one." Russ waves his ball cap as they drive away.

Ken sits up front in the passenger seat. The fields going by the car windows had stands of corn in them at one time, but now the stocks are on the ground, waiting to be tilled under. Birds call from the roadside. Farmers like Russ are out on the land, discing and harrowing fields. Ken breathes in the air. Headingley seems a long way away, but so do the kids and Elva. He no longer knows what he and his little band are going to do next. The Leishman Gang. What he'd like to do is sleep for ten or twelve hours. He closes his eyes. The whirr of rubber on asphalt is seductive. Ken suppresses a yawn. If they can hook up with this Pablo, they can get some cash, arrange for papers that could be useful in Texas or Arizona, places he knows, places where they might find work of some kind until they can figure out what to do in the long term. They need money, they need papers. One thing for certain, Barry will have to go back to Winnipeg. At any moment he can go nuts, be dangerous. Put him on a bus? Does he have relatives in Manitoba? How to go about getting in touch with them? It's too much for Ken to figure out. His head keeps nodding forward, dropping to his chest, he goes in and out of consciousness, images of Elva appear and fade, someone saying, *you've got a record*, another voice saying, *not the beefcake, the briefcase*. Just to sleep. Just to put the feet up and ease the aching back.

It's the record, it follows you everywhere. Fingerprints, mug shot, record. You make one little mistake when you're just starting out, the mistake of the foolish youth, you take stuff from a furniture store, you don't use a gun, no one is hurt, you do the time and you come out and you think that's it, you've paid the debt to society, you can start afresh, make a new life for yourself and your family. But no. They've hung the record around your neck like the albatross. Apply for a position in the RCMP, they turn you down, land a job at an aircraft factory, a job that has promise, promotion to floor manager, and two months after you start the boss comes around with a hangdog look, the routine check with the cops has turned up the record, the aircraft position is sensitive, government contracts, security, blah blah, they can't take a chance on a man with a record. A con. A bum, a bullshitter, a braggart. Every time you try to go straight, wham, same thing, door closes in your face. Half the time they don't even come clean and say why. Apply for a loan, credit at a bank, they say they'll look into it but three weeks later and you haven't heard, you know what's happened. You don't belong, you don't fit in, you're a criminal. One lousy truckload of furniture. Doctors kill people on the surgery table, no problem. Bankers embezzle hundreds of thousands, they're reprimanded, told they can't work for the bank any longer. Do they have a record? Do all the doors close in their faces? They do for you. What is it you're supposed to do, then? Sell pots and pans. It's not your first choice but by the Jesus you learn how to do it and become the best at it, you make more in a year than the banker, you drive the same car as the lawyer and order steaks and wine like he does at the Town and Country. You show them. But then cookware collapses. What then? Tough luck is what, you're back where you started, the record an anchor around your neck. You go to Harry Backlin and he says he can fix it for you to become office manager at Olgat where they distribute cleaning products, but then Olgat goes under. You're buggered again. Bad luck. You tried, is the point, you tried to play the game their way, their fixed game, but okay, the fix was in and you bested them at it anyhows. But in the end you're left with no alternative. It's a bent system. You're out of work, despite your best intentions, your kids need food and clothes and you got nothing. The only way to reach where you want to go is to do it left-handed, as the man says. But it needn't have worked out that way. If they hadn't hung you with the record.

It's just after 6:30 and the gang is walking the streets of Gary. They're in the neighbourhood near the bus station, crumbling sidewalks, paint peeling on warehouse buildings, broken tarmac in the streets, newspapers clogged in the drains and blown against chain-link fences. Dogs nosing bags of trash, bums on corners puffing at cigarette butts. They fit in, a tough neighbourhood and they're a scruffy lot, the four Headingley escapees, the Leishman Gang. Ken remembers reading that Gary has a big and hardened police force, they're used to dealing with crime coming down from Chicago, they carry guns and are not averse to using them. Only a few weeks or so ago a state trooper was gunned down by an unknown assailant. Everyone is nervous, the cops are out for revenge. It's a union town with plants where machine parts are manufactured, and transients, shipping on the Great Lakes, merchant marine. Maybe it will be their kind of town, a place to connect with this Pablo or Paulo. Fly south. Ken can't think any farther ahead than that.

Georges is ahead of him, almost running, usually people have trouble keeping up to Ken's long, restless stride, but Georges wants to check Gary out so he's gone ahead. Ken can see the bulge of the pistol in the back of his pants. Barry has brought a gun too and Joe has his knife. Only Ken is unarmed; he left the pistol on the seat of the plane. You carry a gun, you end up shooting a cop, you end up getting shot yourself. All Ken wants to do is get clean away, try to make a fresh start.

Georges turns down a street. Up ahead there's a tavern. He drops back to the rest of the gang. "Let's try here, Kennet."

"The M & S," Joe says, studying the sign. "A dive."

"A dive suits us." Georges nods his head. "Right, Kennet?"

"Dives have hookers," Ken, says, "and hookers know the lay of the land."

Joe snorts. "Hookers are the lays of the land."

Ken punches him in the shoulder. "They know who's who. Mark my word, there's one in here, she knows who this Pablo guy is."

"Paulo," Georges says. "It's all coming back. *C'est bon, ça.*" He taps his head.

Ken nods. "Mark my word. She'll know."

Inside, the room is dingy and smoke-filled. Georges and Barry sit near the front. Ken and Joe go farther into the tavern, take seats near a pool table and order a round of beer. Joe relaxes back into his chair. If he feels the way Ken does, he could drop off at a moment's notice.

They down a round of draft. The waitress serving them looks just the type Ken has been imagining, fat, blonde hair with black roots, thick lipstick and a loud brassy voice. Slatternly. But friendly in a guarded way. She's been around the block.

"You boys are thirsty," she says, eyeing their empty glasses on the way past. "Another?"

Ken and Joe drink more draft. It's past 7:30. The room is beginning to look green at the edges. The two guys at the pool table are smoking and it stings the eyes. Ken knows that if he stands up he'll get a head rush. Joe has finished his beer and is looking around for the waitress. He signals for more. "Suzie," he tells Ken, "more the type for Georges than me."

When she comes back, Ken asks, "You know a guy named Paulo? The word is a fellow can get in touch with Paulo if he inquires here." Ken holds a five-dollar bill out to her.

The waitress shakes her head but she takes the bill. "Dunno. But wait. I'll ask Chris."

She goes away, but in a few minutes a man in a wheelchair comes out of a room to the side of the bar and gives Ken a studied look. He's got long, greasy hair. He wheels over to them.

"Hey there," Ken says. He reaches out his hand but the other man ignores it.

Instead he asks, "You asking after someone?" Up close Ken sees he's sweating, the pores of his face are oily. His fingers worry the rests of the armchair.

"Looking for Paulo." Ken sips his beer. "I tried a number but the line was disconnect."

"I know a Paulo but he don't come around here."

"Huh." Ken looks at Joe, then back at Chris. "Heard this was the place."

"Heard wrong. You boys from out of town? You don't look familiar."

"We got some business." Ken pushes his hat up his brow.

Chris glances over his shoulder. "Everybody's got business. Depends what kind."

"This is a big deal."

"Yeah, heard that one before. Heard this too: money talks, bullshit walks."

Ken nods. "A certain amount of cash is involved. The right man could be in on that, if he plays his cards right."

Chris leans forward. He's older than he looks at first sight. In his late forties. "Maybe I can make a call."

Ken nods. "Money in it for the right guy. C-note or two."

"Let me see. I'll make a call."

"You do that." Ken tips his beer glass at Chris. "Much obliged."

When Chris is gone he says to Joe, "We give him half an hour but no more. He's shifty."

"Didn't much like him." Joe taps his fingers on the table. "Good as said we were full of shit."

"We'll see. Shameless prevaricator."

Joe studies Ken for a moment. He clears his throat. "Don't like that, a man telling me I'm full of shit." Joe rotates his head on his shoulders, like a boxer in the ring.

"We give him half an hour." Ken glances at his watch. This is turning into a grey downer.

Across the room Georges is looking their way, shifting his eyes toward the toilets. They agreed not to make contact unless necessary. Ken nods at Joe. "Finish that glass," he says, "then get up slow and go into the toilets, tell Georges what's happened. Tell him to go easy on the beer. We have to stay alert. You hear? And no talking to anybody."

"Uh-huh. Got ya, Chief." Joe laughs, then adds, "Anyone ever call you that before?"

"Plenty. You?"

"Plenty also. And much worse."

Ken studies the bar. There's a guy with a brush mustache on a bar stool across from the neon Schlitz sign, looks like an off-duty cop. Two men in ball caps are engaged in conversation at the far end of the bar, from time to time the bartender stops and joins them. Everything is a bit blurry. Ken is exhausted, hasn't really slept since the break-out, more than two days earlier. He watches Suzie scooting about the room, taking orders, plunking beer down on tables, kibitzing with patrons. He looks toward the end of the bar. No sign of Chris.

When Joe returns, he sits down heavily before speaking and when he does he leans toward Ken and says under the hubbub in the bar, "Georges says Barry is about to pass out. Muttering dumb things and calling out. There's a hotel attached to the tavern, the Baltimore Hotel, Georges says we should get a room, let Barry sleep."

"Not a bad idea. Get the kid out of the public eye." Ken checks his watch. Somehow more than an hour has passed. It's 9:30. He's worried about that Chris, a fishy character.

Joe shifts on his chair. "'Nother round?"

Ken shakes his head. What's taking so long? He taps the tabletop with his fingers.

Joe swallows the last of his beer. Glances around. "Could use another."

"We're getting drunk." Ken blows out his cheeks. "Least I am."

Joe grunts. "Tastes good though. Been a long time, eh?"

"Better not. Dulls the thinking."

"Uh-huh. I'm thinking one more."

"And I'm thinking what's up with that Chris and his phone call?"

"Still, you know. Beer. Buh-eer. Been quite a while, eh?"

Something is wrong. Ken presses one hand on one knee. He checks his watch. He can hardly keep his eyes open. He looks toward the place behind the bar where Chris disappeared. No sign of him. Across the room Barry has put his head down on his arms, which are folded on the tabletop. Does it matter if they catch a few winks? Will much change if they start afresh in the morning? Ken is suspicious of Chris but he's totally pooped, he can hardly put two thoughts together. The beer, no sleep, the stress of flying for a full day, the sheer adrenaline of being on the run. It's been almost twenty-four hours since they left the farmhouse near Warren, a fitful, stressful day. He signals Georges to leave first. When he stands, he has to put one hand on the back of a chair to steady himself. Legs like rubber, a head full of cotton wool. At the door he glances quickly back into the room near the bar. Chris is on the phone, speaking with one hand cupped to the mouthpiece. When he sees Ken is watching him, he turns his back. I should check into this, Ken thinks, this is not good. But almost instantly the thought floats away on him, like a thought in a dream, if Joe were to ask him, What were you just thinking? he would not know how to answer, his mind flits here and there, backward in time and forward, the past confused with the present, butterflies of thought.

It's the only way out. You grow up in the run-down neighbourhood with the rusty spoon in your gob, you got few choices, knuckle under, do what you're told at school and everywhere after that, do what the bosses say, accept your position in society, don't try to better yourself, climb the ladder, which means eat shit and smile doing it. Crime is the only way out. It's a stacked deck, is the point. They all say it isn't, the celebrated American Dream, I seen that movie, I read that book, all horseshit, excuse the French. When you come from them circumstances, the system is stacked against you, whatever they say. So now the choices are, you gotta get lucky or you gotta get somewheres through criminal doings. And you don't dare fall foul of the law on your way, that's the kiss of death certain sure. Rocky knows it in the angels movie and it's what you take in with your mother's milk, if you come from a dirt farm or a shabby neighbourhood. Even if you try to climb the ladder their way, they kick you down, your only recourse is snatch and grab, it's been set up that way, it's worked that way long as anyone can remember. It was as true for the old-time highwaymen as it is today. You ain't complaining, you're just saying the truth of it, the life of crime is the poor kid's one chance so he has to grab at it. Rocky was right when he told the priest crime is the only way out for the dispossessed.

They take two rooms at the hotel, the Baltimore, narrow wooden staircase to the second storey, uneven floors, the smell of sweat and musty socks, the stench of piss. Two cot-like beds in each room, basin, dresser, a grimy window looking onto another grubby building with giant air vents on a flat roof. Ken cannot recall when he's last slept in a place so rundown. No matter, the bed looks inviting. Barry is sitting on the edge of one bed, smoking, shoulders hunched forward, muttering words Ken cannot make out, the pistol he's had with him all day next to his pillow, one foot tapping the floor rhythmically. Ken sits on the edge of the other bed. Decides against taking off his shoes, though his feet are hot and sweaty. He closes his eyes. He lifts his hat off his head but before he can put it on the wooden end-table, he hears Georges at the door. "Cops!" He bangs once hard. "There's cops all over. Kennet. It's a set-up!"

"Jesus." Ken jams his hat back onto his head.

"Kennet, you hear? That *maudite* Chris. *Batard!* He betrayed us!"

"Bastard." It flashes through Ken's mind that if he hadn't been so tired he would not have let things happen this way. He's screwed up.

"Kennet! *Merde!*"

"I hear you, Georges." Ken is on his feet. He looks at Barry. "C'mon. We gotta move."

Barry stays put, blows smoke into the air. "Fuck it."

"Gotta move." Ken has his hand on the doorknob. "C'mon, kid. There's a back stair."

"Forget it." Barry pushes the gun under the pillow.

"Jesus Lord, c'mon, kid." Ken tugs at Barry's sleeve. "We got no time."

"Fuck off!" Barry jerks his arm away. "You always gotta be givin' orders. Makin' your calculations. I ain't listening no more."

"Jesus, Barry, we still got a shot, see, you—"

"I ain't takin' no more orders. No more orders. From you, from Georges. That's it. Finish."

"We can get out the back way. C'mon."

"You go. You're the smart one. You got all the bright ideas. Go."

"Jesus." Ken reaches across Barry's inert form. "Give me the gun at least."

"Piss off." Barry sighs deeply and drags on his cigarette, flops onto the bed. Groans.

Ken has the gun in his hand. He glances back at Barry, shakes his head. Bringing the kid was a mistake, one of many. He bangs the door shut behind him, then knocks on the door of the other room, 236. "Georges, it's me, Ken." He pushes the door open. It's dark inside, the light has been shut off. At the far end of the room stands Georges. His pistol is pointed at Ken. His hand is steady but sweat glistens on his brow. He looks sick and done in, roughed up. Behind him the window is open. Joe is not in the room.

"Put that down." Ken's voice sounds weak.

Georges waves the muzzle. "Get out the door, Kennet. Get out the way, now."

Joe's face appears suddenly behind Georges. He's outside at the window, standing on a ledge. "Christ," Ken yells. "Get back in here!"

"I'm not going back." Joe's words echo in the little room.

"There's a back stair." Ken tips his head in that direction. "I figure we can—"

"Me neither." Georges waves the pistol at Ken, motioning him away from the door. "Not going back. Not never." The muzzle is pointed right at Ken's head. "Get out the way."

"Jesus." Ken throws his gun on the floor. "Georges, this is no way."

"They don't take me alive." The pistol is steady but Georges's eyes dart about the room.

"There's a back stair, see, there's still time to—"

Behind him a harsh voice yells, "You in there, come out with your hands up!"

Joe's face disappears.

"This is the police. We've got your pal. Come out now."

Ken turns. The door is partway open but whoever called out is standing to the side. Ken is at a loss. They can't run. The cops have got Barry Duke already. What to do? The window is a crazy idea. He's turned his head from Georges to the door. There's the crack of a pistol shot. Ken drops to the floor. Smoke is coming out of Georges's pistol. There's another shot. Two more. Georges cries out. "*Merde!*"

"Stop!" Ken is on the floor, flat out. In the silence that follows he calls out. "Stop shooting!"

The voice from the hall is loud and brutal. "Come out. Now. You're under arrest."

"I'm clean." Ken smells cordite in the air. His heart hammers in his chest.

"Come out now. Chuck the weapons first. Hands in the air."

Ken sweeps the pistol near to him into the gap at the door.

"All the weapons!"

Ken scrambles onto his knees. "I'm coming out." He's on his feet. One leg gives way and he grabs the door jamb to keep himself erect. That first shot Georges took whizzed by his head, only inches away. He prays Georges does not fire again. But he does not look back.

In the hallway a burly man grabs his arm and drags him away from the doorway. There are two men to each side of the door. Guns levelled at the door. Farther down the hallway are state troopers with semi-automatic rifles, barrels pointed at Ken, fingers on triggers. More cops with sawed-off shotguns crowd the hallway, some with tear-gas masks around their necks. Ken feels sweat running down his cheeks. The cop next to him is chewing his lip. Outside a siren wails. In a room down the hallway a woman is screaming. Several doors down a man wearing only an undershirt peers out the crack of the door. The cop twisting Ken's arm is about to break it. Ken calls out, "I'm unarmed! Jesus!" One knee buckles, he senses he's about to pass out.

He is shoved aside. Another burly cop grabs him, twists one arm behind his back. For a moment his face is slammed against the wall, then the pressure is released and he's turned around. Ken is woozy but through the stars dancing in his eyes he sees Barry has been captured too. A state trooper wearing the kind of hat with a string that ties beneath the chin has him pinned against the wall near the stairway. Ken thought Georges and Joe would follow him out of the room but they haven't. The men at the door of 236 take a quick peek in, then duck their heads. "Shooter gone," one of them calls out.

"Shit," one of the troopers calls.

"Not down?" The guy who first called out to Ken seems to be in charge. He's wearing a white cap with a shield pinned to it.

"None down," a state trooper yells.

"Was one down," another voice calls out, "there was one down."

"None down," the trooper insists.

The guy in the white hat jabs Ken with a pistol. "How many inside? One? Two?"

Ken turns his face aside but refuses to speak. He's slammed into the wall again.

"Talk," the trooper shouts in his ear.

"I—got to—go to—"

"Fuck it." The cop jabs Ken in the ribs with the pistol, a lightning bolt of pain dances through Ken's spine. "Take these two away," the cop growls to the troopers who have collared Barry and Ken. They're shoved rudely down the stairs and through the lobby of the hotel. Above them Ken hears the sounds of boots running fast down wooden stairs, loud shouts. Another gunshot rings out, two more. Something above them falls over with a loud crash. Voices yelling. The sound of glass breaking. Someone shouts, "On the roof!" The sound of more glass breaking. Another shot.

Ken groans. "Guns," he says to Barry. "Jesus Lord. We never should have."

Outside a crowd has gathered.

"There they are."

"Bums," a fat woman right near Ken screeches at them.

"Bastards. Killers."

Someone calls out: "Hope you hang."

The crowd is maybe a hundred people, two and three deep at some places along the far curb, angry faces, fists in the air. A dog is barking. Kids screaming.

This is a black downer, the worst, a deep dark downer. Jet black. There is nothing gentlemanly about it, nothing smooth.

The cops force their way through the crowd pushing and pulling. "Stand back!"

Barry looks into the faces gathered near the cop cars. Some are smiling, others are staring blankly. "Give us a cigarette."

A man with a cane is gesticulating at them. "There were more. Four or five."

"Send 'em back where they come from."

"Give 'em the needle in the arm."

"Give us a cigarette." Barry's wail is desperate.

Ken looks around, amazed at the crowd, the noise. A shiver of fear runs up his back. Is someone in the crowd stupid enough to rush at them with a knife or pull out a gun? Barry has no idea what is happening. The cops would not care. Good riddance. They agree with the enraged voices in the crowd, good riddance to bad rubbish. Ken and Barry could be the guys who shot the state trooper. They deserve to die.

Ken groans. A black hole downer. There's a kind of fog in the air, maybe vehicle exhaust, and it's trapped a sour smell, like the effluence from a pulp mill.

The cop continues shoving. "Keep moving." Ken's wrists are manacled together, the cop behind him puts pressure on the cuffs by jerking upward, taking Ken's breath away.

"Barry," he calls out. "Stay calm, kid."

The yellow and blue lights on top of squad cars lend the night an eerie aspect. Cops are crouched behind squad cars with automatic rifles aimed at the hotel. A spotlight plays on the hotel and the nearby buildings. Cops and cop cars are everywhere, parked at angles, tilted up on sidewalks. Radios crackle. Some of the cops have walkie-talkies. Farther down a guy in a SWAT team uniform has a tear-gas gun. He fires it toward the roofs of the buildings. Once, twice. Smoke drifts off the roof and down into the street. When the spotlight plays through it, the street becomes the scene in a science-fiction movie. People put handkerchiefs over their mouths. Ken feels the tear gas in his nose, then in his eyes. An alarm goes off, clanging loudly from somewhere nearby. Someone yells, "The jewellery store! The bank." Part of the crowd breaks off and runs toward a side street. Troopers who were standing near squad cars run ahead of them, rifles at the ready. A cop is shouting into a bullhorn.

Ken studies the mob. They're angry but they don't seem vicious. Probably just letting off a little steam. Barry and Ken and their escorts make their way forward. As they break through the crowd, a cop jumps out of a squad car near to them and throws open one door. Ken stops before it. His skull clangs with headache.

From the mob a voice yells, "What's they done?"

"Robbed a bank."

"Good on 'em. Bastards, are bankers."

"Shot a trooper. Up in Canada."

"Killed a Mountie," a voice calls out. "It's on the news."

Ken shouts back, "We're not mad-dogs, we've hurt no one."

"Cigarette," Barry shouts. People laugh.

Someone yells, "Give the man on his way to the chair a smoke!" From the crowd come cigarettes, thrown like pencils. They flutter in the air and drop at Ken's feet. Nervous laughter from the crowd.

"Don't smoke," Ken yells. "Bad for the health." The crowd laughs again.

Voices call out: "What'd they do?"

"Bank robbers. Murderers."

Ken shouts again. "We're not killers. We're just men who wanted our freedom." The crowd is surging this way and that. Barry and Ken bump together. Ken raises his voice. "Same as you."

His words are lost in shouts and catcalls.

"We're citizens," Ken insists. "Law-abiding. We didn't want no trouble."

"Not like us at all."

"Bastards, bankers."

"Give us a cigarette," Barry calls out.

A kid darts out of the crowd, snatches a cigarette off the ground, and shoves it in Barry's mouth. A cheer goes up from the crowd. A cop chases the kid away. The crowd jeers.

Ken feels a cop's hand on his neck, pushing down. "We never hurt no one."

Someone at the back of the crowd yells in a strained tone. "Why the big fuss, then!"

Ken calls back. "No one was hurt!"

Barry is pushed into the squad car first, then Ken. The door slams shut behind him. The alarm continues clanging. Ken sits in the back seat of the squad car. The clang of the alarm competes with the clang in his skull. Troopers and cops mill around. Some are wearing gas masks and look like movie creatures from Mars. Tear gas floats through the air, giving the street an unearthly appearance. It stings Ken's eyes, but he cannot rub them because his wrists are shackled. Barry is coughing past the cigarette in his lips, even the cop up front is breathing hoarsely. In a brief moment of silence Ken hears another shot ring out, then two more. The cop cocks his head toward the sounds. For a minute Ken has a déjà vu-like experience: who is this Barry, who is he, who is the cop, where are they? Ken seems to be looking at himself from the outside, as if he were an actor in a movie, someone Ken does not know or understand. How did he come to be here? He coughs and then clears his throat. In a few minutes Georges is brought out of the hotel, he's bleeding, a cop has wrapped a towel around his arm and is holding it firmly as he pushes Georges ahead of him, his other hand clamped to Georges's neck until they come to the back door of an ambulance. Georges is shoved rudely through the doors. Ken looks at the sky. The stars are out, a crescent moon. Suddenly the alarm stops. For a moment the blood surges in Ken's ears, replaced by the hubbub of the crowd and the throb of headache. Individual voices have lost their distinctness. The radio in the squad car crackles. He hears his name spoken loudly by a woman, someone mispronounces *Winnipeg*. Ken tips the brim of his hat down and closes his eyes. It's a bad dream but he's not going to wake up from it and feel better.

Saying you never hurt anyone made no difference. It was true, though. From the furniture store onward every bad thing you did was done with clean hands. You loaded the furniture in the back of a truck and drove off, being careful to lock the store door behind you. It was easy and it was nonharmful. The company didn't even make the robbery public. Not the first one. Same with the Toronto banks. You sat with the bank managers and reasoned with them. They agreed with what you said. No point in playing the hero. You promised there would be no shooting and there wasn't, you said no one would be hurt and you kept your word. The Gentleman Bandit, the newspapers called you. Okay, sending a Christmas card to the first bank saying *From a Satisfied Customer* was cheeky. But no harm was done. It made no difference in the eyes of the cops—or in the way the prosecutors and judges came down on you. *Criminal, public danger, hooligan, ruffian.* These words applied to killers, to thugs who busted into banks and slugged tellers over the head, knife wizards, rapists. You were none of these, you did none of these things, you were polite and gentle, and people warmed to you and called you Ken, and thought of themselves as your friend, even though you had robbed them or hijacked their car. Amiable, that was what one reporter called you, the cordial crook. They praised your demeanour, they approved of you. You liked people and they liked you and you were always straight with them about how what you were doing was only business. Left-handed business, but business nonetheless. If people did as instructed, they would not be hurt. And you hurt no one. Not entirely true. You hurt Elva, you hurt the kids, and in hurting them you hurt yourself. But that was in the personal sphere, not the sphere in which you plied your trade, that was your private cross to bear. For that you should have been chastised, castigated, for that jail time was a worthy outcome. But you did not hurt anyone any more than an embezzler does, you were clean in a way, you never once fired a gun, women especially liked you because, they said, there was gentleness in your eyes, but that did not matter, they threw the book at you, they slammed the door behind you as hard as possible, clang, no more gentleman bandit, no more Ken Leishman. *Finito*.

Bullets end manhunt

Roof-top gun chase: escapee in hospital

You're awake. How long have you been awake without knowing it? You keep your eyes closed, you have one elbow crooked over them to block out the light. Maybe this time you will fall back into sleep. Breathe deep. Listen to your heart, feel the deep, deep surge of blood, ride that slow surge back into dreams.

No, not this time. You open your eyes. Light is coming in from the corridor, there are shadows on the ceiling. You're in a room within a room within a room. Again. The lockup, the can, the joint. A fly is buzzing against the window screen. The grunts and snores of other men. Dirty cons. Why can't you sleep?

You are not who you thought you were. You thought you were a good man, at heart. You would have said of yourself, a good man at heart. A man who wanted to succeed, who made mistakes, who did dumb things in order to succeed. Some of those things made you a bad man in the eyes of some people. And maybe you were. You wave a gun in another man's face, you cannot maintain you're a good man. Not wholly. So you're a bad man, or at least a not-so-good man. You thought you were a good man but you aren't. You thought you were X but you're actually Y. Is this why you cannot sleep? Is this why you wake with a start and spend half the night looking at the ceiling?

"So you can't sleep?" The psychiatrist is sitting on the opposite side of a desk, fiddling with a file folder. He wears a wedding band and a signet ring on the middle finger of the other hand.

"I thought maybe there might be pills or something."

"Maybe. Not today. Today we're just going to talk."

"Hocus-pocus talk. Why I hate my mother. That kind of bullshit." Ken realizes he's been rubbing both thumbs and forefingers together and he places his palms on his knees. He's in a three-cup high, but it's jangly and awful, he's strung out.

"No. We are not going to talk about that, about why you want to kill your father and sleep with your mother, though in your case, Ken, that might turn out to be useful. No. We're just going to sit easy in our chairs and relax. You can take the big comfy chair behind you, if you wish. Get your butt off that hard plastic thing and into the soft, comfy chair. It helps a man to relax. Close your eyes. You can close your eyes, Ken. Think back to a time long before you were in here, cramped cell, stinky cons, crappy food. The horrid routine of the lockup. Put that all out of mind. Think back to that boy you were back there a long time ago who liked to… who liked to what, Ken?"

"Lie on his back and look at the clouds."

"Right. Big fluffy white clouds in a blue prairie sky. One looked like a plane, I bet."

"The silhouette of a horse's head."

"You like horses?"

"Always have. Dreamed of running my own spread, Herefords, horses, a kind of cowboy life. I liked the open prairie and riding a horse, the sun setting in the west, tumbleweeds blowing over the land, the big open sky. No one to answer to, no one's ass to kiss. Being my own boss."

"It was a nice place, a good time."

"The only time I was truly happy."

"See, this is easy. Now we're getting somewhere. Now maybe we will start to be calm inside. Now maybe the headaches will go away."

You find a place along the wall where you can sit down. Your head is buzzing, your eyes sting. You woke at 2:30 and did not sleep again. You close your eyes. Blood pulses in your throat, in the tips of your fingers. You did like to look at the clouds. Hours of lying in a field with a piece of straw in your teeth. Away from other kids and teachers, your grandparents. Even here in the lockup, relaxing against the exercise yard wall with your eyes closed, you can smell clover, hear birds in the field on the other side of the wall. This is good. Your heart has slowed. If you open your eyes you will see a blue sky and fluffy white clouds. You dare yourself to, you dare yourself to have a happy thought. You open your eyes and look upward. The clouds are black.

When the last has been coughed up, you turn on the tap and wash the green away, the bits of brown that stick to the sides of the white porcelain. You run a glass of water and rinse your mouth out, spit, you run another glass and taste the metal from the well, but the water is cold and you swallow it all back. Then you kneel and rest your head on the edge of the toilet bowl. The porcelain is cold, it numbs your temples, the surging blood of your temples slows. You could rest here a long time.

"You're falling, you say?"

"It's an elevator and it's out of control. Falling but not plunging, there's time to think, I know that when it hits the bottom I'll be killed. I put my hands on the walls. They're shiny metal, like stainless steel, smooth and cool to the touch.. Then the elevator flips upside down, my head is pointing down. Only I don't fall on my head, my feet are stuck to the roof somehow. If we hit bottom, the floor of the elevator will fold in like an accordion, my skull will be crushed. I will be dead. Then the elevator is back upright and it's moving somewhat sideways, kind of slip-sliding, I feel nauseous. I have to stop this dream, I say to myself, I force my eyes open."

"Scary stuff. What does it mean?"

"What does it mean? You're asking me? You're the shrink."

"You're the guy who's falling."

"Dunno. Some bullshit or other. I'm scared of falling?"

"A kind of falling."

"Kind of?"

"The final version of falling."

"Final? You think I'm scared about dying?"

"Hmm. It's like the one where you fall off the mountain and can see the ground below as it rushes upward to you. Rocks, a field."

"Rocks and a meadow covered with white flowers. In that one, if I keep falling I'll be killed when I hit the rocks. I'm kind of floating in the air, like you feel in a plane sometimes, drifting, but overall falling. I force myself to wake up. So I'm afraid of dying?"

"We're all afraid of dying. But you actually know in the dream that you aren't going to die. You can wake yourself up."

"So I'm not afraid of death?"

"Maybe. Maybe not. A kind of death."

"Kind of. You're jerking my chain here, doc. Is this a guessing game? You're supposed to help me get rid of headaches, not give me more."

"Umm. Have a sip of water, Ken, relax. Think of it this way. You keep having the one about drowning too. Your mouth is filling with water. You're choking."

"I can feel myself suffocating, and in a moment I won't be able to breathe. My mouth is filling with water, there's pressure in my chest. I have to wake up."

"And you do."

"It's all bullshit. Psychological hocus-pocus."

"You're the one with headaches. You're the one who can't sleep."

You sit with a book in your lap. The words jump on the page. You can't remember the last sentence that you read. The word *construction* looks like *constitution* and then *constipation*. It looks as if the words are typed on top of each other, superimposed. You laugh aloud. You close your eyes. They're stinging. Every afternoon they begin to sting and your head starts buzzing. You can't concentrate. You used to love reading. And writing. Even when you were a kid and you didn't score good grades, you were a good student, you gobbled up those sports books and adventure stories. You love words. Words and books created a special world you could enter, a world that was yours and yours alone. You look back at the book on your lap. The page is black.

You sit in the exercise yard with your back against the wall, sun on your face and it comes to you then, you feel tired, tired right into your bones, *knackered*, Charlie Feagle would have said. Dead tired. Yes, done in. Somewhere deep down inside. At the corner of your eye there's something hovering, a ghost or a demon, a shadow of a shadow of a thing and it makes you tired just to know it there, looming, a spectre. You cannot make out its features, it's not Elva, it's not the kids but it's like that, all of them in one, a ghostly and ghastly thing, it chills you and sets your teeth to chattering and you know it's the end of something, somehow, the end of the old Ken who cared and strived and had dreams and ambition and your teeth chatter and tears course down your cheeks.

He has a knife and sticks it into his temple. It has a short blade, a very thin blade, like a fish-filleting knife, and it slides into his temple. Right up to the hilt. A little blood oozes out. The pressure in his skull drops. Blood oozes along the blade and down his cheek. Thick, like chocolate, but red. The pounding in his skull eases. He slides the knife out, slowly at first and then quick right at the end so the wound closes fast. The pressure in his skull is gone, no more pounding, his thoughts are clear and calm.

You're awake. How long have you been awake without knowing it? You keep your eyes closed, you have one arm crooked over them to block out the light. Maybe this time you will fall back into sleep. Breathe deep. Listen to your heart, ride the slow surge of black blood back into dreams.

No, not this time. You open your eyes. Light is coming in from the corridor, there are shadows on the ceiling. A fly is buzzing against the window screen. The grunts and snores of other men. Cons. Why can't you sleep?

Who you are is not who you are. No. You are who you thought you are and yet also who you are not. You thought you were X. The good husband, the responsible father. But you're Y, the disgrace, the bum. You are X and Y. You thought you were X but you have become Y. No. You are X and Y at the same time. And Z. The boy who had dreams and ambitions, who loved the movies. You thought there was one you, then you thought the one you had become another you, but this is not how it is. You're many yous, X, Y, and Z, and A and C, too. You're Ken who gets along with the guard and Ken who could hit the guard over the head with a lead pipe and escape. You're Ken who loves to play with his kids on the floor and Ken who deserts them and is chucked in jail. It's like there are all these pieces of *Ken* and you can combine them on any day in any way to form a new *Ken*. You thought you were one thing, going down one path, but you're a collection of fragments, scattered—a broken thing.

"The headaches haven't stopped. It's all bull. Like I said."

"Umm. Have a sip of water, Ken. Relax."

"Calm down, relax, take it easy. It's all you ever say. I hate that. Been told that all my life. 'You got strange ideas, Ken, that's a stupid plan, Ken.' "

"You're right. That was wrong of me. That was a silly projection."

"I'm coming apart here. Discombobulated."

"You're on edge today. I can see that. Today is not the day."

"It's all bullshit and you're bullshit too." Ken studies his hands. He's been rubbing thumbs and forefingers together, the skin is cracked, blood is smeared on both thumbs.

"Maybe you should sit in the big chair. There's forty minutes left.

I've got paperwork to do. You can sit quiet and forget about all this. Just enjoy your own thoughts."

"Coming here is crap."

"You like that, don't you, just drifting off into your own thoughts? Musing, it's called."

"A waste of my time, doc. Yours and mine."

"There are magazines. You like sports, don't you, Ken?"

"Bullshit. I'm choking on it." Ken places his palms flat on his knees. Sighs.

"Exactly. You sit quiet and I'll do my paperwork. We don't have to go at this hammer and tongs. Drive ourselves crazy. We're not trying to get somewhere in a big hurry. The one thing we have, you and I, is lots of time."

Why do I say "he" instead of "I"? Why do I say "you" when I'm talking about "me"? It's as if I'm standing outside myself looking at myself from the outside, watching myself do things as if it was another separate person from me doing them. Not me at all, but someone I can watch in an uninvolved way, a character in a movie and I'm a spectator. Why do I flip back and forth from one to the other until I don't know which is which any more, as if it didn't make any difference which was which?

You're leaning against a wall in the exercise yard. A guard sidles over. They like you, you can talk about more than sports and Harley-Davidson motorcycles, you tell stories and jokes and laugh at theirs, you ask about their kids, what they do on weekends. The guard speaks to you but keeps his eyes on the other cons. "Another day in the swamp."

You scuff your shoe in the dirt. "Could use a cold beer, I'm not a drinker but I like a cold beer on a summer day."

The guard grins. "Me too." A lock of hair blows in his eye and he keeps pushing at it with one hand. "You still got them headaches?"

"Pounding in my temples. I think I'm cracking up some days. If there was a pill. If that head shrink quack doc would only give me a pill. I know they'd go away."

"There are pills. I can lay hands to them for you."

"I know them pills, I know what they do to you."

"This and that, red and blue. Yellow. You name the pill, I can get it for you. At a price."

"Price. Yeah. I know the price to be paid. Don't want those. Look at these guys. Half of them are so doped up they don't know their own names. Look. Zombies, their eyes roll in their skulls, spit dribbles from their mouths. They've lost the will to live. Not for this cowboy."

"It can help."

"Not for me. I want to stay sharp. I wanna get out of here some day. You take them pills, something inside you gives up, you don't give a shit anymore. You're dead inside, you may as well be dead. You're never leaving here."

"You change your mind, you let me know."

"No chance. But thanks anyhows."

"So you're saying I don't want to accept the death of the old me?"

"Something like that."

"It sounds like bullshit, doc."

"It's a hypothesis."

"Hypothecate? What the hell. And what does that have to do with anything?"

"Hypothesis, Ken. Theory."

"Bullshit. Why do I even bother? You tell me, head shrink, quack doc."

"You're the one who can't sleep at nights."

"It doesn't make sense. That I'd wish for my own death. What kind of crazy man does that there? The dreaming neither. Don't make sense. I try to make sense of it. But I can't puzzle it."

"We're dealing with stuff that goes a long way back, stuff deep inside you, we're asking, What does it mean to be you? Asking what the very idea of you is. That's what these dreams are all about, Ken. Who is Ken?"

"I feel like I'm going berserk."

"You're not. Here, take a Kleenex. It's not a way we're used to thinking. It takes a little time to become used to thinking this way. A little effort, a little trust."

"It doesn't make sense."

"Think of it this way. Not so much that you can't let the old you die, but more that you can't take on the new you. Say goodbye to the old, welcome the new."

"Oh, now, that's total bull."

"It's an old idea. Jesus said something like it. Put away the old self, put on the new."

"I never put much store in that church bull. And I don't buy it now neither."

"You will. Learn to trust yourself with yourself. You'll be surprised at what you find out."

Tonight it was *The Misfits*, Clark Gable, Marilyn Monroe, Montgomery Clift. We're all misfits, seemed to be the message. Everyone looked gloomy and talked in hushed tones, there were a lot of silences where people stared off into space. The horses were great, the rolling hills.

Marilyn Monroe. What a piece. You wouldn't throw her out of bed for eating crackers. Gable had put on weight, he looked tired. Too much booze, too much sucking young tit. Gable is dead now. But the horses. Magnificent. Even in black and white. The riding into the sun. Almost as good as flying. Last week it was one about a prostitute, this guy is on top of her and she's saying yes, yes, moaning, but all the time she's got one arm crooked behind his head and is looking at her watch. Jane Fonda, what a piece. Hard little tits, tight ass, tight everything. You still like the movies, the old thrill of sitting in the dark and looking at the images dance on the screen. But Gable is dead now, Marilyn Monroe. Bogart is dead. That's all over.

"The question is not that you got caught, Ken, it's that you got caught over and over again."

"Bad luck, you're saying?"

"Not exactly."

"I never seem to turn up nothing but bad luck. Story of my life."

"That's not exactly what I was getting at, luck."

"You're saying I can't find my way out of a room that's all doors."

"Not really that either. Here, move the comfy chair a bit closer so I can hear you."

"Well, what then?"

"Come at it this way. Try to look at it from the outside, Ken. Sometimes people do things with motives they don't even know they have. They want to fail, say. Get caught."

"No. Impossible. Why would I do that? I tried to rob those banks. I had every intention of succeeding, I wanted to have the money from the gold business to set myself up, me and my family. I was trying to get away with it. Sheesh. Doc, what kind of fool do you take me for?"

"But you got caught. For the third time. You must have known, down deep somewhere, that the odds of getting away with the gold heist were pretty slim. You're a smart guy, Ken, you'll admit the odds against you were high. Crapshoot high. And yet you walked right in there, doesn't that seem, well, odd?"

"Fools rush in kinda thing. Not too wise. Is that what you're saying?"

"And then you're hardly locked up in Headingley and pull off this breakout. Daring and really eye-popping, yes, grabbed the headlines across the country, but what were the chances of that succeeding? The real chances that you'd get away with it?"

"We had a shot."

"A shot at adding a pile of time to your sentence. It's almost as if... as if—"

"As if I didn't give a rat's ass? Well, maybe I don't. I been bottom of the pile all my life and I don't give a rat's ass sometimes. Truth be told."

"More than that. As if you sort of wanted to get caught, as if you had to bring shit down on yourself, Ken. Pardon my French."

"This is bull. Psychological bull. All I ever wanted, really wanted, was to get my feet on the ground. It was not some mysterious and stupid deep-down motive that did me in, the record did me in, it haunted me like a ghost. I couldn't never catch a break, you see. That's the real story, the whole narrative, doc."

"Yes. I see that. There's truth in that, to be sure. It's not a very forgiving system."

"It's a bent system."

"But to return to what I was saying, Ken, do you think it's even remotely possible that you wanted your actions to hurt someone, not to solve your problems? No, let me rephrase, hurt yourself, maybe, for letting others down, or to hurt someone close to you as well as solve your financial and other problems?"

"You mean get back at my granddad—or my father? Stick him in it, another Leishman in the way he stuck me in it when I was a kid? Make him read all those headlines with his name in them and hurt the way I once did because of what he did to me?"

"That kind of thing. Maybe you were trying to punish your—your own—"

"It sounds queer to me. Sick. I'm not a sick person, so don't try to lay that on me. I got headaches is all. What I need is some pills for them headaches. And to help me sleep in this godforsaken hole of a tank."

You lie in the dark, looking up at the ceiling, hands folded behind your head. How many more days? You begin to count backward from a possible release date, but then you give it up. Enough of that. Too many hours of your life you've made calculations and counted things up and where has it got you in the end? Wasted time, is all. Wasted energy. You listen to the grunts of other men, the sounds of a guy farting in a nearby cell, you smell the grungy feet of other cons, their sweat, you smell your own armpits. And the thoughts in your brain are suddenly swamped by a great darkness, an inky sea that obliterates everything it sweeps before it, and you roll over onto your side and try to burrow down into the thin mattress and your teeth chatter and you weep.

"You what?"

"Lawyer. Take the courses by correspondence. I'm a good student. I work hard."

"Umm."

"I'm smart, you said so. You did them tests. You were the one got me thinking about it."

"You are a good student. You did well. Exceptionally."

"But you don't think it's a good idea."

"I think—"

"A man's gotta go for it, that's what I think. A man's gotta take the bull by the horns. This is a great country, a land of opportunity. You just have to have initiative. Look at this K.C. Irving, now, the guy out in the Maritimes. K.C. Irving started from nothing and now he's a billionaire. Owns half of the Maritimes. He's a magnate, a tycoon, and all because of what? Because of he believed in himself. He showed a little gumption, a bit of initiative. That's what this here country was built on. Gumption."

"It's a good story."

"It's more than a story. It's the truth. It's the truth of a man who set his mind to a dream and had the determination, the personal presence, the willpower to achieve it."

"You need some luck."

"Certain sure, but I never had much good luck, truth be told. Can't count on that, luck. What you really need is will power and moxie. Set a goal and don't look back. That's the K.C. Irving story. And look at them Kennedys and the guy who started up Standard Oil. What's his name, now, J.P. Morgan."

"John Paul Getty. I think."

"No. You got the wrong end of the stick there, doc."

"Yes. J.P. Morgan was a banker."

"I was sure. But whichever. The point is about what it takes, gumption and self-belief."

"I believe you, Ken, don't get me wrong."

"But?"

"But. Well, it's an ambitious idea. Studying to be a lawyer. You're what—thirty-five? An ambitious plan."

"You don't think I got the brains, you don't believe I can do it? You think it's a stupid plan?"

"If anyone can do it, Ken, you can."

"I've always had the gift of the gab. Everybody says so. I think like a lawyer. Devious. I study the angles. You said that yourself. But now you say not."

"It's a big undertaking. Many courses. Tests, exams. It could take years. A long grind. Lots who start at the law school don't finish. It's not easy. It takes more than high test scores."

"You say I'm setting myself up. Setting myself up for a fall."

"Not exactly, that's not quite it."

"Dreaming too big a dream. Again. My imagination running away with me."

"Something like that. But, Ken, there are other options, alternatives."

"So you say."

"There are. Here's just one. You've flown hundreds of hours, thousands. You love planes and flying."

"And?"

"And—well—you could do that. Fly the big ones."

"You think I should try for a commercial pilot's licence?"

"You've flown the hours already. There are books to read, tests to pass, it's a sizeable undertaking. But in a year. With work. It's—it's an achievable goal. Well within reach."

"Yeah. Commercial pilot's licence."

"There are good jobs when you get out. Airlines."

"I could do that, doc, yeah. Fly. High in the sky."

"It's something you can achieve. An achievable objective. You've always liked flying. And when you're out of this place, practical. You can use it. Make a sound living."

"You're the smartest man in the room," Charlie Feagle said. "You take them tests you'll see. You're quick and you're shrewd." And you were. And devious. All the way back to when you were a kid in school. You'd look around at the kids at their desks and wonder why no one else knew the answer. Even the good kids, teacher's pet, the ones who got to dust the chalk brushes. Same wherever. No one figured out how to sell the cookware as fast as you did, the angles, the variations in the patter, the other peddlers followed the words in the book like a script but you came up with your own patter for each housewife. It was easy, you didn't understand why the other guys didn't do it, then one day it occurred to you, they didn't even see it could be done, they didn't have the smarts. It just came to you. Like how to do the bank in Toronto, how to snatch the gold at the airport, how to intercept the payroll courier on the way to the military base in Shilo. You had this thing. Other guys had big muscles or pretty faces but you had brains, you were smart, what they call a quick study. So why didn't it get you anywhere? Why were you always either on the verge of going under or in the joint? What were the good of brains if that's all they got you? Staring out from between bars half your life. That and headaches and nightmares and pounding in the brain that never ceased.

"Blackouts, doc. You heard me right: I said blackouts."

"Hmm, yes. Go on."

"Well, it's like this. I'm sitting in the yard gazing at the clouds or whatever and everything's good, I'm doing fine, and the next minute I wake up and I'm not sitting anymore, I'm laying on my side feeling woozy. You know, head buzzing, ears ringing, totally out of it."

"And nauseated? Upset gut?"

"Exactly. Like vomit, eh."

"And how long were you out, how much time—?"

"Who knows, doc. A minute, maybe a few minutes. Once I kinda cracked my skull."

"Well, that's no good."

"No it ain't. Got me a little bump just on the temple."

"But you weren't, ah, out for a long time. Just a minute or so."

"Scares the crap outta me."

"Hmm, no doubt. I was reading just the other day, if you've got diabetes, you can black out. Be subject to blackouts. They won't give guys long-distance driving licences who are diabetics. Heavy machine operators. Airline pilots. Not until they're on insulin for a while and stable."

"Diabetes? Me?"

"We could run some tests. Just as a precaution."

"I don't think so, doc, I don't think I got no sugar diabetes. It's just them headaches. If only you could give me a pill."

He plunges his head into a tub of ice water. It's cold on the skin, it starts to freeze, to turn numb, the throbbing in the skull subsides. The water in the tub washes his face, cools his eyes, the ice is cold in the back of the mouth. He is holding his breath and continues to do so while his heart slows. When he takes his head out, the throbbing in the temples will be gone, his thoughts will be cold and calm and clear. Palliated.

Ken is sitting on a bench with a magazine on his lap. He's in a concrete room, a room within a room within a room, a room from which there is no escape. Light leaks in from a tiny window. The concrete is damp and smells of must, soiled bedding, old socks. It's a place not unfamiliar. Stony Mountain Penitentiary. Ken puffs out his cheeks and breathes slowly in and out, willing the wall opposite, which has been creeping towards him all morning, to draw back. He closes his eyes and listens to the sublittoral hum of air ducts, of fluorescent tubing, willing his racing heart to match their steady pulse, to calm his flailing chest, knowing that when he opens his eyes the room will have closed in, that if he reaches out his hand he will be able to finger the rough concrete of the wall opposite with his trembling fingertips.

Ken has been locked up for nearly eight years. He's ten pounds lighter than when he was incarcerated, his hair has thinned further, there are dark pockets under his eyes and creases on his forehead. He's forty-three years old but could be mistaken for fifty-five. Ken glances at his watch. He's no longer as concerned about the passing of time as he was when he was younger, but today is a special day. It's May 3 of 1974 and tomorrow Ken will be released from prison. It has been a long eight years. It started in the pen in Prince Albert, Saskatchewan, but over time Ken finagled to be moved closer to his family in Winnipeg. He sent letters to members of parliament, he made appeals to cabinet ministers, wrote a letter to the editor. Ken has become something of an expert at using the system to his advantage. The move from Prince Albert to Stony is only one thing he has managed. He's become famous in the lockup for knowing how to manipulate and manoeuvre. He's a model prisoner and tuned himself into the sixties and the wave of liberalism sweeping North America. Police are not to be trusted, men should not be locked up like animals, rehabilitation works. Give a man like Ken Leishman another chance.

Some of the early years were dark. Moods, suicidal thoughts, long days spent staring at the walls. Not eating. Refusing to take exercise. Refusing to see visitors. Psychiatrists told him he was suffering depression. There were sleepless nights and longer nights when he was conscious half the time and in a grainy half-awake state for hours on end. And days that slipped away in a fog, days when he could not remember what time it was, whether he'd eaten, if he'd had a shit. Headaches. He lay curled in a fetal position in his cell and grew so cold he shook. He took pills. The headaches subsided but he was in a deep fog all day, listless, he lost the will to live. He went off the pills. He came out of the fog but headaches and nightmares returned.

Somehow he got through it. The letters from Elva helped, though their frequency dropped after the first year and he sometimes wondered if she hadn't made the break with him, was with another man, had papers from a lawyer ready to be served on him as soon as she got up the nerve. He could not blame her. He had failed her so often. She deserved better.

He dug in. Talked to the psychiatrists. He tried to follow what they said, tried to change the way he thought about things. About himself. He wondered if the word sociopath might apply to him, so he read about the psychology of con men. Was he one? He needed to make more of an effort to be normal. He befriended the guards. Took jobs around the prison. He took to reading again. A number of years ago he received his high school diploma after studying for matriculation by correspondence. He signed up for college courses. In the pen he was no longer known as The Flying Bandit, he was the Professor. No, Ken corrected, Doctor of Depravity. He joked with the guards, took his family for outings in the country when given day parole, picnics with his grandfather in Treherne. A prison counsellor told him his story was interesting, would be a big hit in the outside world, he should write it down. He's begun an autobiography. He writes poems and sends them to Elva. She says he should find a publisher. The magazine he has on his lap is *Business Week*. The college courses Ken took were in economics. He signed up for more at Red River. The professors tell him he's quick as well as dedicated and that he could complete a degree at the business school. He thinks he might do that, get a jump-start for once.

He's spent more than twelve years of his life in jail, at his age of forty-three almost one half of his adult life, 107,000 hours staring at concrete and listening to water taps dripping, smelling the repugnant odours of other cons, eating shit food, dreaming and scheming about what he will do when he's once again a free man. Lost time, according to Ken, time he has somehow to recover, a whole lifetime, to his way of thinking, that he and Elva must make up. He will never be able to settle accounts with the kids, which, when he thinks of it, sets his fingers to tapping. Best not thought about, then.

Elva smiles from ear to ear each time they meet. She's still his girl. She thinks they should start over again in a town far away from the city and its bad influence. Buy a small business, she can apply for a loan and with Ken's business sense they will do all right. Ken has his eye on an opening with a small airline operating out of northwestern Ontario. Bush pilots, single-engine aircraft, cargo to the north country and reserves, mercy flights to hospitals in Thunder Bay. The north is still the place he dreams of. Though he lost the fishing lodge, he has good memories of the trees and rocks, the people, the quiet and the beauty, it's a place where a man doesn't feel all hedged in by the crowds in cities, where laws and such aren't followed so strictly to the letter. He will learn to fly with pontoons and take over the business end of the small airline. Make a success of himself, make Elva and the kids proud. Kids. The oldest are in their teens, about to become adults. They'll be having their own kids soon enough. Grandpa Ken.

Searchers find Leishman plane

T here's a second when it seems everything is going to be all right after all, so Ken takes in a shallow breath of relief, but then he realizes it's a false hope, the sound of the wind has fooled him, and the plane tilts abruptly at an acute angle, tipping crazily, sideways, the wing in Ken's side view momentarily elevated above his head, it seems that they're going to flip, but then the plane rights itself. He puffs out his cheeks, holding in breath, then releases it slowly, keeping his heartbeat steady. The Piper Aztec hangs suspended on a wind current for a moment as if all power has gone out of the engine, then suddenly plunges thirty feet, a sudden punch to Ken's gut that takes his breath away. Whoa, he thinks. The nurse kneeling over the woman in the storage compartment behind him lets out a sharp call, "Oh, good heavens!" Ken keeps his hand steady on the stick, eyes focused out of the windscreen into the darkness where moments ago he was sure he'd seen the lights of Thunder Bay in the distance. "Don't let," the nurse behind him cries loudly, her words almost lost in the banging of wind on the plane's fragile body, "Don't let us go down."

"We're okay," Ken calls back. "We'll get through this. Hang in there. We're good."

But they're not, he fears. The little single-engine Aztec is going down. And he doesn't know why. And he can't do anything about it.

He glances up at the sky, a mass of black streaked with grey wisps, like cigarette smoke running through, but rushing at them, billowing in crazy swirls, creating that sensation you get when your car is stopped but the car beside it is rolling backward, and for a moment Ken thinks he will vomit.

At his elbow there's a sharp crunching, it sounds as if the door of the plane may snap open. Or a panel just behind him break off. Ken is glad he cannot see the wing or the plane's tail. Both must be bending to the point of popping. They're dropping too fast. The little Aztec might just explode into pieces. "Lord," Ken whispers under his breath.

"I'll try to bring 'er down," he calls over his shoulder. "Set 'er down on the highway."

This would be a good plan but Ken lost sight of the highway minutes ago and he has no idea where they are. The instruments have gone kerflooey, everything out the window below is a mass of swirling grey and black, the lights he saw earlier have disappeared, there's nothing below in any direction except inky blackness. If there were an open spot somewhere down there where a plane could put down, he would not see it. For a moment he wonders if he should risk dropping down a few hundred feet to risk a better view. Would that bring them too close to the treetops? Not according to the last altimeter reading, but what does that mean, that was minutes ago? His hand hesitates on the stick.

"I'll bring 'er down," he repeats, a shout that cracks his voice, "we're gonna be okay."

He's on a mercy flight from Sandy Lake to Thunder Bay. This is what he does now, steps in when regular pilots are unable to take on such flights—or more often when the weather is so bad it frightens them off. *Medevacs*, they call them, emergency flights. That's when the airline calls him, Sabourin Airways operating out of Red Lake Ontario, where Ken and Elva run the general store, the Trading Post, that's when they need him, when they're desperate and no one else will go. Put the call in to Ken. He doesn't mind. He gets to fly, he gets to do the one thing he's always loved doing. And playing the Soaring Samaritan, as Elva puts it, instead of the Flying Bandit, doing good now for other folks, the solid citizen. He loves feeling the throb of the engine through the floorboards under his feet, he loves being free in the air. Flying high in the sky is the life he was made for. Isn't that what he's always told Elva?

Today is different, though, December 14, 1979, a bitter cold day in the north, and one turning odder by the minute. Today is a day of mild terror bleeding into greater terror, sweat in the armpits, trembling forearms, thumping heart. Wildly tumbling thoughts about Elva and the kids. A day when a single-engine is not a great place to be in the dark with no instruments and no radio, and no notion where you are. Today is a day when Ken thinks he may die.

He's had them before. He and Elva have lived in Red Lake for almost half a decade. It's a bizarre turn of events that they've ended up running the general store in the very town from which the gold was flown to Winnipeg in 1966. Almost more than Elva can bear to think of. "Ken, Ken," she said, when she added it up one day after they'd been in Red Lake a few weeks, "this is just too crazy, this is madness." Her voice had that sing-song quality he fell in love with so many years ago, amazement at the ways of the world, wonder, a depth of wide-eyed wonder that matched her wondrous red hair and made Ken want to hug her.

"It's a Ken Leishman turn-up," he said to her, laughing, wishing he himself could share that quality of wonder.

"It is, Ken, it's a flying bandit turn-up."

Ken the solid citizen, Ken the good man. The folks in Red Lake have taken to him, hardly a surprise, he's always had the gift of the gab, he's always cut a fine figure. And he's a celebrity of sorts. He's the president of the Chamber of Commerce. Folks on the street can say to visitors, "You see that guy in the hat on the other side of the street, why, he's the Flying Bandit—you never heard of the Bandit, the great gold robbery of 1966, well let me tell you…" Ken is a legend. And he's adding to the legend by taking on hazardous rescue missions and returning home unscathed. Like an old Greek god or something.

Yes, there have been scary days in the air before. Once he had to land on a frozen winter road that connected two Native towns, usually separated by water and swamp, thumping and bumping to a halt against pines, a broken wing, a cracked propeller blade, a few scratches to his face, lacerations they said at the hospital. It's the name of the game when you're a bush pilot, put your life on the line, cast your fate to the wind. Literally, Ken thinks, and he snorts, literally cast your fate to the wind. Behind him both women are breathing heavily, short gasps, the patient in pain, the nurse frightened, though trying not to show it. They're both Native, the patient a woman who broke her hip on a trapline, who needs hospital attention in Thunder Bay, the nurse a largish, mothering type who has kids of her own, she told Ken. It's those kiddies Ken is thinking about. For some reason he begins to trip the names of his own children off his tongue: LeeAnne, Wade, Ron. He knows why. It's only days before Christmas and he wanted to do something special for them, part of the strategy he's worked on these past half-dozen years to make things up to Elva and the kids for all those lost Christmases, lost birthdays, lost years. But if the Aztec goes down, it will be another Christmas of disappointment for them. He'll be a failure again.

"Hang in there," he calls out again, a little more loudly, almost fiercely, "we're gonna make it." Though his words, even in a half-shout, are lost in the rattling of the Aztec's whipping fibre panels and juddering windows and rattling floorboards. A sudden lurch downward jolts him back into the seat, knocking his elbow wickedly against the door and his fur hat askew.

Reflexively Ken puts his mittened hand to his brow. He's sweating, his body is reacting, despite what he's repeating to himself. Don't be afraid. Stay calm. You've been through this before. But the body knows better. It senses it's about to cease to be. He half expects to freeze up suddenly, the way a deer about to be brought down by wolves will become paralytic in the final moment. Ken puffs out breath again. There's a sweet taste in his mouth. He's bitten through his lower lip. He tries to swallow down the blood.

"What the hell is going on?" he mutters under his breath. "Lord. What is happening here?" He has to will his hands to stay locked on the stick.

They drop through another air pocket, this drop longer, maybe twenty seconds, and as they hit the bottom, the wind slams the underside of one wing, the little Aztec tilts so abruptly that Ken momentarily thinks they're upside down, like when you lose balance and tumble off a horse, feet up and head down, a metal box beside him flies against the passenger door with a loud crack, some piece of equipment the nurse has been holding over the injured woman clatters onto the floorboards. "My God!" the nurse screams. Ken wants to reassure her but he's hanging on to the stick with both hands so tightly that his neck and back feel as if they're in a vise. A jolt of pain races down his spine and into his leg, turning it abruptly numb. And his mouth has gone totally dry, tongue stuck to palette, so he can hardly swallow. But he can taste the blood.

Are they upside down? No. But the sky is a uniform inky mass, up could be down, left could be right, Ken feels vomit rising in his gullet. He hears the nurse behind him suddenly retch.

Hang on, he'd like to say. But he cannot.

"We're going down," he whispers to himself. "Jesus. Elva. We're going down. This is it."

Under my breath I whisper, *what will be will be*, but I'm not sure it's the way anyone can actually feel in the moment before their death, all quiet acceptance in the face of the inevitable with hands folded in the lap 'cause you know you're joining Jesus in heaven. Grandma was full of that kind of talk come Sunday morning in the parlour but she howled out like Satan his own self on her death bed, *Jesus, Jesus*, it's only natural, no one can blame that irregardless the claims was made beforehand. That acceptance bit is a philosophy, Charlie Feagle told me about it and then I looked it up in a book, there's lots of time to ponderate stuff like that there when you're in the slammer staring at four concrete walls sixteen hours a day. Stoicism, it's called, that particular philosophy, taking what's given you and making the best of it despite it's a shovel full of shit thrown in your face on your birthday or however may be. That's a good one, that philosophy, if you come from poor folks, also for putting in long days in the clink. *Que sera, sera*. Stoicism. I took it to mean no use bucking the system, but it's one hard lesson to learn.

There's one philosophy where you try to do good to other folks and humble yourself before them like certain types of churchgoers, I never had much time for that one myself. Also denying the self worldly pleasures, also hedonism, another fancy word for the old snatch-and-grab that drives most folks to do what they do including kicking their neighbours in the teeth if that's what's called for. And a bunch of others, the Greeks had names for every attitude a man can adopt on the heady subject of the life and death of the barnyard pig, as the fella says, they must have had a lot of time in them bygone days for sitting around discussing such matters to come up with so many sophisticated distinctions.

Fancy philosophies with high-class labels, what do they all amount to in the end, posh talk about why you do what you do, what good does talk like that do for a man in the end?

I'm scared. There I've gone and said it. Took me a whole lifetime to get the words out of my mouth. All that need to get somewhere, all that swagger, all the bullshit and the derring-do, everything I done to prove I was a somebody, it came down to I was scared of life and trying to prove myself. All I wanted was for people to say I was okay, the way a father or mother would, and I grew up without neither to say it to me so I craved to hear it, I wanted to hear that so bad. I needed approval. It's what the psychiatrists were trying to tell me, and Elva too, she understood me like no one else ever did. If only I'd been able to see it before.

I was faking it. To the rest of the world and to myself. I see now that there's basically two types of folks in this crazy mixed-up world and you can attach whatever sobriquet you care to but irregardless it comes down to them that puts thinking first and needing second and them that does pretty much the opposite. Thinking things out with a clear head, I always believed that was me, the sober type who considered this and weighed it up against that and then did the logical thing, the thing that made the most sense. I prided myself on that, being the man who measured things up and acted in a measured way, as the fella says, the rational type that can be counted on. Yeah. But looking back at my life, my career, as they say, I see I was actually doing the opposite much of the time, headstrong when it came to getting what I wanted and wild in a hurry to show I was the best, ditching the steady job at Tommy's Meats to gain the approval of my father, dumb, impulsively stupid where the truly rational man, Charlie Feagle, say, would of studied into things farther before he acted and maybe wouldn't of acted at all. Robbing banks and such like. Kind of drunk but without the whiskey, crazed with lust for money and fame is how it looked, but it really was for approval. So that was me. Ambitious, it's called in nicer circles. Driven by this aching need. A far cry from accepting whatever comes your way, you give it any thought. A gambler's mentality, and I never believed I was much of a gambler, I hated playing cards and rolling dice and had no use for the ponies but here all along I was gambling for bigger stakes, gambling with my life and the life of my wife and kids, risking it all the way a man of sense would never have done.

You'd have to say I was a bit of a fool.

So much left undone, so much that could have been done. Ken is thinking these words as he grips the stick, repeating them to himself, a kind of mantra he cannot let go of, like sticking the end of his tongue into a cavity until it bleeds. The Aztec is tilting wildly now, first one wing dipping, then the other. Saliva runs out of Ken's mouth and dribbles down his chin, he can taste blood, he can taste his own death. He steals a desperate glance out the window. The highway should be down there but they're off course, the highway could be anywhere. And he would not see it if it were. But it's not. Over the past few minutes the plane has been blown eastward, he thinks, away from Thunder Bay, a slow drifting arc, taking them farther and farther off course. This is what Ken cannot understand. They were so close. At 8:25 he was in radio contact with Thunder Bay, telling them he'd be arriving in five minutes, to have the ambulance ready. He was sure he saw the city lights glowing in the distance.

Then his own lights went out. The engine stayed on, miraculously, roaring away in the housing up front, but the lights of the instrument panel went, the radio, it was as if the electricals just shut down. There had been a warning. About twenty minutes back the lights in the cabin had flickered briefly but they had come back on almost immediately. But there was a smell in the cabin, a faint whiff like burnt cordite that dissipated within seconds. A warning Ken did not take. He can manoeuvre the stick a bit but the hydraulics have been affected, it's not possible to do much, what with the winds buffeting the plane and the little machine's natural inclination to follow the pull of gravity downward. They're lost and they're in very serious trouble. Steadily the plane is losing altitude. It's going down. He knows it and the nurse crouched behind him knows it. "Oh God," she moans from time to time, "Oh Jesus God, save us."

Ken has given up trying to reassure her. "Elva," he whispers. He always told her he wanted to go this way, flying, but now that it's happening he's wishing it wasn't so, he realizes what folly it is. He wants to live. There's so much that he didn't do for her. All those years wasted in the slammer. All those hours and days and months and minutes when she waited for him, held the fort, raised the kids, worked at crappy jobs as a waitress, all those years he's never been able to make up to her and now never will make up to her. He thought there would be plenty of time. He's only forty-eight. He's not even going to make it to fifty. Elva. Kids. In a half-whisper he mutters, "Forgive me." She always did, she always has, but what was her reward?

She wanted a house on the river, a house along Henderson Highway with a big yard. But instead he bought a place in River Heights because that's where he thought they should live, where he should live, a man on the way up. She wanted Kildonan Drive, on the river, a yard big enough so that she could have a garden, like when she was a girl in Somerset and grew tomatoes and a flower bed, but he thought that was below her, gardening, it reminded him of grunt work he'd done for his relatives. Elva was too good for grunt work, so he bought a house in River Heights. He bought what he thought she should have wanted not what she did want. Ignorant. Arrogant. He was a terrible husband. But she stood by him. The good wife. He should have taken her to Europe. All her life she wanted to go to Europe and he'd said, "What, Europe, the Rockies aren't good enough, Niagara Falls?" But he'd never taken her there either. She'd had a teacher in Somerset who was French, she taught Elva some words of French, she filled her head with ideas of Paris, Elva was in love with the idea of Paris, it was the one city she looked for in all the movies he dragged her out to. And he had been a shit about it, he had scoffed. He'd said, "Paris, Rome, we'll get there. Yeah, count on it." But he hadn't meant it and it had hurt her. Her dreams. Dashed. Second fiddle to his ambitions. So much left undone.

With the kids too. Birthdays missed, Christmases with no presents.

There's a sharp crack to Ken's rear and he shoots a look backward. Maybe a side panel of the plane's body has broken or broken loose. It's dark back there, he sees nothing except dim shadows and the ashen face of the nurse, looking at him out of round black eyes, imploring. The other woman seems to be gurgling, trying to say something. Ken closes his eyes for a moment. Is it better to go down in a ball of flame and die instantly or to be thrown out of the aircraft when it crashes, break limbs and expire slowly in the snow? He heard a story once about a trapper who fell and shot himself and whose arm was being gnawed by wolves before a fellow trapper came upon them and shot the wolves. Did the guy survive? Ken cannot recall. Being gnawed to death seems a grisly way to go. He thought wolves would go for the jugular but maybe the guy had a stick to beat them off. So, better to go up in a ball of flame. But not much better.

The plane suddenly drops and Ken's heart shoots into his mouth. There's a loud piercing crunch. Have they hit a treetop? Ken pulls hard on the stick but the plane won't go up, instead it slews sideways into an arc, nose pointing down. Ken feels his bowels loosen. He saw a plane go into free fall at an air show once, plummeting like a stone dropped off a bridge, the pilot pulling it out just above the treetops, wonderful, but that was on a sunny day with no wind, the Aztec is pitching forward in herky-jerky leaps, his vision is a blur, the plane is a corkscrew. They're going down. Ken is surprised the little engine hasn't stalled. But they're going down. It's only minutes until they hit the tops of pines or smash into the ground. Let it be a flat spot, Ken prays, let it not be jagged rocks that smash limbs and crush bone. Stupid thinking. One second alive, the next dead in the snow.

Maybe it's for the best. Some men can grow old with dignity, can dodder to the wheelchair and the cane, stumbling along to the final reckoning. But that was not the Bandit, his style was the style of youth, the smart black mustache, the swagger, hat cocked at a jaunty angle. The style of the matinee idol was the Bandit's style. He was not made for false teeth and the seventy-year-old shuffle. Maybe it's fitting he go down in a blaze, he was not the one born to die in bed.

But it's sad, yes, another Christmas that didn't work out for the kids, another failure.

The boys will come looking. He knows it. They're good kids though he's been a rotten dad. They'll come looking. They won't rest until they've found the plane, until they've found whatever is left of him. The Flying Bandit, the legend. He'll be gone but they'll keep looking, it's a heartwarming thought, Ken feels a lump in his throat. He'll be gone, dead, but there will be those who claim the crash was a ruse, a way for the Bandit to slip out from under the law and pull another heist, some crazy Mexican scam, he's always been a schemer, and they'll want to believe the legend goes on, everyone knows about that missing little bar of gold, worth $50,000, they say, enough to start all over in the deep south, pull some derring-do, but the truth is he's gone straight, Ken is no longer the dashing Bandit, he's just a middle-aged guy with a pot belly and thinning hair who wants to be a solid citizen, who wants to do the right thing, who wants to make up all his stupid mistakes to his wife and kids. They're good kids and he's been a rotten dad. Kids? They're grown up now and have made him a grandpa many times over. Grandpa Ken. He'll never see those little tykes again, bounce those giggling warm bodies on his lap, sing them the songs of his childhood, wipe their tears. Jesus. Elva. So many mistakes, so much you should have had and seen.

Ken closes his eyes. He knows what's coming. His mouth opens but no sound comes out. In a moment something will hit the undercarriage, an inevitable blow, but Ken refuses to think about that. Instead he rehearses the words of his favourite poem: "I know that I shall meet my fate somewhere in the skies above…" He conjures up a farm boy lying in a field with a straw in his teeth, fluffy white clouds rolling across a big blue prairie sky, the sun's golden hue spreading across the vista, crickets chirring in ditches, crows flapping over alfalfa fields, a horse nickering in the distance. Ken refuses to open his eyes, he sees the prairie fields from the perspective of a plane in midsummer, a patchwork of yellow, green, black, and brown fields, the sky stretching endlessly from one horizon to the other, his youthful face peering down, distant and beyond, he sighs aloud, then murmurs in a trembling voice, "somewhere in the skies above," and he smiles.

Ken Leishman: Chronology

1931   born near Holland, Manitoba to Irene and Norman Leishman

1930s   lives with, works on farms of various relatives in Manitoba

1945   employed as butcher's apprentice at Tommy Reece's butcher shop, Treherne

1947   employed with father Norman at elevator maintenance, Winnipeg

1950   25 February: marries Elva Shields of Somerset, MB

1950   March: arrested for break, entry, theft at Genser's furniture warehouse, Winnipeg

1950   serves four months of nine-month sentence at Headingley Correctional Facility, MB

1950   LeeAnne, first of seven children born to Elva and Ken Leishman

1951   employed installing and servicing combine cutters at Machine Industries, MB

1952   learns to fly single-engine aircraft; buys an Aeronea single engine

1952   employed selling Queen Anne Cookware, Winnipeg

1952   charged with flying without a licence; receives suspended sentence

1953   acquires interest in hunting/fishing lodge near Swan River, MB

1957   Queen Anne Cookware ceases business; unemployed

1957   17 December; robs branch of Toronto Dominion Bank, Toronto, ON

1958   17 March; caught in act of robbing branch of Bank of Commerce, Toronto, ON

1958   sentenced to twelve years' imprisonment at Stony Mountain Penitentiary, MB meets Harry Backlin, lawyer, while imprisoned

Acknowledgements

I am indebted to the following persons: Sandra Pomes-Bohay, LeeAnne Leishman Dewsnup, Brent Lougheed, Paul Grenkow, and to the following sources: Norma Bailey, *Ken Leishman: The Flying Bandit*, Frantic Films, 2004; Max Haines, the *Winnipeg Sun*, 13 February, 1983; Stanley Handman, *Weekend Magazine*, V8 #29, 1958; Bob Holliday, the *Winnipeg Sun*, 3 August, 2003; Heather Robertson, *The Flying Bandit*, James Lorimer & Co., 1981; Chuck Thompson, the *Winnipeg Sun*, 21 June, 1987; Charles Whibley, *A Book of Scoundrels*, E.P. Dutton, 1912; the *Winnipeg Free Press* Archives, Winnipeg Millennium Library; the *Winnipeg Tribune* Archives, University of Manitoba.

Thanks to the staff at Turnstone Press: Jamis Paulson, Christine Mazur, Sara Harms, and especially Sharon Caseburg for perspicacity, tact, flexibility and good humour.

Special thanks to Kristen Wittman, my wife, for her sharp eye and generous thoughts.

The errors, omissions, and oversights remain mine.